PRAISE FOR HELEN FIELDING'S

Bridget Jones: Mad About the Boy

"Tender and comic."   —*The New Yorker*

"Feels like visiting with your funniest friend."
                    —*Entertainment Weekly*

"Delightful. . . . Bridget Jones was a character made for the Internet, from her confessional tone to her casual creation of memes."   —*Los Angeles Times*

"Sweet and satisfying. . . . Bridget still has her posse of funny friends and her shelf of self-help books."
                    —*USA Today*

"Helen has always had a sharp eye for the obsessions and neuroses of our times, a talent much in evidence here—[Bridget's] liability rests very much on her believability."   —Anna Wintour,
                    editor in chief of *Vogue*

"Very funny."   —*The Boston Globe*

HELEN FIELDING

Bridget Jones: Mad About the Boy

Helen Fielding is the author of *Bridget Jones's Diary* and *Bridget Jones: The Edge of Reason,* and was part of the screenwriting team on the movies of the same name. *Bridget Jones: Mad About the Boy* is her fifth novel. She has two children and lives in London and sometimes Los Angeles.

Also by Helen Fielding

Cause Celeb
Bridget Jones's Diary
Bridget Jones: The Edge of Reason
Olivia Joules and the Overactive Imagination

BRIDGET JONES

Mad About the Boy

BRIDGET JONES

Mad About the Boy

Helen Fielding

VINTAGE CANADA

VINTAGE CANADA EDITION, 2014

Published in Canada by Vintage Canada, a division of Random House
of Canada Limited, Toronto, in 2014, and simultaneously in the United
States of America by Vintage Books, a division of Random House LLC,
New York, a Penguin Random House company. Originally published in
hardcover in Canada by Alfred. A. Knopf Canada, a division of Random
House of Canada Limited, in 2013, and simultaneously in the United
States of America by Alfred. A. Knopf, a division of Random House LLC,
New York. Originally published in Great Britain by Jonathan Cape, an
imprint of The Random House Group Limited, London. Distributed by
Random House of Canada Limited.

Vintage Canada with colophon is a registered trademark.

www.randomhouse.ca

Library and Archives Canada Cataloguing in Publication

Fielding, Helen, author
Bridget Jones : mad about the boy / Helen Fielding.

ISBN 978-0-345-80796-0

I. Title. II. Title: Mad about boy.

PR6056.I35B75 2014   823'.914   C2013-904992-4

Printed and bound in the United States of America

2 4 6 8 9 7 5 3 1

To Dash and Romy

CONTENTS

CONTENTS

BRIDGET JONES

Mad About the Boy

PROLOGUE

Thursday 18 April 2013

2.30 p.m. Talitha just called, talking in that urgent, "let's-be-discreet-but-wildly-overdramatic" voice she always has. "Darling, I just want to let you know that it's my sixtieth on the 24th of May. I'm not SAYING it's my sixtieth, obviously. And keep it quiet because I'm not asking everyone. I just wanted you to keep the date free."

I panicked. "That would be great!" I gushed unconvincingly.

"Bridget. You absolutely can't not come."

"Well, the thing is . . ."

"What?"

"It's Roxster's thirtieth birthday that night."

Silence at the end of the phone.

"I mean, we probably won't still be together by then, but, if we are, it would be . . ." I tailed off.

"I've just put 'no children' on the invites."

"He'll be thirty by then!" I said indignantly.

"I'm just teasing, darling. Of course you must bring your toy boy. I'll get a bouncy castle! Back on air. Mustrunloveyoubye!"

Tried to turn on telly to see if Talitha had indeed, as so often, been calling me live on air during a film clip. Jabbed confusedly at buttons like a monkey with a mobile phone. Why does turning on a TV these days require three

3

remotes with ninety buttons? Why? Suspect designed by thirteen-year-old technogeeks, competing with each other from sordid bedrooms, leaving everyone else thinking they're the only person in the world who doesn't understand what the buttons are for, thus wreaking psychological damage on a massive, global scale.

Threw remotes petulantly onto sofa, at which TV randomly burst into life, showing Talitha looking immaculate, one leg sexily crossed over the other, interviewing the dark-haired Liverpool footballer who has the anger-management/biting problem. He looked as if he wanted to bite Talitha, though for rather different reasons than on the pitch.

Right. No need for panic—will simply assess pros and cons of Roxster/Talitha party issue in calm and mature manner:

PROS OF TAKING ROXSTER TO PARTY
*It would be terrible not to go to Talitha's. She has been my friend since our *Sit Up Britain* days, when she was an impossibly glamorous newsreader and I was an impossibly incompetent reporter.

*It would be quite funny to take Roxster, and also smug-making, because the thirtieth/sixtieth birthday thing would stop all that patronizing pitying-of-single-women-"of-a-certain-age" thing, like they're terminally stuck with their singleness, whereas single men of that age are snapped up before they've had time to draw up the divorce papers. And Roxster is so gorgeous and peach-like, thereby somehow denying reality of ageing process on self.

CONS OF TAKING ROXSTER TO PARTY

*Roxster is his own man, and would doubtless take exception to being treated as some sort of comedy, or anti-ageing device.

*Crucially, it might put Roxster off me, to be surrounded by old people at sixtieth birthday party, and make some sort of completely unnecessary point about how old I am though of course am MUCH younger than Talitha. And frankly, I refuse to believe how old I actually am. As Oscar Wilde says, thirty-five is the perfect age for a woman, so much so that many women have decided to adopt it for the rest of their lives.

*Roxster is probably having his own party with young people squeezed onto his balcony, barbecuing and listening to 70s disco music with ironic "retro" amusement, and is thinking at this moment how to avoid asking me to the party in case his friends find out he is going out with a woman literally old enough to be his mother. Actually, possibly, technically, with the advancement of puberty due to hormones in milk these days—grandmother. Oh God. Why did mind think such a thought?

3.10 p.m. Gaaah! Have got to pick up Mabel in twenty minutes and have not got rice cakes ready. Gaah. Telephone.

"I have Brian Katzenberg for you."

My new agent! Actual agent. But I would be BEYOND late for Mabel if I stopped and talked.

"Can I call Brian back later?" I trilled, trying to smear pretend-butter onto the rice cakes, stick them together and put them in a Ziploc with one hand.

"It's about your spec script."

"Just . . . in . . . a meeting!" How could I be in a meeting, and yet talking on the phone saying I'm in a meeting? People's assistants are meant to say they're in a meeting, not the person themself, who is supposed to be unable to say anything because they're in the meeting.

Set off on school run, feeling, now, desperate to call back and find out what the call was about. Brian has so far sent it to two production companies, both of whom have turned it down. But now maybe a fish has bitten at the fish hook?

Fought overwhelming urge to ring Brian back claiming "meeting" had come to an abrupt end, but decided far more important to be on time for Mabel: and that's the sort of caring, prioritizing mother I am.

4.30 p.m. School run was even more chaos than usual: like *Where's Wally?* picture of millions of lollipop ladies, babies in prams, white-van men having standoffs with over-educated SUV mums, a man cycling with a double bass strapped to his back, and earth mothers on bicycles with tin boxes full of children in the front. Entire road was grid-locked. Suddenly, a frantic woman came running along yelling, "Go back, go BACK! Come ON! Nobody is HELPING HERE!"

Realizing there had been a terrible accident, I, and everyone else, started rearing their cars crazily onto pave-

6

ment and into gardens to make way for Emergency Services. Once road was clear, peered gingerly ahead for the ambulance/bloodbath. But there was not an ambulance, just a very fancy woman, flouncing into a black Porsche, then roaring furiously along the newly cleared road, a smug be-uniformed small child next to her in the front seat.

By the time I got to the Infants Branch, Mabel was the only child left on the steps, apart from the last straggler, Thelonius, who was about to leave with his mum.

Mabel looked at me with her huge solemn eyes.

"Come on, Old Pal," she said kindly.

"We wondered where you'd got to!" said Thelonius's mum. "Did you forget again?"

"No. Hahaha!" I responded to Thelonius's mother's stare. "Better run off and get Billy!"

Managed to get Mabel into the car, leaning over in the traditional body-wrenching movement, fastening the seat belt by waddling my hand in the mess between the seat back and booster seat.

Arrived at Billy's Junior Branch to see Perfect Nicolette, the Class Mother (perfect house, perfect husband, perfect children: only slight imperfection being name, presumably chosen by parents before invention of popular smoking substitute), surrounded by a gaggle of Junior Branch mothers. Perfect Nicorette was perfectly dressed and perfectly blow-dried with a perfectly gigantic handbag. Sidled up, panting, to see if I could get the scoop on the latest Area of Concern, just as Nicolette flicked her hair crossly, nearly taking my eye out with the corner of the giant bag.

"I asked him why Atticus is still in the football Ds—I mean, Atticus has been coming home, literally, in tears—and Mr. Wallaker just said, 'Because he's rubbish. Anything else?'"

Glanced over at the Area of Concern/new sports teacher: fit, tall, slightly younger than me, crop-haired, rather like Daniel Craig in appearance. He was staring broodingly at a group of unruly boys, then suddenly blew a whistle and bellowed, "Oi! You lot. In the cloakroom now or I'll Caution you."

"You see?" Nicolette continued, as the boys formed themselves into a shambolic line, attempting to jog back into school, shouting, "One, sir! Two, sir!" like startled bushmen recruited to form a Spring Uprising, while Mr. Wallaker blew his whistle ludicrously in time.

"He is hot, though," said Farzia. Farzia is my favourite school mum, always having her priorities in place.

"Hot, but married," snapped Nicolette. "And with children, though you wouldn't guess it."

"I thought he was a friend of the headmaster," ventured another mum.

"Exactly. Is he even trained?" said Nicolette.

"Mummy." Looked round to see Billy, in his little blazer, dark hair tousled, shirt hanging out of his trousers. "I didn't get picked for chess." Those same eyes, those same dark eyes, stabbed with pain.

"It doesn't matter about being picked or winning," I said, giving Billy a furtive hug. "It's who you are that counts."

"Of course it matters." Gaah! It was Mr. Wallaker. "He

has to practise. He has to earn it." As he turned away, distinctly heard him mutter, "The sense of entitlement amongst the mothers in this school defies belief."

"Practise?" I said brightly. "Why, I'd never have thought of that! You must be terribly clever, Mr. Wallaker. I mean, sir."

He looked at me with his cold blue eyes.

"What has this got to do with the Sports Department?" I continued sweetly.

"I teach the chess class."

"But how lovely! Do you use the whistle?"

Mr. Wallaker looked disconcerted for a moment, then said, "Eros! Get out of that flower bed. Now!"

"Mummy," said Billy, tugging on my hand, "the ones that got picked get two days off school to go to the chess tournament."

"I'll practise with you."

"But Mummy, you're rubbish at chess."

"No, I'm not! I'm really good at chess. I beat you!"

"You didn't."

"I did!"

"You didn't!"

"Well, I was letting you win because you're a child," I burst out. "And anyway, it isn't fair because you have chess classes."

"Perhaps you could join the chess classes, Mrs. Darcy?" Oh GOD. What was Mr. Wallaker doing still listening? "There is an age limit of seven, but if we stretch that to mental age I'm sure you'll be fine. Did Billy tell you his other news?"

"Oh!" said Billy, brightening. "I've got nits!"

"Nits!" I stared at him aghast, hand reaching instinctively to my hair.

"Yes, nits. They've all got them." Mr. Wallaker looked down, a slight flicker of amusement in his eyes. "I realize this will cause a National Emergency amongst the north London Mumserati and their coiffeurs but you simply need to nit-comb them. And yourself, of course."

Oh God. Billy had been scratching his head recently but I'd sort of blanked it as one thing too many to take on. Could feel my head starting to crawl as my mind cartwheeled. If Billy's got nits, then probably Mabel's got nits, and I've got nits, which means that . . . Roxster has got nits.

"Everything all right?"

"Yes, no, super!" I said. "Everything's fine, jolly good, bye then, Mr. Wallaker."

Walked away, holding Billy's and Mabel's hands, to hear a ping on my mobile. Hurriedly put on my glasses to read the text. It was from Roxster.

<How late were you this morning, my precious? Shall I hop on the bus tonight and bring round a shepherd's pie?>

Gaaah! Cannot have Roxster coming over when we have to nit-comb everyone and wash all the pillowcases. Surely it is not normal to be thinking of an excuse to cancel your toy boy because the entire household has got nits? Why do I keep getting myself into such a mess?

5 p.m. We burst back into our terrace house, with the usual jumble of backpacks, crumpled paintings, squashed bananas, plus a large bag of nit-combing products from the chemist, and clattered past the ground-floor "lounge/

10

office" (increasingly redundant apart from the sofa bed and empty John Lewis boxes) and down the stairs into the warm messy basement/kitchen/sitting room where we spend all our time. I settled Billy to do his homework and Mabel to play with her "Hellvanians" (Sylvanian bunnies) while I put on the spag bog. But now am in total fug about what to text Roxster about tonight, and whether I should tell him about the nits.

5.15 p.m. Maybe not.

5.30 p.m. Oh God. Had just texted <Would love you to come, but have to work tonight, so better not> when Mabel suddenly sprang up and started singing Billy's least favourite song at him, "Forgeddabouder money money money!" Then the phone rang.

Lunged at it, just as Billy jumped up, yelling, "Mabel, stop singing Jessie J!" and a receptionist's voice purred, "I have Brian Katzenberg for you."

"Um, could I possibly call Brian back in—"

"Berbling, berbling!" sang Mabel, chasing Billy round the table.

"I have Brian on now."

"Nooo! Can you just—"

"Mabel!" wailed Billy. "Stop iiiiiiiiiiiiiit."

"Shhh! I'm on the PHONE!"

"Heyyyyyy!" Brian's brisk cheery voice. "So! Great news! Greenlight Productions want to take out an option on your script."

"What?" I said, heart leaping. "Does that mean they're going to make it into a film?"

Brian laughed heartily. "It's the movie business! They're just going to give you a small amount of money to develop it, and—"

"Mummeee! Mabel's got a knife!"

I put my hand over the receiver, hissing, "MABEL! Give me the knife! Now!"

"Hello? Hello?" Brian was saying. "Laura, I think we've lost Bridget . . ."

"No! I'm here!" I said, flinging myself at Mabel, who was now hurtling after Billy, brandishing the knife.

"They want to have an exploratory meeting on Monday at noon."

"Monday! Great!" I said, wrestling the knife off Mabel. "Is the exploratory meeting like an interview?"

"Mummeeee!"

"Shhhh!" I hustled the two of them onto the sofa, and started struggling with the remotes.

"They just have a few issues with the script they want to talk about before they decide to go ahead."

"Right, right." Suddenly felt hurt and indignant. A few issues with my script *already*? But what could they possibly be?

"So, remember they're not going to—"

"Mummeee. I'm bleeeeeding!"

"Shall I call back in a while?"

"No! All fine!" I said desperately, as Mabel yelled, "Call de ambulance!"

"You were saying?"

"They're not going to want a first-time writer who's difficult. You've got to find a way to go along with what they want."

12

"Right, right, so not to be sort of a nuisance?"

"You got it!" said Brian.

"My brudder'th going to die!" sobbed Mabel.

"Er, is everything—"

"No, fine, super, twelve o'clock Monday!" I said, just as Mabel shouted, "I've killed my brudder!"

"OK," said Brian, sounding nervous. "I'll get Laura to email you the details."

6 p.m. Once the furore had been dampened, the minuscule snick on Billy's knee covered in a Superman plaster, black marks placed on Mabel's Consequences Chart, and spag bog placed in their stomachs, I found my mind flashing through multiple matters, like that of a drowning person, only more optimistic. What was I going to wear for the meeting and was I going to win an Oscar for Best Adapted Screenplay? Didn't Mabel have an early finish on Monday and how was I going to pick them up? What was I going to wear for the Oscar ceremony and ought I to tell the Greenlight Productions team that Billy has got nits?

8 p.m. *Nits found 9, actual insects 2, nit eggs 7 (v.g.)*

Just bathed the kids and nit-combed them, which turned out to be brilliant fun. Found two actual insects in Billy's hair and seven eggs behind his ears—two behind one and a magnificent crop of five behind the other. It's so satisfying seeing the little black dots appear on the white nit comb. Mabel was upset as she didn't have any, but cheered up when I let her nit-comb me to reveal I didn't have any either. Billy was waving the nit comb, crowing, "I got seven!" but when Mabel burst into tears, he sweetly put three of his into her hair, which meant we had to nit-comb Mabel all over again.

9.15 p.m. Kids are asleep. Wildly puffed up re meeting. Am professional woman again and going to a meeting! Am going to wear navy silk dress and get hair blow-dried in spite of Mr. bloody Wallaker's supercilious take on coiffeurs. And in spite of gnawing sense that increasing female blow-dry habit is turning women into those eighteenth (or seventeenth?) century men who only felt comfortable in public situations when wearing powdered wigs.

9.21 p.m. Oh, though is it morally wrong to get a blow-dry when I may have undetectable nit eggs at the start of their seven-day cycle?

9.25 p.m. Yes. It is morally wrong. Maybe Mabel and Billy should not go to play dates either?

9.30 p.m. Also feel should tell Roxster truth about nits, as lies are bad in a relationship. But maybe, in this case, lies better than lice?

9.35 p.m. Nits seem to be throwing up unfeasible number of modern moral dilemmas.

9.40 p.m. Gaah! Just went through entire wardrobe (i.e. pile of clothes heaped on exercise bike) plus actual wardrobes and cannot find navy silk dress. Have nothing to wear for meeting now. Nothing. How is it that have all these clothes stuffed into wardrobe and navy silk dress is only one that can actually wear for anything important?

Resolve in future, instead of spending evenings shoving grated cheese into mouth and trying to avoid glugging wine, to calmly go through all clothes, giving anything that have not worn for a year to the poor, and organize everything else into mixy-matchy "capsule wardrobe" so that getting dressed becomes a calm joy instead of hysterical scramble. And then will go for twenty minutes on exercise bike. As exercise bike is not wardrobe, obviously, but exercise bike.

9.45 p.m. Though maybe it is all right to wear navy silk dress all the time in manner of Dalai Lama and his robes. If I could find it. Presumably Dalai Lama has several sets of robes, or on-call dry-cleaner, and does not leave robes in bottom of wardrobe full of outfits he bought but does not wear from Topshop, Oasis, ASOS, Zara, etc.

9.46 p.m. Or on exercise bike.

9.50 p.m. Just went up to check on children. Mabel was asleep, hair all over her face as usual, so that her head looked back to front, and clutching Saliva. Saliva is Mabel's dolly. Billy and I both think she has mixed the name up with Sabrina the Teenage Witch and Sylvanian bunnies, but Mabel considers it to be perfect.

Kissed Billy's hot little cheek, all snuggled in with Mario, Horsio and Puffles One and Two, at which Mabel raised her head, said, "Lovely weather we're havin'," then lay back down again.

I watched them, touching their soft cheeks, listening to their snorty breathing—then, the fatal thought "If only . . ." invaded my head without warning. "If only . . ." Darkness, memories, sorrow rearing up, engulfing me like a tsunami.

10 p.m. Just rushed back downstairs to the kitchen. Worse: everything silent, forlorn, empty. "If only . . ." Stoppit. Can't afford to do this. Switch on the kettle. Don't go over to the dark side.

10.01 p.m. Doorbell! Thank God! But who can it possibly be at this time of night?

PLENTY OF FUCKWITS

Thursday 18 April 2013 (continued)
10.45 p.m. Was Tom and Jude, both completely plastered, stumbling into the hallway giggling.

"Can we use your laptop? We were just in Dirty Burger and—"

"I's trying to do PlentyofFish on my iPhone and we can't get it to download a photo from Google so . . ." Jude clattered down the stairs into the kitchen in her high heels and work suit, while Tom, still dark, buff, handsome and fabulously gay, kissed me extravagantly.

"Mwah! Bridget! You've lost SO much weight!"

(He's said this every time he's seen me for the last fifteen years, even when I was nine months pregnant.)

"'Ere, have you got any wine?" Jude yelled upstairs from the kitchen.

Turns out Jude—who now practically runs the City, but has continued to translate her love of the financial roller coaster into her love life—was spotted yesterday on an Internet-dating site by her horrible ex: Vile Richard.

"And yes!" announced Tom, as we clattered down to join her. "Vile Fuckwit Richard, in spite of having messed this fabulous woman around in a fuckwitted, commitment-phobic manner for a HUNDRED years, then married her, then left her ten months later, has had the NERVE to send her an indignant message about being on Plentyof . . . find it, Jude . . . find it . . ."

Jude fiddled confusedly with the phone. "I can't find it. Shit, he's deleted it. Can you delete your own message once you've—"

"Oh, give it to me, dear. Anyway, the point is, Vile Richard sent her this insulting message, then BLOCKED her so . . ." Tom started laughing. "So . . ."

"We're going to make up a person on PlentyofFish," finished Jude.

"PlentyofDicks, more like," snorted Tom.

"PlentyofFuckwits, more like, and then we're going to use the invented girl to torture him!" said Jude.

We all squeezed onto the sofa and Jude and Tom started sifting through mugshots of twenty-five-year-old blondes on Google Images and trying to download them onto the dating website, while making up insouciant answers to the profile questions. Wished for a moment Shazzer was here to rant feministically, instead of in Silicon Valley being a dot-com whizz with her unexpectedly-after-years-of-feminism dot-com husband.

"What kind of books does she like?" said Tom.

"Put 'Seriously, do you care?'" said Jude. "Men love bitches, remember?"

"Or 'Books? What are they?'" I suggested, then remembered. "Wait! Isn't this completely against the Dating Rules? Number 4? Use authentic, rational communication?"

"Yes! It's FABULOUSLY wrong and unhealthy," said Tom, who is actually now quite a senior psychologist, "but it doesn't count with fuckwits."

Was so relieved to be rescued from the Darkness Tsunami, plunging myself into the creation of Revenge-Girl on PlentyofFish, that I almost forgot my news. "Greenlight Productions are going to make my movie!" I suddenly blurted excitedly.

They stared at me gobsmacked, then interrogation was followed by wild jubilation.

"You go, girl! Toy boy, screenwriter, you've got it all going on now!" said Jude, as I managed to persuade them out of the door so I could go to sleep.

As Jude stumbled into the street, Tom hesitated, looking at me anxiously. "Are you OK?" ·

"Yes," I said, "I think so, it's just . . ."

"Be careful, hon," he said, suddenly sobering up into professional mode. "It's going to be a lot to take on if you're having proper meetings and deadlines and stuff."

"I know, but you said I should start doing work again and be writing and—"

"Yes. But you're going to need some more help with the kids. You're in a bit of a bubble right now. It's fantastic, how you've turned everything round, but you're still vulnerable underneath and—"

"Tom!" called Jude, who was teetering towards a taxi she'd spotted on the main road.

"You know where we are if you need us," Tom said. "Any time, day or night."

10.50 p.m. Thinking about "authentic, rational communication," have decided to call Roxster and tell him about the nits.

10.51 p.m. Though it is a bit late.

10.52 p.m. Also unannounced switch from texting to telephonic communication with Roxster too dramatic: giving undesirable weight and importance to whole nit issue. Will text instead.

<Roxster?>

Very short wait.

<Yes, Jonesey?>

<You know I said I was working tonight?>

<Yes, Jonesey.>

<There was another reason.>

<I know, Jonesey. You are hopeless at lying even via text. Are you having an affair with a younger man?>

<No, but it's equally embarrassing. It's related to your love of the natural world and its insect life.>

<Bedbugs?>

<Nearly . . .>

<*Spontaneous crying, starts hysterically scratching head.* Not . . . nits!!!>

<Can you possibly forgive etc?>

There was a brief pause then texting noise.

<Shall I come round now? Am in Camden.>

Dazzled by Roxster's cheerful gallantry, I texted back.

<Yes, but don't you mind about the nits?>

<No. I've googled them. They're allergic to testosterone.>

THE ART OF CONCENTRATION

Friday 19 April 2013

134lbs, calories 3482 (bad), number of times checked for nits on Roxster 3, number of nits found on Roxster 0, number of insects found in Roxster's food 27, number of insects found in house plague 85 (bad), texts to Roxster 2, texts from Roxster 0, mass emails from class parents 36, minutes spent checking emails 62, minutes spent obsessing about Roxster 360, minutes spent deciding to prepare for film meeting 20, minutes spent preparing for film meeting 0.

10.30 a.m. Right. Am really going to get down to work on presentation of my script, which is an updating of the famous Norwegian tragedy *Hedda Gabbler* by Anton Chekhov, only set in Queen's Park. Studied *Hedda Gabbler* for my English Literature finals at Bangor University, which unfortunately resulted in a Third. But maybe all that is about to be put right!

10.32 a.m. Imperative to concentrate.

11 a.m. Just made coffee and ate remains of children's breakfast, then started mooning about remembering things from Roxster visit last night: appearance of Roxster at 11.15 p.m., gorgeous in jeans and a dark sweater, eyes sparkling, grinning, holding a Waitrose shepherd's pie, two cans of baked beans and a Jamaican ginger cake.

Mmmm. The way his face looks when he's on top of me, the stubble on the beautiful jawline, the slight gap in his front teeth, which you can only see from below, those beefy naked shoulders. Waking up sleepily in the middle of the night to feel Roxster kissing me very gently, my shoulder, my neck, my cheek, my lips, feeling his hard-on pressing against my thigh. Oh God, he is so beautiful and such a great kisser, and such a great . . . Mmm, mmm. Right, must think about the feminist, pre- and anti-feminist, themes in . . . Oh God, though. It is so delicious, it makes me so happy, like I'm in a bubble of happiness. Right, must get on.

11.15 a.m. Suddenly burst out laughing, remembering overblown mid-sex conversation last night.

"Oh, oh, oh, you're so hard."

"Hard because I want you, baby."

"*So* hard . . ."

"You make me hard, baby."

Then, for some reason, I got carried away and gasped, "You make ME hard."

"What?" said Roxster, bursting out laughing. We both collapsed in giggles and then we had to start all over again.

Typically, in his cheerful manner, Roxster seemed unworried by the nits, though we both agreed that in order to have Responsible Sex, we must nit-comb each other first. Roxster was so funny, combing my hair, pretending to find and eat the nits, whilst intermittently kissing the back of my neck. When it was my turn to nit-comb Roxster, however, did not want to draw attention to my age by putting on reading glasses, so ended up studiously nit-combing his gorgeous thick hair, without being able to see anything at all. Fortunately Roxster seemed too keen to get it over with and into the bedroom for him to notice my blindness. And was probably fine because of his testosterone. But surely it is not normal to be too vain to put on your reading glasses to nit-comb your toy boy?

11.45 a.m. Right. My script! You see, *Hedda Gabbler* is really very relevant to the modern woman because it is about the perils of trying to live through men. Why hasn't Roxster texted me yet? Hope it is not because of the insect incident.

Roxster and I were able, unusually, to have breakfast together today, as Chloe the nanny was taking them to school. Chloe, who has been working for me since just after it happened, is like the improved version of me: younger, thinner, taller, nicer, better at looking after the children, and with an age-appropriate life partner called Graham. Nevertheless, consider it better that Roxster does not meet either Chloe or the children at this stage, so he hides in the bedroom until they have all gone off to school.

Roxster was just happily tucking into his first bowl of muesli, when he spat his mouthful out onto the table. Obviously am used to this sort of thing, though not, admittedly, from Roxster. But then he held out the bowl. The muesli was jumping with tiny insects, flailing and drowning in the milk.

"Are they nits?" I said aghast.

"No," he said darkly, "weevils."

23

Unfortunately my response was to start giggling.

"Have you any idea what it's like to put a spoonful of insects in your mouth?" he said. "I could have died. And, more importantly, so could they."

Then, just as he was tipping the bowl into the correct food recycling bin, he cried, "Ants!" There was a neat line of ants coming from the basement door to the food recycling bin. When he tried to move back the curtain to get rid of them, a small cloud of moths fluttered out.

"Aaargh! It's like the Nine Plagues of Egypt in here!" he said.

And even though he laughed, and gave me a very sexy kiss in the hall, he did not say anything about impending weekend and I have a feeling something is wrong—even if only the combined insult to his three great loves: insects, food and recycling.

Noon. Gaah! Is noon already and have not prepared any of my Thoughts.

12.05 p.m. Still Roxster has not texted. Maybe I should text him? Clearly, in textbook terms, the gentleman should text the lady first after intercourse, but perhaps the whole socio-etiquettical system breaks down when an insect plague is involved.

12.10 p.m. Right. *Hedda Gabbler*.

12.15 p.m. Just texted: <So sorry about the Nine Plagues of Egypt and for laughing. Will have entire house and occupants fumigated for your next visit. Are you all right?>

12.20 p.m. Right. Excellent. *Hedda Gabbler*. Roxster has not replied.

12.30 p.m. Roxster has still not replied. This is not like Roxster.

Maybe will check emails. Sometimes Roxster switches electronic mediums just to show off.

In-box is overrun not only by Ocado, ASOS, Snappy Snaps, Cotswold Holiday Cottages, links to amusing You-Tube clips, offers of Mexican viagra, save the dates for Cosmata's Build-A-Bear party, but also rash of parent mass emails over Atticus's missing shoes.

> Sender: Nicolette Martinez
> Subject: Atticus's shoes
>
> Atticus came home wearing
> Luigi's shoe but his other
> shoe is also not his nor is
> it labelled. I would appreciate
> the return of both of Atticus's
> shoes, both of which were
> clearly labelled.

12.35 p.m. Decided to join in group exchange to show solidarity and take mind off work.

```
Sender: Bridget Billymum
Subject: Re: Atticus's shoes
```

```
Just to clarify—did Atticus and
Luigi go home from swimming just
wearing one shoe each?
```

12.40 p.m. Hee hee, have triggered funny mass email response: jokes about children coming home with no trousers, knickers, etc.

```
Sender: Bridget Billymum
Subject: Billy's ear
```

```
Billy came home from football
last night wearing only one
ear. Does anyone have Billy's
other ear? It was VERY clearly
labelled and I would appreciate
its prompt return.
```

12.45 p.m. Tee hee.

```
Sender: Nicolette Martinez
Subject: Re: Billy's ear
```

```
Some parents appear to think
that the boys taking care of
their own property and the
parents clearly labelling it
```

is a matter for amusement. It
is actually important for their
development as self-reliant indi-
viduals. Perhaps if it was their
child's shoes which were missing
they would take a different
view.

12.50 p.m. Oh no, oh no. Have offended Class Mother
and probably horrified everyone else as well. Will send
direct mass apology.

Sender: Bridget Billymum
Subject: Atticus's shoes, Billy's
        ears, etc.

I'm sorry, Nicorette. I was
trying to write and bored and
just joking. Am very bad.

12.55 p.m. Gaaah!

Sender: Nicolette Martinez
Subject: Bridget Jones

Bridget—Possibly the misspelling
of my name was a Freudian slip.
I think we all know you struggle
with the occasional smoking
lapse. If it was intentional it

27

was hurtful and rude. Perhaps we
need to talk all this through
with the head of Pastoral Care.

NicoLette

Shit! I called her Nicorette! Look. Don't dig yourself in further. Just leave it now and concentrate!

1.47 p.m. This is ridiculous! I'm just COMPLETELY blocked.

1.48 p.m. All the class mothers hate me and Roxster has not replied.

1.52 p.m. Slumped at kitchen table.

1.53 p.m. Look. No going over to the dark side. Grazina the Cleaner will be here any second and she can't see me like this. Will leave a note re insect plague and go to Starbucks.

2.16 p.m. In Starbucks now with ham-and-cheese panini. Right.

3.16 p.m. Huge gaggles of posh mothers with prams have taken cafe over, talking really loudly about their husbands.

3.17 p.m. Is so noisy in here. Hate people who talk on their phones in cafes—ooh, phone, maybe Roxster!

3.30 p.m. Was Jude, clearly in meeting, whispering furtively, "Bridget. Vile Richard has totally fallen for Isabella."

"Who's Isabella?" I whispered urgently back.

"The girl we made up on PlentyofFish. Vile Richard's fixed to have a date with her tomorrow."

"But she isn't real."

"Exactly. She's me. He's arranged to meet me, I mean her, at the Shadow Lounge and she's going to stand him up."

"Brilliant," I whispered, as Jude said bossily, "So just put a stop order of two million yen at a hundred and twenty-five and wait for the quarterly profits." Then whispered, "And simultaneously, the guy I met on DatingSingleDoctors is meeting me—the actual me—two blocks away at the Soho Hotel."

"Great!" I said, confusedly.

"I know, right? Gottogobye."

Hope the man from DatingSingleDoctors doesn't turn out to be made up by Vile Richard.

3.40 p.m. Roxster still has not texted. Cannot concentrate. Am going home.

4 p.m. Got home to find terrifyingly pungent old-lady smell. Grazina had diligently followed my scribbled instructions, thrown all the food away, cleaned and sprayed everything and put mothballs in and behind any conceivable entry or exit to all floorboards, walls, doors or items of furniture. Will take me all weekend, and possibly rest of life, to find and destroy all mothballs. No moth could live through this or, crucially, toy boy. But that is, presumably, irrelevant, as STILL NO TEXT.

4.15 p.m. Gaah! There is bang, clatter and voices of every-one coming home. Is Friday night, is time for Chloe to leave and have not prepared my Thoughts.

4.16 p.m. How could Roxster not respond? Even though my last text was a question. Or was it? Will just check my last text again.

<So sorry about the Nine Plagues of Egypt and for laughing. Will have entire house and occupants fumigated for your next visit. Are you all right?>

Lurched in dismay. There was not only a question, an ending of text with a question, but an undeniably presump-tuous presumption that I would see Roxster again.

6 p.m. Went downstairs, attempting to conceal meltdown from Billy and Mabel (who fortunately, as is weekend, were absorbed respectively in Plants vs. Zombies and *Beverly Hills Chihuahua* 2) whilst simultaneously heating up spag bog (actually spag cheese without spag as Grazina has thrown away all the pasta). Finally, when supper was over, something about loading the dishwasher made me crack and send Roxster a fraudulently cheery text saying: <It's the weeeeeeekend!>

Then went into paroxysms of agony, so bad that I had to let Billy just stay permanently killing plants with zom-bies, and Mabel watching *Beverly Hills Chihuahua* 2 for the seventh time so they wouldn't notice. Realized was irresponsible and lazy parenting, but decided not as bad as emotional damage inflicted by awareness of melting-down mother over someone closer in age to—Gaaah! Is Roxster actually closer in age to Mabel than me? No, but I think he might be to Billy. Oh God. What am I thinking? No wonder he has stopped texting.

9.15 p.m. Still no text. Able, at last, to free-fall into well of misery, insecurity, emotional-pillow-pulled-from-under-feet, etc. The thing about going out with a younger man is that it makes you feel that you have miraculously turned back time. Sometimes, when we're on the chair in the bathroom, and I catch sight of us in the mirror, I just can't believe this is me, doing this with Roxster, at my age. But now it's gone away I have burst like a bubble. Am I just using the whole thing to block existential despair about growing old, and the fear that maybe I'm going to have a stroke, and *what would* happen to Billy and Mabel?

It was worse when they were babies. Had constant dread that I would spontaneously die in the night, or fall down the stairs, and no one would come, and they would be left alone, and end up eating me. But then as Jude pointed out, "It's better than dying alone and being eaten by an Alsatian."

9.30 p.m. Must remember what it says in *Zen and the Art of Falling in Love*: when he comes, we welcome, when he goes, we let him go. Also, when Zen students sit on the Cushion they make friends with Loneliness, which is different from Aloneness. Loneliness is Transience and the way that people we love come into our lives and go away again which is just part of Life, or maybe that is Aloneness, and Loneliness is . . . Still no text.

11 p.m. Cannot get to sleep.

11.15 p.m. Oh, Mark. Mark. I know I did all this "Will he call, won't he call?" when we were going out, before we were married. But even then it was different. I knew him so well, I'd known him since I was running round his parents' lawn with no clothes on.

He used to have conversations with me when he was sleeping. That's when I could find out what he was really feeling inside.

"Mark?" That dark, handsome face, sleeping on the pillow. "Are you lovely?"

Sighing in his sleep, looking sad, ashamed, shaking his head.

"Does your mummy love you?"

Very sad, now, trying to say "no" through his sleep. Mark Darcy, the big powerful human rights lawyer, and inside, the little damaged boy, sent away to boarding school at seven.

"Do I love you?" I'd say. And then he would smile in his sleep, happy, proud, nod his head, pull me to him, snuggle me under his arm.

We knew each other inside out, back to front. Mark was a gentleman and I trusted him completely in everything and I went out from that safe place into the world. It was like exploring the scary underwater ocean from our safe little submarine. And now . . . everything is scary and nothing will be safe again.

11.55 p.m. What am I doing? What am I doing? Why did I start all this? Why didn't I just stay as I was? Sad, lonely, workless, sexless, but at least a mother and faithful to their . . . faithful to their father.

DARK NIGHT OF THE SOUL

Friday 19 April 2013 (continued)
Five years. Has it really been five years? To start with it was just a question of getting through the day. Thankfully, Mabel was too little to know anything about it, but, oh, the flashbacks to Billy, running all through the house saying, "I lost Dada!" Jeremy and Magda at the door, a policeman behind them, the look on their faces. Running instinctively to the children, holding them both to me in terror: "What's wrong, Mummy? What's wrong?" Government people in the living room, someone accidentally turning on the news, Mark's face on the television with a caption:

Mark Darcy 1956–2008

The memories are a blur. Friends, family, surrounding me like a womb, Mark's lawyer friends sorting everything, the will, the death duties, unbelievable, like a film that was going to stop. The dreams, with Mark still in them. The mornings, waking at 5 a.m., washed clean by sleep for a split second, thinking everything was the same, then remembering: poleaxed by pain, as though a great stake was ramming me to the bed, straight through the heart, unable to move in case I disturbed the pain and it spread, knowing that in half an hour the children would be awake and I'd be on: nappies, bottles, trying to pretend it was OK, or at least keep things together till help arrived and I could go off and howl in the bathroom, then put some mascara on and brace up again.

But the thing about having kids is: you can't go to pieces; you just have to keep going. KBO: Keep Buggering On. The army of bereavement counsellors and therapists helped with Billy and later Mabel: "manageable versions of the truth," "honesty," "talking," "no secrets," a "secure base" from which to deal with it. But for the *soi-disant* "secure base"—i.e., (try not to laugh) me—it was different.

The main thing I remember from those sessions was, bottom line: "Can you survive?" There wasn't any choice. All those thoughts that crowded in—our last moment together, the feel of Mark's suit against my skin, me in my nightie, the unknowing last kiss goodbye, trying to recapture the look in his eye, the ring at the doorbell, the faces on the doorstep, the thoughts, "I never . . ." "If only . . .," they had to be blocked out. The carefully orchestrated grieving process, watched over by experts with soft voices, and caring upside-down smiles, was less helpful than figuring out how to change a nappy whilst simultaneously microwaving a fish finger. Just keeping the ship afloat, if not exactly upright, was, I thought, 90 per cent of the battle. Mark had every-thing arranged: financial details, insurance policies. We got out of the big house full of memories in Holland Park, and into our little house in Chalk Farm. School fees, home, bills, income, all practical matters perfectly taken care of: no need to work now, just Mabel and Billy—my miniature Mark—all I had left of him to keep alive, and to keep me alive. A mother, a widow, putting one foot in front of the other. But inside I was an empty shell, devastated, no longer me.

By the time four years had gone by, however, the friends were not having it.

PART ONE

Born-Again Virgin

ONE YEAR AGO . . .

These are the extracts from last year's diary, starting exactly one year ago, four years after Mark died, which show how I got myself into the current mess.

2012 DIARY

Thursday 19 April 2012

175lb, alcohol units 4 (nice), calories 2822 (but better eating real food in club than bits of old cheese and fish fingers at home), possibility of having or desire to have sex ever again 0.

"She HAS to get laid," said Talitha firmly, sipping a vodka martini and glancing alarmingly around Shoreditch House for candidates.

It was one of our semi-regular evenings which Talitha, Tom and Jude insist I attend, in an effort to "Get Me Out," rather like taking Granny to the seaside.

"She does," said Tom. "Did I tell you, I got a suite at the Chedi in Chiang Mai for only two hundred quid a night on LateRooms.com. There was a Junior Suite for 179 on Expedia but it didn't have a terrace."

Tom, in later life, has become increasingly obsessed with boutique-hotel holidays and trying to make us tailor our lifestyles to fit in with Gwyneth Paltrow's blog.

"Tom, shut up," murmured Jude, looking up from her iPhone, where she was on DatingSingleDoctors. "This is serious. We have to do something. She's become a Born-Again Virgin."

"You don't understand," I said. "It's a total impossibility. I don't want anyone else. And anyway, even if I did, which I don't, I'm non-viable, completely asexual and no one will ever fancy me again, ever, ever, ever."

I stared at my stomach, bulging under my black top. It was true. I had become a Born-Again Virgin. The trouble with the modern world is that you are bombarded with images of sex and sexuality all the time—the hand on the bum on the billboard, the couples smooching on the beach in the Sandals ad, real-life couples entwined in the park, condoms by the till in the chemist—a whole wonderful magical world of sex, which you no longer belong to and never will again.

"I'm not going to fight it, it's just part of being a widow and the process of turning into a little old lady," I said melodramatically, hoping they would all immediately insist I was Penelope Cruz or Scarlett Johansson.

"Oh, darling, don't be so bloody ridiculous," said Talitha, summoning the waiter for another cocktail. "You probably do need to lose a bit of weight, and get some Botox and do something with your hair, but—"

"Botox?" I said indignantly.

"Oh God," Jude suddenly burst out. "This guy isn't a doctor. He was on DanceLoverDating. It's the same photo!"

"Maybe he's a doctor who's also a dance lover and just covering all the bases?" I encouraged.

"Jude, shut up," said Tom. "You are lost in a morass of nebulous cyber presences, most of whom don't exist and who simply turn each other on and off randomly at will."

"Botox can kill you," I said darkly. "It's botulism. It comes from cows."

"So what? Better to die of Botox than die of loneliness because you're so wrinkly."

"For God's sake, shut up, Talitha," said Tom.

Suddenly found self missing Shazzer again and wishing she was here to say, "Will everyone fucking stop the fuck telling everyone else to shut the fuck up."

"Yes, shut up, Talitha," said Jude. "Not everyone wants to look like a freak show."

"Darling," said Talitha, putting her hand to her brow, "I am NOT a 'freak show.' Grieving apart, Bridget has lost, or shall we say, mislaid, her sense of sexual self. And it's our duty to help her relocate it."

And with a toss of her lush, shining locks Talitha settled back into her chair while the three of us stared at her silently, sucking our cocktails through our straws like five-year-olds.

Talitha burst out again, "The thing about not looking your age is, it's all about altering the 'signposts.' The body must be forced to reject the fat-positioning of middle age, wrinkles are completely unnecessary and a fine head of swingy shiny healthy hair—"

"Purchased for a pittance from impoverished Indian virgins," interjected Tom.

"—however obtained and attached, is all one needs to turn back the clock."

"Talitha," said Jude, "did I actually just hear you articulate the words 'Middle' and 'Age'?"

"Anyway, I can't," I said.

"Look. This really makes me very sad," said Talitha. "Women of our age—"

"Your age," muttered Jude.

"—have only got themselves to blame if they brand themselves as unviable by going on and on about how they haven't had a date for four years. Germaine Greer's 'Disappearing Woman' must be brutally murdered and buried. One needs, for the sake of oneself and one's peers, to create an air of mysterious confidence and allure, rebranding oneself—"

"Like Gwyneth Paltrow," said Tom brightly.

"Gwyneth Paltrow is not 'our age' and she's married," said Jude.

"No, I mean I can't shag anyone," I elucidated. "It wouldn't be fair on the kids. There's too much to do, and men are very high-maintenance matters."

Talitha surveyed me sorrowfully, my customary black loose-waisted trousers and long top swathing the ruins of what was once my figure. I mean, Talitha does have some authority to speak, having been married three times and, ever since I first met her, never without some completely besotted man in tow.

"A woman has her needs," Talitha growled dramatically. "What good is a mother to her poor children if she's suffering from low self-esteem and sexual frustration? If you don't get laid soon, you will literally close up. More importantly, you will shrivel. And you will become bitter."

"Anyway," I said.

"What?"

"It wouldn't be fair to Mark."

There was silence for a moment. It was as if a huge

wet fish had been thrown into the high-spirited mood of the evening.

Later, though, Tom drunkenly followed me into the Ladies', leaning against the wall for support as I flapped my hands around the designer tap trying to get it to turn on.

"Bridget," said Tom, as I started groping under the washbasin for pedals.

I looked up from under the sink. "What?"

Tom had gone into professional mode again.

"Mark. He would want you to find someone. He wouldn't want you to stop—"

"I haven't stopped," I said, straightening up with some difficulty.

"You need to work," he said. "You need to get a life. And you need someone to be with you and love you."

"I do have a life," I said gruffly. "And I don't need a man, I have the children."

"Well, if nothing else, you need someone to show you how to turn taps on." He reached over to the square tap column and turned a bit of the base, at which water started gushing out. "Have a look on Goop," he said, suddenly changing back into funny, flippant Tom. "See what Gwyneth has to say about sex and French-style parenting!"

11.15 p.m. Just said goodnight to Chloe, trying to conceal slight squiffiness.

"Sorry I'm a bit late," I mumbled sheepishly.

"Five minutes?" she said, wrinkling her nose, kindly. "Glad you had a bit of fun!"

11.45 p.m. In bed now. Tellingly, am wearing, instead of usual pyjamas with dogs on, which match the children's, the only vaguely sexual nightie I can still get into. Suddenly have surge of hopeful feeling. Maybe Talitha is right! If I shrivel and become bitter, then what use will that be to the children? They will become child-centric, demanding King Babies: and I a negative, rasping old fool, lunging at sherry, roaring, "WHY DON'T YOU DO ANYTHING FOR MEEEEEEEEE?"

11.50 p.m. Maybe have been going through long dark tunnel, which there is light at the end of. Maybe someone could love me? Is no reason why could not bring a man back here. I could put a hook inside bedroom door, so the children wouldn't walk in on "us," creating an adult, sensual world of . . . gaaah! Cry from Mabel.

11.52 p.m. Rushed into kids' room to see fluffy-headed figure in bottom bunk, sitting up, then quickly bending over, flat-pack style, which is what she always does as she is not supposed to wake up in the night. Mabel then sat straight up again, looked down at her pyjamas, which belched diarrhoea, opened her mouth and was sick.

11.53 p.m. Lifted Mabel into the bath and removed PJs, trying not to retch.

11.54 p.m. Washed and dried Mabel, sat her on floor, then went to find new PJs, remove sheets and attempt to locate clean sheets.

Midnight. Crying from kids' room. Still carrying diarrhoea sheets, diverted to room, only to hear rival crying emerging from bathroom. Considered wine. Reminded self am responsible mother, not slapper in All Bar One.

12.01 a.m. Flapped in fugue-like state between kids' room and bathroom. Level of bathroom-crying notched up. Rushed in, assuming Mabel consuming Bic razor, poison or similar, to find her pooing on the floor with expression both guilty and startled.

Overwhelmed by love for Mabel. Picked her up. Diarrhoea and sick now not only on sheets, bathmat, Mabel, etc., but also on vaguely sexual nightie.

12.07 a.m. Went to kids' room, still holding Mabel, plus diarrhoea ensemble, to find Billy out of bed, hair all hot and messy, looking up as if I was benign God with answer to all things. Billy held my gaze, whilst belching sick in manner of *Exorcist* except head remained in forward stationary position instead of spinning round and round.

12.08 a.m. Diarrhoea erupted onto Billy's PJs. Billy's bewildered expression overwhelmed self with love for Billy. Ended up in diarrhoea/vomit-filled California-style "group hug" embracing Billy, Mabel and diarrhoea sheets, bathmat, PJs and vaguely sexual nightie.

12.10 a.m. Wished Mark was here. Had sudden flashback to Mark in his lawyerly dressing gown at night, the glimpse of hairy chest, the sudden flashes of humour at baby chaos,

45

getting all military trying to organize us all, as if it was some sort of cross-border situation, then realizing the absurdity of it all, and both of us ending up giggling.

He's missing all the little moments, I thought. Missing his own children growing up. Even this would have been funny instead of confusing and scary. One of us could have stayed with them and the other done the sheets, then we could have got into bunk beds again and giggled about it and . . . how could anyone else ever delight in them and love them as he would have, even when they are pooing everywhere and . . . ?

12.15 a.m. "Mummy!" Billy jerked self back to reality. Was difficult situation, undeniably: everyone poo- and sick-smeared, alarmed and retching. Ideal would be to separate children and fabrics/fluids and put both children in warm bath and find sheets. But what if pooing/vomiting contin-ued? What then? Water could become toxic, and possibly cholera-filled, like open sewer in refugee camp.

12.16 a.m. Arrived at makeshift solution: placing plastic mat on bathroom floor with pillows, towels, etc. generally around.

12.20 a.m. Resolved to go down to washing machine (i.e. fridge to get wine).

12.24 a.m. Closed door and ran down.

12.27 a.m. Having cleared head with swig of wine, real-ized was immaterial washing sheets, etc. Only essential objective, surely, was to keep children alive until morning, ideally simultaneously avoiding nervous breakdown.

12.45 a.m. Realized wine, though fortifying head, had done opposite to stomach.

12.50 a.m. Threw up.

2 a.m. Billy and Mabel both now asleep on bathroom floor on and under towels, cleaned to a degree. Resolve simply to sleep next to them in poo- and sick-covered vaguely sexual nightie.

2.05 a.m. Experiencing pleasing sense of triumph, like general who has brought massacre, bloodbath, etc. back from brink, engineering peaceful solution: even starting to hear theme tune from *Gladiator*, seeing self as Russell Crowe, partially obscured by caption: "A Hero Will Rise."

At same time, however, am unable to avoid sense that attempting any sort of erotic scenario with this sort of thing going on might not be a particularly good idea.

A NEW START—A NEW ME

Friday 20 April 2012
173lb, minutes set aside for meditation 20, minutes spent meditating 0.

2 p.m. Right. Have made a decision. Am going to completely change. Am going to return to Zen/New Age/self-help-book study and yoga, etc., starting from the inside not the outside, meditate regularly, and lose weight. Have got all set up with candle and yoga mat in bathroom and am going to quietly meditate and settle mind before taking kids to doctors, remembering to allow time to a) get snacks and b) locate missing car keys.

Also the other things am going to do are as follows:

I WILL
*Lose 30lb.

*Get on Twitter, Facebook, Instagram and WhatsApp instead of feeling old and out of it because everyone except self is on Twitter, Facebook, Instagram and WhatsApp.

*Stop being scared of turning on the television but instead simply locate and read instruction manuals for TV, Virgin box DVD remotes and buttons, so that

TV becomes source of entertainment and pleasure rather than meltdown.

*Do regular Life Laundry, cleansing house of all unnecessary possessions, esp. cupboard under stairs, so is a place for everything and everything in its place in manner of Buddhist Zendo/Martha Stewart's house.

*With above in mind, ask Mum to stop sending me unused handbags, "stoles," Wedgwood "tureens," etc., reminding her that age of rationing ended some time ago and is now space rather than possessions which is in short supply (at least in Western urban world).

*Start writing my *Hedda Gabbler* adaptation in order to have professional adult life again.

*Actually write said screenplay instead of spending half day setting off to look for something then wandering vaguely from room to room worrying about unanswered emails, texts, bills, play dates, go-kart parties, leg waxes, doctors' appointments, parents' evenings, babysitting schedules, strange noise from fridge, cupboard under stairs, reason why telly won't work, then sitting down again realizing have forgotten what was looking for in the first place.

*Not wear same three things all the time, but instead go through wardrobe and put together fashionable "looks" based on celebrities at airports.

*Clear cupboard under stairs.

*Find out why fridge is making that noise.

*Go on email for one hour only per day instead of spending entire day in helpless cyber-circle of email, news stories, Calendar, Google and shopping and holiday websites whilst texting, then not answering any of emails anyway.

*Not add Twitter, Facebook, WhatsApp and whatever to cyber-circle when have got on them.

*Deal with emails immediately and so that email becomes effective means of communication instead of terrifying Unexploded Email In-box full of guilt trips and undetonated time-vampire bombs.

*Be better at looking after the children than Chloe the nanny.

*Establish regular routine with children so everyone knows where they are and what supposed to be doing, esp. self.

*Read parenting self-help books, including *One, Two, Three . . . Better, Easier Parenting* and *French Children Don't Throw Food* in order to be better at looking after the children than Chloe.

*Be kinder to Talitha, Jude, Tom and Magda in return for their kindness to me.

*Go to Pilates once a week, Zumba twice a week, gym three times a week and yoga four times a week.

I WILL NOT
*Drink so much Diet Coke before yoga that entire yoga session becomes exercise in trying not to fart.

*Ever be late for school run.

*Do V-signs at people during school run.

*Get annoyed by dishwasher, tumble dryer and micro-wave beeping in attention-seeking manner to tell you they have finished, wasting time crossly imitating dishwasher by dancing round saying, "Oh, oh, look at me, I'm a dishwasher, I've washed the dishes."

*Get annoyed with Mum, Una or Perfect Nicolette.

*Call Nicolette "Nicorette."

*Chew more than ten pieces of Nicorette per day.

*Hide empty wine bottles from Chloe.

*Eat grated cheese straight out of the fridge, dropping it all over the floor.

*Be shouty or snarly with the children but talk in calm, even, electronic-person-on-voicemail-type voice at all times.

*Drink more than one can (each) of Red Bull and Diet Coke a day.

*Drink more than two non-decaf cappuccinos a day. Or three.

*Eat more than three Big Macs or Starbucks ham-and-cheese paninis per week.

*Keep saying, "One . . . two . . ." in warning voice to children before have decided what to do when get to "three."

*Lie in bed in the morning thinking morbid or erotic thoughts, but get straight up at six o'clock and do self up for school run in manner of Stella McCartney, Claudia Schiffer or similar.

*Wang around hysterically when things go wrong but instead achieve acceptance and calm—and stand like a great tree in the midst of it all.

But how can I accept what happened? . . . Look, I mustn't . . . Gaah! Is time for doctor's appointment and have not got snack ready, written, meditated or located whereabouts of EFFING CAR KEYS! FUCK!

SOCIAL MEDIA VIRGIN

Saturday 21 April 2012

172lb, minutes spent on exercise bike 0, minutes spent cleaning out cupboard 0, minutes spent working out how to use remotes 0, resolutions kept 0.

9.15 p.m. Children are asleep and house is all dark and quiet. Oh God, I'M SO LONELY. Everyone else in London is out laughing uproariously with their friends in restaurants and then having sex.

9.25 p.m. Look. Is absolutely fine being in on own on Saturday nights. Will simply clear out cupboard under stairs then get on exercise bike.

9.30 p.m. Just looked in cupboard. Maybe not.

9.32 p.m. Just looked in fridge. Maybe will have glass of wine and bag of grated cheese.

9.35 p.m. That's better. Am going to get on Twitter! With the advent of social media is no need for anyone to feel isolated and alone ever again.

9.45 p.m. Have got onto Twitter site but do not understand. Is just incomprehensible streams of gibberish half-conversations with @this and @that. How is anybody supposed to know what is going on?

Sunday 22 April 2012
9.15 p.m. OK. Have got self set up on Twitter now. Need to find name. Something young-sounding: TotesAmazog-Bridget?

9.46 p.m. Maybe not.

10.15 p.m. JoneseyBJ!

10.16 p.m. But why does it call it @JoneseyBJ? @? At? At what?

Monday 23 April 2012
176lb (oh God), Twitter followers 0.

9.15 p.m. Cannot figure out how to put up photo. Is just empty egg-shaped graphic. Is fine! Can be photo of self before was conceived.

9.45 p.m. Right. Will wait for followers.

9.47 p.m. No followers.

9.50 p.m. Actually will not wait for followers. A watched pot never boils.

10 p.m. Wonder if I've got any followers yet.

10.02 p.m. No followers.

10.12 p.m. Still no followers. Humph. Whole point of Twitter is you are supposed to talk to people but there isn't anyone to talk to.

10.15 p.m. Followers 0. Feel lurching sense of shame and fear: maybe they are all Twittering to each other, and ignoring me because I'm unpopular.

10.16 p.m. Maybe even Twittering to each other about how unpopular I am, behind my back.

10.30 p.m. Great. Not only am I isolated and alone but also, now clearly, unpopular.

Tuesday 24 April 2012
175lb, calories 4827, number of minutes spent fiddling furiously with technological devices 127, number of technological devices managed to get to do anything they were supposed to 0, number of minutes spent doing anything nice apart from eating 4827 calories and fiddling with technological devices 0, number of Twitter followers 0.

7.06 a.m. Just remembered am on Twitter. Feel wildly puffed up! Part of huge social revolution and young. Last night I just didn't give it enough time! Maybe thousands of followers will have appeared overnight! Millions! I will have gone viral. Cannot wait to see how many followers have come!!

7.10 a.m. Oh.

7.11 a.m. Still no followers.

Wednesday 25 April 2012
178lb, number of times checked for Twitter followers 87, Twitter followers 0, calories 4832 (bad but fault of non-existent Twitter followers).

9.15 p.m. Still no followers. Have eaten the following things:

* 2 chocolate croissants
* 7 Babybel cheeses (but one was half eaten)
* ½ bag of grated mozzarella
* 2 Diet Cokes
* 1.5 leftover sausages from kids' breakfast
* ½ a McDonald's cheeseburger from fridge
* 3 Tunnock's Tea Cakes
* 1 bar Cadbury's Dairy Milk (large)

Tuesday 1 May 2012
11.45 p.m. Have just been whitelisted by Twitter for checking my followers 150 times in one hour.

Wednesday 2 May 2012
174lb, Twitter followers 0.

9.15 p.m. Am not going to do Twitter any more or check followers any more. Maybe will go on Facebook.

9.20 p.m. Just called Jude to ask how to get on Facebook. "Be careful," she said. "It's a good way of keeping in touch but you'll end up looking at endless pictures of exes embracing their new girlfriends, then finding they've de-friended you."

Humph. Not very likely to happen to me. Am going to try Facebook.

9.30 p.m. Maybe will wait a bit before attempting Facebook.

Jude just called me back, laughing. "Really don't do Facebook yet. I just got a thing saying Tom is checking out dating profiles. He must have ticked a box by accident. Everyone can see, including his parents and former psychology professors."

THE FLABBY DIAPHRAGM

Wednesday 9 May 2012
175lb, Twitter followers 0.

9.30 a.m. Emergency! Back has gone. I mean, not actually gone, in sense of still having shoulders attached to bottom. But was just checking Twitter for followers then slammed laptop shut, tossing head dismissively and saying, "Pah!" and whole of left upper back suddenly went into spasm. Is like I didn't notice I had a back before and now it is complete agony and what am I going to do?

11 a.m. Just back from osteopath. Osteopath said it is not fault of Twitter but due to years of lifting children and I should try bending from the legs instead of the back— i.e. squat like an African tribal woman, which seems a bit ungainly, though not to insult the gracefulness of African tribal women who are of course very graceful.

She asked if I had any other symptoms and I said, "Acid." She poked around my stomach exclaiming, "Gosh! This is the flabbiest diaphragm I've ever felt."

Turns out, because of my age, my entire middle section has refused to go back like it was and all my intestines are flobbering about, uncontained. No wonder they are hanging over my black sweatpants like porridge.

"What shall I do?"

"You'll have to start working that stomach," she said. "And you'll have to lose some of the fat. There's a very good new obesity clinic at St. Catherine's Hospital."

"OBESITY CLINIIIIIIIIIC?" I said indignantly, jumping up from the bed and putting my clothes back on. "I might have a bit of baby fat, but I'm not obese!"

"No, no," she said hurriedly. "You're not obese. It's just very effective if you want to lose weight properly. It's very hard when you've got little ones."

"I know," I gabbled. "It's all very well knowing what you're supposed to be eating, but if you're surrounded by leftover fish fingers and chips at five o'clock every night, and then eat them and have your own dinner later . . ."

"Exactly, the clinic puts you on meal replacement so there isn't any argument," said the osteopath. "You just don't put anything else into your mouth."

Not sure what Tom, Jude and Talitha would say about that one, harrumph harrumph.

Left in huff, then had sudden urge to go back in and say, "Will you follow me on Twitter?"

9.15 p.m. Got home and surveyed self aghast in mirror. Am starting to look like a heron. My legs and arms have stayed the same, but my whole upper body is like a large bird with a big roll of fat round the middle that, when clothed, looks like it should be served up at Christmas with cranberry jelly and gravy; when unclothed, as though it's been cooking all night in a pot in a box full of straw in Scotland, and is about to be served up for an extended family's post-Hogmanay breakfast. Talitha is right. The secret is to alter the automatic fat positioning of (unacceptable outdated phrase approaching) Middle Age.

Thursday 10 May 2012
174lb, Twitter followers 0.

10 a.m. Just spoke to Obesity Clinic. Encouragingly, there was some doubt over whether I was actually obese enough to be accepted! Found self, for first time in life, lying about weight to make it heavier than it actually is.

10.10 a.m. Am going to completely transform my body into a lean muscular thing with tight band of muscle round the middle, holding in the intestines.

10.15 a.m. Just reflexively put remains of kids' breakfast into mouth.

Thursday 17 May 2012
175lb, Twitter followers 0.

9.45 a.m. On point of Obesity Clinic departure. Feel have got to lowest ebb ever. Will be like one of those people you see in medical news reports looking ashamed of themselves, having their blood pressure taken in hospital gowns while a trim, streamlined reporter talks in front of them in stern, concerned tones, about the "Obesity Epidemic."

10 p.m. Obesity Clinic was FANTASTIC. After initial awkwardness of having to repeat "The Obesity Clinic" increasingly loudly to the receptionist, eventually reached the clinic, to see a man who was so large he was actually wheeling his fat on a trolley in front of him. He seemed to be being hit on by an only slightly less large woman who was saying to him in a seductive voice, "Were you Childhood Obese?"

People were looking at me, with the sort of admiration I hadn't felt since I was twenty-two and running round in a psychedelic shirt tied up in a knot revealing my flat midriff. Realized they must think I was one of the clinic's success stories nearing the end of my "programme." Felt unaccustomed, leaping sense of self-confidence. Realized this was wrong, and disrespectful to fellow patients.

Also, the very fact of seeing fat as a separate body attachment being wheeled on a trolley started to make me see fat as an actual thing. Realize, in the past, have seen fat as some totally unreasonable, random act of nature rather than a direct product of things-put-in-mouth.

"Name," said the man on reception, who, worryingly, was very fat himself. Surely the people who work at the clinic ought to have got this one down by now?

The whole thing was medical and complex: blood tests, ECGs and consultations. Once we got over the moment of awkwardness when they tried to put me down on the form as a "geriatric mother" it all went absolutely swimmingly. Seems like the whole thing of weighing yourself is not the point. The point is to drop dress sizes. And people who are very, very fat—say fifty or a hundred pounds overweight—can lose a lot—like twelve pounds of fat in one week! And that is actual fat. But if you're just trying to lose 10, 15 per cent of your body weight, anything more than a couple of pounds isn't losing fat, it's (darkly) other things.

You see, crucially, is not about weight but the percentage of fat to muscle. If you just go on a crash diet, and do not lift weights, you end up losing your muscles, which are heavier than your fat. So you weigh less, but are more fat. Or something. Anyway, upshot is: am supposed to go to gym.

My diet is going to be just protein chocolate puddings and protein chocolate bars, then a small portion of protein and vegetables in the evenings, so I mustn't put anything in my mouth which isn't those things. (Apart from penises— why did mind think such a thought? Chance would be a fine thing, though after today it is suddenly looking like that might be a possibility.)

MAKEOVER!

Thursday 24 May 2012

179lb (huh), pounds lost 0, Twitter followers 0, protein chocolate bars consumed 28, chocolate protein puddings consumed 37, number of meals replaced by protein chocolate bars or puddings 0, average number of calories per day eaten combining normal food with protein products 4,798.

Just went to Obesity Clinic for first week's progress weigh-in.

"Bridget," said the nurse, "you're supposed to replace the meals with the protein products, not eat them as well."

Looked sulkily at the chart then blurted out, "Will you follow me on Twitter?"

"I am not," she said, "on Twitter. Now, next week, forget about Twitter and just eat the products. Nothing else. OK?"

9.15 p.m. Children are asleep. Oh God, I'm so lonely, Twitter follower-less, fat, hungry and sick of effing obesity products. Hate this time of day when children are asleep. Should be relaxing and fun instead of just lonely. Right. Am not going to wallow in it. In next three months am going to:

* Lose 75lb
* Gain 75 Twitter followers

* Write 75 pages of screenplay
* Learn to operate television
* Find friend with children same age who lives nearby so whole evening is fun instead of chaos followed by grated-cheese stuffing-fest

Yes! That is what I need. Is not natural for children to be isolated in individual houses with one or two adults focusing far too much attention on their happiness, scared to let them play in the street for fear of paedophiles. Sure there must have been paedophiles when we were growing up, but mass-media-induced fear of paedophiles has changed the whole face of parenting. Need other parents to spontaneously talk and drink wine with while children play, so whole thing would be like extended Italian family having dinner under a tree. For as the saying goes, "It takes a whole village to raise a child."

Also, to get a celebrity ready for the red carpet.

Actually, there is a nice woman I have seen opposite who seems to have children—though "nice" is perhaps the wrong word. She is wildly bohemian, with mane of black hair topped off with things that would be more at home in a garden centre or pet shop than on a head. Whole thing might look strange were it not for her equally outlandish dark bohemian beauty. Have seen her along with other people coming and going: children, teenagers—nannies? mannies? lovers?—a ruggedly handsome man who may be a husband, or a visiting artist, and, from time to time, a baby. Maybe she has kids the same age?

Feeling more jolly now. Tomorrow will be better.

Thursday 31 May 2012
175lb

Yayy! Have lost 4lbs since last week! Am back to weight at start of diet. Though nurse says loss is not really fat but "other things." Also says I need to start e.g., cycling instead of sitting on my arse all day.

Thursday 7 June 2012
171lb

10 a.m. Have embraced the bike-borrowing scheme of our eccentric (i.e., sensible) mayor, Boris Johnson—bought Boris Bike key, and borrowed Boris Bike and everything! Suddenly feel part of cool bicycling London: whole world of carefree young people eschewing cars and being lean and green! Am going to cycle to Obesity Clinic.

10.30 a.m. Just returned, traumatized from bike ride. Completely terrifying. Kept feeling had forgotten to put seat belt on, and getting off whenever a car came. Maybe will go on canal towpath.

11.30 a.m. Just back from canal ride on bike. Went really well until someone threw an egg at me from a bridge. Or maybe it was a bird which went into sudden early labour. Will clean off egg, not do Boris Bikes any more and go to Obesity Clinic on bus. At least will be alive and clean when sitting on arse instead of dead and covered in egg.

Thursday 14 June 2012

167lb!

Keep repeatedly taking off clothes and getting on scales, then taking off watch, bracelet, etc., and staring delightedly at dial. Just makes me want to do diet more.

Wednesday 20 June 2012

1 p.m. Have just been to gym—which is good, though hideous, obviously. Also what is the law which says that when changing room is empty except for one other person, their locker will always be the one directly above yours?

Now am going to go back on Twitter and find people.

1.30 p.m.

<@DalaiLama Just as a snake sheds its skin, so we must shed our past again and again.>

You see? The Dalai Lama and I are one cyber-mind. I am shedding my fat like a snake.

Wednesday 27 June 2012

9.30 a.m. Have started my *Hedda Gabbler* screenplay. Is really very relevant because it is about a girl living in Norway—which I am going to translate to Queen's Park— who decides "her dancing days are over" and nobody lovely is going to actually marry her, so goes for someone boring— like grabbing the last seat when the music stops in musical chairs. Maybe I will also make her lose loads of weight and get millions of Twitter followers.

10 a.m. Maybe not. Twitter followers 0.

Thursday 28 June 2012
159lb, pounds lost 16!

OMG. Have lost 16 lbs! The strange thing is, where hundreds and hundreds of diets over the years have failed or lasted five days, this one is actually . . .

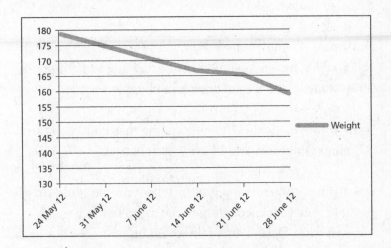

. . . working! It is something about going every week and being weighed and having my fat-to-muscle ratio measured, and knowing I can't cheat and tell myself am on the Hay Diet when I want a baked potato and the Weightwatchers diet when I want a Mars bar. Also just found I can fit into dress I had before I was pregnant (though admittedly tent-shaped) and that has whipped me into a frenzy of optimism.

Thursday 12 July 2012
155lb, pounds lost 20, pages of screenplay written 10, Twitter followers 0.

9.15 p.m. Oh God, I'm so lonely. Right. Am going to really get going on Twitter.

9.20 p.m. Dalai Lama has 2 million followers and yet he follows no one. That is right. A god cannot follow others. Wonder if he actually tweets himself or does he get his assistant to do it?

9.30 p.m. Complete meltdown. Lady Gaga has 33 million followers! Why am I even bothering? Twitter is giant popularity contest which I am doomed to be the worst at.

9.35 p.m. Just texted Tom explaining that Lady Gaga has 33 million followers and I have zero followers.

9.40 p.m. <You're supposed to follow people. Otherwise how are they supposed to know you're on Twitter?>
   <But the Dalai Lama follows no one.>
   <You're not a god or Lady Gaga, dear. You have to be proactive. Follow me: @TomKat37.>

10 p.m. @TomKat37 has 878 followers. How did he manage that?

Friday 13 July 2012
10.15 p.m. I've got a follower! You see. People are starting to notice my style.

10.16 p.m. Oh. <@TomKat37 You see? You've got a follower. Now keep going.>
   Is just Tom.

Tuesday 17 July 2012

152lb., Twitter followers 1.

Noon. Glorious and historic day. Just went shopping to H&M and asked the assistant to bring me a 16 and she looked at me as if I was mad and said, "You need a 14."

I scoffed, "I'll never fit into a 14," and she brought it, and it fitted. I am a 14!

And I have a follower! Am practically viral.

Thursday 26 July 2012

149lb, pages of screenplay 25, Twitter followers 1.

Yayy! Have broken through 150lb glass floor (though may have been through standing on one leg and slightly leaning on washbasin).

Also am on total screenwriting roll. Have decided to call my screenplay *The Leaves in His Hair*, which is Hedda's most famous line in *Hedda Gabbler*. Even though it is only famous because nobody understands what she means.

Monday 30 July 2012

148lb, Twitter followers 50,001.

9.15 p.m. I've got another follower! But a weird follower. It's a follower with 50,000 followers.

9.35 p.m. What is it? It's just sort of hovering there like a spaceship, watching silently. Feel I ought to fire on it or something.

9.40 p.m. It's called XTC Communications.

10 p.m. Just tweeted whole weird-follower scenario to Tom, who tweeted back.
    <@TomKat37 @JoneseyBJ It's a spambot, baby. It's just marketing.>

10.30 p.m. Tee hee. Just replied:
    <@JoneseyBJ @TomKat37 I already have a spambot. You should have seen it today in the harsh rays of the early morning sun.>

Tuesday 31 July 2012
Twitter followers 50,001.

2 p.m. FIFTY THOUSAND AND ONE FOLLOWERS. Feeling fabulous! Just bought lip plumper! It feels a bit funny but actually seems to work.

3 p.m. Wonder if put lip plumper on hands will get fat fingers?

Wednesday 1 August 2012
Twitter followers 1 again.

7 a.m. Humph. Spambot has just, like, gone, taking its 50,000 bloody followers with it. Gaah! Kids are awake.

9.15 p.m. Will just check Twitter.

9.20 p.m. Tom has "retweeted" my spambot tweet and seven followers have come.

9.50 p.m. What should I do now, though? Should I greet them? Welcome them?

9.51 p.m. Follow them?

10 p.m. Paralyzed into silence by social-media embarrassment. Maybe will not do Twitter any more.

Thursday 2 August 2012

142lb, pounds lost 33, muscles grown 5% (whatever that means).

1 p.m. Giddily euphoric! Just went to Obesity Clinic and nurse says I am now ahead of target and model patient. Then went to H&M again to check size and am a 12.

Am thin and not a heron! Am Uma Thurman! Am Jemima Kahn!

2 p.m. Just nipped into Marks & Spencer to purchase celebratory chocolate mousse cake and have eaten whole thing like a polar bear taking great swipes out with his paw.

Friday 3 August 2012

145lb (emergency).

10 a.m. Chocolate mousse cake has, I swear, moved directly from my mouth to my stomach and is just sitting there, under my skin, like the foil bag inside a cheap wine-box. Must abandon screenplay, career, etc., and go to gym.

Noon. Am never going to gym again. Am never going to lose the weight, never and don't bloody well care. Was consumed with rage whilst lying on front with bum in air failing to lift weight bar with ankles. Looked round to see everyone contorted ludicrously in machines like Hieronymous Bosch painting.

Why are bodies so difficult to manage? Why? "Oh, oh, look at me, I'm a body, I'm going to splurge fat unless you, like, STARVE yourself and go to undignified TORTURE CENTRES and don't eat anything nice or get drunk." Hate diet. Is all fault of SOCIETY. Am just going to be old and fat and eat whatever I like and NEVER HAVE SEX AGAIN and WHEEL MY FAT AROUND ON A TROLLEY.

Sunday 5 August 2012

Weight (unknown, daren't look).

11 p.m. Have today consumed the following things.

*2 "Healthy Start" (i.e. 482 calories each) muffins
*Full English breakfast with sausages, scrambled egg, bacon, tomatoes and fried bread
*Pizza Express pizza
*Banana split
*2 packets of Rolos
*Half a Marks & Spencer chocolate cheesecake (actually, if am honest, whole of a Marks & Spencer cheesecake)
*2 glasses Chardonnay

*2 packets cheese and onion crisps
*1 bag grated cheese
*1 12-inch jelly "snake" purchased at the Odeon cinema
*1 bag popcorn (large)
*1 hot dog (large)
*Remains of 2 hot dogs (large)

HARHARBLOODY HAR. Put that in your pipe and smoke it, society!

Thursday 9 August 2012
152lb, weight gained since last week: 10lbs (though maybe chocolate cheesecake is still intact in stomach?)

2 p.m. Could hardly bring self to go to Obesity Clinic as was so ashamed.

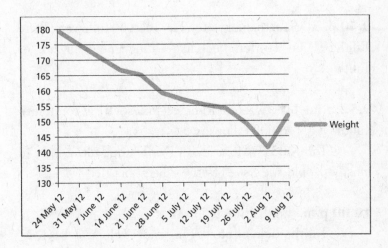

Nurse took one look at scales, marched me into the doctor, and then made me go into the Group Therapy room, where everyone else talked about their "eating relapses." Actually it was great. Mine was definitely the best and everyone seemed deeply impressed.

9.15 p.m. In spite of—or perhaps proving—nurse's lecture ("it takes three days to create a habit and three weeks to break it"), just want to eat cake and cheese again, and go back next week and impress everyone even more.

9.30 p.m. Just called Tom, grated cheese falling out of my mouth, and explained the whole thing.

"Nooo! Don't start trying to out-relapse obese people!" he said. "What about Twitter? Have you followed your followers? Follow Talitha."

9.45 p.m. Tom just tweeted me Talitha's Twitter address.

9.50 p.m. @Talithaluckybitch has 146,000 followers. Hate Talitha. Hate Twitter. Feel like eating cheese again, or Talitha.

9.52 p.m. Just tweeted Tom: <@JoneseyBJ @TomKat37 Talitha has 146,000 followers.>

<@TomKat37 @JoneseyBJ Don't worry dear, they're mostly people she's slept with or been married to.>

10.00 p.m. Talitha tweeted back.

<@Talithaluckybitch @TomKat37 @JoneseyBJ Darling it's really TERRIBLY vulgar to display the green-eyed monster on Twitter.>

Friday 10 August 2012

Twitter followers 75, then 102, then 57, then probably none, by now.

7.15 a.m. 75 followers have mysteriously, silently appeared overnight.

9.15 p.m. 102 now. Feel overwhelmed by responsibility: like am leader of a cult and they will all jump into a lake or something if I tell them to. Maybe will have glass of wine.

9.30 p.m. Must clearly show leadership and address followers.

    <@JoneseyBJ Welcome followers. I am thy leader. Ye art most welcome to my cult.>

    <@JoneseyBJ But please do not do anything weird like jump into a lake, even if I suggest it, as may be drunk.>

9.45 p.m. <@JoneseyBJ Gaah! 41 one of ye followers have drained away as suddenly as ye first appeared.>

    <@JoneseyBJ Comest thou back!>

Thursday 16 August 2012

137lb, pages of screenplay written 45, Twitter followers 97.

4.30 p.m. Twitter followers have surged back and multiplied, rather like Pinocchio's broomstick. Is clearly sign or portent. Weight is coming off again, have finished Act Two of screenplay, well sort of, and just had sighting of bohemian neighbour.

Was trying to park car. This is impossible in our street as is narrow, curved and cars park on both sides. Had just reversed in and out of space fourteen times, then resorted to Braille Parking, i.e., forcing car into space by bumping cars in front and behind. Braille Parking is fine in our street because everyone does it, then every so often a delivery lorry charges through, scraping everyone, someone takes its number and we all get our dents done on the insurance.

"Mummeee!" said Billy. "There's someone in the car you bumped."

The bohemian neighbour was sitting in the front seat, yelling at the kids in the back. I knew we were kindred spirits. She climbed out of the car, followed by her two dark, wild-looking children. They looked the same age as Billy and Mabel: older boy, younger girl! Then the bohemian neighbour looked at her bumper, grinned at me, and disappeared into her house.

We have initiated contact! We are on the friendship road! As long as she does not behave like the spambot.

Thursday 23 August 2012
135lb, pounds lost 40 (unbelievable), dress sizes dropped 3.

Historic and joyful day. Have not got fat anything. Obesity Clinic says have now got down to healthy weight and should go on "Maintenance" and losing more weight is only for aesthetic reasons and not because they think I need it!

And to prove it, I just went to H&M again and I am a 10!

I have written half of screenplay and at least ascertained that have neighbour with children the same age, I have 79 twitter followers and am part of hooked-in generation of social-media people, and I AM A SIZE 10. You see! Maybe am not completely rubbish.

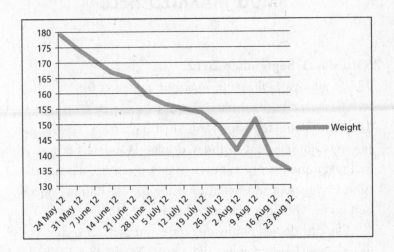

Monday 27 August 2012
Acts of screenplay written 2.25, Twitter followers 87.

Mabel is so funny. She was sitting staring ahead in an eerie manner.

"What are you doing?" said Billy, brown eyes looking at her intently, slightly amused. Mark Darcy. Mark Darcy re-created in child form.

"Havin' a starin' competition," said Mabel.

"Who with?"

"De chair?" said Mabel, as if it was the most obvious thing in the world.

Billy and me started giggling, then suddenly he stopped and looked at me: "You're laughing again, Mummy?"

SMUG MARRIED HELL

Saturday 1 September 2012

135lb, positive thoughts 0, romantic prospects 0.

10 p.m. Giant step backwards. Just back from Magda and Jeremy's annual joint-birthday drinks. Was late because it had taken me twenty minutes to do up my zip, despite the time I had spent in yoga attempting to interlink my hands behind my shoulder blades and trying not to fart.

On the doorstep the memories surged up again: the years when I would stand there with Mark, with his hand on my back; the year I'd just found out I was pregnant with Billy and we were going to tell them all; the year when we took Mabel all wrapped up in her little car seat. It was so lovely going to things with Mark. I never worried about what I was wearing because he'd watch me try everything on before we left and help me choose, and tell me I didn't look fat and do all the zips. He always had something kind and funny to say if I did something stupid, was always batting off any jellyfishing remarks (the kind that suddenly zap you as if from nowhere in the middle of a conversational warm sea).

I could hear the music and laughter inside. Fought the urge to run off. But then the door opened and Jeremy was there.

I saw Jeremy feeling what I was feeling: the yawning gap beside me. Where was Mark, his old friend?

"Ah, there you are! Excellent," said Jeremy, blustering over the pain, as he had consistently done since the moment it happened. That's public school for you. "Come in, come in. Great! How are the children? Growing up?"

"No," I said rebelliously. "They are stunted by grief and will be midgets for the rest of their lives."

Jeremy has clearly never read any Zen books and doesn't know about just being there, and letting the other person be there, just as they are. But for a split second, he stopped the bluster and we just were there as we were, which was: extremely sad about the same thing. Then he coughed and started again as if nothing had happened.

"Come on! Voddy and tonic? Let's take your coat. You're looking very trim!"

He ushered me into the familiar sitting room and Magda waved cheerily from the drinks table. Magda, who I met at Bangor University, is actually my oldest friend. I looked around at all the faces I'd known since my early twenties, once the original Sloane Rangers, older now. All the couples who seemed to get married like a line of falling dominoes when they were thirty-one, still together: Cosmo and Woney, Pony and Hugo, Johnny and Mufti. And there was the same sense I'd had for all that time—of being a duck out of water, unable to join in what they were talking about because I was at a different stage of life, even though I was the same age. It was as though there had been a seismic timeshift and my life was happening years behind theirs, in the wrong way.

"Oh, Bridget! Jolly good to see you. Goodness, you've lost weight. How are you?"

Then there was the sudden flash in the eyes, the remembering of the whole widowhood thing: "How ARE the children? How are they doing?"

Not so Cosmo, Woney's husband, a successful, confident-though-egg-shaped fund manager, who came charging up like a blunderbuss.

"So! Bridget! Still on your own? You're looking very chipper. When are we going to get you married off again?"

"Cosmo!" said Magda indignantly. "Zip it."

One advantage of widowhood is that—unlike being single in your thirties, which, because it is ostensibly all your own fault, allows Smug Marrieds to say anything they like—it does usually introduce some element of tact. Unless, of course, you're Cosmo.

"Well, it's been long enough now, hasn't it?" he crashed on. "Can't carry on wearing widow's weeds for ever."

"Yes, but the trouble is—"

Woney joined in. "It's very hard for middle-aged women who find themselves single."

"Please don't say 'middle-aged,'" I purred, trying to imitate Talitha.

". . . I mean, look at Binko Carruthers. He's no oil painting. But the second Rosemary left him he was inundated with women! Inundated! Throwing themselves at him."

"Hurling themselves," said Hugo enthusiastically. "Dinners, theatre tickets. Life of Riley."

"Yes, but they're all 'of a Certain Age,' aren't they?" said Johnny.

Grrr. "Of a Certain Age" is even worse than "middle-aged" with its patronizing, only-ever-applied-to-women insinuations.

"Meaning?" said Woney.

"Well, you know," Cosmo was bludgeoning on. "Chap gets a new lease of life, he's going to go for something younger, isn't he? Plump and fecund and—"

Caught the quick flash of pain in Woney's eyes. Woney, not an advocate of the Talitha school of branding, has allowed the fat-positioning of middle age freely to position itself all over her back and beneath her bra: her skin, falling exhausted into the folds of her experience, unpolished by facials, peels or light-reflecting make-up bases. She has let her once long and shiny dark hair go grey, and cut it short, which only serves to emphasize the disappearance of the jawline (which as Talitha says, can be quickly glossed over with some well-cut, face-framing layers), and has gone for a Zara version of the structured black frock and high ruffled collar favoured by Maggie Smith in *Downton Abbey*.

I sense Woney has done this, or rather not done any "rebranding," presumably not out of "feminism" as such, but partly out of an old-fashioned British sense of personal honesty; partly because she can't be arsed; partly out of self-belief and confidence; partly because she doesn't define herself by how she looks or her sexuality; and, perhaps, mainly because she feels herself loved unconditionally for who she is: albeit by Cosmo who, in spite of his spherical physique, yellow teeth, hairless scalp and unbridled eyebrows, clearly feels he would be unconditionally loved by any woman lucky enough to have him.

But for a second, at that flash of pain in Woney's eyes, I felt a surge of sympathy, until she went on . . .

"What I mean is that for a single man of Bridget's age, it's a total buyer's market. No one's knocking at Bridget's door, are they? If she was a middle-aged man, with her own house and income and two helpless children, she'd be inundated by people wanting to take care of her. But look at her."

Cosmo looked me up and down. "Well, yes, we ought to get her fixed up," he said. "But I just don't know who would, you know, at a certain age . . ."

"Right," I burst out. "I've had enough of this! What do you mean, 'middle-aged'? In Jane Austen's day we'd all be dead by now. We're going to live to be a hundred. It's not the middle of our lives. Oh. Yes. Well, actually it is the middle. Come to think of it. But the point is, the whole expression 'middle-aged' conjures up a certain look." I panicked, glancing at Woney, feeling myself plunging helplessly into a deepening hole. ". . . a certain, a certain, past-it-ness, non-viability. It doesn't have to be like that. I mean, why are you assuming I don't have a boyfriend, just because I don't blab on about it? I mean, maybe I do have boyfriends!"

They were all staring at me, slavering almost.

"Do you?" said Cosmo.

"Do you have boyfriends?" said Woney, as if she were saying, "Do you sleep with a spaceman?"

"Yes," I lied smoothly, about the admittedly imaginary boyfriends.

"Well, where are they, then?" said Cosmo. "Why don't we ever see them?"

"I wouldn't want to bring them here because they'd think you were all too old, set in your ways and rude,"

I was about to blurt out. But I didn't because, ironically enough, as for the last twenty years or more, I didn't want to hurt their feelings.

So instead I used the immensely skilful social manoeuvre I've been employing for the last two decades and said, "I need to go to the toilet."

Sat down on the loo seat, saying, "OK. It's OK." Put some more lip plumper on, and headed back down. Magda was on her way to the kitchen, holding—symbolically enough—an empty sausage plate.

"Don't listen to bloody Cosmo and Woney," she said. "They're just in a frightful state because Max has gone off to university. Cosmo's on the verge of retiring, so they're going to be staring at each other across their Conran Shop 70s-style table for the next thirty years."

"Thanks, Mag."

"It's always so nice when things go badly for other people. Especially when they've just been rude to you."

Magda has never stopped being kind.

"Now, Bridget," she said. "Don't listen to that lot. But you do have to start moving on, as a woman. You have to find someone. You can't carry on feeling like this. I've known you for a long time. You can do it."

10.25 p.m. Can I? Can't see any way out of feeling like this. Not at this moment. You see, things being good has nothing to do with how you feel outside, it is all to do with how you are inside. Oooh, goody! Telephone! Maybe . . . a suitor?

10.30 p.m. "Oh, hello, darling"—my mother. "I'm just ringing quickly to see what we're doing about Christmas, because Una doesn't want her cranio-facial at the spa because she's had her hair done, and it's in fifteen minutes—though why she had her hair bouffed when she's got a cranio-facial and Aqua-Zumba in the morning I have no idea."

I blinked confusedly, trying to make sense of what she was talking about. Ever since Mum and Auntie Una moved into St. Oswald's House, the phone calls have been the same. St. Oswald's House is an upscale retirement community near Kettering, only we are not allowed to call it a "retirement community."

The not-a-retirement community is built around a grand Victorian mansion, almost a stately home. As described on the website, it has a lake, grounds which "boast a variety of rare wildlife" (i.e., squirrels), "BRASSERIE 120" (the bar/bistro), "CRAVINGS" (the more formal restaurant) and "CHATS" (the coffee bar), plus function rooms (for meetings: not toilets), "guest suites" for visiting families, a collection of "superbly appointed" houses and bungalows, and, crucially, "an Italianate garden designed by Russell Page in 1934."

On top of this lot there is "VIVA," the fitness facility—with pool, spa, gym, beauty salon and hairdresser, and fitness classes—the source of most of the trouble.

"Bridget? Are you still there? You're not wallowing in it, are you?"

"Yes! No!" I said, attempting the bright, positive tones of someone who is not wallowing in anything.

"Bridget. You're wallowing. I can tell from your voice."

Grrr. I know Mum did go through a dark time after

84

Dad died. The lung cancer took him in six months from diagnosis to funeral. The only positive thing was that Dad did get to hold newborn Billy in his arms, just before he died. It was really hard for Mum when Una still had Geoffrey. Una and Geoffrey had been Mum and Dad's best friends for fifty-five years and, as they never tired of telling me, had known me since I was running round the lawn with no clothes on. But after Geoffrey's heart attack there was no holding Mum and Una back. If they feel it now, Mum about Dad, or Una about Geoffrey, they rarely show it. There's something about that wartime generation which gives them the capacity to just cheerfully soldier on. Maybe something to do with the powdered eggs and whale-meat fritters.

"You don't want to mope around when you're widowed, darling. You want to have fun! Why don't you come over and jump in the sauna with Una and me?"

It was kindly meant, but what did she imagine I was going to do? Run out of the house, abandon the children, drive for an hour and a half, rip off my clothes, have my hair bouffed, then "jump in the sauna"?

"So! Christmas! Una and I were wondering, are you going to come to us or . . ."

(Have you noticed how when people are giving you two options, the second one is always the one they want you to do?)

". . . Well, the thing is, darling, there's the St. Oswald's cruise this year! And we wondered if you might like to come? With the children of course! It's to the Canaries, but it's not all old people, you know. There are some very 'with-it' places they visit."

"Right, right, a cruise, great," I said, suddenly thinking that if the Obesity Clinic had made me feel thin, maybe an over-seventies cruise might make me feel young.

Mind, however, now also contained image of me chasing Mabel along a cruise-liner deck through a morass of bouffed hairdos and electric wheelchairs.

"You'll be perfectly at home, because it's actually for over-fifties," Mum added, unknowingly putting the kibosh on the plan in a microsecond.

"Well, actually, we think we might have plans here! You're welcome to join us, of course, but it'll be chaos, and if the other option is a cruise in hot weather, then—"

"Oh, no, darling. We don't want to leave you at Christmas. Una and I would love to come to you! It'd be super having Christmas with the little ones, it's such a hard time for us both."

Gaaah! How could I possibly handle Mum, Una and the kids, with no help as Chloe was going on a t'ai chi retreat to Goa with Graham? Did not want it to end up like last year, with me trying to stop my heart from breaking into pieces at doing Santa without Mark and sobbing behind the kitchen counter, whilst Mum and Una squabbled over lumps in the gravy and commented on my parenting and housekeeping, as if, rather than inviting them for Christmas, I had called them in as Systems Analysts.

"Let me think about it," I said.

"Well, the thing is, darling, we have to reserve the berths by tomorrow."

"Go ahead and book it for just you, Mum. Honestly, because I haven't worked out—"

"Well, you can cancel with fourteen days' notice," she said.

"OK, then," I said. "OK."

Great, an over-fifties cruise for Christmas. Everything looks so dark and gloomy.

11 p.m. Was still wearing my prescription sunglasses. That's better.

Maybe I have just been like a wave building momentum and now I have crashed and another will come along soon! For as it says in *Men Are from Mars, Women Are from Venus*, women are like waves and men are like rubber bands which ping away to their caves and come back.

Except mine didn't come back.

11.15 p.m. Look, stoppit. For, as it says on the Dalai Lama's Twitter:

<@DalaiLama We cannot avoid pain, we cannot avoid loss. Contentment comes from the ease and flexibility with which we move through change.>

Maybe will go to yoga and become more flexible.

Or maybe will go out with friends and get plastered.

A PLAN

Sunday 2 September 2012

Alcohol units 5 (but hard to tell with mojitos—maybe 500?).

"It's time," said Tom, settling into his fourth mojito in Quo Vadis. "We're taking her to the Stronghold."

The Stronghold has recently become a regular part of Tom's micro-universe. Run by a client from his therapy practice, it is an illegal American-style speakeasy in Hoxton.

"It's like being in an incredibly well-directed music video," Tom enthused, eyes shining. "There's every age group: young and old, black and white, gay and straight. Gwyneth's been seen there! And it's a 'pop-up.'"

"Oh, please," said Talitha. "How many minutes till the edginess of 'pop-up' anything has popped down?"

"Anyway," said Jude. "Who bothers to meet people in real life any more?"

"But Jude, there are actual live people there. And Americana bands, and sofas—you can talk and dance, and make out with people."

"Why would you do all that before you've found out in one click whether they're divorced or separated-with-kids, like bungee jumping more than going to the movies, know how to spell, know not to use the expression 'lol' or 'special lady' without irony, and whether they think the world would be a better place if people with low IQs were not allowed to reproduce?"

"Well, at least you'll know they're not a photograph from fifteen years ago," said Tom.

"We're going," said Talitha.

Upshot is, we are off to the Stronghold in Hoxton on Thursday.

Wednesday 5 September 2012

Acts of screenplay written 2.5, attempts to find babysitter 5, babysitters found 0.

9.15 p.m. Disaster. Forgot to ask Chloe about babysitting tomorrow, and she is going to watch Graham compete in the South of England t'ai chi semi-final.

"I'd love to help, Bridget, but t'ai chi means an enormous amount to Graham. I can definitely do the school run on Friday morning, though, so you can sleep in."

What am I going to do?

Cannot ask Tom as he is coming to the Stronghold, ditto Jude and Talitha, plus Talitha does not do children since she says she has done that and only uses hers if she needs a walker for charity auctions.

9.30 p.m. Just called Mum.

"Oh, darling, I'd love to but it's the Viva Supper tomorrow! We're doing Ham in Coca-Cola. Everyone is doing things in Coca-Cola now!"

Am slumped at kitchen table, trying not to think about everyone doing things in Coca-Cola in the Viva spa. It's SO UNFAIR. Am trying my best to rediscover myself as a woman but now am up shit creek without a . . . Oh! What about Daniel?

A DANIEL IN SHINING ARMOUR

Wednesday 5 September 2012 (continued)

"Jones, you little devil," growled Daniel when I called. "What are you wearing, what colour are your knickers and how are my godchildren?"

Daniel Cleaver, my former Emotional Fuckwit "boyfriend" and Mark's former arch-enemy, has, to his credit, really done his best to help since Mark was killed. After years of bitter one-upmanship, when Billy arrived the two of them finally made it up and Daniel is actually the children's godfather.

Daniel's best isn't exactly everyone's best: the last time he had them to stay, it turned out he just wanted to impress some girl by boasting that he had godchildren and . . . suffice it to say he dropped them off at school three hours late, and when I picked up Mabel later, her hair was in an incredibly complex plaited chignon.

"Mabel, what fabulous hair!" I said, imagining Daniel had brought John Frieda in to do full hair and make-up on Mabel at 7.30 a.m.

"De teacher did it," said Mabel. "Daniel brushed my hair wid a fork," adding, "it had maple syrup on it."

"Jones? Are you still there, Jones?"

"Yes," I said, startled.

"Babysitting call, Jones?"

"Would you . . . ?"

"Absolutely. When were you thinking?"

I cringed: "Tomorrow?"

There was a slight pause. Daniel was obviously doing something.

"Tomorrow night is absolutely fine. I find myself at a loose end, having been rejected by all human women under the age of eighty-four." Awww.

"We might be quite late, is that OK?"

"My dear girl, I am nocturnal."

"You won't . . . I mean, you won't bring a model or—"

"No, no, no, Jones. I shall *be* a model. A paragon of babysitting. Ludo. Wholesome vitamin-packed fare. And by the way . . ."

"Yes?" I said suspiciously.

"What kind of knickers *are* you wearing? At this moment? Are they mummy pants? Mummy's lovely mummy panties? Will you show them to Daddy tomorrow night?"

Still love Daniel, though obviously not to the point that I would get involved with any of his crap.

THE PERFECT BABYSITTER

Thursday 6 September 2012
133lb (v.g.), alcohol units 4, sexual encounters in last 5 years 0, sexual encounters in last 5 hours 2, embarrassing sexual encounters in last 5 hours 2.

The day of the Stronghold outing was upon us. Billy was wildly excited that Daniel was coming. "Will Amanda be here?"

"Who's Amanda?"

"The lady with the big boobies who was there last time."

"No!" I said. "Mabel, what are you looking for?"

"My hairbrush," she said darkly.

Managed somehow in the excitement to get them bathed and asleep, and scrambled to get ready before Daniel arrived.

I had opted for jeans (a brand chillingly called *Not Your Daughter's Jeans*) and a cowboy shirt, thinking it would fit in with the Americana theme.

Daniel arrived late, in his usual suit, hair shorter now, still gorgeous with that irresistible smile, bearing armfuls of unsuitable gifts—toy guns, semi-naked Barbies, giant bags of sweets, Krispy Kreme doughnuts—and a suspicious-looking half-hidden DVD, which I decided to ignore as I was cataclysmically late now.

"Ding-dong! Jones," he said. "Have you been on a diet? I thought I'd never see you looking like this again."

It's horrifying how differently some people treat you when you're fat, to when you're not. And when you're all done up and when you're just normal. No wonder women are so insecure. I know men are too. But when one is a woman, with all the tools at a modern woman's disposal, one can literally look like a completely different person from one half-hour to the next.

Even then, you think you don't look like you should. Sometimes look at billboards of beautiful models, and the real people underneath, and think it's a bit like if we were on a planet where all the space creatures were short, green and fat. Except a very few of them were tall, thin and yellow. And all the advertising was of the tall, yellow ones, airbrushed to make them even taller and yellower. So all the little green space creatures spent their whole time feeling sad because they weren't tall, thin and yellow.

"Jones? Are you still inhabiting your head? I said, I suppose a fuck would be out of the question?"

"Yes!" I said, jerking back to the present. "Yes, it would. Though this is in no way a sign of my lack of gratitude for the babysit." Rattled through a gabble of instructions and thanks and shot out of the door, feeling outraged as a feminist by Daniel's complex fattist pass, but uplifted as a female.

When I arrived at Talitha's, however, Tom burst out laughing. "Seriously? Dolly Parton?"

"You can't rely on your arse in jeans at our age," said Talitha briskly, sweeping in with a tray of mojitos. "You've got to have something else going on."

"I don't want to look like mutton," I said. "Or a prostitute."

"Well, quite, but you need something to start the idea of sexuality. Legs or boobs. Not both."

"What about one leg and one boob?" said Tom.

Eventually I ended up in a very expensive short black silk tunic of Talitha's and insanely high Yves Saint Laurent thigh boots.

"But I can't walk in them."

"Honey," said Talitha, "you're not going to need to walk."

In the cab started to think about how much Mark would have loved the thigh boots.

"Stoppit," said Tom, seeing my face. "He would want you to have a life."

Next I started to panic about the children. Talitha, who has known Daniel since *Sit Up Britain* days, took out her phone and texted:

<Daniel. Please reassure Bridget that the children are fine and asleep and you will text the moment they're not.>

No reply. We all stared nervously at the phone.

"Daniel doesn't text," I said, suddenly remembering. Then added, giggling, "He's too old."

Talitha put her mobile on speakerphone and called him.

"Daniel, you bloody old bastard?"

"Talitha! My dear girl! The very thought of you finds me suddenly, unaccountably, over-aroused. What are you up to at this moment and what colour are your panties?"

Grrr. He was supposed to be BABYSITTING.

"I'm with Bridget," she said, drily. "How's it going?"

"Yup, all perfectly splendid. Children fast asleep. Am

patrolling the doors, windows and corridors like a sentry. I shall be impeccable."

"Good."

She clicked off the phone. "You see? It will all be fine. Now stop worrying."

THE STRONGHOLD

The Stronghold was in a brick warehouse with an unmarked metal door and a buzzer with a code. Tom punched in the code, and we teetered in our insane heels up a concrete staircase which smelt as if somebody had weed in it.

But once we got in, as Tom gave our names for the guest list, I felt a reckless surge of excitement. The walls were brick, there were bales of straw round the edges which made me slightly wish I'd remained as Dolly Parton, and battered sofas. There was a band playing and a bar in the corner, manned by youths who were adding to the atmosphere by looking around nervously, as if a sheriff was going to tie up his horse, burst in in a cowboy hat and break it all up. It was hard to make the people out in the artistic lighting, but it was instantly clear that they weren't all teenagers, and that there were some . . .

". . . very hot men in the room," murmured Talitha.

"Come on, girl," said Tom. "Get back on that horse."

"I'm too old!" I said.

"So? It's practically pitch black."

"What am I going to talk about?" I gabbled. "I'm not au fait with popular music."

"Bridget," said Talitha, "we are gathered here to rediscover your inner sensual woman. This has nothing whatsoever to do with talking."

It felt like going back to being a teenager with the same leaping sense of doubt and possibility. It reminded me of the parties I used to go to when I was sixteen, when as soon as the parents had dropped us off, the lights would go out and everyone would get on the floor and start snogging anyone with whom they had made the most perfunctory eye contact.

"Look at him," said Tom. "He's looking at you! He's looking at you!"

"Tom, shut urrp," I said out of the side of my mouth, folding my arms across my chest and trying to tug the tunic down to reach the thigh boots.

"Pull yourself together, Bridget. DO SOMETHING."

I forced myself to look across, with an attempt at smoulderingness. The cute guy was, however, now making out with a stunning iBabe in short-shorts and an off-the-shoulder sweater.

"OhMyGod, that's disgusting—she's an embryo," said Jude.

"Call me old-fashioned, but I did read in *Glamour* that one's shorts should always be longer than one's vagina," murmured Talitha.

We all became crestfallen, our confidence collapsing like a house of cards. "Oh God. Do we just look like an ensemble of elderly transvestites?" said Tom.

"It's happened, just as I always feared," I said. "We've ended up as tragic old fools convincing ourselves the vicar is in love with us because he's mentioned his organ."

"Darlings!" said Talitha. "I forbid you to continue in this vein."

Talitha, Tom and Jude went off to dance, while I sulked

on a hay bale, thinking, "I want to go home and snuggle my babies, and hear their quiet breathing and know who I am and what I stand for," shamelessly using the children to gloss over me being old and past it.

Then a pair of legs in jeans sat down beside me on the hay bale. I caught a scent of a MAN, darling, as Talitha would put it, as he leaned in to my hair. "Do you want to dance?"

It was as simple as that. I didn't need to formulate a plan, work out what to say, or indeed do anything but look up into his attractive brown eyes and nod. He took my hand, and hoisted me up with a strong arm. He kept hold of my waist as we walked towards the floor, which was fortunate, given the thigh boots. Thankfully, it was a slow dance or I would have broken an ankle. He had a crinkly smile, and looked in the darkness like the sort of man who appears in adverts for SUVs. He was wearing a leather jacket. He put his hand on my waist and pulled me in to him.

As I laid my arm on his shoulder I suddenly realized what Tom and Talitha were on about. Sex is just sex.

Flashes and pulses of long-forgotten lust started running through me, like Frankenstein's monster when he was plugged into the electricity, only more romantic and sensual, and I found myself instinctively slipping my fingers to feel the hair on the stranger's collar, the skin on the back of his neck. He pulled me even closer to him, making it unmistakable that he was into sex at least with someone. As we turned slowly to the music, I saw Tom and Talitha staring at me with a mixture of awe and astonishment. I felt like a fourteen-year-old who'd pulled her first boy. I made a face to stop them doing anything stupid as I felt him, slowly, irresistibly, in manner of Mills & Boon hero, moving his lips to find mine.

And then we were kissing. Suddenly everything started going crazy. It was like driving a very fast car in a pair of stilettos. Nothing had stopped functioning despite years in the garage. One minute I was blocked at every turn and in a flash there were zero restraints and what was I doing? What about the children and what about Mark and who was this impertinent man anyway?

"Let's go somewhere quieter," he murmured. It was all a plot. Why else would he have asked me to dance? He was planning to murder me and then eat me!

"I've got to go! Now!"

"What?"

I looked up at him, terrified. It was midnight. I was Cinderella and I had to get back to the cots and the nannies, and the sleeplessness and sense of being totally asexual and staring down the barrel of single life till the end of my days . . . but wasn't that better than being murdered?

"Awfully sorry! Must be going. Jolly good! Thanks!"

"Go?" he said. "Oh God. That face."

Even as I was stumbling down the wee-smelling stairs I was becoming puffed up by his last phrase. "That face!" I was Kate Moss! I was Cheryl Cole! Once in the minicab, however, explaining the whole incident, a glance at my wild expression and drink-bloated features, mascara smeared under the eyes, somewhat ruined the concept.

"He means tormented by the face of a geriatric mother who's decided he's planning to murder her because he's kissed her!" shrieked Tom.

"And then eat her," added Talitha, as everyone fell about laughing.

"What were you thinking?" said Jude, giggling hysterically. "He was hot!"

"It's all right," said Talitha, recovering her composure and trying to settle elegantly back into the minicab seat, which smelt of curry. "I got his number."

12.10 a.m. Just got back and crept into house. Everything was quiet and dark. Where was Daniel?

12.20 a.m. Tiptoed downstairs and turned on the light. The basement looked like a bomb had hit it. The Xbox was still going, there were Sylvanian bunnies arranged in a line from one end to the other, Barbies, toy dinosaurs and machine guns, cushions, pizza cartons, Krispy Kreme doughnut bags and chocolate wrappers all over the floor, and a tub of melted chocolate fudge Häagen-Dazs upside down on the sofa. They would probably throw up in the night but at least they'd had a good time. But where was Daniel?

Crept up to their room. They were fast asleep, chocolate all over their faces but breathing peacefully. No Daniel. Started to panic.

Rushed down to the sofa bed in the sitting room—nothing. Rushed back up to my bedroom, opened the door and let out a noise. Daniel was in the bed. He raised his head and squinted through the darkness.

"Good God, Jones," he said. "Could those possibly be . . . thigh boots? Could I take a closer look?"

He pulled back the sheet. He was half-naked.

"Come on in, Jones," he said. "I promise I won't lay a finger on you."

The whole combination of being slightly drunk, aroused by a recent kiss and Daniel half-naked and devilish in the half-light made me flash back to being a thirty-something singleton. A split second later I was giggling and lurching into bed in the thigh boots.

"Now, Jones," began Daniel, "these are very, very naughty boots, and this is a very, very silly little tunic"—and then another split second later I fast-forwarded back to the present moment and remembered . . . well, everything, really.

"Gaah! Can't do this! Terribly sorry. Jolly good!" I gabbled, leaping out of the bed.

Daniel stared, then started laughing. "Jones, Jones, Jones, you're completely bonkers as usual."

I waited outside the door while he got up and dressed, and then, in the midst of my apologies and thanks for the babysitting, there was another moment when I felt so confused and turned on I almost jumped on him again and started devouring him like an animal. Then his mobile rang.

"Sorry, sorry," he said into the phone. "No, my plumptious, just got terribly stuck at work, look, I know, FUCK!" Cross Daniel now. "Look! Jesus! I said I had a presentation. It's a huge big deal for the project and . . . OK, OK, I'll be back in fifteen minutes, yes . . . yes . . . mmm . . . I long for your orb-like radiance . . ."

Orb-like radiance??

". . . I long to plunge myself into . . ."

Sighing with relief that I hadn't succumbed to the old routine, I managed to get him out of the door, then wrestle Talitha's thigh boots off. I cleared up the sitting room enough to not make Chloe hand in her notice in despair tomorrow, and sank into the empty bed.

12.55 a.m. But now feeling all restless and aroused. Feel like it has gone from total Man-Desert to, in the space of one evening, literally raining men.

AFTERMATH

Friday 7 September 2012

7 a.m. Am stark naked with clouting headache and have got to do school run.

7.01 a.m. No! Do not have to do school run. Was special treat this morning to lie in but have woken up anyway.

7.02 a.m. Gaah! Just remembered what happened last night with Leatherjacketman. And Daniel.

7.30 a.m. Traumatized by sounds of Chloe downstairs doing all the things that I am supposed to do: the one Weetabix that Mabel is allowed to put one teaspoonful of sugar on herself, the two slices of bacon for Billy with ketchup but no bread.

7.45 a.m. Feel terribly guilty: like hung-over Joan Crawford figure, about to drift down in a housecoat, with lipstick smeared all over my face, saying, "Hello, darlings, I'm your mummy. Remember? What are your names again?"

8 a.m. Door bangs, noises stop.

8.01 a.m. Door opens, noises restart: a search for Mabel's book bag.

8.05 a.m. Door slams again.

8.15 a.m. Silence. Bed is all cool and white and is delicious just lying here naked doing nothing. Feel like a spell has been broken, like Sleeping—well, not Beauty exactly—Sleeping Quite Old Person with Two Children, awoken by a kiss. Spring has touched the withered, wintry branches. Leaves and blossoms are bursting out and unfurling left, right and centre.

8.30 a.m. Texting ping! Maybe Talitha! Texting Leatherjacketman's number! Maybe even Leatherjacketman himself, making joke to defuse whole situation and asking me out! Am sexually viable!

It was the Infants Branch.

<Please remember to bring the Zoo Trip Permission Slip in this afternoon.>

WOMEN CHANGE THEIR MINDS

Saturday 8 September 2012

Annoying electronic devices in house 74, electronic devices which beep 7, electronic devices I know how to operate 0, electronic devices requiring passwords 12, passwords 18, passwords that can remember 0, minutes spent thinking about sex 342.

7.30 a.m. Just woke up from delicious, sensual dream all mixed up with Daniel and Leatherjacketman. Suddenly feel different—sensual, womanly—and yet that makes me feel so guilty, as if I'm being unfaithful to Mark and yet . . . is so sensual feeling like a sensual woman, with a sensual side which is sensually . . . oh. Children are awake.

11.30 a.m. Entire morning has been totally sensual and peaceful. Started day with all three of us in my bed, cuddling and watching telly. Then had breakfast. Then played hide-and-seek. Then coloured in Moshi Monsters, then did obstacle course, all in pyjamas, while roast chicken emitted delicious fragrance from the Aga.

11.32 a.m. Am perfect mother and sensual woman with sensual possibilities. I mean, maybe someone like Leatherjacketman could join in with this scenario and . . .

11.33 a.m. Billy: "Can we do computer, now it's Saturday?"

11.34 a.m. Mabel: "Want to watch *SpongeBob*."

11.35 a.m. Suddenly overwhelmed with exhaustion and desire to read papers in echoing silence. Just for ten minutes.

"Mummeee! De TV is broken."

Realized, horrified, Mabel had got hold of the remotes. I started jabbing at buttons, at which white flecks appeared, accompanied by loud crackling.

"Snow!" said Mabel excitedly, just as the dishwasher started beeping.

"Mummy!" said Billy. "The computer's run out of charge."

"Well, plug it in again!" I said, shoving my head into the cupboard full of wires under the telly.

"Night!" said Mabel as the TV screen went black, and the tumble dryer joined in the beeping.

"This charger doesn't work."

"Well, go on the Xbox!"

"It's not working."

"Maybe it's the Internet connection."

"Mummy! I've unplugged the Airport, I can't get it in again."

Realizing my thermostat was veering dangerously towards red, I scampered off up the stairs saying, "Time to get dressed, special treat! I'll get your clothes." Then ran into their bedroom and burst out, "I hate fucking technology. Why can't everyone just FUCKING SHUT UP AND LET ME READ THE PAPERS?"

Suddenly, horrified, saw that the baby monitor was on! Oh God, oh God. Should have got rid of it ages ago

107

but paranoid as single parent, fear of death, etc., etc. Ran downstairs to find Billy racked by sobs.

"Oh, Billy, I'm so sorry, I didn't mean it. Was it the baby monitor?"

"Nooooooooo!" he yelled. "The Xbox is frozen."

"Mabel, did you hear Mummy in the baby monitor?"

"No," she said, staring delightedly at the television. "De TV is mended."

It was showing a page asking for the Virgin TV password.

"Billy, what's the Virgin password?" I said.

"Isn't it the same as your bank card, 1066?"

"OK, I'll do the Xbox, you put in the password," I said just as the doorbell rang.

"That password won't work."

"Mummeee!" said Mabel.

"Shh, both of you!" I rasped. "There's SOMEONE AT THE DOOR!"

Ran up the stairs, head a mass of guilty thoughts— "I'm a terrible mother, there is a hole inside them left by the loss of their father which they are trying to fill with technology"—and opened the door.

It was Jude looking glamorous, but hung-over and tearful.

"Oh, Bridge," she said, falling into my arms. "I just can't stand another Saturday morning on my own."

"What happened . . . tell Mummy . . ." I said, then remembered Jude was a grown-up financial giant.

"The guy I met on Match and went out with the day before the Stronghold? The one I made out with?"

"Yes?" I said, trying to vaguely remember which one.

"He didn't call. And then last night, he copied me in

on a global text saying his wife has just had a baby girl, six pounds twelve ounces."

"OhMyGod. That's disgusting. That's inhuman."

"All these years I didn't want children and people kept saying I'd change my mind. They were right. I'm going to get my eggs unfrozen."

"Jude," I said. "You made a choice. Just because some guy is a fuckwit it doesn't mean it was the wrong choice. It's a good choice for you. Children are . . . are . . ." I glanced murderously back down the stairs.

She held out her phone, showing an Instagram picture of the fuckwit holding his baby. ". . . Cuddly and sweet and pink and six pounds twelve ounces and all I do is work and hook up and I'm all on my own on a Saturday morning. And—"

"Come downstairs," I said lugubriously. "I'll show you cuddly and sweet."

We clomped back down. Billy and Mabel were now standing cherub-like, holding out a drawing saying, "We Love You, Mummy."

"We're going to empty the dishwasher, Mummy," said Billy. "To help you."

Shit! What was wrong with them?

"Thank you, children," I purred, bustling Jude back upstairs and outside the front door, before they did something worse, like emptying the recycling bin.

"I'm going to defrost my eggs," sobbed Jude as we sat down on the steps. "The technology was primitive then. Crude even. But it might work if . . . I mean, I could get a sperm donor and—"

Suddenly the upstairs window in the house opposite

shot open and a pair of Xbox remotes hurtled out, landing with a smash next to the dustbins.

Seconds later, the front door was flung open and the bohemian neighbour appeared, dressed in fluffy pink mules, a Victorian nightdress and a small bowler hat, carrying an armful of laptops, iPads and iPods. She teetered down the front steps and shoved the electronics in the dustbin, with her son and two of his friends following her, wailing, "Noooooo! I haven't finished my leveeeeeel!"

"Good!" she yelled. "When I signed up for having children, I did NOT sign up to be ruled by a collection of inanimate thin black objects and a gaggle of TECHNO-CRACKHEADS refusing to do anything but stare with jabbing thumbs, while demanding that I SERVICE them like a computer tech crossed with a five-star hotel concierge. When I didn't have you, everyone spent their whole time saying I'd change my mind. And guess what? I've had you. I've brought you up. And I've CHANGED MY MIND!"

I stared at her, thinking, "I have to be friends with that woman."

"Children of your age in India live entirely successfully as street urchins," she continued. "So you can just sit on this doorstep and instead of putting your ENTIRE BRAINS into getting to the next level on MINECRAFT, you can apply them to CHANGING MY MIND about letting you back in. And don't you dare touch that dustbin or I shall enter you in the HUNGER GAMES."

Then, with a toss of her bowler-hatted head, she flounced back into the house and slammed the door.

"Mummeee!" Shouting and crying erupted from my own basement. "Mummeee!"

"Want to come back in?" I said to Jude.

"No, no it's fine," Jude said, happy now, getting to her feet. "You're completely right. I have made the right choice. Just a bit hung-over. I need to have breakfast and a Bloody Mary at Soho House and read the papers and I'll be fine. Thanks, Bridge. Love you. Byee!"

Then she teetered off in her Versace knee-high gladiator sandals looking hung-overly fabulous.

I looked back across the street. The three boys were sitting in a line on the doorstep.

"Everything all right?" I said.

The dark-haired son grinned. "Yeah, it's fine. She just gets like this. She'll be all right in a minute."

He glanced behind him to check the door was still closed, and pulled an iPod out of his pocket. Then the boys started giggling and bent over the iPod.

Huge wave of relief washed over me. I bounded cheerfully back, suddenly remembering that the password for everything was 1890, the year in which Chekhov wrote *Hedda Gabbler*.

"Mummeeeee!"

I grabbed the Xbox remote, grabbed the Virgin remote, and typed "1890" into both of them at which the screens burst miraculously into life.

"There!" I said. "There's your screens. You don't need me. You just need screens. I am going. To make myself. A cup. Of coffee."

I flung the remotes onto the armchair, and flounced,

bohemian-neighbour-like, towards the kettle, at which Billy and Mabel started giggling.

"Mummy!" laughed Billy. "You've turned everything off again."

8.30 p.m. Ended up all cosy and good and Billy had his Xbox time and Mabel watched *SpongeBob* and cuddled me on the sofa, then we all went up on Hampstead Heath and I kept thinking about Leatherjacketman, and how gorgeous it was having the kiss, and feeling sexy again and thinking maybe Tom is right that I do need to be a woman and have someone in my life, and maybe it wouldn't be wrong, and maybe I will call Talitha and get his number.

CRASHING WAVE

Sunday 9 September 2012

135lb, calories 3250, number of times checked for texts from Leatherjacketman 27, texts from Leatherjacketman 0, guilty thoughts 47.

2 a.m. Everything is terrible. Texted Talitha. Turns out she not only took Leatherjacketman's number, but GAVE HIM MY NUMBER. Feel stab of insecurity in my stomach. If she gave him my number—then why hasn't he called?

5 a.m. Should never, ever have got involved with men again. Had completely forgotten the nightmare of "Why hasn't he called?"

9.15 p.m. Children are asleep and all ready for Monday morning. But I am in total meltdown. Why hasn't Leatherjacketman texted? Why? Clearly Leatherjacketman thinks I am crazy and old. Is all my own fault. I should be simply a mother—the children should come home every day to find a casserole bubbling on the Aga and steamed jam roly-poly for pudding. I'd read them *Swallows and Amazons*, put them to bed and then . . . What, though? Watch *Downton Abbey*, fantasize about sex with Matthew, and start again in the morning with the Weetabix?

9.16 p.m. Just called Talitha and explained the whole thing. She is coming round.

9.45 p.m. "Get me a drink, please."

I fixed her her usual vodka and soda.

"This has all been set off because one guy you've met for five seconds hasn't texted you. You've opened yourself to the possibility of life, and now it seems to have been snatched away from under your nose. Why don't you text him?"

"Never pursue a man, it will only make you unhappy," I said, reciting our mantra from being single in our thirties. "Anjelica Huston never, ever called Jack Nicholson."

"Darling, you have to understand that you have no idea what you're talking about. Everything has changed since you were single. There was no texting. There were no emails. People spoke on telephones. Plus, young women are more sexually aggressive now, and men are naturally more lazy. You have to, at the very least, encourage."

"Don't send anything!" I said, lunging at the phone.

"I won't. But it's all fine. When I swapped your numbers, I had a discreet word with him and told him you'd been widowed . . ."

"You WHAT?"

"It's better than being divorced. It's so romantic and original."

"So, basically, you're using Mark's death to procure me a man?"

There was the thud of feet on the stairs. Billy appeared, in his striped pyjamas.

"Mummy, I haven't done my maths."

Talitha looked up vaguely, then returned to the phone.

"Say, 'Hello, nice to see you again,' to Talitha and look at her eyes," I said reflexively. Why do parents do this? "Say Please." "Say Hello!" "Say Thank you for having me." If you haven't trained them to do these things before they get into a live situation then there's really no point in—

"Hello, Talitha."

"Hello, darling," said Talitha without looking up. "He's adorable."

"You did do your maths, Billy. Remember—the problems? We did them when you came home from school on Friday."

"OK, how about this?" Talitha looked up, then looked back at the phone again.

"But there was another sheet," said Billy. "Look—here. It's Craft and Design."

Not Craft and Design. Billy has spent the last six weeks constructing a small mouse out of bits of felt, then he gets "sheets," which ask mysterious conceptual questions. I looked at the latest sheet: "What do you want to achieve by making the mouse?"

Billy and I looked at each other desperately. How global do they expect you to go with a question like that, I mean in a philosophical sense? I handed Billy a pencil. He sat down at the kitchen table and wrote, then handed me the sheet.

To make a mouse.

"Good," I said. "Very good. Now shall I take you back up to bed?"

He nodded and put his hand in mine. "Goodnight, Talitha."

"Say goodnight to Talitha."

"Mummy. I just did."

Mabel was asleep on the bottom bunk, head on back to front, clutching Saliva.

"Will you cuddle me?" said Billy, climbing into the top bunk. I thought about Talitha getting increasingly impatient downstairs then climbed in with him, Puffle One, Mario and Horsio.

"Mummy?"

"Yes," I said, heart wavering, fearing he was going to ask about Daddy or death.

"What is the population of China?" Oh God, he looks so like Mark when he is worrying about these questions. What was I doing messing about texting some unshaven leather-jacketed stranger who probably—

"Mummy?"

"Four hundred million," I lied smoothly.

"Oh. Why is the earth shrinking by one centimetre a year?"

"Um . . ." I thought about this. Is the world shrinking by one centimetre a year? Like, the whole planet or just the land bits? Is it to do with global warming? Or the awesome power of waves and . . . Then I felt the slight relaxing sigh of Billy falling asleep.

Rushed back downstairs, panting. Talitha looked up with a self-satisfied expression: "OK. I hope you appreciate this. This was a really tough one."

She handed me the phone.

<I've finally recovered from my embarrassment at fleeing from Prince Charming and his Stronghold. It was all so outrageously sensual, I feared I would spontane-

ously combust or turn into a pumpkin. What are you up to?>

"You haven't sent it?"

"Not yet. But it's good. You have to take care of their ego. What do you think the poor guy felt like, with you running off like that and not explaining yourself?"

"Doesn't that sound—"

"It's a question, and carrying on the thread. Don't over-think it, just—"

She took hold of my finger, and pressed "Send."

"Nooo! You said you wouldn't—"

"I didn't. You sent it. Could I possibly have another teensy teensy little vodka?"

Mind reeling I headed for the fridge, but just as I opened the door there was a text ping. Talitha grabbed it. A self-satisfied smirk spread across her immaculately made-up features.

<Hi. Is that Cinderella?>

"Now, Bridget," she said sternly, watching the confusion of feelings on my face, "you have to be brave and get back in the saddle, for everyone's sake, including . . ." She nodded in the direction of upstairs.

Ultimately, Talitha was right. But it couldn't have gone more disastrously wrong with Leatherjacketman. As she herself said, as we sat on my sofa in the bloody aftermath:

"It's all my fault. I forgot to warn you. When you come out of a long relationship, the first one is always the worst. There's too much hanging on it. You think you're going to be rescued. Which you're not. And you think they're the barometers of whether you're still viable. Which you are, but they're not going to prove that to you."

I broke every single one of the Key Dating Rules with Leatherjacketman. But, in my defence, at that point, I didn't know that the Dating Rules even existed.

HOW NOT TO DO DATING

Wednesday 12 September 2012

133lb (lost 2lb through texting thumb-action), minutes spent fantasizing about Leatherjacketman 347, number of times checked for texts from Leatherjacketman 37, texts from Leatherjacketman 0, number of times checked Unexploded Email In-box from Leatherjacketman even though Leatherjacketman does not have email address 12 (insane), total cumulative minutes late for school runs 27.

2.30 p.m. Mmm. Just back from lunch with Leatherjacketman in Primrose Hill. He was looking even more like a car-advert man, in a brown leather jacket this time, and aviator shades. It was an unseasonably warm, bright autumn day, the sky blue, the sun shining, so we could sit outside at a pavement cafe.

FINE

I love him. I love him.

NOT FINE

He's about my age and divorced with two kids. And he's called Andy—such a cool name.

ANDY??

As I sat down at the table, he took off his shades. His eyes were like pools. Pools of pale, pale water like a tropical sea . . .

DO NOT GET CARRIED AWAY

. . . only brown. I love him. The Dating Gods have smiled down on me.

TRY TO RETAIN SOME VESTIGE OF OBJECTIVITY

He REALLY understands the problems of single parenting. He said things like "How old are your kids?"

All through lunch felt like some dangerously aroused puppy who was going to start shagging his leg.

DO NOT JUMP TO CONCLUSIONS OR FANTASIZE

It'll be so great having sex together on Sunday mornings, I was thinking, then breakfast together with all the kids—laughing, moving in together, selling both our places and getting a house they can all walk to school from. Just as I was thinking, ". . . then we could just have one car and not have an issue with the parking permits," he interrupted: "Do you want a coffee?"

I blinked at him, disorientated, teetering on the brink of saying, "Do you think we could manage with just the one car?"

ON THE FIRST DATE: LET HIM PAY

When the bill came, I made a terrible fuss about getting my credit card out and saying, "No, let me," and "Shall we split it?"

"I'll get it," he said, looking at me in a funny way—maybe he already knew he loved me too?

RESPOND TO WHAT IS ACTUALLY HAPPENING, NOT WHAT YOU WISH WAS HAPPENING

After lunch, I couldn't bear it to end, and suggested we go for a walk on the Hill. It was so lovely. When we got to his car, I was hoping against hope that he was going to kiss me again but he just gave me a quick peck on the cheek and said, "Take care."

I panicked. "Do you think we should see each other again?" I blurted out.

Maybe it was a bit forward but THINK it was completely fine.

IT WASN'T

"Sure," he smirked. "I was just waiting for you to run off screaming." Then he smiled his crinkly car-advert smile and got into the car.

He's so funny!

DO NOT ALLOW HIM TO DISRUPT YOUR LIFE OR EQUILIBRIUM

Oh, look, this is hopeless. Cannot just lie in bed MAS-TURBATING all day when have a screenplay to write and children to care for.

Thursday 13 September 2012

DO NOT OBSESS OR FANTASIZE WHEN DRIVING

8.30 a.m. Hmmm. The thing is, when I said, "Do you think we should see each other again?" he didn't say, "No," he said, "Sure."

So that means "Yes," doesn't it? But then why didn't he say something about the next time when we said goodbye? Or why hasn't he texted? GAAAH!

9.30 a.m. Rounded a bend to find a taxi had just stopped in front of me, completely selfishly, with no rhyme or reason whatsoever. Was huge line of cars behind me.

Pulled round the taxi, looking crossly at taxi driver. Then realized, as looked ahead, was yet another car steaming towards me, driven by man who was pointing and mouthing at me, "You go back. You. Go. Back!" as if was idiot or similar.

"Honestly, men drivers!" I thought, doing a V-sign at the man. (Apart from Leatherjacketman who am certain is very respectful.) "Oh, oh, look at us! We're alpha males! We're just going to bear down on defenceless women, bullying them into reversing."

"Mummy," said Billy. "The taxi has stopped so that that other car can get round us."

Suddenly realized what Billy meant. The oncoming car was ALREADY THERE and the taxi driver, who is after all an experienced roadsman, was now stopping to let the already-oncoming car come past. And now I was like the alpha female SUV driver (except not in SUV) who had swerved round the experienced roadsman taxi driver and tried to drive the oncoming car backwards like an angry snowplough brandishing an Oxbridge First in PPE (except Third in English from Bangor).

Tried to mouth "Sorreee!" while reversing backwards, but the man glared at me with exactly the same disbelieving "what-is-the-world-coming-to?" expression that I myself am so accustomed to adopting during the morning school run.

"Well!" I said brightly once we'd rounded the corner. "What lessons have we got today, Billy? PE?"

"Mummy."

I looked round at him. The same eyes. The same tone when I'm being not altogether at my best.

"What?" I said.

"Are you just saying that because you feel silly?"

Friday 14 September 2012

DO NOT ALLOW HIM TO MAKE YOU GENERALLY DISTRACTED AND CRAZY

Just made contact with Aspirational Bohemian Neighbour and was so distracted that completely fucked it up. Was just walking back from car when saw her going into the house wearing a woollen hat with several points with bobbles on the end, platform Doc Martens and a garment which looked like cross between a German officer's coat from the Second World War and a crinoline with a frill at the bottom.

"Hello," she suddenly said, "I'm Rebecca. Don't you live across the road?"

"Yes," I said delightedly, then launched into a nervous monologue: "Your children look like they might be the same age as mine? How old are they? What a nice hat! . . ."

It all went very well and ended with Rebecca saying, "Well, maybe knock on the door and come for a play date—doesn't-the-very-word-make-you-want-to-shoot-yourself?—sometime."

"Hahaaha! It does. Yes," I said, miming embarrassingly, shooting my own head. "That would be cool. Byeee!" Then crossed the road and went into the house thinking, "Yayy! We can be friends and maybe I could introduce her to Leatherjacketman and . . ."

"Wait!" Rebecca suddenly called.

I turned.

"Isn't that your daughter?"

Shit! Had completely forgotten I had Mabel with me. She was standing, bemused, outside Rebecca's house, abandoned on the pavement.

NOTICE HOW HE MAKES YOU FEEL. SOMEWHERE AMIDST LIST—"HORNY," "TAKING STOMACH MEDICINE DUE TO ANXIETY"—THERE SHOULD BE THE WORD "HAPPY"

9.15 p.m. Still no text. Whole Leatherjacketman scenario is making me horribly anxious with a sick feeling in my stomach.

124

THE NUMBER ONE KEY DATING RULE

Saturday 15 September 2012

DO NOT TEXT WHEN DRUNK

8.15 p.m. YAYY! Telephone!

9 p.m. "Oh, hello, darling!"—my mother—shit! Tailspinned, wondering if Leatherjacketman could still send a text while Mum was on the phone.

"Bridget? Bridget? Are you still there? Have you decided about the cruise?"

"Um, well, I think it might be a bit—"

"I mean, most people from St. Oswald's will be with their grandchildren. It *is* a special time of year, when people *do* spend it with the grandchildren. Julie Enderbury and Michael are taking the whole family to Cape Verde."

"Well, what about Una's grandchildren?" I counterpointed.

"It's the in-laws' turn."

"Right, right."

In-laws. Admiral Darcy and Elaine are actually incredibly sweet with Billy and Mabel and manage to play it right by inviting them one at a time, to rather well-thought-out and short treat-like occasions. But I don't think they could handle having us for Christmas. Even when Mark was alive he used to invite them to our big house in Holland Park, but he always got a cook to do the Christmas dinner, which he said was nothing to do with my cooking, but so that everyone could relax and enjoy being together. Oh, though. Why would they not "relax," if I was cooking? Maybe it *was* to do with my cooking.

"Bridget? Are you still there? I just don't want you to be on your own," Mum said. "I mean, there's still time to decide."

"Great! Then we can sort it out," I said. "Christmas is ages away."

Now she's gone off to her Aqua-Zumba. Wish Dad was here, to mitigate Mum and giggle with me about everything and hug me. Wish could get blind drunk on entire bottle of wine.

9.15 p.m. Ooh, just heard Chloe come in from her night out in Camden. She's staying on the sofa bed so she can get to t'ai chi early tomorrow.

9.30 p.m. Think will have small glass of wine, now she is here, just to get spirits up.

ALERT! ALERT! DO NOT EVEN OPEN WINE WITHOUT WRAPPING PHONE UP IN NOTE SAYING "NO TEXTING" AND PUTTING ON HIGH SHELF

9.45 p.m. Much better now. Will put music on. Maybe Queen's "Play the Game." Gay perspective is always good, esp. in musical form. Mmmm. Leatherjacketman. Wish he would text me then we could see each other and have sensual . . .

10 p.m. Maybe tiny nother glass of wine.

ALERT! ALERT!

10.05 p.m. Love Queen.

10.20 p.m. Mmm. Dancing . . .
"This is your life! . . . Don't play hard to get . . ."

10.20 p.m. You see, s true. "Love runs . . . pumping through my veeeeiiiiins!" Love Letherjackiema. You an't go ound getting bogged in defensiveness. Love is loike a stream.

DO NOT USE WORDS OF POP SONGS TO GUIDE BEHAVIOUR, ESPECIALLY WHEN DRUNK

10.21 p.m. Youse? Dfon't polay hard to get. So why shunni text him . . . ?

GAAAH! You see, this is the trouble with the modern world. If it was the days of letter-writing, I would never have even started to find a pen, a piece of paper, an envelope, a stamp, and Leatherjacketman's home address and gone outside at 11.30 p.m. with two children asleep in the house to find a postbox. A text is gone at the brush of a fingertip, like a nuclear bomb or Exocet missile.

10.35 p.m. Just pressssd d SEND. Issfineisn' tit.

DO NOT TEXT WHEN DRUNK

CONTINUING DATING INCOMPETENCE

Sunday 16 September 2012

133lb (stuffing feelings).

"No!" said Talitha, sitting in my living room with Tom, me and Jude. "It is not 'fine.'"

"Why?" I said, staring eerily at my text.

<So great to see you Wednesdyy. Let's get togethr again soon!> Tom read it out then snorted.

"Well, number one, you're clearly drunk," said Jude, looking up briefly from OkCupid.

"Number two, it's eleven thirty at night," said Tom. "Number three, you've already told him you'd like to see him again, so you're sounding desperate."

"Number four, you used an exclamation mark," said Jude crisply.

"And it's emotionally inauthentic," said Tom. "It has the gushing, fraudulently breezy tone of a schoolgirl who's persuaded the netball captain to sit next to her at lunch, and is trying to force her to be friends, whilst attempting to sound casual about it."

"And he didn't reply," added Jude.

"Have I ruined everything?"

"Just leave it as the naivety of a newborn bunny amidst a pack of ravenous coyotes," said Tom.

Almost immediately the text pinged.

<How's your babysitting schedule? More organized than your spelling? What about next Saturday night?>

I looked at them with the expression of an anti-Iraq War demonstrator hearing that there were no weapons of mass destruction. Then I floated up onto a cloud—non-biochemical—of excitement.

"'How's your babysitting schedule?'" I said, dancing around. "He's so CONSIDERATE."

"He's trying to get into your knickers," said Jude.

"Don't just stand there," said Tom excitedly. "Answer the text!"

I thought a bit, then texted:

<Saturday night perfect, just need to obtain a sturdy rope to tether the children.>

<I prefer duct tape.> came straight back.

"He's funny," said Tom. "And there's just a hint of S&M. Which is nice."

We all looked at each other happily. A triumph for one was a triumph for all.

"Let's open another bottle," said Jude, padding over to the fridge in her baggy onesie and big fluffy socks. She stopped to kiss me on the head on the way. "Well done, everyone, well done."

ESCALATING DATING INCOMPETENCE

**ON THE FIRST DATE—JUST GO ALONG WITH WHAT HE
SUGGESTS**

Wednesday 19 September 2012

134lb, pounds gained 1, dating rules broken 2.

9.15 p.m. Chloe can't do Saturday night, and instead of
putting my energy into finding someone else, have obsessed
and fantasized so much about the dinner, and what am
going to wear, and the way he will look up at me when I
appear in the navy silk dress, that have not organized anything else. Gaah! Text from Leatherjacketman! <Fancy a
movie on Saturday? Argo?>

9.17 p.m. *Argo? Argo?* A movie is not a PROPER DATE!
Argo is a guy movie! The navy silk dress would be overdressed at a movie. And anyway Chloe can't do Saturday
and . . .

9.20 p.m. Just sent: <How about dinner? Would like to get
to know you better.>

DON'T MAKE IT ALL ABOUT THE BABYSITTER

9.21 p.m. Me: <Also—babysitter problems Saturday night. Any chance we could do Friday??>

10 p.m. Oh God, oh God. Leatherjacketman has not replied. Maybe he is out? With another woman?

11 p.m. Leatherjacketman: <Can't do Friday. How about the week after? Friday? Or Saturday?>

11.05 p.m. Texted back <Yes! Saturday!> then slumped. He wants to wait a whole week? How can he bear it?

Sunday 23 September 2012
9.15 p.m. Agonizing. Leatherjacketman has ignored me all weekend. Has clearly gone off me. If was ever on me in first place.

10 p.m. Am going to try to get things going again.

DON'T PREARRANGE FIRST-TIME SEX

<So sorry about moving things around. Will wear high heels on Saturday to make up for it! And babysitter is staying over.>

Monday 24 September 2012
136lb, pounds gained 2, texts from Leatherjacketman (possibly as result of pounds gained, even though has not seen yet) 0.

9.15 p.m. Leatherjacketman has not replied. Thinks am desperate slut.

Tuesday 25 September 2012
135lb, texts from Leatherjacketman 1 (bad).

11 a.m. Just got reply!
    <Great. How about ENO in Notting Hill. 7.45? Looking forward to the heels.>
    He hates me.

Saturday 29 September 2012
Number of times changed outfit for date 7, minutes late for date 25, positive thoughts during date 0, texts sent to Leatherjacketman 12, texts received from Leatherjacketman 2, Dating Rules broken 13, positive outcomes of entire experience 0.

BE ON TIME, REMEMBERING THAT THIS IS MORE
IMPORTANT THAN CHANGING OUTFITS AND PUTTING ON
MAKE-UP, RATHER LIKE WHEN CATCHING A PLANE

7 p.m. Spent so long putting on outfits and taking them off again, that minicab went away, has not come back and now I cannot find taxi in street. Have sent series of hysterical texts to which only reply has been: <Plenty of taxis here.>

8 p.m. In the Electric Bar. Ended up bringing car but was so late that have had to dump it in residents' bay where am sure to get a ticket. Leatherjacketman is not here.

MAKE SURE YOU BOTH THINK YOU'RE GOING TO THE SAME PLACE AT THE SAME TIME

8.10 p.m. Oh, shit! Shit! He didn't say the Electric. He said ENO.

8.15 p.m. Deranged now. Just sent him text saying have gone to wrong place and now have to run to ENO.

WHEN YOU ARRIVE, BE RELAXED AND SMILE, LIKE A GODDESS OF LIGHT AND CALM

Turned up at ENO forty minutes late to be confronted by a greeter lady who clearly thought I was a mad person who should be ushered out.

I realized I couldn't either see Leatherjacketman or remember his real name.

Eventually located him, engrossed, horrifyingly, at a long table of cool advertising-style people, had to actually go over and touch his shoulder to get his attention, at which he tried to introduce me but obviously couldn't remember my name either.

He tried to get me to join them. But the restaurant couldn't fit in another chair, so we had to go to a table for two, with Leatherjacketman repeatedly glancing over at his sophisticated friends, clearly thinking how much more fun they were than me.

When leaving, the sophisticated friends invited us both on to a party, at which, thinking, "Nooooo!" I said, "Yes! That would be great!"

I lost him immediately at the scary party, hid in the toilet.

DO NOT GET DRUNK OR OTHERWISE INTOXICATED

When I found him, he was smoking pot. I have not smoked pot for fifteen years and then it was two puffs, which made me so paranoid that I thought people were ignoring me when they were actually talking to me. Nevertheless gave in to Leatherjacketman's friends' peer pressure and had two drags on the joint. Immediately became completely stoned and paranoid.

Perhaps noticing this, he whispered, "Shall we go in here?" gesturing at a closed door. Nodded mutely.

We were in a spare bedroom, covered in coats. He closed the door, pushed me against it, kissing my neck, sliding his hand up my skirt, murmuring, "Did you say your babysitter was staying over?"

Nodded mutely.

DO NOT TRY TO HAVE SEX BEFORE YOU'RE READY

Not only was I stoned, not only was I paranoid, but I hadn't had sex for four and a half years and I was absolutely terrified. What if he thought I was revolting without my clothes on? What if I slept with him and he didn't ring me again? What if I couldn't remember how to do it?

"Are you OK?"

DO NOT KEEP DISAPPEARING INTO THE TOILET FOR AGES OR HE WILL THINK YOU HAVE A DRUG OR DIGESTIVE PROBLEM

Nodded mutely, then managed, "I'll just go to the loo."

He looked at me strangely and sat back down on the bed.

When I reappeared he was still sitting on the bed. He got up and shut the door again and started kissing my neck again while sliding his hand back up my dress.

"Shall we go to my place?" he said.

I nodded mutely, just managing to get out, "But . . ."

DO NOT CONFUSE HIM

"Look, if you don't want to do this . . ."

"No, no, I do, I do. But . . ."

YOU DECIDE WHEN YOU'RE GOING TO HAVE SEX, NOT HIM. DECIDE AND BE CLEAR ABOUT IT

"You did say you had a babysitter overnight."

DON'T CREATE PRESSURE

"It's just I haven't slept with anyone for four and a half years."

"FOUR AND A HALF YEARS?? Jesus. No pressure."

"I know. It's just, I've finally met someone I like."

"What??"

DON'T EXPRESS YOUR VULNERABILITIES. WAIT TILL THEY KNOW YOU WELL ENOUGH TO UNDERSTAND

"I mean, I've met you but I hardly know you, and what if you don't like it when I've got no clothes on? And maybe I won't be able to remember what to do, and I'm a widow, and I might think I'm being unfaithful and start crying and then have to wait for the phone to ring and you might not call!"

"What about me? I've met someone I like too."

ALWAYS BE CLASSY, NEVER BE CRAZY

"Who?" I said indignantly. "You've met someone else in the last two weeks? Who is she? How could you?"

"I meant you. Look. Think of it from the guy's point of view. *Does* she want me to call? *Does* she want to sleep with me?"

"I know, I know, I do . . ."

"Good, so . . ." He started kissing me again. He was trying to pull me back on the bed now, with me sitting rather awkwardly on his thigh.

DON'T MAKE HIM FEEL CAGED

"But," I burst out again, "if we have sex will you promise you'll call me and see me again, or maybe we could actually arrange the next date now?! So we don't have to worry about it!"

"Look." For a second, I swear he couldn't remember my name again. "You're a great girl. I just don't think you're ready for this. I don't want to feel responsible for upsetting

136

anyone. Let me put you in a cab for tonight and, yes. I'll call you."

"OK," I said miserably, then followed him, nodding mutely as he said his goodbyes. He put me in a taxi. I turned to wave and saw him going back off towards the party.

CREATE BEAUTIFUL MEMORIES

Caught a glimpse of myself in the taxi mirror. My hair was all messed up, I had the same Alice Cooper eyes with smudged mascara and deranged expression I had left him with in the Stronghold.

11.20 p.m. Have just ended up creeping back into the house, so Chloe wouldn't find out the date was a disaster.

Sunday 30 September 2012
133lb, minutes slept 0, pounds lost through stress and misery 2, pounds lost in parking/towaway fines 245.

5 a.m. Have been awake all night. Am horrible failure, revolting, old and crap with men.

8 a.m. Just attempted to creep out to get the car before it was towed away, only to be caught by Mabel, Billy and Chloe coming up from the kitchen to go to the park.

"Mummy," said Billy, "I thought you'd gone away for the night."

"Didn't go so well, then?" said Chloe sympathetically, looking fresh-faced and perfect.

The car had been towed away and had to go to a

hideous trough between the A40 and the main train line to Cornwall to pay more than Chloe's wages for a week to get it back. Am so sad, the one time I found someone I liked, I completely messed it up. I'll never find anyone again. I'm not only man-repellent, I'm incompetent. But maybe he'll text. Or call.

Friday 5 October 2012
134lb, calls from Leatherjacketman 0, texts from Leather-jacketman 0.

9.15 a.m. He hasn't.

Monday 8 October 2012
130lb (wasting away, look old), calls from Leatherjacketman 0, texts from Leatherjacketman 0.

7 a.m. He still hasn't. Must throw self into work and get on with screenplay.

Tuesday 9 October 2012
Texts to Leatherjacketman 1, texts from Leatherjacketman 0, number of words of screenplay written 0, Dating Rules broken 2.

He still hasn't.

IF HE PULLS AWAY, DON'T FIGHT IT. STEER INTO THE SKID

11 p.m. Maybe I will text Leatherjacketman.

2.30 a.m. Me: <Hey. Thanks for the great party last Saturday. I had such a good time!>

Wednesday 10 October 2012
Texts from Leatherjacketman 0.

No reply.

Friday 19 October 2012
Texts from Leatherjacketman 1, encouraging-in-any-way texts from Leatherjacketman 0, words of screenplay written 0.

10 a.m. Leatherjacketman: <Hey, no worries. We've all been there.>

Saturday 27 October 2012
No communication from Leatherjacketman.

Sunday 28 October 2012

DO NOT TEXT AT ODD TIMES OF DAY OR NIGHT IN MANNER OF STALKER

5.30 a.m. Maybe will text Leatherjacketman!
    <How are you?>

One soul reaching out to another, I thought, amid the smouldering remains of the silly old mess we'd accidentally created, like silly billies in the midst of a deep unbreakable connection: Leonardo da Vinci's Adam reaching out, in that painting, for God's fingertips.

Friday 2 November 2012

Possibilities of anything ever happening with male of species again 0.

11.30 a.m. Text from Leatherjacketman.

<Great but very overloaded—heading off to Zurich tomorrow, might be there for a while. Have a good Christmas.>

And that was the end of that.

"You have to laugh about it," said Talitha. "Don't let him have possession of your self-esteem. Or your sexual viability. Or anything."

Clearly, however, something had to be done.

INTENSIVE DATING STUDY

Night after night, when the children were in bed, I studied, as if for an Open University course on how to get off with people. The children seemed to sense that a great project was in the works, and treated it with appropriate respect. Mabel, when she burst into my bedroom at midnight, clutching Saliva and saying she'd had a nasty dream, would whisper, "Exthcuthe me, Mummy, but a giant ant ith eatin' my ear," whilst peeping respectfully from the tangle of hair, at the piles of epic tomes all over the bed. I did of course tweet as I went along, increasing my Twitter followers to a staggering 437.

Bibliography:

I started with my historical archive—the obvious classics from my thirties:

* *Men Are from Mars, Women Are from Venus*
* *Finding the Love You Want*
* *Letting Love Find You*
* *What Men Want*
* *What Men Secretly Want*
* *What Men Really Want*
* *What Men Actually Want*

How Men Think

What Men Think About When Not Thinking About Sex

But somehow it just wasn't *enough*. I went on Amazon and there were seventy-five pages of dating self-help books to choose from.

* *The Single Trap: The Two-step Guide to Escaping It and Finding Lasting Love*
* *The Three Most Successful Online Dating Profiles Ever*
* *Quadruple Your Dating*
* *It Takes All 5: A Single Mom's Guide to Finding the Real One*
* *Make Him Beg to Be Your Boyfriend in 6 Simple Steps*
* *100% Love: 7 Steps to Scientifically Find the True Love of Your Life*
* *Fearless Love: 8 Simple Rules That Will Change the Way You Date, Mate and Relate*
* *The Love Laws: 9 Essential Rules for Lasting, Loving Partnership*
* *10 Dating Lessons from* Sex and the City
* *Attraction Magnets: 12 Best Conversation Topics for Dating and Pickup*
* *20 Rules of Internet Dating*
* *The Red Flag Rules: 50 Rules to Know Whether to Keep Him or Kiss Him Goodbye*
* *The 99 Rules of Online Dating*

* *The New Rules: The Dating Dos and Don'ts for the Digital Generation* (same authors as the original *Rules*)
* *The Old Dating Rules* (different authors from the original *Rules*)
* *The Unwritten Rules*
* *The Unspoken Rules*
* *The Spiritual Rules for Dating, Relating and Mating*
* *Changing the Rules*
* *Love Has No Rules*
* *Breaking the Rules*
* *Dating, Fornication and Romance: Who Knew There Were Rules?*
* *The Anti-Rules—Now That You've Got Him, How Do You Get Rid of Him?*
* *The 30-Day Dating Detox*
* *Zen and the Art of Falling in Love*
* *Geisha Secrets*
* *Why Men Love Bitches*
* *You're Irresistible*
* *He's Just Not That Into You*
* *The Strategy*
* *The Automatic 2nd Date: Everything to Say and Do on the 1st Date to Guarantee a 2nd Date*
* *Getting to Third Date*
* *Date Dream Girl: Third Date and Beyond*
* *Getting to Fifth Date after Fourth Date and Sex*
* *Now What? Getting Beyond the Fifth-Date Hurdle*
* *When Mars and Venus Collide*
* *The Art of War for Dating*
* *The Worst-Case Scenario Survival Handbook: Dating*

* *Dating Dead Men*
* *Romantic Suicide*
* *Dating: It's Not Complicated*

It might sound confusing, but actually it wasn't! There was more consensus than disagreement amongst the dating masters. I studied diligently, marking up the books and making notes, searching for commonalities as if between the world's great religions and philosophical tenets, distilling them down to a molten core of key principles:

THE DATING RULES
*Do not text when drunk.

*Always be classy, never be crazy.

*Be on time.

*Use Authentic Communication.

*Do not go to the wrong place.

*Do not confuse him. Be rational, congruent and consistent.

*Do not obsess or fantasize.

*Do not obsess or fantasize when driving.

*Respond to what is actually going on, not what you wish was going on.

*On first date just go along with whatever he suggests (unless Morris dancing, dogfight, obvious booty call, etc.)

*Be sure he makes you feel happy.

*Try to retain some vestige of objectivity.

*When he comes we welcome, when he goes we let him go.

*Don't get stoned or pissed out of brain.

*Be calm smiling goddess of light.

*Allow things to unfold like a petal at their own pace, e.g., do not demand to make third date in insecure panic in middle of sex on second date.

*Wear something sexy but that you feel comfortable in.

*Stay calm, confident and centred re whole thing— consider meditation, hypnotherapy, psychotherapy, antipsychotic medication, etc.

*Don't come on too obviously strong, but do do sensual things like stroking stem of wine glass up and down.

*Don't pre-arrange first-time sex.

*Don't try to have sex too soon.

*Don't make him feel caged.

*Never mention any of the following: exes, how fat you are, how insecure you are, problems, issues, money, cellulite, Botox, liposuction, facial peels/lasers/ microdermabrasion, etc., control undergarments, possible shared parking permits when married, seating plans for wedding reception, babysitters, marriage/ religion (unless you've just realized he's a polygamous Mormon, in which case get blind drunk and bring up all of the previous in one hysterical gabble and excuse yourself because you feel fat and have to get back for the babysitter).

*Create beautiful memories.

*Do not text while drunk.

Of course this immense body of knowledge was entirely theoretical: rather as with a philosopher who sits in an ivory tower (NB an actual ivory tower, not IvoryTowers .net, the dating website), developing theories about how life ought to be lived, without actually living it.

The only thing I had to work with was the experience with Leatherjacketman. Examining the mistakes I made there, from my newly well-read perspective of informed understanding, allowed me to heal my sense of incompetence, grossness, failure and unlovableness and give me hope that, even if all is lost, if indeed it had ever been found, with Leatherjacketman, it was perhaps not lost with all other males of the species for ever.

However, there was another section—RULES FOR GETTING DATES—which was entirely empty.

WALLOWING IN IT

Monday 26 November 2012

132lb, Twitter followers impressed with knowledge of dating self-help books and Dating Rules 468, romantic prospects 0.

12.30 p.m. Just got back from Oxford Street. Whole thing is mutated as if by an avalanche of lights, sparkly baubles, romantic shop-window tableaux and festive songs on a loop, inducing the panicky feeling that Christmas has suddenly fast-forwarded itself and arrived, and I've forgotten to buy the turkey. What am I going to do? I'm not ready for the impending hysterical-taste-of-others exam, the sense of needing to do all the things you already have to do plus another twice-as-big layer of Christmas things on top. Worse, the forcing down the throat of perfect nuclear family, hearth-and-home tableaux, the tragic emotions, the helpless flashbacks to Christmases past, and doing Santa on your own and . . .

1 p.m. House seems dark, lonely and forlorn. How can I possibly get on with writing screenplay when feel like this?

1.05 p.m. That's better, was wearing prescription sunglasses again. But still cannot face the thought of getting the tree, and getting out all the decorations that Mark and I bought together and . . . at least we have the St. Oswald's House cruise to look forward to . . .

1.20 p.m. Oh God. What am I going to do about that? I have to let Mum know in just under four weeks. The children will drown, and it'll be impossible, but if I don't go, I'll just be on my own with the kids, trying to make it all work, and I'm just alone. Aloooone!

Sunday 2 December 2012
9.15 p.m. Just called Jude and explained psychological meltdown. "You have to get online."

9.30 p.m. Have signed up for a free trial on SingleParent Mix.com. Have followed Jude's advice and slightly lied about my age as who is going to even look at a profile over fifty? Though don't tell Talitha I even thought that. Have not put a photo up or a profile or anything.

9.45 p.m. Ooh, I've got a message! A message! Already! You see there ARE people out there, and . . .

Oh. It's from forty-nine-year-old man called "5times anight."

Well, that's . . . that's . . .

Just clicked on message: <Hiya sexy! lol :)>

Just clicked on picture. Is of a plump, heavily tattooed man, wearing a short black rubber dress and a blond wig.

Mark, please help me. Mark.

9.50 p.m. Come on, come on. Keep Buggering On. I have just got to, got to get over this. I MUST stop thinking, "If only Mark was here." I must stop thinking of the way he used to sleep with his arm across my shoulder, like he was protecting me, the physical intimacy, the scent of the arm-

149

pit, the curve of muscle, the stubble on the chin. The way I felt when he answered the phone about work and went into his busy and important mode, then he'd look at me in the middle of the conversation with those brown eyes, so sort of smouldering, yet vulnerable. Or Billy saying, "Do puzzles?" and Mark and Billy spending hours doing incredibly complicated puzzles because they were both so clever. I can't carry on having every sweet thing which happens with the children tinged with sadness. Saliva being picked to play the little baby Jesus in Mabel's first nativity play (Mabel was a hen). Billy's first grown-up carol concert. Billy and Mabel buying me the Nespresso machine I'd been wanting for Christmas (helped by Chloe) as a "surprise," then Mabel telling me about it every night in a furtive whisper. I can't have another Christmas like that. I can't have another year like this. I can't carry on like this.

10 p.m. Just called Tom. "Bridget, you have to grieve. You haven't grieved properly. Write Mark a letter. Wallow in it. W.A.L.L.O.W."

10.15 p.m. Just went upstairs. I found Billy and Mabel cuddled up together in the top bunk. Awkwardly I climbed up the ladder and got in with them and then Billy woke up and said, "Mummy?"

"Yes," I whispered.

"Where is Dada?" Feeling my insides wrenching apart with pain for Billy, I pulled him to me, terrified. Why were we all feeling like this tonight?

"I don't know," I began. "But . . ." Billy had fallen back

to sleep. Stayed squeezed in the top bunk, holding them close.

11 p.m. In tears, now, sitting on the floor surrounded by cuttings, photographs. I don't care what Mum says, I'm just going to wallow in it.

11.15 p.m. Just opened the cuttings box, took one out.

Mark Darcy, the British human rights lawyer, was killed in the Darfur region of Sudan when the armoured vehicle in which he was travelling struck a landmine. Darcy, the internationally recognized authority in cross-border litigation and conflict resolution, and Anton Daviniere, a Swiss representative of the UN Human Rights Council, were both killed in the incident, Reuters reports.

Mark Darcy was a leading international figure in victim representation, international crisis resolution and transitional justice. He was regularly called upon by international bodies, governments, opposition groups and public figures to give advice on a broad array of issues, and was a leading supporter of Amnesty International. His intervention, prior to his death, secured the release of the British aid workers Ian

Thompson and Steven Young, who had been
hostages of the rebel regime for seven
months and whose execution was believed
to have been imminent.

Tributes have been pouring in from
heads of state, aid agencies and indi-
viduals.

He leaves behind a widow, Bridget, a
son, William, aged two, and a daughter,
Mabel, three months old.

11.45 p.m. Sobbing now, the box, the cuttings and photos
fallen on the floor, memories, sucking me down.

Dear Mark,

I miss you so much. I love you so much.

*It just sounds trite. Like when you try to write a
letter to the bereaved. "My deepest sympathy for your
loss." Still, when people wrote to me after you died, I
was glad even if they didn't really know what to say
and stumbled around.*

*But the thing is, Mark, I just can't manage on my
own. I really, really can't. I know I've got the kids and
friends and I'm writing* The Leaves in His Hair *but
I'm just so lonely without you. I need you to comfort
me, counsel me like we said at our wedding. And hold
me. And tell me what to do when I get all mixed up.
And tell me I'm all right when I feel I'm crap. And do
my zip up. And do my zip down and . . . oh God, the
first time you kissed me and I said, "Nice boys don't
kiss like that," and you said, "Oh yes, they fucking*

well do." I so fucking miss you and miss fucking you.

And I wish our life . . . I can't bear that you're not seeing them grow up.

I JUST HAVE TO GET ON AND MAKE THE BEST OF IT. Life doesn't turn out how everyone wants and I'm very lucky to have Billy and Mabel and that you made sure we would be all right, and the house and everything. I know you had to go to the Sudan, I know how long you'd worked on getting the hostages out, I know you did everything to make sure it was safe out there. You wouldn't have gone if you'd thought there was a risk. It wasn't your fault.

I just wish we could do it together, and share all the little moments. How is Billy ever going to understand how to be a man without his father? And Mabel? They don't have a dad. They don't know you. And we could have just been at home together for Christmas if only . . . stop it. Never say could've, should've or if only.

I'm sorry I'm such a crap mother. Please forgive me. I'm so sorry I spent four weeks studying dating books, and making a fraudulent cyber version of myself available to a man wearing a rubber minidress, and for being upset about anything which isn't about not still having you. I love you.

Love,

Bridget xxxx

11.46 p.m. Just heard a thud. One of them is out of bed.

Midnight. Mabel had got down from the bunk bed and was standing, silhouetted, in her little pyjamas, against the window. I went and knelt beside her.

"There's the moon," she said. She turned to me, solemnly, and confided, "It followth me."

The moon was full and white above the little garden. I started to say, "Well, the thing is, Mabel, the moon—"

"And . . ." she interrupted. "Dat owl."

I looked to where she was pointing. There, on the garden wall, was a barn owl, white in the moonlight, staring at us, unblinking. I'd never seen an owl before. I thought owls were extinct, except in the countryside and zoos.

"Shut de curtainth," said Mabel and started closing the curtains in a bossy, businesslike way. "It's all right. Dey're watching over us."

She clambered up into the top bunk. "Do de Baby Printheth."

Still freaked out by the owl, I held her hand and said the bedtime verse Mark had made up for her when she was just born:

"For the Baby Princess is as sweet as she is fair, and as gentle as she is beautiful, and as kind as she is lovely. And wherever she goes, and whatever she does, Mummy and Daddy will always love her. Just because she's lovely, and because she's—"

"—Mabel!" she finished.

"And the thoughts," said Billy sleepily.

I could hear Mark's voice as I whispered, "All the thoughts are going away. Just like the little birds in their nests, and the rabbits in their rabbit holes. The thoughts don't need Billy and Mabel tonight. The world will turn

154

without them. The moon will shine without them. And all Billy and Mabel need to do is rest and sleep. And all Billy and Mabel need to do is . . ."

They were both asleep. I opened the curtains to see if the owl really had been there. There it was, still, gazing at me unblinking. I looked back for a long time, then closed the curtains.

CHRISTMAS

Friday 7 December 2012

Twitter followers 602 (have broken 600 ceiling), words of screenplay written 15 (better though utter rubbish), Christmas invitations (start of day) 1, Christmas invitations (end of day) 10, ideas re what to do re sudden plethora of invitations largely unsuitable for small children 0.

9.15 a.m. Right. Christmas Resolutions:

I WILL

*Stop feeling sad and thinking about or attempting to live through men, but think about children and Christmas.

*Have a Christmassy Christmas and make a new start.

*Make everything Christmassy and enjoy Christmas.

*Not be scared of not making a Christmassy enjoyable Christmas.

*Be more Buddhist about Christmas. Even though is Christian festival and, by its very nature, therefore, not Buddhist.

*Order piles of plastic crap from Amazon from "Santa," impossible to open in their Plastipaks, with twelve bits of wire fastening each thing to the cardboard backing. But instead encourage Billy and Mabel to choose one or two gifts each from "Santa" which are meaningful. Perhaps made of wood.

*Go on the St. Oswald's House Christmas cruise, but instead take action to make a Christmassy Christmas.

3.15 p.m. Right! Action stations! Have sent email to just about everyone I know, Magda, Talitha, Tom, Jude, Mark's parents, several of the mothers from school, saying, "What are you doing for Christmas?"

4.30 p.m. Just back from school run. Was just getting everyone organized when Rebecca the neighbour came and rang the doorbell. She was wearing a pair of tartan knickerbockers, a low-cut frilly top, a heavy leather belt with chains and studs and, in her hair, a robin in a nest which I recognized from the Graham and Green Christmas decoration display.

"Hello. Do you lot want to come over?"

We were all wild with excitement! At last! We clumped downstairs into Rebecca's *Downton Abbey*–like kitchen: dark wood floorboards, a rough-beamed ceiling, old wooden school table, photographs, hats, paintings, a huge statue of a bear and worn French windows opening onto a hidden world of brick pathways, long field-like grass, a life-size cow with a crown on its head, a laminated motel sign saying "*Vacancy*" and chandeliers in the trees.

We had a really good fun evening sitting at the kitchen table drinking wine and shoving bits of pizza at the children while the girls dressed up Rebecca's cat in scarves and dolly's dresses and the boys threw fits when we asked them to come off the Xbox.

"Is it normal to be too frightened of your own son to tell him to come off?" said Rebecca, staring vaguely at them. "Oh, fuck it. GET OFF THE BLOODY XBOX!"

There's nothing nicer than a friend who claims her own children are more badly behaved than your own.

I explained my whole theory about parenting being better if it was like a large Italian family having dinner under a tree while children play. Rebecca poured more wine and explained her theory of child-rearing, which is that you should behave as badly as possible so that the children will rebel against you and turn out like Saffron in *Absolutely Fabulous*. We made plans about Casual Kitchen Suppers, and holidays we would never go on, going on ferries between the Greek Islands with some sort of InterRail Pass only for ferries, and everyone—children included—carrying *nothing* but a toothbrush, swimsuit and floaty sarong.

Finally, as we were about to leave at 9 p.m., Rebecca said, "What are you doing for Christmas?"

"Nothing."

"Well, come to us!"

"We'd love to!" I said, quite carried away.

10 p.m. Gaaah! Just checked email. Have set off giant guilt trip amongst all friends and acquaintances, going from

158

nothing to do at Christmas to impossible multiple bookings. The following plans are now in place:

Tom: We are taking the children to join him at Drag Queen Christmas Market in Berlin.

Jude: We are taking the children to her mother's tiny council house in the rough part of Nottingham she refuses to leave (don't ask) and then going grouse shooting with Jude's father (exactly) and his friends in the north of Scotland.

Talitha: We are bringing the children to join, as she put it, "an ill-defined group of dubious Russian money-launderers on a luxury vodka boat on the Black Sea."

Admiral and Elaine Darcy: We are causing them to cancel their Christmas in Barbados in order to spend it with my children messing up their pottery collections, and scouring their immaculate Queen Anne house in Grafton Underwood for an Internet connection.

Daniel: We are joining him on a romantic weekend in bedroom at undecided European city with someone called Helgada.

Billy's friend Jeremiah's mum: We are celebrating Hanukkah with Jeremiah's dad, grandma, four aunts, seventeen cousins and the rabbi in Golders Green, though there'll be quite a lot of time when they are all at the synagogue.

Cosmata's mum: We are going to watch her oldest child perform as an extra in Wagner's *Ring* cycle in Berlin.

Mum and Una: Still the St. Oswald's House over-fifties Christmas cruise.

I mean, maybe the children would enjoy the Drag Queen Christmas Market?

Oh God, oh God. Just when I have made friends with Rebecca I have proved myself to be a total flake.

10.15 p.m. Just called Magda.

"Come to us," she said firmly. "You can't possibly do any of those things with two kids, or stay in your house relying on a neighbour you've only just met. Come to us in Gloucestershire. I'll get the couple next door over from the farm—they've got kids the same age and that's all kids need. Plus, there's nothing they can spoil and we've still got all the Xboxes. Never mind anyone else. Just email them back quickly, and say you've found a perfect kid-friendly plan. And tell your mum you'll do a special Christmas at St. Oswald's House when you get back. It'll all be perfectly fine."

Monday 31 December 2012

Christmas *has* been perfectly fine. Mum was perfectly happy with the post-Christmas-Christmas plan and had a whale of a time on the cruise, calling up, gabbling about "Pawl" the pastry chef and some man going into everyone else's berths. Rebecca thought the whole overbooking thing was hysterical and said we should definitely do the Drag

Queen Market or the money-launderer's vodka boat and if not she was available for wine and burnt food.

Christmas Eve and Christmas Day were really nice at Magda and Jeremy's. Magda did Christmas Eve with me; the stockings, helping wrap the giant pile of plastic crap, which "Santa" had of course ended up ordering from Amazon, and putting it under the tree. And I seriously think Billy and Mabel thought it was great. Billy doesn't really remember Christmas with Mark, and Mabel never had one. Billy only had two of them and he was so little . . . And the rest of the time we've been in and out of Rebecca's house, crossing the road with pans of burnt food, and moaning about computer games, and her and the kids in and out of ours and next year is going to be so much better!

PART TWO

Mad About the Boy

2013 DIARY

Tuesday 1 January 2013
Twitter followers 636, resolutions made about not making resolutions 1, said resolution kept 0, resolutions made 3.

9.15 p.m. Have made a decision. Am going to completely change. This year am not going to do any New Year's Resolutions but instead focus on being grateful for myself as I am. New Year's Resolutions would be expressing dissatisfaction with status quo rather than Buddhist gratitude.

9.20 p.m. Actually, maybe will just do Capsule New Year's Resolutions in manner of soon-to-be Capsule Wardrobe.

I WILL
*Focus on being a mother instead of thinking about men.

*If by any unlikely chance do run across any attractive men, put the Dating Rules into practice and be an accomplished dater.

*Oh, fuck it. Find someone really great to shag who is really good fun and makes me feel gorgeous, not horrible, and have SEX.

PERFECT MOTHER

Saturday 5 January 2013

9.15 a.m. Right! Caring for two children will become effortless now I have read *One, Two, Three . . . Better, Easier Parenting*, which is all about giving two simple warnings and a consequence, and also *French Children Don't Throw Food*, which is about how French children operate within a cadre which is a bit like in school where there is a structured inner circle where they know what the rules are (and if they break them you simply do One Two Three Better, Easier Parenting and then outside you don't fuss about them too much and wear elegant French clothes and have sex).

11.30 a.m. Entire morning has been totally lovely. Started day with all three of us in my bed cuddling. Then had breakfast. Then played hide-and-seek. Then drew and coloured in Plants and Zombies from Plants versus Zombies. You see! It's easy! All you have to do is devote yourself completely to your children and have a *cadre*, and, and . . .

11.31 a.m. Billy: "Mummy, will you play football?"

11.32 a.m. Mabel: "Noo! Mummy, will you pick me up and thwing me round?"

11.40 a.m. Had just escaped to toilet when both cried "Mummy" simultaneously.

"I'm on the TOILET!" I retorted. "Hang on a minute."

Shouting ensued.

"Right!" I said brightly, pulling myself together and emerging from the loo. "Let's go out, shall we?"

"I don't want to go out."

"I want to do compuuuteerrrrrrrrrr."

Both children burst into spontaneous crying.

11.45 a.m. Went back into the toilet, bit my hand really quite hard, hissing, "Everything is completely intolerable, I hate myself, I'm a rubbish mother," tore up a piece of toilet paper pettily and, for lack of a grander gesture, threw it into the toilet. Smoothed myself down and stepped out again, smiling brightly. At which I distinctly saw Mabel waddle up to Billy, whack him on the top of the head with Saliva, then sit down to innocently play with her Hellvanians while Billy burst into loud spontaneous crying again.

11.50 a.m. Oh GOD. I really, REALLY want to go on a mini-break with someone and have sex.

11.51 a.m. Returned to toilet, put towel over face and muttered, shamefully, into towel, "Look, will everyone just SHUT UP?!"

The door burst open. Mabel stared solemnly. "Billy's exasperating me," she said, then ran back into the room yelling, "Mummy's eatin' a towel!"

Billy rushed eagerly, then suddenly remembered: "Mabel hit me with Saliva."

"I didn't."

"You did."

"Mabel, I saw you hit Billy with Saliva," I joined in.

Mabel stared at me under lowered brows, then burst out, "He hit me wid a . . . wid a HAMMER."

"I didn't," wailed Billy. "We haven't got a hammer."

"We have!" I said indignantly.

Both started spontaneous crying again.

"We don't hit," I said despairingly. "We don't hit. I'm going to count to . . . to . . . It's not OK to hit."

Ugh. Ridiculous expression: "Not OK," suggesting am too idle or passive-aggressive to locate or use word categorizing what hitting actually is (very bad, effing annoying, etc.), so, instead, hitting has to make do with mere exclusion from vague generalization of things which "are OK."

Mabel, regardless of hitting's OKness or otherwise, grabbed a fork from the table, jabbed Billy, and then ran off and hid behind the curtain. "Mabel, that's a One," I said. "Give me the fork."

"Yes, master," she said, throwing down the fork and running to the drawer to get another one.

"Mabel!" I said. "The next thing I'm going to say is . . . is . . . TWO!"

I froze, thinking, "What am I going to do when I get to Three?"

"Come on! Let's go up to the Heath," I said in a jolly way, deciding it wasn't the moment to hit the hitting issue head on.

"Nooooo! I want to do Wizard101."

"Not goin' in de car! Want to watch *SpongeBob*."

Was suddenly wildly indignant that own children's values were so entirely off-key, due to American cartoons, computer games and general consumer culture. Had flashback to own childhood, and urge to inspire and teach them with song from the Girl Guides.

"There are white tents upon the hillside / And the flag is flying freeeee!" I sang.

"Mummy," said Billy, with Mark-style sternness.

"There are white tents upon the hillside / And that's where I long to beeee . . ." I warbled. "Pack your kit, girls! / Feeling fit, girls! / For a life of health and joy!"

"Thtoppit," said Mabel.

"For it's off to camp again / In a lorry not a train."

"Mummy, stop!" said Billy.

"Camp ahoy!" I finished with a rousing flourish. "Camp ahoy!"

Looked down to see them staring at me nervously, as if I was a zombie from Plants versus Zombies.

"Can I go on the computer?" said Billy.

Calmly, deliberately, I opened the fridge, reaching for the enormous stash of chocolate-from-Granny on the top shelf.

"Chocolate buttons!" I said, dancing about with the buttons in an attempt to mimic a fairy-themed party entertainer. "Follow the trail of buttons to see where it leads! Two trails," I added, to ward off conflict, laying a careful line of exactly matching chocolate buttons up the stairs and towards the front door, ignoring the fact that tradesmen may previously have trailed dog-poo traces into the carpet.

The two of them obediently trotted up the stairs after me, stuffing the no-doubt-dog-poo-smeared buttons into their mouths.

On the way in the car, I thought about what I should do about the hitting. Clearly, according to *French Children Don't Throw Food*, it should be outside the cadre (but then so should putting chocolate buttons in a trail out of the house) and according to *One, Two, Three . . . Better, Easier Parenting* there should simply be a scorched-earth, zero-tolerance, three-strikes-and-you're-out Donald Rumsfeld kind of policy.

"Mabel?" I said in preparation, as we drove along.

Silence.

"Billy?"

Silence.

"Earth to Mabel and Billy?"

They both seemed to be in some sort of trance. Why couldn't they have had the trance in the house so I could have sat down for a minute and read the Style section from last week's *Sunday Times* whilst believing myself to be reading the News Review?

Decided to let the trance just happen: to go with the flow and make the most of any moment of calm to clear my head. It was really quite jolly driving along, the sun was shining, people out and about, lovers in each other's arms and . . .

"Mummy?"

Hah! I seized the moment, adopting a statesmanlike, Obama-esque tone. "Yes. Now. I have something to say: Billy—and particularly Mabel—hitting is not allowed in our family. And I say to you now: every day when a person doesn't hit—or jab—they will get a gold star. I say to you: any time a person does hit they get a black mark. And I say to you, as a non-violent person and as your mother:

170

any person who gets five gold stars by the end of the week will get a small prize of their choice."

"A Hellvanian bunny?" said Mabel excitedly. "A Fuckoon Family?"

"Yes, a Raccoon Family," I said.

"She didn't say Raccoon. She said the F-word. Can I have crowns on Wizard101?"

"Yes."

"Wait. How much is a Raccoon Family? Can I get crowns that are worth the same as a Raccoon Family?" Mark Darcy the top negotiator in child form. "How much money does Mabel lose for saying the F-word?"

"I didn't say de F-word."

"You did."

"I didn't. I THAID Fuckoon."

"How many Wizard101 crowns does Mabel lose for saying the F-word again?"

"Here we are at the super-dooper Heath!" I said rousingly, pulling into the car park.

Is amazing how everything calms down once one is in the outdoors with blue skies and crisp winter sunshine. Headed for the climbing trees, standing close by as Billy and Mabel hung upside down, motionless, from the conveniently broad, low boughs. Like lemurs.

Wished, for a fleeting second, they *were* lemurs.

1 p.m. Suddenly had urge to check my Twitter followers and pulled iPhone out to take a look.

1.01 p.m. "Mummeee! Mabel's stuck in the tree!"

Looked up in alarm. How had they got up there in

thirty seconds when they'd just been hanging upside down? Mabel was now way up, clinging to the tree trunk like not so much a lemur as a koala, but slithering alarmingly.

"Hang on, I'm coming."

I took off my parka and hoisted myself awkwardly into the tree, positioning myself under Mabel and putting a firm hand under her bottom, wishing I hadn't come in quite such low-rise jeans, and high-rise thong.

"Mummy, I can't get down either," said Billy who was crouched, wobbling, on a branch to my right like an unsteady bird.

"Um," I said. "Hang on."

I leaned my full weight against the tree, placing one foot on a slightly higher branch to lift me towards Billy and putting my hand on Billy's bottom, whilst keeping the other hand under Mabel's bottom, simultaneously feeling the low-rise jeans descending lower over my own bottom. "Calm and poised! Just hold on tight and . . ."

None of us could move. What was I going to do? Were we going to be frozen against the tree for ever, like a trio of lizards?

"Everything all right up there?"

"Is Mr. Wolkda," said Mabel.

I peered awkwardly down over my shoulder.

It was indeed Mr. Wallaker, running, in sweatpants and a grey T-shirt, looking like he was on an assault course.

"Everything all right?" he said again, stopping suddenly below us. He was oddly ripped for a schoolteacher, but staring in his usual annoying, judgemental way.

"Yes, no, everything's great!" I trilled. "Just, um, climbing a tree!"

"Yes, I see that."

Great, I thought. Now he'll tell everyone at school I'm a completely irresponsible mother letting the children climb trees. Jeans were now slipping below my bottom-cleavage, my black lacy thong on full display.

"Right. Good. Well. I'll be off then. Bye!"

"Bye!" I called gaily over my shoulder, then reconsidered. "Um . . . Mr. Wallaker?"

"Yeeees?"

"Could you just . . . ?"

"Billy," said Mr. Wallaker, "let go of your mum, hold onto the branch, and sit down on it."

I released my frozen arm from Billy and put it round Mabel's back.

"There you go. Now. Look at me. When I count to three, I want you to do what I say."

"OK!" said Billy cheerfully.

"One . . . two . . . and . . . jump!"

I leaned back and nearly screamed as Billy jumped out of the tree. What was Mr. Wallaker doing?

"Aaaaaaand . . . roll!"

Billy landed, did a strange military-style roll and stood up, beaming.

"Now, Mrs. Darcy, if you'll forgive me . . ." Mr. Wallaker hoisted himself into the lower branches. "I'm going to take hold of . . ." Me? My thong? ". . . Mabel," he said, reaching his arms past me to put his big hands round Mabel's plump little form. "And you wriggle out and jump down."

Trying to ignore the exasperating frisson brought on by the scent and closeness of Mr. Wallaker, I did what he said and jumped down, trying to pull up the jeans. He took

173

Mabel in one strong scoop of his arm, leaned her on his shoulder and placed her on the grass.

"I thaid Fuckoon," said Mabel, looking at him gravely.

"I nearly said that, too," said Mr. Wallaker. "But we're all all right now, aren't we?"

"Will you play football with me?" said Billy.

"Got to get home, I'm afraid," he said, "to er . . . the family. Now try to avoid the upper branches."

He started running off again, pumping his arms up and down with palms extended. Who did he think he was?

Suddenly found self shouting after him: "Mr. Wallaker?"

He turned. Did not know what had intended to say. Mind whirring frantically, I shouted, "Thank you." Then added, for no reason whatsoever, "Will you follow me on Twitter?"

"Absolutely not," he said dismissively, then started running off again.

Humph. Grumpy bastard. Even if he did get us down from the tree.

A NEEDLE IN A TWITTERSTACK

Saturday 5 January 2013 (continued)
Twitter followers 652, Twitter followers I might fancy 1.

4 p.m. Whole Mr. Wallaker tree/"back to the wife and kids" thing has left self feeling abnormal, and that everyone else is spending Saturday afternoon in nuclear family, while Dad plays ping-pong with the lad, and Mum shops and does mani-pedis with her immaculately dressed little girl. Ooh, doorbell!

9 p.m. Was Rebecca! Had lovely evening sitting at her kitchen table while kids ran around. Was still feeling a bit abnormal, as Rebecca has a husband, or at least a "partner" as they are not married. He is tall, handsome, though frequently a bit wrecked-looking and always dressed in black, and a musician. Told Rebecca about the everyone-else-in-nuclear-families-paranoia at which she snorted.

"Nuclear families? I never see Jake from one month to the next. He's always off on some gig or tour, and when he appears it's frequently like having some kind of teenage stoner in the house."

Then we all came back to our house, and watched *Britain's Got Talent* while I cooked (i.e., microwaved popcorn) and now the children are asleep. Billy and Finn are over the road, and Mabel and Oleander are here.

Sunday 6 January 2013

Twitter followers 649 (feel like tweeting disappeared followers saying, "Why? Why?").

8 p.m. Another good day with Rebecca and the kids. Another good evening with me, Mabel and Billy on my bed watching the *Britain's Got Talent* results while I checked Twitter on my iPhone, tweeting my followers (649) with piercing aperçus on the ongoing programme: e.g.,

<@JoneseyBJ Aww #Chevaune song v. moving totes amazog.>

8.15 p.m. Ooh. Have got response to my aperçu from someone called @_Roxster!

<@_Roxster @JoneseyBJ #Chevaune song "totes amazog"? My tears are getting mixed up with my sick.>

"Mummy," said Billy.

"Mmmm?" I said vaguely.

"Why are you smiling like that?"

DO NOT TWEET WHEN DRUNK

Thursday 10 January 2013
Twitter followers 652, Twitter followers who came back 1, new Twitter followers 2, alcohol units (do not want to even think about it. But—quavering voice—don't I deserve a little happiness?).

9.30 p.m. Chloe staying over again after her night out with Graham in Camden. Is nice sitting down at the end of the day and updating myself with current affairs and Twitter with a well-earned glass or two of white wine.

10 p.m. Woah. Fantastic story: *"Beef Lasagne 100% Horse."*

10.25 p.m. Hee hee. Just tweeted.
<@JoneseyBJ Warning: Fish fingers found to be 90% Sea Horse.>
Sure will be retweeted and bring more followers like spambot tweet!
Maybe will have another glass of wine. I mean, Chloe is here, so is fine.
Love that the tone of my Twitter feed is so loving and friendly. Not like some, where everyone is slagging each other off. Really, is like going back to the days of Robin Hood with all these little fiefdoms and oh . . .

10.30 p.m. Everyone is slagging me off. And my tweet.

<@_Sunnysmile @JoneseyBJ You think that's a new joke? Don't you read anyone except yourself on Twitter? Self-obsessed or what?>

Really need another glass of wine now.

10.45 p.m. Right, am going to tweet back to @sunny or whatever she's called 'erself and tick her off. So people aren't allowed to make up their own jokes any more?

11 p.m. <@JoneseyBJ @_Sunnysmile If you don't stop being mean I will de-follow you.>

11.01 p.m. <@JoneseyBJ @_Sunnysmile Here one spreads joy & positive energy by tweeting. Rather like birds do.>

11.07 p.m. <@JoneseyBJ "They toil not, neither do they tweet." Hmm. No, they do tweet though. Thasu point with birds.>

11.08 p.m. <@JoneseyBJ Anyway f*** em. Stupid birds flapping around tweeting all over s place. Oh oh look at me! I'm a bird!>

11.15 p.m. <@JoneseyBJ Hate birds. Look at that movie "The Birds!" Birds can turn MAN-EATING.>

11.16 p.m. <@JoneseyBJ Peecking people's eyes out with 60s hairdos. Vicious nasty birds.>

11.30 p.m. <@JoneseyBJ 85 followess gone waway. Why? Why'wasi hwohave I don? comebac!k>

<@JoneseyBJ Noo! Follwers draining away as if through sieve.>

<@JoneseyBJ Nooo! Hate bireds Hatetweetings Hate drainqineaway follwoers. An goingsoto bed!>

TWUNKEN AFTERMATH

Friday 11 January 2013

Twitter followers lost 551, Twitter followers remaining 101, number of words of screenplay written 0.

6.35 a.m. Will just check my Twi—Gaaah! Just remembered twunking incoherent drunken rant last night, slagging off birds for no reason to hundreds of complete strangers. Oh God. Have clouting hangover and have got to do school run. Oh, is OK because Chloe is doing school run. Am going back to sleep.

10 a.m. Look, this can be salvaged, like any other PR disaster. With exception, possibly, of current Lance Armstrong PR disaster.

10.15 a.m. Right. *The Leaves in His Hair*. Must get on.

11.15 a.m. Actually, maybe I could have a career in PR! Oh, shit, is 11.15, must get on with screenplay. First, though, clearly I quickly need to make a full and frank Twitter apology to my few remaining followers.

    <@JoneseyBJ Very sorry re #twunk last night re birds.>

11.16 a.m. <@JoneseyBJ Birds delight our ears and eyes with their feathers and song! And control worms. Leave birds alone!>

11.45 a.m. Maybe will just throw in quote from Dalai Lama for good measure:

<@JoneseyBJ Just as a snake sheds its skin so we can shed our past and begin anew. (@DalaiLama)>

9.15 p.m. Right. Children are asleep. Am going to get back on Twitter.

9.16 p.m. OMG. Tweet from @_Roxster! Yesss! At least Roxster has not left in disgust.

<@_Roxster @JoneseyBJ @DalaiLama Once the hangover has cleared? Do you realize you've been singled out in a #Twunk thread?>

9.17 p.m. Oh God. Everyone is ridiculing me and retweeting my drunken birds tweet. Must try and do damage control.

<@JoneseyBJ #twunkbirds Look, sorry, I really wish I hadn't—what is the past tense of tweet? Tweeted? Twittered?>

<@_Roxster @JoneseyBJ I believe the appropriate term is "Twat.">

<@JoneseyBJ @_Roxster Are you being grammatical or rude?>

<@_Roxster @JoneseyBJ The former *pretentious voice*: from the Latin, Twitto, Twittarse, Twittat.>

He's funny. And pic is handsome. And young-looking. I wonder who he is?

<@JoneseyBJ @_Roxster Roxster, if you carry on like this, your 103 remaining Twitterati will be demanding sick bags.>

<@_Roxster @JoneseyBJ Why? Are they all hung-over because they too were twunking about birds last night?>

Mmmmmmmmmmmmmmmmmmmmmm. Cheeky young whippersnapper.

<@JoneseyBJ @_Roxster Please stop being so impertinent, or I shall have to tweak you.>

<@_Roxster @JoneseyBJ Tweak or tweet? Best not the latter. You've just lost 48 more followers.>

<@JoneseyBJ @_Roxster Oh no! They think I'm a really neurotic Twitterer and fat.>

<@_Roxster @JoneseyBJ Did you just say "and fart"?>

<@JoneseyBJ @_Roxster No, Roxster, I said "and fat." You seem unhealthily obsessed with farting and vomiting.>

Roxster just retweeted me from one of his followers: <@Raef_P @Rory See you in five, yar? Outside the Fartage?> adding:

<@_Roxster @JoneseyBJ Posh bastards are skiing in France.>

<@JoneseyBJ @_Roxster But what is Fartage?>

<@_Roxster @JoneseyBJ Waxing.>

10 p.m. Waxing? France? Suddenly have lurching fear that Roxster is not a cute younger man who finds me entertaining, but gay, and is drawn to me and Talitha as tragic ironic ruined drag acts, like Lily Savage.

10.05 p.m. Just called Talitha to get her opinion.

"Roxster? That rings a bell. Is he one of my followers?"

"He's MY follower!" I said indignantly, then conceded, "Though he may have jumped across from you."

"He's adorable. Roxster. Roxby someone. I had a man on the show who was plugging designer food-recycling caddies and Roxby came with him. He works for some green eco-charity. Nice young chap. Very handsome. Go for it!"

10.15 p.m. <@JoneseyBJ @_Roxster Do you go to France and get waxed, Roxster?>

<@_Roxster @JoneseyBJ *Deep masculine voice* Jonesey, I am very far from gay. I am talking about waxing snowboards.>

<@JoneseyBJ @_Roxster "Oh oh, look at me, I'm a young person. I do snowboarding in baggy trousers showing my underpants.">

<@JoneseyBJ @_Roxster "Instead of skiing elegantly with a fur-lined hood.">

<@_Roxster @JoneseyBJ Do you like younger men, Jonesey?>

<@JoneseyBJ @_Roxster *Icy, almost to point of glacier-esque* Excuse me? What EXACTLY are you implying?>

<@_Roxster @JoneseyBJ *Hides behind sofa* How old are you, Jonesey?>

<@JoneseyBJ @_Roxster Oscar Wilde: Never trust a woman who will tell you her age. If she tells you that she will tell you anything.>

<@JoneseyBJ @_Roxster How old are you, Roxster?>

<@_Roxster @JoneseyBJ 29.>

SCREENWRITER

Monday 14 January 2013

Twitter followers 793 (am #Twunken heroine), tweets 17, disastrous social occasions agreed to 1 (or maybe 3 all in one), words of screenplay written 0.

10 a.m. Right, must get down to work!

10.05 a.m. Maybe will just check news.

10.15 a.m. Oooh. Really like Michelle Obama's new haircut with fringe, or "bangs," as they are known. Maybe I should get fringe or bangs? Also, of course, delighted by Obama's second term of presidency.

10.20 a.m. Really has started to seem as if nice people are in charge: Obama, that new Archbishop of Canterbury who had a proper job before and speaks out against the banks being greedy, and William and Kate. Right, work. Ooh, phone!

11 a.m. Was Talitha. "Darling! Have you finished your screenplay?"

"Yes!" I said. "Well, sort of." The truth is, what with the whole Leatherjacketman thing, and the dating study thing, and then the Twitter thing, *The Leaves in His Hair* seems to have rather *gone to seed*. Oh, though, can leaves go to seed? Maybe if sycamores?

"Bridget? Are you still there? Is it in some sort of shape?"

"Yes!" I lied.

"Well, send it to me. Sergei's doing some 'dealings' in the film business and I think I can use it to get you an agent."

"Thanks," I said, very touched.

"Send it today?"

"Um. Yes! Just give me a couple of days?"

"OK," she said. "But get on with it, OK? Between tweets to toy boys? Remember, we do not let Twitter become an obsession."

11.15 a.m. Right. Is absolutely imperative not to tweet today, but finish screenplay. Have just got to do the ending. Oh, and the middle bit. And sort out the start. Maybe will just look quickly at Twitter to see if @_Roxster has tweeted again. Gaah! Telephone.

"Oh, hello, darling"—my mum. "I'm just ringing about the Cruise Slideshow Event and Hard-Hats-Offing a week on Saturday. It was super doing the Christmas-After-Christmas at Chats and I thought . . ."

Tried to resist the temptation to immediately tweet hilariously about the Mum/Cruise Event conversation whilst being in the middle of it. Of course Mum would never be on Twitter.

"Bridget?"

"Yes, Mum," I said, trying to drag myself away from Twitter.

"Oh! So you ARE going to come?"

"Um," I said. "Can you just run through it again?"

She sighed. "It's the Hard-Hats-Offing for the completion of the new Gatehouse Lodges! All the St. Oswald's establishments do them when they've finished a new build. We all wear hard hats, and then just toss them in the air!"

"When is it again?"

"A week on Saturday. You will come, darling, because Mavis is having Julie and Michael and all the grandchildren."

"So I can bring the kids?"

There was a slight pause. "Yes, of course, darling, that's the whole idea but . . ."

"But what?"

"Nothing, nothing, darling. You'll make sure Mabel wears the dress I sent?"

I sighed. No matter how many cool shorts-tights-and-biker-boots outfits from H&M kids, or sticky-outy party dresses from Mum I try to coax Mabel into, Mabel has her own ideas about what she wants to wear: usually some sort of Hamish-meets-Disney look involving a glittery T-shirt, leggings and an ankle-length tiered skirt. Feel am from totally Other Generation, which doesn't understand the look of the young people.

"Bridget!" said Mum, understandably, perhaps, exasperated. "You must come, darling, it doesn't matter how badly they behave."

"They don't behave badly!"

"Well, the other grandchildren are older because of you having them so late in life, and of course when you're on your own with them it's harder to—"

"I'm not sure I can make Saturday week."

"Everyone else will have their grandchildren there and it's terribly hard for me being on my own."

"OK. Now, Mum, I've got to go."

"Did I tell you about the trouble we've been having . . . ?" she started to gabble, as she always does when I say I have to go. "We've got one of these men going into all the bedrooms. Kenneth Garside? He keeps getting into bed with all the women."

"Do you like Kenneth Garside, Mum?" I said innocently.

"Oh, don't be silly, darling. You don't want a man when you get to my age. They just want looking after."

It's an interesting thing, the ages at which men and women want each other more than the other does:

Twenties: Women have the upper hand because pretty much everyone wants to shag them so they have a lot of power. And twenty-something men are super-horny but haven't made it in their careers yet.

Thirties: Men definitely have the upper hand. Thirties is the worst possible time for a woman to be dating: whole thing increasingly loaded by biologically unfair ticking clock: a clock which will hopefully soon be transformed, by the perfection of Jude-style egg-freezing, into silent digital clock with no need for an alarm. Meanwhile, men sense it like sharks scenting blood and are also simultaneously perfecting their careers, so the balance tips more and more in their favour until . . .

Forties: Not sure about this because I was with Mark most of the time. Maybe about equal? If you take babies out of the equation. Or maybe men think they're on top because they think they want younger women and think age-equivalent women want them. But actually secretly the women equally want younger men. And the younger men like the older women because they're refreshingly not looking to them to be breadwinners and not thinking about babies any more.

Fifties: It used to be the age of Germaine Greer's "Invisible Woman," branded as non-viable, post-menopausal sitcom fodder. But now with the Talitha school of branding combined with Kim Cattrall, Julianne and Demi Moore, etc. is all starting to change!

Sixties: Balance completely shifting, as men realize they've got as far as they're going to get in their careers and that they've never really made friends in the way women do, but just talked about golf and stuff. And women take better care of themselves—look at Helen Mirren and Joanna Lumley!

Seventies: Definitely women have the upper hand, and still do themselves out nicely, and make a nice home and cook and—

"Bridget, are you still there?"

Upshot of it is, have agreed to take the children to Hard-Hats-Offing for the new Gatehouse Lodges and the Cruise Slideshow Event followed by Family Tea at Chats. And have still not even made a start on screenplay.

Tuesday 15 January 2013

11.55 p.m. Have spent all of last night and all of today writing writing writing and just emailed *The Leaves in His Hair* to Talitha.

Wednesday 16 January 2013

134lb (bad: too much time sitting on arse), agents, though, 1!

11 a.m. Just had phone call from agent! Unfortunately had mouth full of grated cheese but did not matter as did not seem imperative to talk.

"I have Brian Katzenberg for you," said the assistant.

"So," Brian Katzenberg crashed straight in. "We have Sergei in common, and I know Sergei wants to get this spec out."

"Have you read it?" I said excitedly. "Do you like it?"

"I think it's fascinating and I'm going to get it out to appropriate people immediately. So you can let Sergei know that straight away and it's a pleasure to meet you."

"Thank you," I stammered.

"So you'll tell Sergei I did it?"

"Yes!" I said. "Will do!"

11.05 a.m. Just called Talitha to thank her.

"You will tell Sergei?" I said. "He seemed very anxious that I tell him straight away."

"Oh God. Yes, I'll tell Sergei. Fuck knows what's going on there. But, darling, I'm very proud of you for finishing."

LET IT SNOW!

Thursday 17 January 2013
Texts about snow 12, tweets about snow 13, snowflakes 0.

8 p.m. Text from school.

<Dear Parents. Heavy snow is expected tomorrow. Please check your texts and do not start your journey before 8 a.m. We will text you if school is cancelled for a Snow Day.>

8.15 p.m. Plain excitement. We can all bunk off and go sledging! Clearly no one can go to sleep. We keep opening the curtains to check if you can see it in the street lamps.

8.30 p.m. Still no snow.

8.45 p.m. Still no snow. Look, is really time the children went to sleep now.

9 p.m. Eventually got them to sleep by saying, "Go to sleep, go to sleep, if you don't go to sleep you won't be allowed to ENJOY the lovely snow!" repeatedly like parrot. Obvious lie, as who else am I going to go in the snow with?

9.45 p.m. Still no snow. Maybe will check Twitter.

9.46 p.m. @_Roxster is tweeting about the snow!

    <@_Roxster Anyone else excited about the snow?>

9.50 p.m. <@JoneseyBJ @_Roxster Me. But where is it? "Oh, oh, look at me! I'm snow but I don't exist!">

10 p.m. Tweet from @_Roxster!

    <@_Roxster @JoneseyBJ Jonesey, are you twunking again? Or do you like snow as much as me?>

10.15 p.m. Carried on flirting with @_Roxster.

    <@JoneseyBJ @_Roxster Are you getting fartaged in preparation?>

    <@_Roxster @JoneseyBJ Definitely.>

    Talitha joined in. <@Talithaluckybitch @JoneseyBJ @_Roxster Very funny, you two. Now GO TO SLEEP.>

10.30 p.m. Mmmm. Love Twitter. Love feeling that there is someone else out there who cares about all the little exciting things you yourself get excited about.

11 p.m. Still no snow.

Friday 18 January 2013

Number of times checked for snow 12, snowflakes 0, tweets from @_Roxster 7, tweets pretending to be to all followers but actually to @_Roxster 6 (slightly less than him, v.g.)

7 a.m. Woke up and all rushed excitedly to the window. No snow.

7.15 a.m. Tempting to all stay in PJs for Snow Day, even if no snow, but forced self to force everyone, including self, to get dressed just in case School Snow Day text did not happen.

7.45 a.m. No text. Maybe tweet, though, from @_Roxster?

7.59 a.m. Still no school text. Still no tweet from @_Roxster. Trying to deal with own as well as everyone else's disappointment, shoved three bacon-wrapped chipolatas in mouth, adding as an afterthought, "Anyone else want one?"

8 a.m. No text from school. We had better go.

9 a.m. Dropped off Mabel and got to Junior Branch to find infectious excitement, and Mr. Wallaker organizing lines of boys crouching behind imaginary snow-walls and hurling imaginary snowballs at each other. Resisted temptation to tweet about scene to @_Roxster lest it put him off me that I have kids.

"Snow today, Mrs. Darcy!" said Mr. Wallaker, suddenly looming up beside us. "Going to be climbing trees?"

"I know! I've been waiting for it all night," I said, smoothly ignoring the tree reference. "But where is it?"

"On its way from the west! It's snowing in Somerset. Do you enjoy snow?"

"Punctual snow," I said darkly.

"Maybe it's been held up on the M4," he said. "It's closed by snow at Junction 13."

"Oh!" I said, brightening.

"Wait," said Billy suspiciously. "How could snow be held up by snow?"

There was a slight twitch of amusement in Mr. Wallaker's eyes, then Billy's face broke into a grin. It was really annoying, as if they were somehow sharing a joke at my expense.

"Have a nice day!" I said confusedly—we weren't exactly in California—and slithered off through the ice to get on with my Twitter, I mean writing. Why did I put on high-heeled boots?

9.30 a.m. Back home. Right! *The Leaves in His Hair*.

9.35 a.m. Quickly tweeted @_Roxster, I mean my followers, Mr. Wallaker's joke.

9.45 a.m. <@JoneseyBJ Apparently the snow has been held up by snow on the M4 but will be here shortly.>

10 a.m. Five people have retweeted my tweet! Twelve more followers have come.

10.15 a.m. Keeps saying, "WARNING! SNOW!" on the telly.

10.30 a.m. The snow has started!

11 a.m. Is just getting thicker and thicker. Can't stop going up to window to look out at it.

11.45 a.m. Just keep staring at the miracle of the snow. Is like someone has beautifully drawn white shading on all the trees. Is an inch and a half thick on the table outside—like icing on a cake. Or cream . . . Maybe not an inch and a half. Consider going out with ruler to measure, then realize ridiculous. Must get on with myriad tasks.

Noon. OMG is tweet from @_Roxster.

<@_**Roxster** @JoneseyBJ Shall we bunk off work, get fartaged and go sledging??>

Blink at tweet in shock. Is @_Roxster actually asking me out? Does he mean it? But I'm looking completely crazed with hair standing up on end and . . . But I could wash my hair! And put on sledging things and you only live once and it's snowing! Tweeted: <@**JoneseyBJ** @_Roxster Yes! Can you?>

Just as I had tweeted there was a text:

<INFANTS AND JUNIOR BRANCH. Due to the snow please pick up your children as soon as possible and get them safely home. School will close at 1.30.>

12.15 p.m. What am I going to do? Cannot expect twenty-nine-year-old dream god to suddenly want to come sledging with two children and older woman with mad hair. Whole point of older woman is you are supposed to be *soignée* in black silk stockings like in French-style parenting and Catherine Deneuve and Charlotte Rampling. Must go get children but how can I stand @_Roxster up, and the Dating Rules say it's like dancing and you're just meant to follow but . . .

Another text:

<Both Infants and Junior Branch children are gathered in the school hall. Please pick up your children as soon as possible.>

Is genuine emergency!!

12.30 p.m. Rushed downstairs to get sledges out of cupboard, quickly wiping off spiders, etc.

12.50 p.m. Opened door to see road was completely covered in snow. It is a major blizzard, clearly a very serious and dangerous situation! Wildly excited. But what about @_Roxster? Must put children first.

1 p.m. OK, have got full ski gear on now, not sure if helmet is required but goggles certainly. Have thrown snow boots, salopettes, jackets, gloves, survival kit, shovel, torch, water, chocolate and sledges in back of car.

5 p.m. Eventually got to school after thrilling slithery journey. Was necessary, even so, to take goggles off and put glasses on to check for @_Roxster tweets.

<@_Roxster @JoneseyBJ Sorry, Jonesey—was being inauthentically devil-may-care. Have job cannot get out of to play in snow. Unlike, clearly, you.>

Crushed. Am stood up for snow date.

Waddled up hill into school, in manner of Lance Armstrong when landing on moon—I mean, Neil Armstrong—owing to ski pants on top of my jeans and jacket and everything, thinking, "OK, do not need to reply to @_Roxster now as he has, technically speaking, stood me up for sledging. And I responded not reacted so have perfectly followed dating rules and—"

Burst through door into school hall, where the Infants and Juniors were gathered, to see Perfect Nicorette dressed as a sort of Snow Queen in white snow boots, perfectly blow-dried hair, enormous black patent handbag covered in bling, and long white coat with white fur thing draped around it, laughing flirtatiously with Mr. Wallaker. Huh. Man-Tart. Married and flirting with Nicorette. Mr. Wallaker turned as I walked in, and patently burst out laughing.

He wouldn't laugh if he knew I had a possible sledging date with a toy boy, would he? Am Catherine Deneuve and Charlotte Rampling.

"Mummeee!" Billy and Mabel ran over, eyes shining. "Can we go sledging?"

"Yes! I've got the sledges in the car!" I said and, giving Mr. Wallaker an imperious look, I pulled my goggles back over my eyes and swept mysteriously—as best I could given outfit—out of the hall.

10 p.m. Fantastic day. Sledging was completely brilliant. Rebecca and everyone from over the road came up to Primrose Hill too and it was completely magical, really like a Christmas card. The snow was deep and fluffy and hardly anyone was up there at first and you could really get the sledge to go quite fast on the paths. And @_Roxster tweeted in the middle.

<@_Roxster @JoneseyBJ Do you want to sledge later? Can make it tonight if you can.>

<@_Roxster @JoneseyBJ Though worry re you in treacherous conditions. Would another night be better?>

Was too difficult to reply as fingers were frozen, had to put glasses on to read tweets and simultaneously run after sledges to stop collisions, etc., so just left it for a while, savouring the feeling of being the last one to receive a message and @_Roxster wanting to have a date with me!

As it got later, more and more people were on the Hill, and it started getting icy so we all came back to our place, had hot chocolate and supper together and it was really very jolly, and while Rebecca was watching the kids I snuck off to my Twitter for five minutes, glancing briefly in the mirror and realizing tonight really would not be a good night for a date with a toy boy.

In the midst of all the incoherent stream of tweets about snow and the M4 there was another one from @_Roxster.

<@_Roxster @JoneseyBJ Jonesey? Have you died in the snow?>

<@JoneseyBJ @_Roxster Nearly. Was epic off-piste powder. Another night would be great.>

<@_Roxster @JoneseyBJ Any particular night?>

You see, straightforward, authentic communication! That's the way. Tweeted back.

<@JoneseyBJ @_Roxster Let me consult my extremely full diary . . .>

<@_Roxster @JoneseyBJ You mean huge body of dating advice manuals?>

OMG. Was Roxster reading my tweets back in the days of Leatherjacketman?

<@JoneseyBJ @_Roxster *Smoothly ignoring imperti-
nent young whippersnapper* When did you have in mind?>

<@_Roxster @JoneseyBJ Tuesday?>

Headed back down to the kitchen beaming. Everything is
marvellous! Have date with gorgeous, funny, hunky twenty-
nine-year-old toy boy and house full of rosy-cheeked children, sweet-smelling food, sledges and willies (I mean
wellies—where did that come from?).

DO NOT TWEET ABOUT
DATE DURING DATE

Sunday 20 January 2013

Twitter followers 873, tweets from @_Roxster 7.

11 a.m. Tweeting is going sensationally. More and more followers have come since the whole #twunkbirds thread thing. Cannot help noticing that Roxster has gone rather silent since the agreement about the date. But maybe, being a man, he feels that a level has been accomplished, as with Xbox, and there is no need to keep on at it.

11.02 a.m. Actually had better just send a tweet to let everyone know what's going on.

<@JoneseyBJ *Trills smugly, annoyingly, full-of-joys-of-spring-and-I've-got-a-date-with-mysterious-stranger-off-Twitter* Morneeeee-ing, everyone!>

11.05 a.m. OMG, have lost two followers. Why? Why? Was there something in the *tone*? Had better send another one.

<@JoneseyBJ Sorry, have clearly turned off several followers with early-morning smugness. Obviously date will all go wrong and will be stood up.>

11.15 a.m. Great, have lost three more followers. Must remember not to overtweet in the morning. Or maybe at all since seem to get more followers when do not tweet than when do tweet.

Roxster has tweeted! You see, this is my reward for epic self-control.

<@_Roxster @JoneseyBJ *Insulted, appalled* Stand you up, Jonesey??>

<@JoneseyBJ @_Roxster Roxster! You're back!>

<@JoneseyBJ @_Roxster Was just trying to counteract boasty tone of previous tweet which had alienated followers. So you're still on?>

<@_Roxster @JoneseyBJ Jonesey, I may be a youth but I am not a callow one, nor a charlatan.>

Then another: <@_Roxster @JoneseyBJ OK. How about I meet you outside Leicester Sq. tube @7.30? Then we could go to Nando's. Or fish and chips?>

9.45 p.m. Immediately went into meltdown. Leicester Sq. tube?? Leicester Sq. tube?? But it's freezing. Then remembered the key dating rules.

JUST GO ALONG WITH WHATEVER HE SUGGESTS

<@JoneseyBJ @_Roxster *Purrs* Why, that would be delightful!>

<@_Roxster @JoneseyBJ *Growls* See you there, baby.>

You see? You see? So much better than trying to manipulate the situation.

9.50 p.m. Suddenly in panic re meeting stranger off Twitter at Leicester Square tube when am single mother.

9.51 p.m. Just called Tom, who is going to pop round.

10.50 p.m. Unfortunately, had to wait for opinion as Tom was having meltdown of his own about a Hungarian architect called Arkis. He insisted on showing all the texts and pictures and Arkis's messages on the Scruff app on his iPhone. "Scruff is *so* much better than Grindr. It used to be Beardy but now it's got more Fashion Beardy, small clothes and big glasses, but not in a George Michael sense."

"So what's the problem?" I said, in a crisp professional manner, as if I were the psychotherapist and not Tom.

"I think Arkis might be all text and no trousers. He just keeps sending really flirty, sexual texts late at night but nothing else."

"I see. Have you suggested meeting?" I enquired.

"I said I'd like to get to know him better but I sent it at 1 a.m. because I was looking for validation and I just got the opposite of validation because Arkis didn't reply for two days, then didn't mention it and just started talking about my Scruff pictures again, and now I'm wandering around with this horrible pain below my ribcage because I think he thinks—"

"I know, I know," I said eagerly. "It was *exactly* like that with Leatherjacketman. It's like the love interest assumes this huge power—like a giant standing over you in judgement, possessed of all the rules of dating competence, and about to mark you down as a desperate stalker."

"I know," he said sadly. "But he did say he wanted to see *Zero Dark Thirty*."

"So? Suggest you go! Durr!" I said loftily. "Otherwise it's like a staring competition of who'll blink first."

Once Tom appeared satisfied with the psychological underpinnings of the plan, I moved smoothly onto my own worry, at which he said crisply:

"Of course you must meet @_Roxster, as long as it's in a public space. Talitha says he's fine. We'll all be on the end of the phone. And it's perfectly normal and healthy to meet in cyberspace."

Love the way Tom and I swap positions at being the expert on dating mores as if on a seesaw—even though clearly neither of us has any idea what we are talking about in the first place. Sometimes it seems like just a sea of humanity out there with millions of seesaws all going on at the same time like nodding-donkeys. And everyone's on one end or other of the seesaw at different times.

11 p.m. Heaven is rewarding me today. Roxster just tweeted again.

<@_Roxster @JoneseyBJ It's freezing out there, Jonesey. Shall we make it the bar at the Dean Street Townhouse instead?>

Aww. He's been thinking about it. He's so gorgeous and nice. Tweeted back:

<@JoneseyBJ @_Roxster Perfect. See you there.>
<@_Roxster @JoneseyBJ Can't wait, baby.>

Tuesday 22 January 2013

133lb (still!), number of outfits tried on and thrown on floor 12, tweets sent when supposed to be getting ready 7 (very stupid), though Twitter followers 698 (advantages of live-action tweeting must be weighed against disadvantages of lateness).

6.30 p.m. Right. Almost ready. Talitha, Jude and Tom are primed about where I am going and standing by to rescue me in case anything goes wrong. Determined not to make same mistake this time and be late. Only thing is, cannot help self from tweeting as I get ready. Is almost as if I have duty to all followers to let them know what I'm doing all the time.

<@JoneseyBJ Which is more important? Look nice or be on time? I mean, if it's an either/or situation?>

Wow—lots of responses and @ mentions:

<@JamesAP27 @JoneseyBJ On time of course. How can you be so vain? That's so unattractive.>

Humph. Right. We'll see about him.

<@JoneseyBJ @JamesAP27. Is not vanity but CONCERN for others i.e., not startling or scaring them.>

6.45 p.m. Shit shit, have put waterproof mascara on lips as same Laura Mercier packaging as lip gloss and will not come off. Oh God. Am going to be late with black lips.

7.15 p.m. OK. In minicab now, still rubbing at lips. Have time for a few more tweets.

<@JoneseyBJ Calm assured—in taxi now—receptive responsive Woman of Substance . . .>

<@JoneseyBJ . . . goddess of joy and light! *Rasps at cab driver* Noooo! Don't go down f***ing Regent St!>

<@JoneseyBJ *Holds nose, talks in police radio voice* Going into the Dean Street Townhouse. Going INTO the Townhouse.>

<@JoneseyBJ Wish me luck. Over and out. Roger.>

<@JoneseyBJ *Whispers* He's FANTASTIC.>

<@JoneseyBJ There is a lot to be said for the younger man as long as not young enough to be legal grandson.>

<@JoneseyBJ He's smiling! He's stood up like a gentleman.>

Roxster was indeed gorgeous, was even more handsome than his photo but, crucially, merry-looking. He looked as if he was going to burst out laughing all the time. "Hellooo." Was just about to instinctively reach for my phone to tweet <He has the loveliest voice> when he put his hand on top of mine on my phone . . .

"No tweeting."

"I haven't . . . !" I said insanely.

"Jonesey, you've been twatting or twunking all the way here. I've been reading it."

DATE WITH TOY BOY

I shrank down sheepishly into my coat. Roxster laughed.

"It's all right. What would you like to drink?"

"White wine, please," I said sheepishly, instinctively reaching for the phone.

"Very good. And I'm going to have to confiscate this until you've settled down."

He took my phone, put it in his pocket and summoned the waitress, all in one easy movement.

"Is that so you can murder me?" I said, eyeing his pocket with a mixture of arousal and alarm, thinking that if I needed to summon Tom or Talitha I would have to wrestle him to the ground and lunge at it.

"No. I don't need the phone to murder you. I just don't want it being tweeted live to the breathless Twitterati."

As he turned his head I guzzled the spectacle of the fine lines to his profile: straight nose, cheekbones, brows. His eyes were hazel and twinkly. He was so . . . young. His skin was peachy, his teeth white, his hair thick and shiny, slightly too long to be fashionable, brushing his collar. And his lips had that fine white line outlining them that only young people have.

"I like your glasses," he said as he handed me the wine.

"Thank you," I said smoothly. (They're progressive glasses so I can see out of them normally and also read.

205

My idea in wearing them was that he wouldn't notice I was so old that I needed reading glasses.)

"Can I take them off?" he said, in a way that made me think he meant . . . clothes.

"OK," I said. He took them off and put them on the bar, brushing my hand slightly, looking at me.

"You're much prettier than your photo."

"Roxster, my photo is of an egg," I said, slurping at the wine, remembering too late that I was supposed to sit back and let him look at me stroking the stem of the wine glass arousingly.

"I know."

"Weren't you worried I might turn out to be a sixteen-stone cross-dresser?"

"Yes. I've got eight of my mates planted in the bar to protect me."

"That's spooky," I said, "I've got a parade of hit men lined up in all the windows across the street in case you try to murder me and then eat me."

"Have they all been fartaged?"

I was just taking a slurp of wine and laughed in the middle, then choked with the wine still in my mouth, and sick started coming up my throat.

"Are you all right?"

I waved my hand around. My mouth was a mixture of sick and wine. Roxster gave me a handful of paper napkins. I made my way to the loos, holding the napkins over my mouth. Got inside just in time and spurted the sick/wine into the washbasin, wondering if I should add "Do not be sick in own mouth at start of date" to the Dating Rules.

I washed my mouth out, remembering with relief that

there was a kid's toothbrush somewhere at the bottom of my handbag. And some gum.

When I got out Roxster had found us a table and was looking at his phone.

"I thought I was supposed to be the one who was obsessed with vomit," he said, without looking up. "I'm just tweeting your followers all about it."

"You're not?"

"Noooo." He handed me back my phone and started laughing. "Are you all right?" He was laughing so much now he could hardly speak. "Sorry, I just can't believe you were sick in your own mouth on our first date."

In the midst of giggling, I realized he had just said "our first date." And "first" clearly implied that there would be others in spite of sick-in-own-mouth.

"Are you going to fart next?" he said, just as the waiter arrived with the menus.

"Shut up, Roxster," I giggled. I mean, honestly, he did have a mental age of seven, but it was fun because it made me feel so at home. And maybe this was someone who wouldn't be completely appalled by the bodily functions on display in our household.

As we opened the menus, I realized I didn't have my glasses any more.

I looked at the blurry letters, panicking. Roxster didn't notice. He seemed completely overexcited by the food. "Mmm. Mmm. What are you going to have, Jonesey?"

I stared at him like a rabbit caught in headlights.

"Everything all right?"

"I've lost my glasses," I mumbled sheepishly.

"We must have left them on the bar," he said, getting

up. Marvelling at his impressive young physique, I watched him go to where we had been standing, look around, and ask the barman.

"They're not there," he said, coming back, looking concerned. "Are they expensive ones?"

"No, no, it's fine," I lied. (They were expensive ones. And I really liked them.)

"Would you like me to read the menu to you? I could cut up your food for you as well if you like." He started laughing. "Have to watch out for your teeth."

"Roxster, this is a very undesirable line of teasing."

"I know, I know, I'm sorry."

After he'd read me the menu, I tried to remember the Dating Rules, rubbing my finger delicately up and down the stem of the wine glass, but there didn't seem to be any point, as Roxster already had my knee between his strapping young thighs. Realized, even in the midst of excitement, was DETERMINED to find the glasses. Is so easy to let something like that go out of sexual distraction and embarrassment and they were really, really nice glasses.

"I'm just going to look under the bar stool," I said, when we'd ordered.

"But your knees!"

"Stoppit."

We both ended up crawling about under the stools. A pair of very young girls, who were sitting where we had been, were very snotty about it. Suddenly felt myself dying with embarrassment at being on a date with a toy boy and forcing him to look under young girls' legs for my reading glasses.

"There aren't any glasses, OK?" said one of the girls,

staring at me rudely. Roxster rolled his eyes then dived under her knees again, saying, "Just while I'm down here . . ." and began groping around on the floor. The girls were unamused. Roxster reared up triumphantly, brandishing the glasses.

"Found them," he said and put them on my nose. "There you are, darling."

He kissed me pointedly on the lips, gave the girls a look, and led me back to the table while I tried to recover my composure, hoping he couldn't taste the sick.

Conversation seemed to flow quite effortlessly. His real name is Roxby McDuff and he does work for the eco-charity, met Talitha on the show, and jumped across from Talitha's Twitter to my Twitter. "So you just, like, follow cougars?"

"I don't like that expression," he said. "It implies the hunter, rather than . . . the hunted."

My discombobulation must have been obvious, because he added softly, "I like older women. They know what they're doing a bit more. Have a bit more to say for themselves. How about you? What are you doing out with a younger man off Twitter?"

"I'm just trying to widen my circle," I said airily.

Roxster looked straight at me, without blinking. "I can certainly help you with that."

JOY MIXED WITH SICK

Tuesday 22 January 2013 (continued)

When it was time to go, we stood awkwardly in the street.

"How are you going to get back?" he said, which instantly made me feel a bit sad, because obviously he wasn't planning to come back with me, even though obviously I wouldn't have asked him to. Obviously.

"Taxi?" I said. He looked surprised. Realized I only ever come out into Soho with Talitha, Tom and Jude and we always share a taxi but that that must seem helplessly extravagant to a young person. There were, however, no taxis to be found.

"Do you want me to summon a helicopter, or should we get the tube? Do you know how to get the tube?"

"Of course I do!" I said. But to be honest, it was all unfamiliar, being in the crowds of Soho late at night without the friends. It was quite exciting, though, as Roxster took my arm and led me to Tottenham Court Road tube.

"I'll see you down," he said. When we got to the barriers I realized I didn't have my Oyster card. I tried to pay at the machines, but it was all impossible.

"Come here," he said, taking out a spare card, swiping me through the barriers and leading me to the right platform. The train was approaching.

"Quick, give me your mobile number," he said. "I now haven't murdered you."

I gave it to him really quickly and he typed it in. The doors were opening, people were pouring out.

Then quite suddenly, as if from nowhere, Roxster kissed me on the lips. "Mmm, sick," he said.

"Oh, no! But I brushed my teeth."

"You brought a toothbrush? Are you always sick on your dates?"

Then seeing my horrified expression he laughed and said, "You don't taste of sick." People were crushing themselves into the train. He kissed me again, gently, looking at me with his merry hazel eyes, then again this time with the mouth a little open, then delicately finding my tongue with his. This was MUCH better than stupid Leatherjacketman with his sex-crazed—

"Quick, the doors are closing!" He pushed me towards the train and I squeezed in. The doors closed and I watched him as the train pulled out, just standing there, smiling to himself: gorgeous, gorgeous toy boy.

Came up from the tube into Chalk Farm, euphoric and completely over-aroused. There was a ping on text. It was from Roxster.

<Have you made it home or are you riding round in circles, confused?>

Texted back: <Help, I'm at Stanmore. Have you got the sick out of your teeth yet?>

No reply. I shouldn't have put the thing about the sick. Another text!

<No, because I can't find my reading glasses. Are you shortly going to reuse the sicky toothbrush?>

<Just using it. Mmmmmmmmmmmmmmmmmmmmmmm-mmmmmmmmmmmm>

211

11.40 p.m. Just bustled Chloe out of the house, rather rudely, so could carry on texting.

Here it comes! I love being back in the world of flirting again. It's so romantic. Oh.

<I love the taste of your sick.>

Sent back: <Oh, Roxster. You haven't been reading your dating books, have you?>

Long pause. Oh no. That was the wrong tone. Not flirty. Schoolmistress. Blown it already.

11.45 p.m. Just went upstairs to check the children: Billy beautiful, asleep with Horsio. Mabel snuggled up, head on back to front, with Saliva. Never mind. I'm rubbish at dating but at least I'm keeping the children alive.

11.50 p.m. Rushed back downstairs to check phone. Nothing.

This is all wrong. Am a single mother, cannot afford to be tossed this way and that by vagaries of texting total stranger young enough to be legal son.

11.55 p.m. Text just came.

<You looked beautiful, it was a great kiss and I had a wonderful time.>

Surge of happiness. But then realized he hadn't suggested another date. Should I reply or leave it? Leave it. Jude says you should always be the last one in the texting thread.

11.57 p.m. I wish he was here, I wish he was here. Though of course would never bring a young whippersnapper man back to the house. Obviously.

Wednesday 23 January 2013

5.15 a.m. Such a good job he isn't here. Mabel just burst into my bedroom with a loud clatter. Only instead of being in pyjamas with her head on back to front she was fully dressed in her school uniform. Poor little thing, I think she was so obsessed with me creating the *appearance of lateness*, by being flappy in the mornings, that she decided to get dressed well in advance. I do see her point, but the thing is, when Chloe does the school run, she arrives at 7 a.m. all shiny and fully dressed, calmly helps the children to dress, prepares breakfast, allows them to watch TV without becoming randomly infuriated by the plot lines and over-excited high-pitched screaming on *SpongeBob SquarePants* then has them out of the door by eight and waiting on the wall when the school door opens.

I mean, I did all that yesterday and we were on the wall, freakishly, by 8.05, which I guess was good? Spending ten minutes sitting on a wall? I suppose it improves social interaction with the other parents.

Anyway, I snuggled her down to sleep in all her clothes, finally got back to sleep myself, then slept through the alarm.

GETTING TO SECOND DATE

Thursday 24 January 2013

9.15 p.m. Children are asleep. Almost forty-eight hours have passed since Roxster's last text.

Determined not to ask for friends' advice because—cf. Dating Rules—if I need friends to orchestrate the whole relationship there is clearly something wrong with it.

9.20 p.m. Just called Talitha and read her Roxster's last text.

<You looked beautiful, it was a great kiss and I had a wonderful time.>

"And you left it at that?"

"Yes. He didn't suggest meeting again or anything. It's like he was saying he had a great time and drawing a line under it."

"Oh, darling."

"What?"

"What am I going to do with you? How long is it since he sent this text?"

"Two days."

"TWO DAYS? And he sent it at night, at the end of the date? OK. Hang on. Put this."

Text pinged up from Talitha.

<I've finally recovered from my embarrassment at vom-

iting on our first date. I had a wonderful time too. And it was a great kiss. What are you up to?>

"It's really good—but 'What are you up to?' Isn't that a bit . . . ?"

"Don't overthink it. Just send it. Frankly, I won't blame him if he takes three days to reply out of pique."

I sent it. Then regretted it at once and headed for the fridge. Just as I'd taken out a bag of grated cheese and the wine bottle the text pinged.

<Jonesey! I was worried you'd choked on your own sick. I'm in the Holiday Inn, Wigan. Have meeting with the District Council recycling department. What are you up to? Looking for your glasses?>

<Roxster, that's just silly. If I was looking for my glasses I wouldn't be able to read the text.>

<You might have had someone from Help the Aged round to help you. Busy weekend lined up, Jonesey?>

Roxster is fantastic. I don't even need to text Talitha or check Dating Rules to see if that's an invitation. It is! It definitely is! Oh no, but it's St. Oswald's House Hard-Hats-Offing this weekend. And I can't tell Roxster my mum's in a retirement community because his mum might be the same age as me.

<Yars, yars, incredibly busy and glamorous. *Sheepish* I'm going to see my mum on the outskirts of Kettering.>

Then, remembering I had to make it easy for him to create a date, I added:

<However, I am around next week and it is imperative that you be punished for your impertinence.>

There was a worrying pause.

<How about next Friday night? But I am going to put a book down my pants.>

<Will it be a dating self-help book?>

<50 Shades of Widening Your Circle. Is Friday good?>

<Friday is perfect.>

<Good. Night-night, Jonesey. I have to get my beauty sleep ready for Wigan Council.>

<Night-night, Roxster.>

HARD-HATS-OFFING!

Saturday 26 January 2013

134lb (worrying slide back into obesity to be blamed on Mum), texts from Roxster 42, minutes spent imagining date with Roxster 242, babysitters to enable self to have date with Roxster 0.

10.30 a.m. The day of the St. Oswald's House Hard-Hats-Offing is upon us. The phone rang just as I was struggling to persuade Mabel out of the glittery T-shirt and purple leggings she'd somehow put on when I was upstairs (Mabel refuses to accept that leggings are more in the tights department than the trousers department and really need something else on top) and into the dress-and-cardi set Mum had sent for her, straight out of the 1950s, white, covered in red hearts with a sticky-out skirt and a big red sash tied in a bow at the back.

"Bridget, you're not going to be late, are you? It's just that Philip Hollobine and Nick Bowering are speaking on the dot of one, so we can still have lunch."

"Who are Philip Hollobine and Nick Bowering?" I said, marvelling at my mother's ability to airily bandy about names-one-has-never-heard-of, as if name-dropping top Hollywood celebrities.

"You know Philip, darling. Philip? The MP for Kettering! He's ever so good with the St. Oswald's events, though

Una says it's just because he knows he'll get his face in the paper because Nick's in with the *Kettering Examiner*."

"Who's Nick?" I said, hissing, "Just TRY it, darling," to Mabel, in an eerie, down-the-generations echo of my mother trying to force me into Country Casuals two-pieces.

"You know Nick, darling. Nick! He's the overall CEO of *TGL*," adding quickly, "*Thornton Gracious Living*! I also want you to meet"—her voice suddenly dropped an octave— "Paul, the pastry chef." Something about the way she said "Pawl," with a French accent, made me sense trouble. "You're not going to wear black, are you? Wear something nice and bright! Red—Valentine's Day coming soon!"

11 a.m. Eventually managed to get Mum off the phone and Mabel into the actually adorable red-and-white dress.

"I used to wear dresses like this," I said wistfully.

"Oh. Was you born in de Victorian Times?" asked Mabel.

"No!" I said indignantly.

"Oh. Wad it de Renaissance Era?"

Quickly turned mind to Roxster and our texting. Have even told him about the kids and he seems unfazed. Texting really puts an enjoyable spin on everything and I realize, with a sense of shame and irresponsibility towards followers, seems totally to have replaced my obsession with Twitter.

Realize Twitter has a bad effect on character, making me obsessed with how many followers I have, self-conscious and regretful as soon as I have sent a tweet, and guilty if I do not report any minor events in my life to the Twitter followers, at which a number of them immediately disappear.

"Mummy!" said Billy. "Why are you staring into space like that?"

"Sorry," I said, glancing, panicked, at the clock. "Gaaah! We're late!" Then immediately started running about parroting discombobulated orders—"Put your shoes on, put your shoes on." In the midst of it all, I got a text from Chloe saying she really, actually, definitely couldn't babysit on Friday night.

Text represents total disaster, throwing whole Roxster date into grave peril. Rebecca is going to her "in-laws" (even though not married) for the weekend, Tom is in Sitges for a birthday party (he got a suite with a 40 sq. metre terrace and a chromotherapy tub for £297 plus tax), Talitha doesn't do children, Jude is on a second date, which is great—but what am I going to do?

As we roared, late, towards Kettering, I suddenly had a genius idea: maybe I could ask Mum to babysit! Maybe she could have Billy and Mabel at St. Oswald's House for the night!

THE BARNACLE'S PENIS

Saturday 26 January 2013 (continued)

Arrived at 12.59 to find St. Oswald's House transformed into a cross between Show Home event and a royal tree-planting ceremony. There were red-and-white *Thornton Gracious Living* flags everywhere, red balloons, glasses of white wine and girls in stiff Employee of the Month–type suits holding clipboards and looking around hopefully for new people who might be fun-loving, yet slightly incontinent.

Ran, as directed, round the side of the house and emerged into the Italianate garden to see that the ceremony was already under way. Nick or Phil, over a PA system, was addressing a gaggle of elderly people wearing novelty hard hats. Handed Mabel the basket of chocolate hearts we'd brought, which she immediately dropped onto the gravel. There was a moment of calm, then a) Billy trod on them, b) Mabel burst into bereft sobs so loud that Nick or Phil stopped his speech and everyone turned to stare, c) Billy burst into his own bereft sobs, d) Mum and Una strode furiously towards us with mad bouffed hair and wearing identical pastel Kate Middleton's mother coat-dress outfits, and e) Mabel tried to pick up the chocolate hearts but her distress and humiliation were so heart-rending that I gathered her into my arms like the Virgin Mary, realizing, too late, that several of the chocolate globs were now sandwiched between Mabel's Shirley Temple red-and-white ensemble and my pastel Grace Kelly–style J.Crew coat.

"It doesn't matter," I whispered as Mabel's plump little body shook with sobs. "The hearts were just for showing off, it's you that counts," just as Mum bustled up saying, "Oh, for heaven's sakes, let ME take her."

"But . . ." I began but it was too late. Mum's ice-blue Kate Middleton's mother coat was now smeared with chocolate too.

"Oh, my godfathers," said Mum, putting Mabel down crossly, at which Mabel burst into even louder sobs, wrapping her chocolate-smeared self round my cream trousers as Billy started yelling, "I want to go hooooooooooooooooooooome!"

My phone pinged: Roxster!

<Jonesey. I'm in the Natural History Museum. Do you know that the barnacle has the largest penis in relation to its body of any creature in the natural world?>

Startled, I dropped the phone, narrowly missing Mabel's head. Mum bent to pick it up.

"What's this?" she said. "This is a very peculiar message."

"Nothing, nothing," I gabbled, lunging at the phone. "Just . . . the fishmonger!!"

In the background the speech of Nick or Phil was reaching some kind of crescendo, climaxing with a yell of "Hard Hats Off!" echoed by the group of elderly residents, throwing their hard hats into the air, at which Billy burst into more tears, wailing, "I wanted to do Hard-Hat-Offing." Mabel said, "Dammit!" then Billy, furious with stress in a way I understood only too well, turned to me and said, "This is all your fault. I'm going to kill you!"

221

Before I knew what was happening, I too had erupted with stress like a steam kettle and burst out, "I'm going to kill you first!"

"Bridget!" said Mum apoplectically.

"He started it!" I retorted.

"No, I didn't. You started it by being late!" said Billy.

The whole thing was a total, total fucked-up nightmare. But there was no reprieve. We all retreated into the Ladies' outside the Function Room to clean ourselves up. Managed to sneak into the cubicle and reply to Roxster about the giant barnacle penis.

<Really? Ding-dong! In what state?>

<Hang on, I'll just see if I can arouse the barnacle.>

Emerged from the Ladies', chocolate stains smeared and therefore worse, to a stress-free interlude when Mum went off to get changed and the children were briefly entertained by a clown making animals out of balloons. The clown was clearly bored as Mabel and Billy were the only grandchildren under the age of thirty-five, apart from a couple of great-grandchildren, who were babies. Texted Roxster about the clown and balloon animals at which he texted back:

<Can you ask him to make me one of a barnacle with an erection?>

Me: <Does it have to be to scale?>

Tee-hee. The fantastic thing about texting is that it allows you to have an instant, intimate emotional relationship giving each other a running commentary on your lives, without taking up any time whatsoever or involving meetings or arrangements or any of the complicated things which take place in the boring old non-cyber world. Apart from sex, it would be perfectly possible to have an entire relationship that is much closer and healthier than many traditional marriages without actually meeting in person at all!

Maybe this will be the way forward. Sperm will simply be donated, frozen through the dating website which originally introduced you. But then, hmm, the women will end up doing what I end up doing, trying to run crazily between one child who's done something messy and complicated in the toilet and the other who's got sandwiched between the fridge and the fridge door. Maybe the way forward is cyber children, rather like those Japanese Tamagotchi pets, which give you the illusion of parenthood for about two days until you get bored with them, combined with cuddly soft toys. But then the human race would die out and . . . Ooh, another text from Roxster.

<I think to scale would be tricky. But I would like him to use a pink, flesh-coloured balloon.>

Me: <Barnacles are not pink.>

Roxster: <I think you'll find the Titan Acorn Barnacle, native to the west coast of America, has a vivid pink hue. But I'm sure the clown is fully aware of this.>

"Bridget, are you still talking to the fishmonger?" My mother was now dressed in another Kate Middleton's mother coat and dress, only this time in Titan-Acorn-Barnacle pink. "Why don't you just go to Sainsbury's?—they have a smashing fish counter there! Anyway, come on! You know Penny Husbands-Bosworth is married now?" she gabbled, sweeping me away from the children-and-balloon scenario.

"Ashley Green! You remember Ashley? Pancreatic cancer! Wyn had hardly made her exit through the crematorium curtains before Penny was ringing Ashley's doorbell with a sausage casserole."

"I don't think I should leave the—"

"They'll be fine, darling, with their balloons. Anyway, Penny was saying we really should get you together with Kenneth Garside! He's on his own. You're on your own and—"

"Mother!" I hissed, as she dragged me into the alarmingly named Function Room. "Is this the man who kept going into everyone's bedrooms on the cruise?"

"Well, all right, yes, darling, he is. But the point is he's clearly got a VERY high sex drive, so he needs a younger woman and . . ."

"Mother!" I burst out, just as a Roxster text pinged up on my phone. I opened it. Mum grabbed the phone.

"It's the fishmonger again," she glowered, showing me the message.

<It's 20 ft when flaccid, 40 when erect.>

"Who is this fishmonger?—Oh, look! Here's Kenneth now."

Kenneth Garside, wearing grey slacks and a pink sweater, did a little dancey step towards us. And for a second it could have been Uncle Geoffrey. Uncle Geoffrey, Una's husband, Dad's best friend, with his slacks and golfing sweaters and little dancey steps and "How's your love life? When are we going to get you married off?"

I started spiralling into grief about Dad, and what he would have made of all this. Then Kenneth Garside snapped me out of it by flashing an enormous set of very white false teeth in the midst of his orange face, and saying creepily,

"Hello, beautiful young lady. I'm Ken69. That's my 'press age,' my secret preferences and my Internet-dating profile name. But maybe I won't be needing that now I've met you!"

Euww! I thought, then instantly shrank at my own hypocrisy, as my mind careered into mental arithmetic, demonstrating, horrifically, that the age difference between me and Roxster was four years more than the gap between me and Kenneth Garside's "press age."

"Hahaha!" said Mum. "Oh, there's Pawl, I'll just have a quick chat to him about the profiteroles," she said, diving off towards a man in a chef's outfit, leaving me with Kenneth Garside's dazzling false teeth, just as Una, mercifully, started banging on a wine glass with a spoon. "Ladies and gentlemen! The Cruise Slideshow Event is about to begin!"

"Can I offer you my arm?" said Kenneth, grabbing my arm and parading me into the Ballroom, where rows of ornate cream chairs with gold edges were filling up in front of a giant screen showing a picture of the cruise liner.

As we sat down, Kenneth Garside said, "What have we got on our trousers?" and started rubbing at my knee with his handkerchief, as Una took to the platform and began.

"Friends! Family! This year's St. Oswald's cruise marked the high spot of an already full and fulfilling year."

"Stoppit," I hissed to Kenneth Garside.

"It's all computerized now!" Una continued. "So! Without further ado, I'm going to talk over the 'Macslideshow' and some of us can relive while others dream!"

The cruise-ship shot morphed into a mosaic of pictures, zooming in on a photo of Mum and Una boarding the ship and waving.

"Gentlemen Prefer Blondes!" said Una into the mic,

cueing the slideshow soundtrack of Marilyn Monroe and Jane Russell singing "Two Little Girls from Little Rock" over a shot of Mum and Una in a horrifying *Gentlemen Prefer Blondes* homage, lying side by side on a double bed in the cabin, looking coquettishly towards the camera, one leg each raised in the air.

"Oh, my word," said Kenneth.

Then suddenly the soundtrack was masked by a familiar electronic tune and the slideshow was replaced by a lurid cartoon of a dragon belching fire at a one-eyed purple wizard. Sat, frozen, realizing that this was Wizard101. Could it possibly . . . could Billy possibly have got on a computer and . . . ? Suddenly the Wizard101 page disappeared to be replaced by my EMAIL IN-BOX PAGE, saying "Welcome, Bridget," with a list of subjects, the first one, from Tom, entitled "St. Oswald's House Cruise Event Nightmare." What was Billy DOING?

"Excuse me, excuse me," I said, panicking, making my way along the row, amidst the general consternation, trying to avoid Mum's eye.

Rushed out into the hallway and back to the balloon room, to find Billy, oblivious, tapping furiously at a Mac-Book Air, which was attached to a lot of wire and Ethernet hubs on a side table.

"Billy!"

"Wait! I just got to finish this leveeeeel! I didn't go on your email. I was trying to retrieve my password."

"Come off that," I rasped. I managed to forcibly get him off, close the Wizard101 and Yahoo windows, and drag him back to the balloons, just as a man in wire glasses rushed in and up to the laptop, looking traumatized.

"Has anyone touched this?" he said, eyes darting incredulously around the room. I looked at Billy's face, hoping Billy would remain silent or lie. He frowned thoughtfully, and I could see him remembering all my bloody lectures about the importance of honesty and telling the truth. "Not now!" I wanted to yell. "It's all right to lie when Mummy needs you to!"

"Yes, it was me," said Billy ruefully. "And I didn't mean to go on Mummy's email but I forgot my password."

9.15 p.m. At home. In bed now. On top of the whole appalling disaster, the question still remains of what I am going to do about babysitter on Friday. Tried suggesting Friday night to Mum, after the furore had died down, but she just looked at me coldly and said it was Aqua-Zumba.

9.30 p.m. Tried Magda, but she is going to be on a short break to Istanbul with Cosmo and Woney.

"I wish I could, Bridge," she said. "We always had my mother for babysitting emergencies, it must be tricky having had the children older. Is it that the kids are too young for you to help her, and she's too old to help you?"

"No," I said. "She's got Aqua-Zumba."

Am going to have to try Daniel.

10.45 p.m. Called Daniel.

"Who are you shagging, Jones?"

"No one."

"I demand to know."

"I'm not, it's just—"

"I shall punish you."

227

"I just thought you'd like to have them to stay."

"Jones. You have always been the most cataclysmically awful liar. I am wild with sexual jealousy. I feel tragic, a past-it old fool."

"Daniel, don't be ridiculous, you're incredibly attractive and virile and young-looking and irresistibly sexy and—"

"I know, Jones, I know. Thank you, thank you."

Upshot is Daniel is coming round on Friday at six thirty to take them to his place!

TO SLEEP WITH OR NOT TO SLEEP WITH?

Wednesday 30 January 2013

Pros of sleeping with Roxster 12, cons of sleeping with Roxster 3, percentage of time spent deciding whether or not to sleep with Roxster, preparing for possibility of sleeping with Roxster and imagining sleeping with Roxster compared with actual time it would probably take to sleep with Roxster 585%.

9.30 p.m. Just called Tom. "OF COURSE YOU HAVE TO SLEEP WITH HIM," he said. "You have to lose your Born-Again Virginity, or it'll just turn into a bigger and bigger obstacle. Talitha says he's a good chap. And besides, it's an opportunist crime. How often do you get the house to yourself?"

Called up Talitha to cross-check with her view:

"What did I tell you about not sleeping with anyone too soon?"

"You said, 'not before you feel ready,' not 'too soon,'" I elucidated, then reiterated Tom's argument, adding, to give strength to my position: "We've been texting for weeks. Surely it's rather like in Jane Austen's day when they did letter-writing for months and months and then just, like, immediately got married?"

"Bridget. Sleeping with a twenty-nine-year-old off Twitter on the second date is not 'rather like in Jane Austen's day.'"

"But it was you who said, 'She has to get laid.'"

"Well, all right, I know. And Roxster seems a sterling chap. Just go with your gut, darling. But keep safe, keep in touch and use a condom."

"Condoms! I'm not going to sleep with him! What are you supposed to do about being naked?"

"You get a slip, darling."

"A slip—like the zoo form?"

"Go to La Perla—no, don't go to La Perla, the expense is eye-watering. Go to Intimissimi or La Senza and get yourself a couple of little short black silk sexy slips. I think, when you were last doing this, they were called 'petticoats.' Or maybe one black, one white. With a slip, you can show off your arms and legs and décolletage, which are always the last to go, but keep the central area—which we might want to gloss over—glossed over. OK?"

Thursday 31 January 2013

10 a.m. Just logged onto email.

```
Sender:  Brian  Katzenberg
Subject: Your  screenplay
```

10.01 a.m. Yayy! Screenplay has been accepted!

10.02 a.m. Oh.

```
Sender: Brian Katzenberg
Subject: Your screenplay

We have a couple of responses on
your script. They are passing.
The themes are fascinating but
they're wanting more of a romcom
feel. I'll keep trying.
```

10.05 a.m. Sent fraudulently cheery email back saying:

```
Thanks, Brian. Fingers crossed.
```

But now am slumped in despair. Am failure as screenwriter. Am going to go shopping for underwear.

Noon. Just back from purchasing slip, though am not going to sleep with Roxster. Obviously.

2 p.m. Just back from leg and bikini wax. Though am not going to sleep with him, obviously.

At the beauty salon, Chardonnay said I should have a Brazilian because that is what the young men expect these days and suggested I buy a course of laser treatments.

"But," I said, "what if Brazilians go out of fashion and the thing is to have a fulsome giant bush like French people again?"

At this, Chardonnay revealed that she had had the whole thing lasered so she was like a baby girl. But, as she says, she worries now, what if she sleeps with someone who doesn't like the full Brazilian? And admitted that she had toyed with the idea of putting that potion onto it that makes bald men's hair grow back.

3.15 p.m. In total agony. Opted for a sort of modified Brazilian known as "landing strip." Is no possibility of ever having sex with anyone after this, which is fine as am not going to sleep with him anyway. Obviously.

Friday 1 February 2013
9.30 a.m. Leaped furtively into Boots after school drop-off to purchase condoms, since could not do it with children in tow. (Though, on other hand, presence of children might have suggested condom-purchase was sign of responsible attitude to world overpopulation, rather than loose behaviour.)

Was just standing at till, when had a sense of someone glancing at basket. Looked up to see Mr. Wallaker at the next till, now staring implacably ahead, though he had obviously seen the condoms, because of the slight twitch at the corner of his mouth.

Completely brazened it out by also looking straight ahead and saying, "Terrible weather for the rugby match today, isn't it?"

"Oh, I don't know, it's sometimes rather enjoyable in the mud," he said, picking up his Boots bag with a tiny snort of amusement. "Enjoy your weekend."

Humph. Bloody Mr. Wallaker. Anyway, what was he bloody well doing in the chemist at half past nine on a weekday morning? Shouldn't he be at school organizing one of his military uprisings? He was probably buying condoms as well. Coloured condoms.

On the way home started to panic about leaving the kids with Daniel and called him up.

"Jones, Jones, Jones, Jones, Jones. Whatever can you be suggesting? The darlings will be meticulously cared for, almost to the point of overindulgence. I shall take them," he said grandly, "to the cinema."

"What movie?" I said nervously.

"*Zero Dark Thirty.*"

"WHAT?"

"That was what we human people laughingly call 'a joke,' Jones. I have tickets to *Wreck-It Ralph*. At least, I shall shortly have tickets to *Wreck-It Ralph* now that you have reminded me about the whole splendid occasion. And then I shall take them to a fine eating establishment, such as McDonald's Restaurant, and then I shall read them children's classics until they fall purringly to sleep. And if you send a hairbrush I shall use it to spank them if they misbehave. So anyway. Who ARE you shagging?"

Just then the text pinged: Roxster.

<Do you fancy seeing a movie tonight? How about *Les Misérables*?>

MOVIE?? I tailspinned. Doesn't he KNOW I'm doing all this incredibly complicated hoop-jumping-through just so we can sleep together? Slips and bikini waxes and condoms and Daniel and thinking about packing?

Reminding self of Dating Rules, I took some calming breaths and texted back: <That sounds great. Is it a romantic comedy?>

<Are you thinking of Lay Mister Arbres—the famous Anglo-French erotic tree-hugging romp?>

And texting continued with an increasingly risqué tone.

5 p.m. Massive packing-up preparations for Daniel sleep-over included Saliva, various bunnies, Horsio, Mario, Puffles One, Two and Three, Sylvanian bunnies, pyjamas, toothbrushes and toothpaste, crayons and colouring/puzzle books, full box of DVDs in case Daniel ran out of things to do, suitable books to avoid bedtime story from *Penthouse Forum*, emergency phone number list, full first-aid kit and manual, and, crucially, hairbrush.

Daniel turned up in a Mercedes with the top down. Had to fight urge to ask him to put the top up. Isn't it, surely, unsafe to drive children round with the top down? What if a great big plank fell off the back of a lorry onto them? Or they went under a motorway bridge and someone dropped a block of concrete on them?

"Shall we put the top up?" Daniel said to Billy, reading my face as Billy protested, "Noooooo!"

"Just . . . move these . . ." Daniel said, smoothly picking up some magazines from the front seat, the top one bearing a large caption over a very odd photo saying *LATIN LESBIAN CAR WASH!*

"Have to learn some time," he said cheerfully, climbing into the car and sitting Billy in the front seat. "OK, I'll press the brake and you do the buttons."

The children—anxious, freaking-out mother completely forgotten—squealed with excitement as the roof started closing. Until Mabel suddenly looked worried, and said, "Uncle Daniel. You've forgotten to thtrap uth in."

Once I'd managed to persuade Daniel to put Billy in the back seat and they were all strapped in, I waved as the three of them zoomed off without a backward glance.

And then the house was empty. I cleared all the soft

toys and plastic dinosaurs and embarrassing self-help books out of my bedroom, then started on de-childing the living room, but gave up as too monumental a task, and also am not going to sleep with him anyway. Then I ran a hot bath and put sweet-smelling potions in and music on, reminding self that the most important thing was to a) be in a calm yet sexual mood (which wasn't a problem) and b) turn up in the right place at the right time.

SECOND DATE WITH TOY BOY

Friday 1 February 2013 (continued)
I have literally no idea what goes on in *Les Misérables* and really must watch it again sometime. I hear it's terribly good. All I could think about was how horny I felt with Roxster's knee so close to mine. His hand was on his left thigh, and I kept my hand on my right thigh so that it would only have been a matter of inches for his hand to touch mine. Was incredibly arousing, wondering if he was feeling as aroused as me, but not being quite certain. Suddenly, after quite a long time, Roxster reached across and casually put his hand on my right thigh, his thumb moving the silk of the navy-blue dress across my bare leg. It was a highly effective move, and not one which was, I thought, open to misinterpretation.

As people continued to throw themselves into weirs and die of bad haircuts to song on the big screen, I glanced across at Roxster. He was looking calmly at the screen, only a slight flicker in his eyes betraying the fact that anything but operatic-misery-watching was going on. Then he leaned across and whispered:

"Shall we go?"

Once outside we started kissing frantically, then pulled ourselves together and decided we should at least go to a restaurant. The magic of Roxster was that, even in the din of a succession of insanely noisy Soho restaurants with no free tables, he was such fun to talk to. Eventually, after many drinks, and much talking and laughing, we ended up in the restaurant he had booked in the first place for after the movie.

During the meal, he took hold of my hand and slid his thumb between my fingers. I in turn wrapped my fingers around his thumb and stroked it up and down in a manner which just stopped on the right side of the line of being an advertisement for a handjob. Throughout, neither of us gave any hint in our conversation that we were anything other than the jolliest of chums. It was wildly sexy. Went to the loos as we left and called Talitha.

"If it feels right, darling, go for it. Any red flags, call me. I'm on the end of the phone."

When we got outside—Soho again, but Friday night this time, so *seriously* no taxis—he said, "How are you going to get home? The tubes have stopped."

I reeled. After all the preparation, and the thumb stroking, and calling friends, we actually were just jolly friends. This was terrible.

"Jonesey," he grinned. "Have you ever been on a night bus? I think I'm going to have to see you home."

On the night bus, I felt as though parts of other people were going into parts of me I didn't even know existed. I felt like I was being more intimate with members of the night-bus community than I'd ever been with anyone in my whole life. Roxster, however, looked worried, like the night bus was his fault.

"OK?" he mouthed.

I nodded cheerfully, wishing I was squeezed up against

Roxster instead of the weird woman with whom I was practically having the sort of lesbian car-wash sex explored in Daniel's magazine.

The bus stopped and people started getting off. Roxster muscled through to an empty seat, and sat down, in a way which seemed uncharacteristically ungallant. Then, when everyone had settled down, he got up and installed me in his place. I smiled up at him, proud at how handsome and beefy he was, but saw him looking down with a horrified expression. A woman was silently retching onto my boot.

Roxster was now trying to control his laughter. It was our stop, and, as we got off, he put his arm round me.

"A night without vomit is a night without Jonesey," he said. "Hang on." He strode into the late-night supermarket and reappeared with a bottle of Evian, a newspaper and a handful of paper napkins.

"I'm going to have to start carrying these with me. Stand still."

He poured the water over my boot and knelt down and wiped off the sick. It was terribly romantic.

"Now I smell of sick," he said ruefully.

"We can wash it off at home," I said, heart leaping that there was a reason for him to come in, even if it was vomit.

As we got close to the house I could see him looking all around, trying to place where we were, and what sort of place I lived in. I was so nervous when we got to the door. My hands were shaking as I put the key in the lock and couldn't get it to open.

"Let me do it," he said.

"Come in," I said, in an absurdly formal voice, as if I was a 1970s cocktail hostess.

"Shall I go somewhere till the babysitter goes?" he whispered.

"They're not here," I whispered back.

"You have *two* babysitters? And yet you've left the children alone?"

"No," I giggled. "They're with their godparents," I added, changing Daniel into "godparents" in case Roxster somehow sensed that Daniel is a sexually available man, at least until you get to know him.

"So we've got the house to ourselves!" Roxster boomed. "Can I go and wash the sick off?"

I showed him to the loo halfway up the stairs, then rushed down to the kitchen basement, brushed my hair and put more blusher on, dimming the lights, realizing as I did that Roxster had never actually seen me in daylight.

Suddenly had vision of self as one of those older women who insist on spending their entire time indoors with the curtains drawn, lit only by firelight or candlelight, then completely miss their mouth with the lipstick whenever anyone comes round.

Then I had a terrible moment of guilt and panic about Mark. I felt like I was being unfaithful, like I was about to step off a cliff and like I was far, far away from everything that I knew and everything that was safe. I leaned over the sink, feeling as though I was going to be . . . well . . . fittingly, I suppose . . . sick, then suddenly I heard Roxster bursting out laughing. I turned.

Oh, shit! He was looking at Chloe's chart.

Chloe had decided that Billy and Mabel would be far better in the mornings if they had a STRUCTURE, and so had drawn up a chart of what is supposed to happen, more or less moment-by-moment, when she takes them to school. This was absolutely fine, except it was ridiculously large, and one of the entries, which Roxster was now reading out, said:

7.55 a.m. to 8 a.m. Hugs and Kisses with Mummy!

"Do you even know their names?" he said. Then seeing my face, he laughed and held his hand out for me to smell.

"They're perfect," I said. "Vomit-free. Would you like a glass of . . . ?" but Roxster was already kissing me. He wasn't rushing at it. He was gentle, almost tender, but in control.

"Shall we go upstairs?" he whispered. "I want hugs and kisses with Mummy."

I started off being nervous, wondering if my bum looked fat from behind and below, but realized Roxster was focused, instead, on turning the lights off as we went. "Tsk tsk, what about the National Grid, Jonesey?" Ah, the young people and their concern for the planet!

When I opened the door to the bedroom the room looked beautiful, just lit by the light from the landing and Roxster at least didn't turn that one off. He stepped inside, pushing the door half closed behind him. He took off his shirt. I gasped. He looked like an advert. He looked like he'd been airbrushed with a six-pack. There was no one in the house, the lights were low, he was good, he was safe, he was gorgeous beyond belief. Then he said, "Come here, baby."

DEFLOWERED

Saturday 2 February 2013

11.40 a.m. Roxster has just left because the kids are due back in twenty minutes with Daniel. Could not resist putting on Dinah Washington's "Mad About the Boy" and dancing moonily around the kitchen. I feel so happy and fantastic and as though nothing is a problem any more. I keep wandering around, picking things up and putting them down again in a daze. It is as if I have been bathed in something, like sunshine, or . . . milk, well, not milk. Moments from last night keep coming back to me: Roxster lying back on the bed, looking at me as I walked out of the bathroom in my slip. Removing the slip. Saying I looked better without the slip. Me watching Roxster's beautiful face above me, lost in what we were doing, the slight gap between his front teeth. Then suddenly the very adult shock wave of the thrust, the unexpected shock and thrill after so, so long of feeling the fullness of him inside me, a moment's pause to savour it, then starting to move and remembering the ecstasy two bodies can create together. It's just amazing what bodies can do. And then, when I came, far too soon, Roxster watching my face with a horny, disbelieving expression, then feeling him starting to shake with laughter.

"What?" I said.

"I was just wondering how long this was going to go on for."

Roxster getting hold of my feet under the duvet and suddenly pulling me right down to the bottom of the bed and bursting out laughing. And then starting again at the bottom of the bed.

Me trying to pretend not to be having an orgasm in case he started laughing at me again.

Then finally, hours and hours later, stroking his thick, dark hair as he briefly rested on the pillow, taking in every detail of his perfect features, the fine lines, the brow, the nose, the jawline, the lips. Oh God, the fun, the closeness, the ecstasy of being touched after so long by someone so beautiful, so young and so good at it. Resting my head on his chest and talking in the darkness, and then Roxster taking my upper lip and lower lip and holding them together, saying, "Shhhhhhhh," and me trying to say through his fingers, "But I don't bant to btop talking." And Roxster whispering kindly, like I was a child or a lunatic: "It's not stopping talking, it's more like saving up talking, till the morning."

And then . . . Oh, shit—doorbell.

I opened the door, beaming. The kids looked wild, mad-haired, dirty-faced, but happy. Daniel took one look at me and said, "Jones. It must have been a very good night indeed, you look twenty-five years younger. Will you jiggle on my knee and just quickly run through the details of the whole thing carefully and precisely while they watch *SpongeBob SquarePants*?"

Sunday 3 February 2013

9.15 p.m. Has been a wonderful rest-of-weekend. The kids were happy because I was happy. We went out and climbed trees and then came back and watched *Britain's Got Talent*. Roxster texted at 2 p.m. and said it had been wonderful apart from the sick he'd found on the sleeve of his jacket. And I said it had been wonderful apart from the mess he'd made on the sheets. And we both agreed our mental ages were very low and have been demonstrating it in text form ever since.

I'm so lucky, at this time of my life, to have had that one night, with someone so young and gorgeous. I'm so grateful.

9.30 p.m. Oh God. Suddenly, for some reason, reminded of a line in the movie *The Last King of Scotland* where someone says, "I prefer sleeping with married women. They're so grateful." Think it was Idi Amin.

BACK IN THE PRESENT MOMENT

DARK NIGHT OF THE SOUL

Saturday 20 April 2013

Texts from Roxster 0, number of times checked for texts from Roxster 4567; nits found on Billy 6, nits found on Mabel 0, nits found on me 0; minutes spent thinking back about Mark, loss, sadness, death, life without Mark, trying to be a woman again, Leatherjacketman, dating disasters, child-rearing and whole of last year 395; thoughts prepared for Monday screenplay meeting with Greenlight Productions 0; minutes of sleep 0.

5 a.m. But it wasn't only the one night. Roxster and I just hit it off and a week turned into two weeks, and six weeks, and now it has been eleven weeks and one day.

The thing is, although in theory it was practically difficult with Roxster, it was also been surprisingly easy. Practically it was tricky because Roxster lives with three other boys the same age. So obviously we couldn't really go back there, with me plunged into some *Beavis and Butt-head*–type situation, trying to deal with crispy sheets and sinkfuls of washing-up, whilst pretending to be a family friend of Roxster's mother, who had come to stay with him in his bed in his crispy sheets.

Equally I didn't want to introduce the kids to Roxster so soon and certainly didn't want them to find me in bed with him. But—thanks to the hook on the bedroom door—we found our way. And it was so lovely. It has been so lovely. So lovely having a separate adult life, and meeting in pubs and little restaurants and going to movies and for walks on the Heath and having fantastic sex, and someone who cares about me. Although he hasn't met the kids, they've become part of our dialogue, and part of the texting that is the running commentary on both our lives, what we're doing, what we're eating, what time I've got them to school, what Roxster's boss has done now and more about what Roxster's eating.

Looking back, I think I've been almost delirious, permanently shag-drunk, in a haze of happiness. And now it is five on Saturday morning, I have been awake all night thinking about all these things, the kids will be up in an hour, I've got the film meeting on Monday and have done no preparation, I probably have nits and there is still no text from Roxster.

10 p.m. Still no text, am melting down again. Have left messages and texts for Jude, Tom and Talitha but nobody seems to be there. Jude is on her date with PlentyOfDance or perhaps PlentyOfDoctor Man whilst simultaneously standing Vile Richard up with an imaginary girl. Oh, telephone!

Was Talitha, coming to the rescue. Refusing to listen to my wails of: "It's because I'm *middle-aged!*" She said, "Nonsense, darling!" reminding me how in *Men Are from Mars, Women Are from Venus*, it says men *of any age* need to retreat to their caves sometimes.

"And also, darling," she added, "you did see him on

Thursday night. You can't expect to have the poor boy every other day."

Then just as I got into bed the phone pinged. Leaped at it hopefully.

Was Talitha again.

<Now stop worrying. It's just relationship weather. Remember everything you've learned. You are an expert Dating Sailor, and I promise you, you will successfully navigate this little squall.>

Sunday 21 April 2013

136lb (oh no, this has to stop), calories 2850 (ditto, but is Roxster's fault), minutes spent playing with children 452, minutes spent worrying about Roxster while playing with children 452 (hope Social Services not reading).

3 p.m. Still no sex. I mean, text. But feeling much more composed about Roxster today. Calm, Buddhist, almost Dalai Lama–like. When he comes, we welcome. When he goes, we let him go.

3.05 p.m. FUCK ROXSTER! FUCK HIM! Suddenly doing death-by-texting after all that, that CLOSENESS. It's inhuman. I didn't like him anyway. I was just . . . just . . . USING HIM FOR SEX . . . like a, like a TOY BOY. And it's a REALLY good job the children didn't meet him—because now it is all over, so at least it won't affect them. But where am I going to find someone I just get on with like that and who is so funny, and sweet and gorgeous and—

"Mummy?" Billy interrupted. "How many elements are there?"

"Four!" I said brightly, snapping back into the reality of the messy Sunday afternoon in the kitchen. "Air, fire and wood. And um—"

"Not 'WOOD'! Wood isn't an element."

Oh. Suddenly realize "wood" came from a book I read about Elemental Design—when I had the fantasy of redoing the house into a Buddhist Zendo—and it said the house had to have water, wood, earth and fire. No problem with the last one anyway!

"There are five elements."

"No, there aren't!" I said indignantly. "There are four elements."

"No. There are five elements," said Billy. "Air, earth, water, fire and technology. Five."

"Technology isn't an element."

"Yes, it is!"

"No, it isn't!"

"It is. It's in Wii Skylanders: air, earth, water, fire and technology."

Stared at him in horror. Has technology become another element now? Is that it? Technology is the fifth element, and my generation just don't understand it, like the Incas just completely forgetting to invent the wheel? Or maybe the Incas invented the wheel and it was the Aztecs to whom the idea of the wheel just never occurred?

"Billy?" I said. "Who invented the wheel? Was it the Incas or the Aztecs?"

"Mummeeeee! It was in Asia in 8000 BC," Billy said without looking up.

He had somehow got onto his iPod without me noticing.

"What are you DOING?????" I burst out. "You've had your time. Your next time isn't till four o'clock!"

"But I wasn't doing Skylanders for the whole forty-five minutes. I was only playing for thirty-seven minutes because it was loading and you SAID you would save my time when I went to the toilet."

I grasped my hair and pulled it, trying not to think about the nit eggs. I just don't know what to do about technology. It's banned in the week, and at the weekend it's maximum two and a half hours with no more than forty-five minutes at a time and at least an hour in between, but the whole thing gets like a complicated algorithm of finishing levels, and loading, and going to the toilet, and playing cyber wizards with someone across the road, and it just drives me MAD because it turns them into non-present creatures and I might as well still be in BED as . . .

"Billy," I said in my best voicemail voice. "You have had your screen time. Would you please hand me the iPad, I mean iPod?"

"It's not an iPod."

"Hand it over," I said, staring Medusa-like at the evil thin black object.

"It's a Kindle."

"I said ENOUGH SCREENS!"

"Mummy. It's your Kindle. It's a book."

I blinked rapidly, confused. It was technological and black and thin and therefore Evil, but . . .

"I'm reading *James and the Giant Peach* by Roald Dahl."

. . . it was also a book.

"Well!" I said brightly, trying to recover my dignity. "Anyone want a snack?"

"Mummy," said Billy, "you're so silly."

"OK, I'm sorrreeeee," I said, like a sulky teenager. I got hold of him and hugged him perhaps a little too passionately.

Suddenly there was a ping. Lunged at the phone. Roxster! It was Roxster!

<Jonesey, I'm so sorry I've been out of touch. I left my phone on the kitchen table when I went to Cardiff on Friday and I don't have your number anywhere else. I've been tweeting and emailing you like a frenzied beast. Have the ants got into your computer?>

Oh God. That's right. Roxster had said he was going to Cardiff to watch the rugby this weekend. That was why he wanted to see me on Thursday, when I found out Billy had nits. The Cardiff rugby thing was this weekend!

Had delicious texting exchange culminating in:

<Shall I come round tonight to have make-up sex? Even though we didn't actually have break-up sex? But maybe we could do that after?>

Am going to say no. Have meeting tomorrow and is really important to be prepared, rested and fresh and that is the sort of professional, prioritizing Power Mother I am. After the children are asleep I shall prepare my thoughts for the Power Meeting.

11.55 p.m. Mmmmm. There is nothing like make-up sex to help you forgive your toy boy for going to watch the rugby and leaving his phone behind.

POWER MOTHER

Monday 22 April 2013

132lb (evaporated through sex), shags 5, minutes spent preparing thoughts for meeting 0, ideas of things to say in meeting 0 (oh God).

11.30 a.m. Film Company Reception Area.
Oh, God. What was I thinking having sex all night? The whole make-up/break-up thing somehow whipped Roxster and me up into a sexual frenzy and neither of us could stay asleep. Was just actually hanging upside down from the side of the bed with Roxster holding both my legs in the air whilst thrusting in between them when suddenly—

"Mummeeee!" The door handle started rattling.

Oh God, it was so difficult to stop.

"Mummeee!"

Roxster pulled back in alarm so that I crashed down backwards onto the floor . . .

"Mummy! What was that bang?"

"Nothing, darling!" I trilled, upside down, "Comeeee-ing!" at which Roxster whispered, "And I'm certainly about to."

I tried to turn myself round unladylikely, with my bum in the air, and Roxster started giggling as he hoisted me back up onto the bed, whispering, "Please don't fart."

"Mummee, where are you? Why is the door locked?"

I dived over the bed, trying to straighten my slip while Roxster hid over the other side. I undid the hook, opened the door a crack, and hurriedly stepped out, shutting it behind me.

"It's all right, Billy, Mummy's here, and everything's fine. What's the matter?"

"Mummy," said Billy, looking at me strangely, "why are your boobies hanging out?"

Once I'd taken them to school, the morning was complete nightmare trying to sort out complex matrix of pickups and nits and play-date dilemmas with Chloe, blow-drying hair (presumably spraying bathroom with early-cycle nit eggs), and eventually locating navy silk dress in bottom of wardrobe requiring ironing and wiping off of chocolate stain, and now I am here waiting for the film meeting and have not done any mental preparation at all.

Offices are incredibly scary. Reception area is like an art gallery. Reception desk is like an enormous concrete, free-standing bath, and there is a man lying face-down on the floor—perhaps another aspiring screenwriter whose "exploratory option meeting" had failed?

12.05 p.m. Oh. Is a sculpture, or perhaps more of an *installation*.

12.07 p.m. Calm and poised. Calm and poised. Everything is fine. Just need to remind self of what is actually in script.

12.10 p.m. Maybe will win BAFTA award for Best Adapted Screenplay. "I would like to thank Talitha, Sergei, Billy, Mabel, Roxster . . . anyway, enough about them! I was born thirty-five years ago and . . ."

12.12 p.m. Look, stoppit. Must marshal thoughts. The important thing is that this updating is a feminist tragedy. The key narrative thread is that Hedda, instead of just being independent like Jude, settles for a dull, unattractive academic, who stretches his budget to buy them a house in Queen's Park. Then, disappointed by the intellectual honeymoon in Florence, because she really wants to go to Ibiza, and disappointed by the rubbish sex, because she really wanted to marry her hot alcoholic lover, she comes back to find self also disappointed by the dingy, rainy house in Queen's Park and eventually ends up shooting herself and . . . Gaah!

5 p.m. Was startled from reverie by a tall girl with dark hair, dressed entirely in black. A shorter youth stood behind her, with hair cut short at one side and long at the other. They smiled over-brightly as if I'd already done something wrong and they were trying to smooth me over before they killed me, and left me like the man on the floor.

"Hi, I'm Imogen and this is Damian."

There was a moment of awkward silence as we squashed into the stainless-steel lift looking at each other, through maniacal grins, wondering what to say.

"It's a very nice lift," I burst out, at which Imogen said, "Yes, isn't it?" and the doors opened directly into a spectacular boardroom looking out over the rooftops of London.

"Something to drink?" said Imogen, pointing to a low sideboard sporting an array of designer waters, Diet Cokes, coffee, chocolate biscuits, Nutribars, oatmeal biscuits, a bowl of fruit and chocolate Celebrations, and, oddly for that time of day, croissants.

Just as I was helping myself to coffee and a croissant, to create a pleasing air of a Power Breakfast, the door burst open and a tall, imposing man in large black glasses and immaculately ironed shirt swept in, looking very busy and important.

"Sorry," he said in a deep voice without looking at anyone. "Conference call. OK. Where are we?"

"Bridget, this is George, the head of Greenlight Productions," said Imogen, just as my handbag started making a loud quacking noise. Oh God. Billy had obviously done something with the text alert.

"Sorry," I laughed gaily, "I'll turn that off," and started grappling amongst the bits of cheese in my bag to try and find the phone. The thing is, though, the quacking wasn't a text alert, it was some sort of alarm so it kept on going and my bag was so full of rubbish I couldn't find the phone. Everyone stared.

"So . . ." said George, gesturing at the chair beside him, as I managed to pull out the phone, wipe off a bit of squashed banana and turn it off. "So . . . we like your script."

"Oh, that's great," I said, furtively placing the phone on "vibrate" and on my knee in case Roxster, I mean Chloe or the school, texted.

"There are some really lovely things in there," said Imogen.

"Thank you!" I beamed. "I've made some notes for our discussion and—"

The phone vibrated. Was Chloe.

<Cosmata's mum says fine to bring Mabel to play date as Cosmata and Thelonius have nits too, but Atticus's mum says no to nits for Billy play date. Also Billy has been sick at school and they want someone to get him now but I can't and Cosmata's mum doesn't want sick germs in her house, so can't take Billy to pick up Mabel from Cosmata's.>

Mind reeled over Latin-verb-declension-like morass of children's names—Cosmo, Cosmas, Cosmata, Theo, Thea, Thelonius, Atticarse—and hideous pickup/sick dilemma, wondering what Power Mothers did in similar situations.

"Basically we think the whole tone and the updating of the Hedda story is great," Imogen was saying.

"The Hedda *character*," added George tersely. Imogen coloured slightly, seeming to take this as some kind of rebuke, then continued: "We think the idea of a woman dissatisfied with her lot, and torn between a sensible-choice husband and a wildly creative—"

"Exactly, exactly," I said as the phone vibrated again. "I mean, even though it was a long time ago, women are still making these decisions. And I think Queen's Park has exactly the sort of—"

Glanced furtively at the text. Roxster!

<What are you wearing and how is the film meeting?>

"Right, right, what we're thinking is—we set it in Hawaii," George interrupted.

"HAWAII?" I said.

"Yes."

Realizing this might be a crucial juncture, I gathered my courage, and added: "Although, it is meant to be more Norwegian. So like, in November, all dark and miserable, in a dark, depressing house in Queen's Park."

"It could be Kauai," said Imogen encouragingly. "It rains all the time there."

"So instead of being in, like, a dark depressing house it's—"

"On a yacht!" said Imogen. "We want to bring in a sort of 60s/70s glamorous feel."

"Like *The Pink Panther*," interjected Damian.

"You mean it's going to be a cartoon?" I said, furtively texting <Navy silk dress. Nightmare.> under the desk.

"No, no, you know, like the original *Pink Panther* with David Niven and Peter Sellers," said Imogen.

"Wasn't that set in Paris and Gstaad?"

"Well, yes, but it's the *feel* we're after. The mood," said Imogen.

"A yacht in Hawaii with a Paris/Gstaad sort of feel?" I said.

"Where it's raining," said Imogen.

"Dark, dark, cloudy skies," added Damian.

I slumped. The whole thing was meant to be about everything being disappointing and shabby. But, importantly, as Brian the Agent says, if you're a screenwriter you don't want to be sort of a nuisance.

The phone vibrated. Roxster.

<GBH x. Is that the navy silk dress I had my head up last week?>

"So . . ." said George. "Hedda is Kate Hudson."

"Right, right." I nodded, writing "Kate Hudson" in my iPhone notes and quickly texting <GBH?> while trying not to think about Roxster's head up my dress.

"The boring husband is Leonardo DiCaprio and then the alcoholic ex is . . .?"

"Heath Ledger," Damian said quickly.

"But he's dead," said Imogen just as Roxster texted: <Great Big Hamburger. I mean, Hug.>

"Yeah, yeah, yeah, yeah, yeah," Damian was saying. "Not Heath Ledger but someone *like* Heath Ledger only . . ."

"Not dead?" said Imogen, staring at Damian coldly. "Colin Farrell?"

"Yup," said George. "I can see that. I can see Colin Farrell. If he's on the straight and narrow, which I think he is. So what about the other girl?"

"The friend—the one Hedda Gabbler was at school with?" said Imogen. The phone vibrated.

<Billy has stopped being sick so I can get first, but Cosmata's mother still doesn't want him to come to the door. Can I leave him in the car?>

"Alicia Silverstone," said Damian. "It should be like *Clueless*."

"Nope," said George.

"No," Damian disagreed with himself.

"You know what?" George was looking thoughtful. "Hedda could be more of a Cameron Diaz. What about Bradley Cooper for boring husband?"

"Mmm! Yes!" I said. "But isn't Bradley Cooper quite sex—"

"Jude Law in *Anna Karenina,*" concurred Imogen, with a knowing smile. "Or cast the whole piece older and have George Clooney playing against type?"

Felt in some strange twilight world where we were just bandying about incredibly famous people, who would have absolutely no interest in being in it at all. Why would Cosmata's mother think that nits and sick germs could hop from the pavement into the front door and why would George Clooney want to be in an updated version of *Hedda Gabbler*, set on a yacht in Hawaii, playing against type, written by me?

"What if she doesn't die?" said George, getting to his feet and starting to walk around. "She dies, right, in the book?"

"The play," said Imogen.

"But that's the whole point," I said.

"Yeah, but if it's a romcom?"

"It's not a romcom, it's a tragedy," I said, then immediately regretted my presumptuousness.

The phone vibrated again. Chloe.

<You can't park in Cosmata's street. And her mother won't come round the corner because of the baby.>

"She shoots herself," said Imogen.

"Shoots herself? *Shoots herself?*" said George. "Who does that?"

"But you can't say 'Who does that?' about someone shooting themselves," Imogen was saying.

"That's exactly what they say! In the original play!" I said, trying to overcome feelings of annoyance with Cosmata's mother. "'Good God! People don't do things like that!'"

There was a silence. I knew I'd said completely the wrong thing.

Imogen was looking daggers at me. I had to stop looking at the texts and CONCENTRATE. I was clearly in the middle of some incredibly complex power struggle, which I didn't fully understand, and one or other of the children would have to remain abandoned and Roxster's food obsession unsatisfied. Imogen had supported me over the fact that you couldn't question whether people shot themselves or not—because clearly they do sometimes and not just in plays—but then I, instead of supporting her in her support, had supported George by saying that his views were supported by the opinions of . . .

"I mean, I agree with you, Imogen," I said. "People shoot themselves all the time. Not actually all the time, but they do shoot themselves sometimes. Look at, look at, um." I looked wildly around for inspiration, wishing I could google "Modern Celebrities Who Have Shot Themselves." Instead I quickly texted Chloe: <Get surgical mask for Billy.>

"Right," said George, sitting down again, in an important, businesslike way. "So. We'll give you a couple of days. No Kate Hudson shooting herself. It's a comedy. It's the comedy we like."

I stared at George aghast. *The Leaves in His Hair* is not a comedy. It is a tragedy. Had the tragedy in my writing somehow inadvertently come out as comic? The fact that Hedda Gabbler shoots herself is fundamental. But, as Brian said, in the movie business, artistic integrity has to go together with pragmatism and . . . There was another text from Roxster!

<Maybe suggest they make "Nits" as a Pixar-style animation.>

Actually, that wasn't a bad idea. Suddenly the previously

mentioned *Pink Panther* concept combined with Roxster's "Nits" suggestion triggered a brilliant notion in my mind.

"What about *Tom and Jerry*?" I burst out. George, who had now opened the door to leave, stopped in his tracks and looked back.

"I mean, *Tom and Jerry* is a comedy, but terrible things happen to both Tom and Jerry. I mean, more Tom—he gets flattened, he gets electrocuted, yet somehow . . ."

"He always comes back to life!" said Imogen, smiling at me.

"You mean she's resuscitated?" said George.

"Like *Fool's Gold* meets *ER* meets *The Passion of the Christ*!" enthused Damian, adding hurriedly, "but without the Jewish controversy."

"Try it, send us the rewrite by Thursday and see how it comes off the page," said George in his deep voice. "Right, I've gotta go. I've got a conference call."

The phone vibrated. Roxster: <Is there any food in the meeting?>

Once euphoric farewells were made—"You did *really* well in there! I love your dress"—and hugs exchanged, whilst I tried to keep my head oddly at an angle because of the nits (I mean, what if they got in Damian's lopsided haircut?), I sat down in reception and looked at my latest texts.

Chloe: <Billy OK now. So will let Cosmata's mother pick up Mabel then I'll pick up Billy and take to pick up Mabel?>

Roxster: <Have just left office for calming cold shower—over food, you understand, not dress/meeting fantasy. Supply full food list?>

Instead of processing the whole meeting, calling Brian to get him to get them to give me more time, then rushing home to see how Billy is, and having a serious think about telling Chloe she has to make decisions herself if I am in important meetings, I replied to Roxster with a complete list of every item of food in the meeting, adding: <I doubt your head would have been up my dress.>

NITS IN THE WORKS

Tuesday 23 April 2013

Minutes spent writing script 0, minutes spent dealing with people's nits instead of getting on with work 507, people whom family might have infested with nits (including Tom, Jude, all Jude's recent dates, Talitha, Roxster, Arkis, Sergei, Grazina the Cleaner, Chloe, Brian the Agent—but only if nits can get down phone—and entire Greenlight Productions team) 23 (not counting people above people might have infested with nits).

9.30 a.m. Right. This is my first official rewriting day on *The Leaves in His Hair*. Feel marvellous and proud! Almost like it was just a sort of hobby before but now it is real.

10.05 a.m. Grrr. This is really quite difficult, though. Don't want to be a Prima Donna, but setting *Hedda Gabbler* on a yacht in Hawaii is somehow changing the mood and meaning of the whole piece. It brings up all sorts of difficulties, which weren't there with the terrace house in Queen's Park. Ooh, goody. Text!

10.45 a.m. Was Tom. <Is your head itching? Because mine is. Maybe psychosomatic, but didn't we have rather a head-nuzzling hug when I left the other night?>

Freaked out, I texted back: <Sure is psychosomatic. I haven't got them.>—but even as I texted, my head started to itch.

Tom again. <But I finally slept with Arkis on Saturday. Should I tell him?>

Paroxysms of guilt. Tom sleeping with Arkis is the product of months of discussion and strategizing and I have potentially ruined it!

11 a.m. Just texted Tom list of nit products, combs, etc., offered to nit-comb him if he wanted to come round.

11.15 a.m. Jude just rang, talking in a wobbly, sepulchral voice.

"Vile Richard has blocked Isabella."

"Who's Isabella?"

"The made-up girl on PlentyofFish.com, remember? She stood him up on Saturday and now . . ."

Jude was really upset.

"What?"

"Vile Richard replaced his profile with a message saying he's no longer available because he's met someone else. I just feel really, really hurt, Bridget. How could he meet someone else so quickly?"

Tried to explain to Jude that Isabella wasn't real, and Vile Richard clearly hadn't met someone else, he was just trying to get back at Isabella for standing him up, even though Isabella didn't exist, at which Jude seemed to brighten and said: "The guy I met on Saturday was nice, though, you know the one from the dance-lover site. Though he hates dancing. He says they must have passed his profile on from a snowboarding site."

At least she didn't mention anything about nits.

Noon. Right. Now Jude is all calm and happy again, will get on with *The Leaves in His Hair*.

The trouble is, people don't LIVE on yachts, do they? Or maybe they do? Like people who live on barges on the canal. But don't yacht-type people live in big houses and just go on holiday on the yachts? And, more to the point, honeymoons.

12.15 p.m. Texted Talitha.

<Do people live on yachts?>

Talitha texted back.

<No, only crew or money-launderers.>

12.30 p.m. Another text from Talitha.

<By the way, is your head itching? Because mine is. Didn't I borrow your hairbrush last time we went out? Slightly worried about implications with my extensions.>

Oh God. Talitha's hair extensions! Can you nit-comb hair extensions?

Just had another text from Jude.

<By the way, is your head itching? Because mine is.>

4.15 p.m. Shit! Shit! There is bang, clatter and voices of everyone coming home.

5 p.m. Mabel burst in, holding out a letter. She sat down on the sofa and sobbed, big tears dribbling down her cheeks.

Why do all the class names in Infants sound like the sort of Cotswold holiday cottages I keep googling instead of writing *The Leaves in His Hair?*

> *. . . has been found to be infested with head lice. Please obtain suitable nit comb and products and check your children carefully before bringing them to school.*

"Ith me," sobbed Mabel. "I's infestered Briar Rose with headlies. I'm 'a child in Briar Rose.'"

"It isn't you," I said, hugging her and probably reinfestering her, or vice versa, with headlies. "Cosmata has head lice. And we didn't find any on you. Maybe they just put 'a child' when they meant lots of people."

Wednesday 24 April 2013
175lb (feels like again), pieces of Nicorette chewed 29 (NB of smoking substitute, not Class Mother), Diet Cokes 4, Red Bulls 5 (terrible, am practically on ceiling), packets of grated cheese 2, slices of rye bread 8, calories 4897, sleep 0, pages written 12. Humph.

12.30 p.m. Right. There is absolutely no need to panic. If a story is sound, and has themes relevant to modern life, then the actual setting ought to be immaterial.

1 p.m. Whole thing about Hedda and the boring husband going on a honeymoon not on a yacht and then coming back and living on a yacht seems completely nonsensical.

1.15 p.m. Wish head would stop itching.

1.20 p.m. Maybe they could have been on a road trip in the American West? Yes, surely as a car would be a nice change from a yacht?

4.30 p.m. Think will call Brian the Agent and talk it through with him. I mean, that's what you do with agents, right?

5 p.m. Explained the whole thing to Brian the Agent, while maniacally scratching head.

"So here's the thing," said Brian. "Apparently, Greenlight hired a yacht in Hawaii for the *Puff the Magic Dragon* stoner movie, and now the stoner movie has fallen over, so they need another vehicle for a Hawaiian yacht."

"Oh," I said, crestfallen. I mean, I thought the reason Greenlight so loved *The Leaves in His Hair* was . . .

"So what do we do?" Brian said cheerfully. "We make *Hedda Gabbler* work on a Hawaiian yacht, right?"

"Right," I said, nodding emphatically, even though Brian could not see emphatic nodding, infestering surrounding area with nits, as was on phone. Which was fortunate as otherwise would have also infestered Brian Katzenberg.

Thursday 25 April 2013
5 a.m. In bed writing crazily. Surrounded by revolting mess of Nicorette packets, coffee cups, pages of script all over

floor, Diet Coke, Red Bull cans, etc., etc. Feel completely disgusting. Stomach is just huge bulge of grated cheese, rye bread, Diet Coke and Red Bull, and head is constantly itching. And still have not finished any coherent pages and is all spelt wrong and spacing mad, etc., etc. Also cannot even text Roxster to cheer self up because he is asleep.

10 a.m. Somehow spurred on by adrenalin rush of deadline, finished "pages" and have emailed them off, even throwing in an extra, admittedly idiotic, scene I did in about twenty minutes flat, of Hedda throwing herself off the boat at the end, then Lovegood her alcoholic ex-lover doing the same and them both appearing putting on scuba gear at the bottom of the ocean like in *For Your Eyes Only*. But still, will give pleasing sense of more pages having been written.

Now am going back to sleep.

NIT-INFESTERED POWER MEETING

Friday 26 April 2013
12.30 p.m. Greenlight boardroom. Oh God. There was a tense atmosphere when I walked in. They were all talking amongst themselves and suddenly stopped.

"Bridget, hello! Come and sit down!" said Imogen. "Thank you for the pages. There are some lovely things in there." (Have subsequently come to realize that "There are some lovely things in there" means "It's crap.")

There was a flat, tired air of weariness, quite different from the excitement of last week. Felt overwhelming urge to scratch my head.

"How is the road trip a good idea when these are people who like yachts?" George bulldozed in.

"That's exactly what I thought!" I said, quickly giving my head a scratch as if to illustrate the dilemma, but actually to squash the worst bit of itching. "If Hedda's going to come back and be disappointed by her new yacht, how can she already have been on a honeymoon on it?"

"Yes, but they don't have to go on a road trip, they could go to . . . to . . ."

My phone vibrated. Talitha.

< The hair extensions place won't take out my extensions because they don't want to infect the salon with nits. >

"Vegas!" said Damian eagerly.

"Not *Vegas*," said George disparagingly. "People get married in Vegas, they don't have their honeymoons in Vegas."

"What about Costa Rica?" said Damian.

The phone vibrated again.

Was Tom.

<Are nits the same as crabs?>

"Or the Mayan Riviera?" said Imogen.

"Not Mexico. Kidnappings," said George.

"But does it matter?" I ventured, trying not even to start with the chilling implications of Tom's text. "Because we're not going to actually see them on the honeymoon, only when they get back."

Everyone stared at me, as if this was a totally brilliant, original thought.

"She's right," said George. "We don't need to see the honeymoon."

Suddenly had sinking sense that George was not actually interested in the quality of my writing so much as the filming locations. Felt should quickly text Tom back reassuringly about the crabs/nit distinction, though did not have a definitive answer. Simultaneously sensed I must seize my advantage, and take control of the meeting.

"Look," I said, in what I could already tell was going to be an annoying, schoolmarmy voice, scratching my head, and having a lurching fear that the reason Roxster hadn't texted was that he too now had nits or maybe even—

"I think the yacht is a *great* idea," I fraudulently enthused, "but it does throw up some issues with the adaptation. It's important that we remember that *The Nits in His Hair* is making an—"

271

"*The Nits in His Hair?*" said Imogen, suddenly reaching her hand to her head.

"I mean *The Leaves in His Hair*," I said hurriedly. Damian was scratching his head now and George, who is bald, was looking at us as if we were completely mad. The phone vibrated. Roxster! No, it was Tom again.

<Could nits become crabs . . . I mean, if they . . . crawled?>

"The important thing," I ploughed on, "is it's important that we don't lose the important . . . Look," I said grandly, opening my laptop, "I've made some notes about the important themes."

Everyone gathered round to look at my screen, though keeping a distance from my head. Just as I was adding, to fill the embarrassing silence while I got the laptop to start up, "You see, this is, essentially, I believe, a *feminist* piece," the screen popped with the pink and lilac home page of Princess Bride Dress Up.

Gaah! How had Mabel got on my laptop?

Started fiddling around trying to find notes, then George said impatiently, "Look, while you're looking for this stuff, why don't we go off and read the pages and we can order in some lunch?"

"Read the pages?" I said, mind reeling. "But haven't you already read the pages?"

I mean, we'd just been *discussing* the pages. WHAT was the point of me staying up all night drinking Red Bull and chewing Nicorette, if they haven't even read the pages and—

"We'll see you after lunch," said George, and now they have all left the boardroom.

1.05 p.m. Humph. Anyway. At least I can freely scratch my head now, and google crabs and head lice and try and make some emotional peace with the fact that insect life has terminally put Roxster off me.

1.15 p.m. Just typed in "Are nits crabs?" on Ask.com and was reading—

> Head lice and "crabs," also called pubic lice, are different things.
> Head lice (usually found on the head) have longer and thinner body compared to pubic lice which have bigger and more robust bodies.
> Head lice live on the head only and cannot live in the pubic region.
> Crab lice live in the pubic region.
> There is also a third kind of lice that lives in other hairy regions of the . . .

—when George's assistant appeared behind me with a lunch menu before I had time to switch the screen back to Princess Bride Dress Up.

Snapped the laptop shut, ordered a Thai chicken salad and, once she'd gone—presumably to tell the entire company that I had pubic lice—emailed the crabs/lice link to Tom.

1.30 p.m. No one has come back. Starting to panic now as I am doing school pickup today. I mean, surely it was reasonable to think a meeting about ten pages would not take quite as long. Ooh, text. Roxster?

Was Tom.

<Thanks for the links. None of this is actually helping.>

Gaah! George and Damian and Imogen are all coming back.

2.45 p.m. Meeting is over and have seconds to spare to get to Infants Branch by 3.15. Cheeringly, meeting was slightly more *positive* after they'd read the pages, and eaten some food (you see, is exactly the same with Billy and Mabel!), except they want me to rewrite everything I've already rewritten because the humour is "not coming off the page," and the only bit George actually wants to leave as it is is the ludicrous, *For Your Eyes Only* scuba-diving ending.

Of course, when they returned after lunch, I *still* did not have feminist notes up on screen. Instead when they gathered round they were greeted with:

Head lice and "crabs," also called pubic lice, are different things . . .

Think managed to click it off before they actually read it, though they may have seen the pictures of the two kinds of lice.

Ensuing discussion was punctuated by texts from Talitha who had, of course, immediately found a Celebrity Nit Nurse in Notting Hill and was texting me a running commentary.

<Hasn't found any yet.>

<Oh my God, I've got nits, though at £130 to clear my head I'm not sure I believe her.>

Was too polite to ask Talitha to stop texting, because felt guilty and clearly needed to support her.

Talitha texts got worse and worse.

<Celebrity nit nurse will not guarantee my head is clear because they might be nesting in the bonds in my extensions.>

<What am I going to do about blow-dry habit? Have to go on TV! Cannot even have girls on show "touch up" my hair. Also what if Sergei now has nits?>

<The salon won't take the extensions out because of the nits, so the only way is if I take them out myself with a bottle of extension oil.>

Talitha really must be in a state because normally she would never do anything to make you feel guilty. Have ruined Talitha's life and career. And character.

Felt was the least I could do to offer to take them out for her if she comes round.

Talitha then came up with the *brilliant* plan of us all going to the Celebrity Nit Nurse tomorrow. "So at least that's one less thing for you to worry about! And it will be a nice outing for us all! It'll be fun!"

11 p.m. Fantastic evening taking out Talitha's hair extensions. Was incredibly challenging, as had to rub oil into the glue bits, and pull out, then inspect for nits. Was a bit like Anne Hathaway dying of a bad haircut in *Les Misérables*, except more moaning and crying. We didn't find any actual insects as the Celebrity Nit Nurse had got all of those, but we did find quite a lot of dark dots actually in the glue.

Worst is that hair extensions will cost hundreds of pounds to put in again.

"It's all my fault. I'll pay for them," I said.

"Oh, don't be ridiculous, darling," Talitha said. "That's

not the point. The point is, I can't put them back in for a week in case we missed any, because the nit cycle is a week. What am I going to do?"

She seemed suddenly to lose heart, looking at herself with nit oil smeared in her real hair. "Oh, good, I look a hundred years old. What is Sergei going to say? And I have to go on TV. Oh, darling, this is what I always feared would happen. I'll get trapped on a desert island where they have no hair-extension specialist or Botox aesthetician and all my artifice will drain away."

Trying not to think about my eighteenth-century wig theory, I pointed out that this was most unlikely to happen— no one looks at their best with their hair smeared down with hair-extension and nit oil—and washed Talitha's hair and blow-dried it. Actually, she looked really sweet. It was all fluffy, like a little chicken.

"I mean, the whole point about celebrities is that they *change their look!*" I said encouragingly. "Look at Lady Gaga! Look at Jessie J. You could wear . . . a pink wig!"

"I'm not *Jessie J!*" said Talitha, at which Mabel, who had been watching solemnly, burst out, "Kerching, kerching! Berbling, berbling!" while looking at us expectantly, as if we were going to say, "No, YOU are Jessie J!" Then, crestfallen, she whispered, "Why does Talitha look so sad?"

Talitha surveyed our faces.

"It's all right, darlings," she said, as if we were both five-year-olds. "I'll simply get some pieces put in at Harrods. They'll come in useful later. As long as they don't have nits in them."

11.30 p.m. Talitha just texted: <Sergei loves my real hair. He's completely turned on. Phew. I always thought he'd hate me if we were stuck on a desert island and he saw the "real me.">—which is quite a sophisticated thing to say, because she was completely eradicating any sense of passive-aggressive guilt inducement, and actually making it seem as if I'd done her a favour.

Talitha really is a sophisticated human being. She has this theory about people who are in "primitive states," i.e. they don't really know how to behave.

Also am sure that if Talitha actually thought it was my fault, i.e. I'd knowingly hugged and nuzzled her, whilst aware I might have nits, without telling her I knew I might have nits, then she'd have been completely straight about it.

Tom texted: <Nits are definitely not the same as crabs, appear to have neither, and Arkis thinks it's funny: bonding experience.>

Saturday 27 April 2013

Nits and nit eggs extracted 32, pounds forked out per dead nit £8.59.

Nit-nurse expedition was, as Billy put it, "extreme, extreme fun" and everyone thoroughly enjoyed themselves. Caring assistants, entirely swathed in white, sucked at all our hair with a vacuum, said they'd found nothing, and then blew us very fiercely with a very hot hairdryer. It was "extreme, extreme fun," that is, until the bill came—275 quid! We could all have gone to Euro Disney for that!—with the right amount of well-timed googling.

"How does this actually work?" I said. "Couldn't I do it at home using the mini-vacuum, then blasting us all with a really hot hairdryer?"

"Oh no," said the Celebrity Nit Nurse airily. "It's all very specially designed. The vacuum comes from Atlanta, and the Heat Destroyer is made in Rio de Janeiro."

FIRE! FIRE!

Wednesday 1 May 2013

Blimey. This morning, instead of staying in the bedroom when I went down to deal with the kids, Roxster said, "I think I should come down to breakfast."

"OK," I said, pleased, a little nervous in case a knife-wielding bloodbath broke out between the children, at the same time wondering if Roxster was driven by a desire to participate in family life, or simply the notion of food. "I'll just get things ready, then come down!"

Everything was going perfectly! Billy and Mabel were dressed and sitting nicely at the table and I decided to cook sausages! Knowing how much Roxster likes a full English breakfast!!

When Roxster appeared, looking fresh-faced and cheerful, Billy made no reaction and Mabel carried on eating, while staring solemnly at Roxster, never taking her eyes off him. Roxster laughed. "Hello, Billy. Hello, Mabel. I'm Roxster. Is there anything left for me?"

"Mummy's cooking sausages," said Billy, glancing towards the cooker. "Oh," he said, eyes lighting up. "They're on fire!"

"Dey're on fire! Dey're on fire!" Mabel said happily. I rushed over to the cooker, followed by the children.

"They're not on fire," I said indignantly. "It's just the fat underneath. The sausages are fine, they—"

The smoke alarm went off. Oddly, the smoke alarm had never gone off before. It was the loudest noise you've ever heard. Deafening.

"I'll try and find where it is," I said.

"Maybe we should put the fire out first," bellowed Roxster, turning off the gas, removing the sausages and the tinfoil in a smooth movement, dumping them in the sink, shouting above the din, "Where's the food-recycling bin?"

"Over there!" I said, looking frantically through various files on the cookery bookshelf to see if I could find the instruction leaflet for the smoke alarm. There was nothing apart from instructions for a Magimix, which we didn't have any more. Also, where did the fire alarm, as it were, *stem from*? Suddenly looked round to see that everyone had disappeared. Where had they gone? Had they all collectively decided I was rubbish, and run off to live with Roxster and his flatmates, where they could play video games all day, uninterrupted, and eat perfectly barbecued sausages whilst listening to popular music which was actually current instead of Cat Stevens singing "Morning Has Broken"?

The smoke alarm stopped. Roxster appeared down the stairs, grinning.

"Why has it stopped?" I said.

"I turned it off. There's a code written on the box— which would be bad if you were a burglar, but good if you're a toy boy and there are burning sausages."

"Where are the children?"

"I think they went upstairs. Come here."

He hugged me against his muscly shoulders. "It doesn't matter. It's just funny."

"I make such a bugger of things."

"No, you don't," he whispered. "Fires, insect plagues, sort of thing which can happen to anyone." We started kissing. "We'd better stop this," he said, "or we'll have more burning sausages to extinguish."

We went upstairs in search of the children, to find they had calmly gone to their bedroom and were playing with their dinosaurs.

"Well! Shall we go to school?" I said brightly.

"OK," said Billy, as if nothing at all unusual had happened.

So the motley crew of me, Billy, Mabel and Roxster emerged from the front door to be greeted by an uptight lady from up the road who looked suspiciously and said, "Have you had a fire?"

"You betcha, baby," said Roxster. "Bye, Billy. Bye, Mabel."

"Bye, Roxster," they said cheerfully at which he patted me on the bottom and headed off to the tube.

But now, maybe I am having a panic attack. Does this mean things are moving to a more serious level? And surely is inadvisable to have Roxster bond with the children in case . . . Maybe I will text him and invite him to Talitha's party!

10.35 a.m. Impulsively sent text: <Talitha has invited you to her glamorous 60th birthday party on May 24th. Will be v. glam with LOTS OF FOOD! Do you fancy going?>—but now instantly regretting.

281

10.36 a.m. No reply. Did not mention had remembered was Roxster's thirtieth same night (lest thought self stalker-esquely focused on him), but why did I say sixtieth? Why? What could be more off-putting? Why cannot one delete sent texts?

10.40 a.m. Roxster has not replied. Gaah! Telephone! Maybe Roxster is calling to break up with me for having sixty-year-old friend.

11 a.m. Was George from Greenlight. Had rather testy conversation which seemed to go, in the space of a few minutes, from George being in a limousine, to George being in a gift shop, to George getting on a plane whilst simultaneously giving me notes on the rewrite and saying things like, "No! Don't wrap it up! I've got a plane to catch, actually do wrap it."

In the end I said, hoity-toitily, as I opened another text from Roxster, "George, I'm actually finding it rather difficult to make sense of your notes when you seem so distracted."

But I'm not sure he heard this because his phone cut out.

Hurrah. Text from Roxster said: <I can't think of a better way to celebrate my 30th than Talitha's 60th, especially if the food will be as good as you say it will. As long as we can celebrate my birthday properly in your boudoir afterwards.>

And then another saying: <Can we have dinner again at home? Shepherd's pie.>

<Yes, Roxster.>

And another.

<I heart shepherd's pie.>

<I know, Roxster.> I texted patiently.

And another.

<Just to be absolutely clear, you really mean two dinners? Counting the party?>

THE TROUBLE WITH SUMMER

Tuesday 7 May 2013
136lb (oh no, oh no, disaster), outfits suitable for summer 0, outfits suitable for modern world 1 (navy silk dress).

9.31 a.m. Summer is here! Finally, the sun is out, the trees are in blossom and everything is marvellous. But oh no! My upper arms are not ready.

9.32 a.m. Also feel familiar sense of panic that must make the most of it as it might be the last and only sunny day of the year. And what about the summer season coming up when everyone will be going to festivals in Effortless Festival Chic like Kate Moss or to Ascot dressed like Kate Middleton and wearing a fascinator? I haven't got any summer events to go to or a fascinator.

9.33 a.m. Oh, phew. It's started raining again.

Wednesday 8 May 2013
9.30 a.m. School run has become impossible outfit obstacle. It is that confusing time before summer has got its confidence going, when you keep leaving the house either in winter woollies, at which it turns out to be sunny and 26 degrees, or wearing a floaty summer dress, and then it starts

hailing, leaving you freezing to death whilst noticing your toenail polish is revolting. Must turn attention to clothes and grooming. Also writing.

Thursday 9 May 2013
7 p.m. Gaah! Just watched *Good Luck Charlie* on Disney Channel with Mabel and realized the mum in *Good Luck Charlie* wears outfits exactly like I have been wearing all winter—apart from the navy silk dress: black jeans tucked into boots, or tight black flared sweatpants when at home, a white scoop-necked vest and a V-necked sweater on top in either black, grey or some other muted colour. Has what I thought was my monochrome, slightly edgy dressing become, in Mabel's eyes, the equivalent of Mum and Una's former Country Casuals two-pieces? Maybe will try to be more eclectic, like *Good Luck Charlie* teenage daughter.

Monday 13 May 2013
Minutes spent on outfit websites 242, minutes spent looking at Yahoo! stories 27, minutes spent arguing with Mr. Wallaker 12, minutes spent listening to Jude 32, minutes spent on homework chart 52, minutes spent doing any work whatsoever 0.

9.30 a.m. Right. Must get down to some serious writing now, but will just have a quick look at websites for River Island, Zara and Mango, etc. to get ideas for updated summer outfits.

12.30 p.m. Right! Work! Will just check Unexploded Email In-box.

12.45 p.m. Ooh, Yahoo! story: *"Biel Disappoints in Less-Than-Sexy Pantsuit."* Pah! Are women now judged by the Distance-From-Sexiness of their pantsuits? V. relevant to Hedda updating. Vital to read.

1 p.m. In frenzy of indignation. I mean, honestly, the only role models women have these days are these . . . these RED CARPET GIRLS who just turn up at events wearing clothes that people have loaned to them, then have their photos taken, which appear in *Grazia*, then go home again to sleep until lunchtime and get some more free clothes. Not that Jessica Biel is a Red Carpet Girl. Is actress. But still.

1.15 p.m. Wish I was a Red Carpet Girl.

2.15 p.m. Maybe will go out and get *Grazia* magazine so as not to disappoint in less-than-sexy mother-from-*Good Luck Charlie* outfit. Not, of course, that mother in *Good Luck Charlie* is less than sexy.

3 p.m. Just back from newsagent's with new *Grazia* magazine. Realize whole of my style is outdated and wrong and must wear skinny jeans, ballet pumps and shirt buttoned up to the collar, and blazer for school run plus enormous handbag and sunglasses in manner of celebrity at airport. Gaah! Is time to pick up Billy and Mabel.

5 p.m. Back home. Billy came out of school looking traumatized.

"I came second bottom in the spelling test."

"What spelling test?" I stared at him aghast as the other boys poured down the steps.

"It was an epic fail," he said sadly. "Even Ethekiel Koutznestov got better than me."

Terrible sense of failure. Whole homework thing is completely incomprehensible with random bits of paper, pictures of multi-armed Indian gods and half-coloured-in recipes for toast in different books.

Mr. Pitlochry-Howard, Billy's anxious, bespectacled form teacher, hurried up to us.

"The spelling test is nothing to worry about," he said anxiously. Mr. Wallaker wandered up to eavesdrop. "Billy's a very bright boy, he just needs—"

"He needs more organization at home," said Mr. Wallaker.

"But, you see, Mr. Wallaker," said Mr. Pitlochry-Howard, blushing slightly, "Billy has had a very difficult—"

"Yes, I know what happened to Billy's father," Mr. Wallaker said quietly.

"So we must make some allowances. It will be fine, Mrs. Darcy. You are not to worry," said Mr. Pitlochry-Howard. Then he pottered off, leaving me glowering at Mr. Wallaker.

"Billy needs discipline and structure," he said. "That's what will help him."

"He does have discipline. And he gets enough of your sort of discipline on the sports field. And in the chess class."

"You call that discipline? Wait till he gets to boarding school."

"Boarding school?" I said, thinking of how Mark had

made me promise not to send them away like him. "He's not going to boarding school."

"What's wrong with boarding school? My boys are at boarding school. Pushes them to their limits, teaches them valour, courage—"

"What about when things go wrong? What about someone to listen to them when they don't win? What about fun, what about love and cuddles?"

"Cuddles?" he said incredulously. "Cuddles?"

"Yes," I said. "They're children—they're not productivity machines. They need to learn how to manage when things don't go right."

"Get on top of the homework. More important than sitting in the hairdresser's."

"I will have you know," I said, drawing myself up to my full height, "that I am a professional woman and am writing an updating of *Hedda Gabbler* by Anton Chekhov, which is shortly to go into production with a movie company. Come along, Billy," I said, sweeping him off towards the school gates muttering, "Honestly. Mr. Wallaker is so rude and bossy."

"But I like Mr. Wallaker," said Billy, looking horrified.

"Mrs. Darcy?"

I turned, furious.

"*Hedda Gabbler*, you said?"

"Yes," I said proudly.

"By Anton Chekhov?"

"Yes."

"I think you'll find it's by Henrik Ibsen. And I think you'll find Gabbler is spelt, and indeed pronounced, with just the one b."

6 p.m. Oh, fuck. Just googled *Hedda Gabbler* and it IS by Henrik Ibsen and spelt with one b but *"Hedda Gabbler by Anton Chekhov"* is now all over the front page of everyone's script. Never mind. If nobody at Greenlight has noticed it, there's no point telling them now. I can always pretend it was intelligent irony.

9.15 p.m. Kitchen table is covered in charts. These are the charts as follows:

CHART ONE—DAY HOMEWORK IS ISSUED
e.g., Monday: maths, word problems and suffixes, for Tuesday morning. Tuesday: Indian god colouring and evaluate Craft and Design—bread, mice, etc.

CHART TWO—DAY HOMEWORK IS TO BE DELIVERED

CHART THREE
Possibly redundant chart, attempting to incorporate elements of both Chart One and Chart Two using different colours.

CHART FOUR—WHAT HOMEWORK SHOULD IDEALLY BE DONE ON WHICH DAY
e.g., Monday: draw and colour "family crest" for the "ic" Suffix Family. Colour in Indian god's arms.

Ooh, doorbell.

11 p.m. Was Jude, in a traumatized state, falling inside and wandering shakily downstairs.

"He wants me to tell him to lick things," she said dully, slumping on my sofa, clutching her phone, staring morbidly ahead.

Obviously I had to stop everything and listen. Turns out Snowboarderguy, with whom it has been going quite well for three weeks now, has suddenly revealed he is into sexual humiliation.

"Well! That's all right!" I said comfortingly, putting a delicate swirl in the froth of her decaffeinated Nespresso ristretto cappuccino, feeling, as always with my new Christmas Nespresso machine, slightly like a barista in Barcelona.

"You could tell him to lick . . . you!" I said, handing her the beautifully constructed beverage.

"No. He wants me to say things like, 'Lick the soles of my shoes, lick out the toilet bowl.' I mean, it's just not hygienic."

"You could get him to do useful things like housework. Maybe not the toilet bowl, but washing-up!" I said, trying to put the gravity of her situation above my own hurt feelings at not having my cappuccino-froth design praised, or at least commented upon.

"I'm not having him lick my washing-up."

"He could lick it to get the worst off, then put it in the dishwasher?"

"Bridget. He wants to be sexually humiliated, not wash the dishes."

Was desperate to cheer her up, particularly as everything was now going so well for me.

"Isn't there something humiliating you might enjoy?"

I said, as if persuading Mabel to go to a children's party. "What about . . . blindfolds?"

"No, he says he doesn't like the *50 Shades* stuff. It has to be, like, I'm just making him feel disgusting. Like he said he wanted me to tell him he had a really small penis. It's just not normal."

"No," I had to concede. "That's not really normal."

"Why did he have to wreck it? Everyone meets online now. Turning out to be nuts is such a cliché."

She threw her iPhone crossly onto the table, which knocked into the cappuccino and completely ruined my design on the froth.

"It's a zoo out there," she said, staring morbidly into space.

DIRECTION!

Tuesday 14 May 2013
1 p.m. Just nipped to Oxford Street, delighted to find that Mango, Topshop, Oasis, Cos, Zara, Aldo, etc., have all read the same edition of *Grazia* as me! Looking at the real-life clothes after so long looking at the websites was almost like seeing film stars in real life after seeing them in magazines. Now have full celebrity-at-airport outfit comprising skinny jeans, ballet pumps, shirt, blazer and sunglasses though not the—perhaps requisite—enormous overpriced handbag.

Wednesday 15 May 2013
Minutes wasted trying and failing to look like Red Carpet Girl 297, minutes spent putting navy silk dress back on 2, number of times worn navy silk dress in last year 137, cost per wearing of navy silk dress since purchase minus £3 per hour—therefore navy silk dress actually more profit-making than self. Which is good. Also Buddhist.

10 a.m. Just setting off for Greenlight meeting in new outfit! *The Leaves in His Hair* seems to be galloping on apace. A director is attached: "Dougie!" The meeting, as usual, is "exploratory," like at the dentist when you know you're going to end up being drilled.

10.15 a.m. Just caught sight of self in shop window. Look completely ridiculous. Who is this person in shirt buttoned up to neck and skinny jeans, which make thighs look fat? Am going to go back home and change into navy silk dress.

10.30 a.m. Back home. Am going to be late.

11.10 a.m. Bumped into George in the corridor as I was running hysterically along in the navy silk dress. Screeched to a halt, thinking George had come out of the meeting to tell me off for being late and always wearing the same outfit, but he just said, "Oh, *Leaves* meeting, right, right, sorry, conference call. I'll be with you in ten or fifteen."

11.30 a.m. It's much more relaxed, now, with Imogen and Damian, and we waited happily in the boardroom for George and Dougie, eating croissants, apples and miniature Mars bars. Tried to bring up skinny jeans issue but Imogen started talking about whether it was better to get clothes from Net-a-Porter in the fancy packaging, because it was so nice opening the black tissue paper, or to go for plain eco-packaging because it was easier to send them all back and also save the planet, and I tried to join in pretending I actually buy things off Net-a-Porter instead of just looking at them and going to Zara, when George BURST through the door, minus Dougie, with his usual "I'm on the move" swooping movement, and talking in his deep powerful voice, whilst clicking through his emails.

"The trouble with George is that he always seems to be

somewhere else," I started thinking piously, whilst feeling my phone vibrate. "He's always either just about to talk to someone else, or talking to someone else or emailing someone else or just getting on or off a plane." I glanced down to open my text, thinking, "Why? Why? Why can't George just be where he is? 'Oh, oh, look at me, I'm in the air, I'm a bird, why don't we all have breakfast in China?'"

Text was from Roxster.

<Shall I sneak round after the kids are in bed tonight? So I can give you another blow-by-blow account of last night's rugby?>

The whole George distraction issue means you have to fit everything you want to say to him into the length of—appropriately enough—a tweet. Though, actually, maybe that's good in some ways. You see, I've noticed that, whereas men, as they get older, get all grumpy and grunty, women start talking too much and gabbling on and repeating themselves. And, as the Dalai Lama says, everything is a gift, so maybe George being so busy is a way of teaching me not to gabble on but—

"Hello?" George loomed up right in front of me, jerking me back into the present moment.

"Hello," I said confusedly, quickly pressing "Send" on my text to Roxster. <Blowjob by blowjob?> Why was George saying "Hello?" when we'd already said hello in the corridor ten minutes ago?

"You're sitting there like this," said George, then did exactly the same imitation Billy does of me with a vacant expression and my mouth hanging open.

"I'm thinking," I said, turning off my phone, which emitted a quack. Hurriedly turned it back on. Or off.

"Well, don't," he said. "Don't think. Right. We'll have to make this quick, I'm just leaving for Ladakh."

You see! Ladakh?

"Oh! Are you making a film in Ladakh?" I asked innocently whilst preconceivedly judging him for going to Ladakh for NO REASON except to go to Ladakh, and glancing down to see who the quacking text was from.

"No," said George, busily looking in all his pockets for something. "No, it's not Ladakh, it's . . ." A panicked gleam came into his eyes. "Lahore. I'll be back in five."

He swept back out of the door, presumably to ask his assistant where he was actually going. Text was from Jude.

<He's just said he wants me to wee on him.>

Quickly texted Jude back.

<Everyone has their little "kinks." Maybe you could just do a modified version of making him feel disgusting, sometimes, as a special treat?>

Jude: <Like wee on him?>

Me: <No. Say: I am NOT prepared to wee on you, but I will . . .>

Suddenly two texts came in. The first was Jude's reply:

<"Tread on your balls?" That's one of the things he wants. I mean, it would puncture them.>

Clicked the other text, thinking maybe Roxster? It was from George.

<Are you interested in meeting your new director at all, or are you just going to sit here texting?>

Looked up and nearly choked. George had somehow got back into the boardroom without me noticing, and was sitting opposite with a small, hip-looking guy in a black shirt, greying stubble-beard and Steven Spielberg round glasses, but with one of those slightly raddled, alcoholic-looking faces, which is different from Steven Spielberg's cheery "I'd never have a facial peel but I look as though I have!" glow.

I blinked at them, then suddenly leaped to my feet, holding out my hand across the boardroom table with a gay smile.

"Dougieeeeeeeee! It's so nice to meet you at last. I've heard SO much about you! How are you? Have you come far?"

Why do I turn into a Girl Guide/Her Majesty the Queen whenever I feel uncomfortable?

Fortunately, just then George's assistant rushed in, looking flustered and whispered, "It's not Lahore, it's Le Touquet." At which George abruptly left, leaving Dougie and I to spend quite a lot of quality "exploring time." This consisted of me actually—for once!—being allowed to talk properly about the feminist themes in *Hedda Gabler*, while Imogen looked on with a fixed smile.

Dougie, on the other hand, seemed really enthusiastic. He kept shaking his head in admiration and saying, "Yup, you've got it." I really think Dougie is going to be an ally in making sure that *Leaves* (as we now simply call it) stays true to its basic heart.

However, after Dougie had left, miming two thumbs on a phone and saying, "We'll talk," the conversation almost seemed to turn against Dougie.

"He, like, *rurely* needs this," said Damian dismissively.

"*So* needs it," said Imogen. "Look, Bridget, this is absolutely, you know, lips-sealed, but I think we have an actress!"

"An actress?" I said excitedly.

"Ambergris Bilk," she whispered.

"Ambergris Bilk?" I said disbelievingly. Ambergris Bilk wanted to be in my movie? Oh. My. God.

"I mean, has she read it?"

Imogen gave me an indulgent, closed-mouth twinkly smile, the same sort of smile I use when telling Billy he's earned his Wizard101 crowns for emptying the dishwasher (though not, of course, licking the plates).

"She loves it," said Imogen. "The only thing is, she's not one hundred per cent sure about Dougie."

THE TROUBLE WITH OUTFITS

Thursday 16 May 2013

10.30 a.m. Mmmm. Another dreamy night with Roxster. Tried to engage him in conversation about the skinny-jeans issue but he had no interest in the matter whatsoever and said he liked me best with no clothes on.

11.30 a.m. Just had a "conference" call with George, Imogen and Damian, to talk about me meeting Ambergris Bilk, who is over in London. Love conference calls, and the ability they give one to mime throat-slitting and toilet-flushing actions whenever anyone says something which vaguely annoys you.

"So here's the thing," said George. There was a loud mechanical roar in the background.

"I think we've lost him," said Imogen. "Hang on."

Just had another look at *Grazia*. Scarf is the thing I am missing with the skinny-jeans look, clearly. A floaty bohemian scarf, double-looped round the neck. Hmm. Also what am I going to wear for Talitha's party? Maybe New Spring Whites? Gaah! They're back. Greenlight, I mean. Not New Spring Whites.

"Right," said George. "We want you to meet Ambergris and . . ."

"What?" I said, straining to hear above the roaring sound.

"I'm in a helicopter. We want you to meet Ambergris and we . . ."

He disappeared again. What was he about to say? Wee on her?

12.30 p.m. Imogen from Greenlight just called back to say that George wants me to talk to Ambergris Bilk about the script, but not to say anything negative about Hawaii because Ambergris is into Hawaii. "And," added Imogen coldly, "he wants you to make nice about Dougie."

Hooray, am going to meet an actual film star. I shall wear a floaty scarf!

5 p.m. Just got back from school run. It's true. I now realize *everyone* has floaty bohemian scarves double-looped round their neck. Is odd, though, when remember all the years Mum and Una spent trying to "get me into scarves" and I dismissed them as old-lady accessories rather like brooches. Now, is almost as if everyone has just read *Grazia* and said, like zombies indoctrinated by Red Carpet Girls, "I must wear a floaty bohemian scarf, I must wear a floaty bohemian scarf."

Friday 17 May 2013
Minutes getting dressed and groomed for school run 75.

5.45 a.m. Have got up an hour early to get styled and groomed for school run in manner of Stella McCartney, Claudia Schiffer or similar. Feel my look is marvellous, still with skinny jeans and ballet pumps, but now with floaty scarf looped round neck.

7 a.m. Woke Billy and helped Mabel up from bottom bunk. Just as was getting the clothes out of the wardrobe I realized Billy and Mabel were giggling.

"What?" I said, turning round to look at them. "What?"

"Mummy," said Billy, "why are you wearing a tea towel round your neck?"

9.30 a.m. Back from school run with latest edition of *Grazia*, and found an article headed: *"Is This the End of the Skinny Jean?"*

Am going to go back to dressing like the mother in *Good Luck Charlie*.

HEADY GLAMOROUS TIMES

Monday 20 May 2013

Film stars met 1, mini-breaks planned 1, parties about to go to with Roxster 1, rides in posh car 2, compliments from film star 5, calories consumed with film star 5476, calories consumed by film star 3.

2.30 p.m. Everything could not be better. I am about to be picked up in a "car" to go and meet Ambergris Bilk in the Savoy. Have tried on various versions of the skinny-jeans/scarf/shirt-buttoned-up-to-neck celebrity-at-airport look but finally have opted for the navy silk dress, even though it is becoming a little worn. Talitha has helped me order some dresses from Net-a-Porter for her party and have got a really nice one which is J.Crew and not that expensive.

Also in three weekends' time Roxster and I are going on a mini-break. A mini-break! Just the two of us, for the whole of Saturday afternoon, Saturday night and Sunday. Am so excited. Have not been on a mini-break for five years! Anyway, must get on with notes for meeting.

5.30 p.m. In car on way back from meeting. Was initially disappointed when Ambergris arrived, as had expected her to sweep in in skinny jeans, shirt buttoned up to the neck, blazer, floaty bohemian scarf and enormous overpriced handbag, so that I could see how it was done, and everyone would look at and admire us. Instead I hardly recognized her when she suddenly slunk into the booth wearing grey sweats and a baseball cap.

There was a sort of bonding prologue—which I am getting used to amongst women in the movie business—taken up with Ambergris complimenting me on my outfit, the fact that it was just the navy silk dress seeming irrelevant. I felt that I too must then compliment her on her sweats.

"They look so . . . sporty!" I gushed wildly, just as an absolutely enormous tea arrived on a three-tier cake stand. Ambergris took a tiny smoked-salmon sandwich and toyed with it for the rest of the conversation, during which I consumed the entire bottom layer of sandwiches, three scones with jam and clotted cream, a selection of miniature tarts and pastries, and both the free glasses of champagne.

Ambergris expressed awe and wonderment at my script, placing her hand on top of mine, saying, "I feel humbled."

Spirits soaring with the notion that my voice was really going to be coming to the fore, I moved on to making nice about Dougie: brushing over the anxieties Ambergris clearly shared with Damian and Imogen, that he "so needed it" and hadn't actually made anything which anyone had heard of.

"Dougie really understands my voice," I said, putting a reverential warmth into the word "Dougie." "You should do a meeting with Dougie." (I so have the lingo down now.)

It was agreed that Ambergris would do a meeting with Dougie and, all too quickly, it was time for Ambergris to go. I felt like we were best friends already. Also felt that was about to throw up from consuming an entire tea for two plus both of our glasses of champagne.

5.45 p.m. Just rang up Greenlight "from the car!" to boast about the success of the meeting, only to find that Ambergris has already called—from her car!—to say how intelligent and empathetic she thinks I am!

TALITHA'S PARTY

It was the hottest day of the year and the sun was still high when we met for Talitha's party. Roxster looked at his most gorgeous: in a white T-shirt, lightly tanned, a half-shadow outlining his jaw. The invitation said: "Casual Summer Party." Was slightly worried about New Spring Whites dress, even though Talitha had chosen it, but when Roxster saw me he said, "Oh, Jonesey. You look perfect."

"You look perfect too," I said enthusiastically, practically panting with lust. "Your outfit's absolutely *perfect.*" At which Roxster, who clearly had no idea what he was wearing, looked down, puzzled, and said, "It's just a pair of jeans and a T-shirt."

"I know," I said, giggling inwardly at the thought of Roxster's ripped torso in a sea of suits and panama hats.

"Do you think there'll be a full buffet or just finger food?"

"Roxster . . ." I said warningly. He nuzzled up to me with a kiss. "I'm only here for you, baby. Do you think it'll be hot dishes or just cold? Joke, joke, Jonesey."

We walked, hand in hand, along a narrow old brick passageway, emerging into a huge hidden garden: sunlight on a blue swimming pool, white armchairs and mattresses for lounging, and a yurt—the quintessential English summer party with just a hint of Moroccan boutique hotel.

"Shall I get us some food—I mean, drinks?"

I stood, lost, for a moment as Roxster trotted off in search of food, staring, scared, at the scene. It was that moment when you first arrive in a sea of people and your mind's all jangly and you can't recognize anyone you know. Suddenly felt I was wearing the wrong thing. I should have worn the navy silk dress.

"Ah, Bridget?" Cosmo and Woney. "Arriving all on your own again. Where are these 'boyfriends' we've heard so much about then, eh? Maybe we can find you one tonight."

"Yes," said Woney conspiratorially. "Binko Carruthers."

They nodded in the direction of Binko, who was looking around with his usual deranged expression, wild hair and plump body erupting at various points from, horrifyingly, instead of his usual crumpled suit, a pair of aquamarine flares and a psychedelic shirt with a frill down the front.

"He thought it said sixties birthday party, not sixtieth," giggled Woney.

"He said he'd be willing to take a look at you," said Cosmo. "Better get in quick, before he's hoovered up by desperate divorcees."

"Here you go, baby." Roxster appeared at my side, holding two large flutes of champagne in one hand.

"This is Roxby McDuff," I said. "Roxby, this is Cosmo and Woney."

There was a corresponding flicker in Roxster's hazel eyes at the names, as he handed me my glass.

"Pleased to meet you," he said cheerfully, raising his glass to Cosmo and Woney.

"Is this your nephew?" said Cosmo.

"No," said Roxster, pointedly putting his arm round my waist. "That would be a very odd relationship."

Cosmo looked as though the rug of his entire socio-sexual world view had been pulled from under him. His face was like a fruit machine with different ideas and emotions whizzing past, failing to find a final combination to rest on.

"Well," Cosmo said finally. "She's certainly looking blooming."

"I can see why," said Woney, staring at the muscled forearm round my waist.

Just then Tom came up overeagerly. "Is this Roxster? Hi. I'm Tom. Happy birthday." Adding, to Cosmo and Woney, "It's his thirtieth today! Ooh, there's Arkis, must run."

"Later, Tom," said Roxster. "I'm ravenous. Shall we get some food, honey?"

As we turned, he slid his hand to my bum, and kept it there as we walked towards the buffet.

Tom glided up again, now with Arkis in tow—who was every bit as handsome as his Scruff app photos. I grinned gleefully.

"I know, I know. I saw," said Tom. "You look revoltingly smug."

"It's been so terribly hard," I said in a quavering voice. "Don't I deserve a little happiness?"

"Just don't get too smug," he said. "Pride comes before a fall."

"You neither," I said, nodding at Arkis. "*Chapeau.*"

"Let's just enjoy, eh?" said Tom, and we clinked glasses.

It was one of those heady evenings: languid, humid, sunlight still dappling on the pool. People were laughing, drinking and lying on mattresses, sucking on chocolate-coated strawberries. I was with Roxster, Tom was with Arkis, Jude was on her third date with, now, a wildlife photographer from *Guardian* Soulmates, who actually looked nice and not at all like he wanted to wee on her, and Talitha was looking stunning, in a floor-length one-shoulder peach gown, carrying a little dog—which Tom thought was an *absurd* touch—and trailed by her doting Silver Fox Russian billionaire. She joined us as Tom, Jude and I stood by the pool with our respective amours. Tom attempted to pat Talitha's little chihuahua. "Did you get it from Net-a-Porter, darling?" At which it tried to bite him.

"She's a present from Sergei," breathed Talitha. "Petula! Isn't she adorable? Aren't you adorable, darling? Aren't you, aren't you, aren't you? You must be Roxster. Happy birthday."

"Happy birthday to both of you," I said, feeling tearful. There we were: the nucleus of Dating Centrale, the command centre of our emotional struggles, all, for once, happy and partnered up.

"It's a fantastic party," said Roxster, beaming, excited through a combination of food, champagne, Red Bull and vodka cocktails. "It's literally the best party I've ever, ever been to in my entire life. Literally, I've never been to a better party ever, ever. It's an absolutely brilliant party, and the food is—"

Talitha touched his lip with one finger. "You're adorable," she said. "I demand the first dance for our birthday."

One of the black-suited party planners was hovering in the background. He touched Talitha's arm and whispered something.

"Will you have her a minute, darling?" she said, holding out the little dog to me. "I must just talk to the band."

I've never really been sure about dogs, ever since I was rushed by Una and Geoffrey's miniature labradoodle when

I was six. Also, what about those pit bulls, which just ate a teenager? Somehow this anxiety must have communicated itself to Talitha's chihuahua, because, as I took hold of her, she barked, nipped my hand and leaped out of my arms. I stared, aghast, as she flew through the air, wriggling, light as a feather, up, up, then down, down, into the swimming pool, where she disappeared.

There was a split second of silence, then Talitha shrieked, "Bridget! What are you *doing*? She can't swim!"

Everyone stared as the little dog foundered to the surface in the middle of the pool, yapping, then disappeared under the water again. Suddenly, Roxster pulled his T-shirt over his shoulders, revealing his ripped torso. He dived straight into the pool, an arc of blue water, spray and muscle, then resurfaced, wet and glistening, at the other end of the pool having completely missed the dog, which took a last gulp of air, then sank. Roxster looked confused for a moment, then dived back under the water and emerged, holding a whimpering Petula. White teeth flashing in a grin, Roxster placed the little dog gently at Talitha's feet, put his hands on the edge of the pool, and hauled himself effortlessly out of the water.

"Jonesey," said Roxster. "We don't throw dogs."

"Oh my God," said Tom. "Oh. My. God."

Talitha was fussing over Petula. "My darling. My poor darling. You're all right now, you're all right."

"I'm sorry," I said. "She just jumped right out of my—"

"Don't apologize," said Tom, still staring at my boyfriend.

"Oh, my darling." Talitha was turning her attention to Roxster now. "My poor, brave darling. Let me help you out of those wet things—"

"Don't you dare re-dress him," growled Tom.

"Actually, I think I need another Red Bull," grinned Roxster. "With a vodka."

Talitha started dragging him off through the crowd, but he grabbed my hand and pulled me with him. The face that stayed with me from the sea of open mouths was Woney's.

Ushering Roxster into the house, Talitha turned to me and murmured, "Now that, my darling, is what I call rebranding."

More smartly dressed now, in one of the Silver Fox's immaculate outfits, Roxster seemed oblivious to his rebranding role, and more interested in the celebrities he could spot in the crowd, most of whom I'd never heard of. Darkness was falling, lanterns were giving a soft, twinkling glow, the guests were getting drunker, the band was playing, people were starting to dance. I was—though smug—worried that there was something slightly wrong about using Roxster to rebrand: though I hadn't deliberately used him, it had just happened. In fact, to tell the truth, I was actually falling helplessly in . . .

"Come on, let's dance, baby," said Roxster. "Let's do it."

He grabbed another vodka cocktail, a beer and a Red Bull, knocked them down, and asked for refills. Roxster was wild, he was exuberant. Roxster was, let's face it, rapidly becoming paralytic.

He bounded onto the dance floor, where everyone was doing generationally appropriate hip-shaking and jigging, some women standing with their legs apart and moving their shoulders provocatively. I had never actually seen Roxster dance before. The band was playing a Supertramp hit and I stared at him in astonishment, as a space cleared around him, and I realized that his chosen dance style was *pointing*. He knew all the words to Supertramp, he was singing along, strutting like John Travolta, pointing in every direction and then, right on cue, just before the instrumental break, pointing at the stage as if conducting the band. Noticing me jigging uncertainly on the spot, he grabbed my hand and gave me his drink, gesturing eagerly for me to down it. I glugged it in one, and joined in the pointing, giving in to the fact that Roxster was going to whirl me round unsteadily, bear-hug me, knock me over and fondle my bum, then point, with everyone watching. What was not to like?

Later I stumbled, feet clearly needing a bunion operation, off to the loo, and returned to find the dance floor empty—I thought. Except that Jude was standing, clearly out-of-her mind drunk, staring at the dance floor and smiling fondly. Roxster was dancing happily on his own, a Kronenbourg in one hand now, pointing cheerfully with the other.

"That was the best night of my entire life," he said to Talitha as we left, taking her hand and kissing it. "Literally the best food ever, ever, ever! And the party, of course. It was the best, you're the best . . ."

"I'm so glad you came. Thank you for saving my dog," breathed Talitha, like a gracious duchess. "Hope he's still up to it, darling," she murmured in my ear.

Once out in the street, and away from the departing guests, Roxster stopped in the lamplight and held both my hands, grinning, then kissed me.

"Jonesey," he whispered, looking into my eyes. "I . . ." He turned away and did a little dance. He was so drunk. He turned back and looked sad for a moment, then happy, then burst out, "I heart you. I've never said this to a woman before. I wish I had a time machine. I heart you."

If there is a God, I'm sure He has more to deal with, what with the Middle East crisis and everything, than giving tragic widows perfect nights of sex, but it did feel as though God had taken His mind off His other troubles that night.

The next morning, when Roxster had gone off to his rugby match and the children had been deposited at their respective magic and football parties, I climbed back into bed for an hour, savouring moments from the night before: Roxster emerging from the pool, Roxster in the lamplight, happy, saying, "I heart you."

Sometimes, though, when a lot of things happen all at once your mind gets confused and you can only dissect all the bits of information later.

"I wish I had a time machine."

It bubbled up through all the other words and images from the night before. The split second of sadness in his eyes, before he said, "I heart you . . . I wish I had a time machine."

It was the first time he had ever mentioned the age difference, apart from jokes about my knees and teeth. We had been caught up in the excitement, the exuberance of realizing that, in the flotsam and jetsam of cyberspace, we'd both found someone we really liked, and it wasn't just a one-night stand, or a three-night stand, it was a real connection full of affection and fun. But in his moment of inebriated joy he had given himself away. It mattered to him, and with that came the elephant in the room.

PART THREE

Descent Into Chaos

HORRIBLE NO-GOOD VERY BAD DAY

Tuesday 4 June 2013

134lb, calories 5822, jobs 0, toy boys 0, respect from production company 0, respect from schools 0, respect from nanny 0, respect from children 0, entire bags of cheese eaten 2, entire packets of oatmeal cookies eaten 1, entire large vegetables eaten 1 (a cabbage).

9 a.m. Mmm. Another highly erotic night with Roxster. Though at the same time, feel lurch of unease. Billy and Mabel weren't quite asleep when he arrived, and they came downstairs crying, because Billy said Mabel had thrown Saliva and "blinded" him in one eye. Took ages to get them back to sleep.

When I came down again, Roxster, not realizing I was there, looked a bit pissed off.

I said, "Sorry!" and he looked up and laughed in his usual merry way and said, "It just wasn't how I imagined I was going to be spending the evening."

Anyway, once the food was on the go he was back to normal. And it was dreamy. The bathroom chair and mirror really came into their own. And the mini-break is next weekend! We are going to find a pub in the country and go hiking and shagging and eating and everything! Chloe has done the school run so can get early start on *Leaves*—which is starting to look less like an impossible dream and more like a fantastic reality—a movie, written by me, starring Ambergris Bilk! So everything's fine. Definitely. Must just get on with rewriting it.

9.15 a.m. Mmmmm. Keep getting flashbacks to last night in the bathroom.

9.25 a.m. Just sent Roxster text saying: <Mmmmm. Was so lovely having you to stay.>

9.45 a.m. Only thing is, why hasn't he replied? "I wish I had a time machine." Oh God, why do I have all these images of myself that I immediately go to—like I'm a stalker, or a tragic deluded grandmother waddling around a discotheque in leggings and a sleeveless top with flappy arms, frizzy hair, a sticking-out stomach and a novelty tiara.

9.47 a.m. Right. Have got to pull self together, get up and get on. Cannot be floating around in lingerie having some completely unnecessary push-me-pull-you inner dialogue about why toy boy hasn't responded to text, when have screenplay to write and children to take responsibility and schedule things for.

But why hasn't he texted back?

9.50 a.m. Will check email.

9.55 a.m. Nothing. Just a forwarded email from George from Greenlight. Maybe something nice?

10 a.m. OMG. Just opened the forwarded email and detonated a bomb.

```
FWD:  Sender:  Ambergris  Bilk
To:  George  Katernis

Just  spoke  with  Dougie.  He's
sooooooooo  awesome.  Am  so  totally
Leaves  now.  So  glad  he's  on  the
same  page  about  putting  a  proper
screenwriter  on  it.
```

For a few moments I stared blankly at the screen.

"A proper screenwriter."

A PROPER SCREENWRITER?

Then I picked up a quarter of a cabbage which Chloe had for some reason left on the kitchen table (did she persuade them to eat some sort of cabbage recipe from the Gwyneth Paltrow cookbook for breakfast?), started shoving the cabbage into my mouth, biting at fronds, and walking very fast round the kitchen table dropping bits of cabbage down the front of my slip and onto the floor. There was a ping on the phone: Roxster.

<It was, wasn't it? But now I am very confused about our relationship. Terribly, terribly confused, baby.>

There was another ping on the text: Infants Branch.

<Mabel has a septic finger. Her nail is almost off. From the look of it, it must have been like this for several days.>

10.15 a.m. Calm and poised. Will simply open fridge, take out grated mozzarella and shove into mouth, along with more cabbage.

10.16 a.m. OK, is all in mouth now. Will just have swig of Red Bull to top it off. Oh! Telephone! Maybe Roxster regretting the text?

11 a.m. Was Imogen from Greenlight. "Bridget. There's been a terrible mistake. George has just forwarded you an email in error. Could you possibly delete it before you . . . Bridget? Bridget??"

Was not able to reply owing to contents of mouth. Rushed over to the sink and spurted out the Red Bull, grated mozzarella and cabbage, just as Chloe appeared at the top of the stairs. I turned round and grinned at her, bits of the cabbage and grated mozzarella falling from my teeth, like a vampire caught eating a person.

"Bridget? Bridget?" Imogen was still saying into the phone.

"Yes?" I said, waving a cheery hello at Chloe, whilst trying to spray the sink with the extendable tap to get rid of the cheese and cabbage.

"Have you heard about Mabel's finger?" whispered Chloe. I nodded calmly and gesticulated towards the phone under my chin. As I listened to Imogen, repeating the story about the inadvertently-forwarded-by-George email, my eye was caught by the newspaper, still folded where Roxster had been reading it.

The Tragic Fate of the Toy Boy

by Ellen Boschup

Suddenly there are more toy boys everywhere! As the advances of medical science preserve the appearance of youth, and more and more middle-aged women are devoting their time and resources to doing just that, more and more are turning to "the younger man"—Ellen Barkin, Madonna and Sam Taylor-Wood to name but a few. For these older, preying women, or "cougars" as they are appropriately known, the advantages are obvious: youth; vigorous, energetic, frequent, satisfying sex; and the sort of baggage-free companionship they would never find in their sagging, balding, middle-aged male counterparts, too idle and self-absorbed to fight the advances of the years.

"Bridget?" Imogen was still saying. "Are you all right? What's going on? Earth-to-Bridget. Bridget? Net-a-Porter? Mini Mars bars?"

"No! Super! Thanks for letting me know. I'll call you later. Bye!"

I clicked off the phone and returned, reeling, to the article.

For the young, defenceless boys who are
their prey, it may seem like an attractive trade. These women, when the lights
are off, anyway, seem impressively pre-
served. Like pickled lemons. There's no
pressure over babies, no demands on the
toy boy to succeed at his career. Instead
there is a gateway into a glamorous,
sophisticated world beyond his wildest
dreams. The benefit of an experienced
lover, a woman who knows what she wants
in bed, who enhances his reputation—
an entrée into society, and access to
luxury travel. Where's the downside?
When he's drunk his fill, he can simply
leave his cougar to fall ravenously on
her next unsuspecting prey. However, as
more and more of these Unfortunates are
discovering . . .

"Everything all right, Bridget?" said Chloe.

"Yes, super. Could you go upstairs and tidy Mabel's
drawers, please?" I said with an unaccustomed air of calm
authority.

Once Chloe had gone, I lunged at another piece of
cabbage, continuing to read as I shoved it into my mouth
along with a piece of Nicorette.

. . . far from leaving when they choose,
and moving on enhanced, these abused
boys are left broken and sexually

exhausted, self-esteem in tatters, with a key phase of their career and family-building life wasted. But hang on a minute! Some of these youths, it is true, like Ashton Kutcher, use their cougar as a kingmaker to advance their own careers and profiles. Far more of them, however, are abandoned, back in their sordid flats and bedsits, scorned by their friends, family and colleagues for consorting with women old enough to be their grandmothers, dumped back in their own world which now seems devoid of a glamour they will never . . .

I slumped at the table, head on my arms. Bloody Ellen Boschup. Don't these people realize what harm they cause with their glib social generalizations? Plucking bogus phenomena and flimsy constructs out of the air at meetings—"Whatever Happened to the Dining Room?" "Suddenly There Are More Dining Rooms Everywhere!!"—then writing sententious social commentary as if it's the conclusion to years of in-depth research rather than 1200 words to file on a deadline, ruining people's lives and relationships, based on something they overheard in the gastropub and a couple of blurry photographs in *Heat* magazine.

"Should I go and pick up Mabel and take her to the doctor?" asked Chloe. "Are you all right, Bridget?"

"No, no, I'll . . . go and get her," I said. "Could you text the school and tell them I'll be there in a mo?"

I walked insouciantly into the toilet and slumped, mind racing. If only there was just one thing to deal with. Roxster's "confusion," the horrible article, the "proper screenwriter" or the septic-finger shame I could probably handle individually but not all at the same time. Clearly the septic finger had to take precedence, but could I allow anyone to see me in such a disturbed state? If I picked Mabel up like this, wild-eyed and bonkers, and took her to the doctor, would the school or the doctor put her into care?

Equilibrium was what I needed. I needed to clear my mind, because, as it says in *How to Stay Sane*, the mind is plastic.

I took some deep breaths in and out and went, "Maaaaa," to pray to the mother of the universe.

I looked at myself in the mirror. It really wasn't good. I washed my face, straightened my hair with my fingers, emerged from the toilet and walked past Chloe with a gracious, lady-of-the-house smile, glossing over the fact that I was still dressed in a slip at eleven in the morning and she may have just heard me saying "Maaaaa" in the toilet.

1 p.m. Mabel seemed quite excited about the finger. It actually wasn't as bad as they'd made out, but still, it was hard to see how a responsible mother could have missed it if it really had been like that all the time.

At the doctor's, stood in front of the two receptionists for four minutes while they calmly continued to type as if a) I wasn't there and b) they were both writing contemplative poems. In the meantime Mabel was trotting happily around the waiting room, and picking up leaflets from the plastic wall display.

"I'm going to weed!" she said, and started reading out, "Guh oh nuh oh ruh."

"Well done, darling," I said, finally sitting down and desperately checking my texts to see if Greenlight or Roxster or indeed anyone had anything to say to make me feel better.

"Guh, oh, nuh, oh, ruh, ruh, huh, oh, eh, ah."

"So clever!" I murmured.

"Gonorrhoea!" she shouted triumphantly, opening the leaflet. "Oh, there's pictures! Weed Gonorrhoea to me?"

"Oh! Hahaha!" I said, grabbing the leaflets and stuffing them in my handbag. "Let's see if there are some more lovely leaflets," I said, staring glassily at an array of them in a variety of cheery colours: "*Syphilis*," "*Non-Specific Urethritis*," "*Male and Female Condoms*" and—rather late in the day—"*Pubic Lice*."

"Let's play with the toys!" I trilled.

"I can't believe I didn't notice it," I said, when we finally got in to the doctor.

"They can flare up in a few moments," the doctor said supportively. "She just needs some antibiotics and she'll be fine."

After the doctor's we went and bought some Disney Princess plasters from the chemist, and Mabel decided she wanted to go back to school.

2 p.m. Just got home, relieved to have house to self, and sat down to . . . What, though? Work? But I've been sacked, haven't I? Everything looks dark and gloomy.

Oh, wait, am still wearing prescription sunglasses again.

3.15 p.m. Just spent twenty minutes staring melodramatically into space, trying not to imagine shooting myself like Hedda Gabler, then started googling skull or dagger pendants on Net-a-Porter instead. Then suddenly realized with a start it was time for Mabel and Billy's school pickup.

6 p.m. I was in a complete flap when Mabel and I got to Billy's school because we were late, and I had to go to the office first about Billy's bassoon lessons. "Have you got the form?" said Valerie, the school secretary. Started rifling through the mess that was my handbag, putting papers down on the counter.

"Ah, Mr. Wallaker," said Valerie.

I looked up and there he was, smirking as usual.

"Everything going well?" he said, still looking down at the mess. I followed his gaze. *"Syphilis—Looking After Your Sexual Health." "Gonorrhoea—Signs and Symptoms." "Sexual Health Direct! A User's Guide."*

"They're not mine," I said.

"Right, right."

"They're Mabel's!"

"Mabel's! Well, in that case, that's fine." He was actually shaking with mirth now. I grabbed the leaflets and stuffed them back in my bag.

"Hey!" said Mabel. "Dothe are my leafletth. Give them to me!"

Mabel reached into my bag and grabbed *"Gonorrhoea—Signs and Symptoms."* I tried, undignified, to snatch it back, but Mabel wasn't letting go.

"They're *my* leafletth," said Mabel accusingly, adding, for effect, "Dammit!"

"And they're very useful leaflets," said Mr. Wallaker, bending down. "Why don't you take this one as well and give the rest to Mummy?"

"Thank you, Mr. Wallaker," I said firmly but pleasantly, then, nose in the air, swept off graciously towards the school gates, nearly tripping over Mabel on the steps, but nevertheless making a reasonably elegant exit.

"Bridget!" roared Mr. Wallaker suddenly, as if I was one of the boys. I turned, startled. He had never called me Bridget before.

"Haven't you forgotten something?"

I stared at him blankly.

"Billy?" He turned to Billy who was trotting up, looking at Mr. Wallaker with a conspiratorial grin. They both looked at me, smirking.

"She even forgets to get up sometimes," said Billy.

"I bet," said Mr. Wallaker.

"Come along, children!" I said, trying to regain my dignity.

"Yeth, Mother," said Mabel with an unmistakable dollop of irony which was, frankly, annoying in one so small.

"Thank you, Daughter," I said smoothly. "Hurry along! Goodbye, Mr. Wallaker."

When we got home, Billy and I slumped on the sofa as Mabel played happily with her sexual health leaflets.

"I got rubbish marks for my homework," said Billy.

"I got rubbish marks for my screenwriting."

I showed him the email about the "proper screenwriter." Billy handed me his art book with his colouring of Ganesha the Elephant God and the teacher's notes:

"*I like your mix of yellow, green and red on his head. However, I am not sure that the multicoloured ears quite work.*"

We stared at each other dolefully, then both started giggling.

"Shall we have an oatmeal cookie?" I said.

We got through the whole packet, but it's just like eating muesli, right?

OVERSTUFFED LIVES

Wednesday 5 June 2013

134lb, hours in day 24, hours required to do all things supposed to do in day 36, hours spent worrying about how to fit in all things supposed to do in day 4, number of things supposed to have done actually done 1 (go to toilet).

2 p.m.

LIST OF JOBS

*Put washing on

*Respond to Zombie Apocalypse invite

*Call Brian Katzenberg about the Ambergris Bilk email

*Blow up bike

*Grated cheese

*Figure out weekend: Saturday afternoon is Atticus's African drumming party for Billy but Bikram's mum says she will do pickup or drop-off if we do the other, then Cosmata's Build-A-Bear party for Mabel on Sun at the same time as Billy's football. Figure out who is going to pick kids up from which party with Jeremiah's mum and Cosmata's mum and also ask Jeremiah's mum if Jeremiah wants to come to football.

*Call Mum (my mum)

*Call Grazina and see if she can fill in gaps at weekend, then check trains to Eastbourne

*Figure out what to do re Roxster mini-break

*Find bank card

*Find Virgin remote

*Find telephone

*Lose 3lb

*Respond to mass emails re Sports Day vegetables

*Find out if still supposed to go to Greenlight meeting tomorrow

*Greek or Roman myth party/photo

*Half-leg and bikini wax in case mini-break still on

*"Ic" Suffix Family "crest"

*Core Stability

*Fill in form about Billy's bassoon lessons and take to school

*Find bassoon form

*Toilet light bulb

*Exercise on exercise bike (clearly this is not going to happen)

*Send back Net-a-Porter dress that didn't wear for Talitha's party

*Find out why fridge is making that noise

*Find and destroy Mabel's gonorrhoea leaflets

*Find end scene from draft 12 about scuba-diving

*Teeth

Oh God. All these jobs will not actually fit into an hour, which is now twenty minutes.

OK. Am simply going to do "Quadrant Living" like it says in *The Seven Habits of Highly Effective People* and simply arrange the jobs into "four quadrants":

IMPORTANT URGENT

*~~Respond to Zombie Apocalypse~~
*Go to toilet
*~~Call Brian Katzenberg about the Ambergris Bilk e-mail~~
*Half-leg and bikini wax in case mini-break on
*Blow up bike
*Grated cheese
*Teeth
*~~Eyebrows~~
*~~Grated cheese~~
*Figure out what to do about Roxster and the mini-break
*Respond to 3c school mum mass emails about Sports Day picnic
*Call Grazina and see what time she can start on Saturday, then google romantic country pubs
*~~Arrange to send back Net a Porter dress that didn't wear for Talitha's party~~
*Find out where Cosmas lives

IMPORTANT NOT URGENT

*Exercise on exercise bike, clearly this is not going to happen
*Find form about Billy's bassoon lessons, fill in and take to school
*~~Call Jeremiah's mum~~
*Call Mum (my mum)
*Deal with social emails
*~~Arrange to send back Net a Porter dress that didn't wear for Talitha's party~~
*Figure out who is going to pick kids up from which party with Jeremiah's mum and Cosmata's mum and also ask Jeremiah's mum if Jeremiah wants to come to football.
*Grated cheese
*~~Teeth~~
*Eyebrows
*Ancient myth party photo

NOT IMPORTANT URGENT

*Respond to Zombie Apocalypse
*Find Virgin remote
*Find Visa card
*~~Find Teeth~~
*Find telephone
*Lose 3lbs
*Find and destroy Mabel's gonorrhoea leaflets
*~~Figure out who is going to pick kids up from which party with Spartacus's mum and Cosmata's mum and also ask Jeremiah's mum if Bikram wants to come to football.~~
*Figure out schedule for weekend
*Saturday afternoon is Atticus's African drumming party for Billy but Bikram's mum says she will do pick-up or drop-off if we do the other, then Mabel's Bear party with Cosmata's for Mabel on Sun at the same time as Billy's football.
*John Lewis kettle

NOT IMPORTANT NOT URGENT

*Find out whether am still supposed to go to Greenlight meeting tomorrow
*~~Grated cheese~~
*Call Bikram's mum
*Put washing in
*Call Brian Katzenberg about the Ambergris Bilk email
*Dance Fever
*~~Respond to 3c school mum mass e-mails about Sports Day picnic~~
*Find bassoon form
*Fix Core Stability
*Book dentist's appointment for Billy and Mabel
*~~Call Mum (my Mum)~~
*Arrange to send back Net-a-Porter dress that didn't wear for Talitha's party
*Go to toilet

2.45 p.m. You see. Much better!

2.50 p.m. Perhaps will go to the toilet. That is at least one of them.

2.51 p.m. Right, have been to the toilet now.

2.55 p.m. Oooh! Doorbell!

I opened the door, and Rebecca from across the road fell into the hallway, wearing a tiara, mascara smeared under her eyes, staring into space, clutching a list and a polythene bag full of egg sandwiches.

"Do you want a fag?" she said, in a strange, other-worldly voice. "I can't go on."

We went downstairs and slumped, staring into space, sucking on our fags like fishwives.

"The annual Latin play," she said in a strange, disconnected voice.

"Staff presents," I concurred dully. "Zombie Apocalypses." Then burst into a coughing fit as have not had a fag for five years apart from two puffs on a joint at Leatherjacketman's party.

"I think I'm having a full-on breakdown without anyone actually noticing," said Rebecca.

Suddenly leaped to my feet, stubbing out the fag, in inspirational frenzy.

"It's just a question of prioritizing into quadrants. Look!" I said, thrusting my quadrant sheet under her nose.

She stared at the form, then burst into hysterical high-pitched giggles like someone in a mental hospital.

I suddenly had a brainwave. "It's a State of Emergency!" I said excitedly. "A cut-and-dried State of Emergency. Once a State of Emergency is declared, normal service is suspended and you don't have to expect anything to be all right and you just need to do whatever you need to do to get through the emergency."

"Great!" said Rebecca. "Let's have a drinky. Just a little teensy-weensy one."

I mean, it was only half a glass and really everything suddenly seemed much better, till she leaped up saying, "Oh my bloody God and fuck. I'm supposed to be on the school run," and ran out of the door, just as Roxster texted: <You've gone awfully quiet, Jonesey.>

Rebecca then reappeared for her egg sandwiches just as I remembered I was supposed to be on the school run as well. Ran upstairs, then downstairs, looking for the rice cakes, simultaneously texting Roxster: <I'm just confused by your text saying you're confused.>

3.30 p.m. Back in car now. Oh, shit, have forgotten rice cakes.

Gaah, text from Roxster.

<Just a panic attack. Shall I call you tonight to discuss, my Precious Cornish Pasty?>

HE'S having a panic attack?

Ended up rushing from car to school in ungainly half-walking, half-running gait in middle of which Scandinavian tourists chose me—for unexplained reasons—to ask for directions. Panicking that they were trying to steal my time, I carried on walking determinedly whilst gesturing directions back to them. Oh God. Have let down country by being inhospitable to foreigners (though Scandinavia is in EU, I think?). But what is world coming to when one is more scared of passers-by stealing one's time than one's handbag?

9.30 p.m. No phone call from Roxster.

Oh God, oh God, he's going to call and break up with me for not having a time machine.

10 p.m. Hate it when people delay phone calls because you know they are putting it off as they have to say what you don't want to hear. Though Roxster hates phone calls anyway because I do too much talking and will not delay talking until the morning. Oh, phone call! Roxster!

10.05 p.m. "Oh, hello, darling." My mother. "Do you know, Penny Husbands-Bosworth has started lying about her age—she says she's eighty-four. It's completely ridiculous. Pawl, you know, the pastry chef, says she's just doing it so everyone will say how young she looks and . . ."

10.09 p.m. Have managed to get Mum off phone but now feel guilty and also think maybe Roxster called while she was . . . Oooh! Text!

10.10 p.m. Was from Chloe.

<Just firming up the details for weekend. So I'll do Sat morning till Grazina arrives, then Grazina will watch Mabel while Bikram's mum takes Billy to African drum-

ming party, then on to Ezekiel's Ancient Myth one (shall I do Greek myth photo—any particular god/costume? Greek or Roman?). Then Grazina will do till 5 on Sunday, drop Billy at football and do both Mabel pickups from Cosmata's Build-A-Bear party with Billy. I'll take over at 5 . . . The only thing is I need to leave at 6 to go to a t'ai chi event with Graham . . .>

Aaaaaargh! How has child-rearing got so . . . so complicated? Is as if you have to keep them on some sort of permanent high of engagement and happiness.

10.30 p.m. Suddenly enraged with Roxster, blaming the whole socio-global child-rearing dysfunctional collapse on him. "BLOODY Roxster! Me and Chloe have had to arrange all this complex matrix of African drummers and bears and extra people taking care of the children because of Roxster, and now will have nowhere to go and no one to see, simply because of Roxster. Will be like a . . . like a GIANT CUCKOO, de trop in own house ALL BECAUSE OF ROXSTER!"—conveniently overlooking the fact that it was me who had wanted to go on the childcare-demanding mini-break in the first place.

10.35 p.m. Impulsively sent positively glacial text to Roxster, saying: <Could you kindly let me know whether or not you wish to go on the mini-break this weekend? I have a number of matters to resolve if we are still intending to go.>—then immediately regretted it as totally non–*Zen and the Art of Falling in Love* and hideous, anal and mean-spirited tone. Can completely see why Roxster might be having doubts as is twenty-one-year age difference, especially if adopting anal tone.

10.45 p.m. Muted text came back from Roxster.

<I would, Jonesey, but just a little concerned about what will happen next.>

Impulsively sent back: <But the mini-break is all set up now and it's the first chance we've had to go away together on our own and it will be so romantic and . . . and everything.>

A few minutes' wait—then a texting ping.

<OK, fuck it! Sod the panic attack, baby, let's do it!>

Yayyy! We're going on a mini-break.

11 p.m. Talitha just called to see what was happening and said, "Careful, darling. Once they have wobbles like that, they're not just enjoying the moment any more, they're thinking about the long term. And Roxster's far too young to know what a disastrous mistake that is."

Feel like putting hands over ears saying, "Lalalala, don't care. You only live once. We're going on a mini-break! Hurrah!"

Thursday 6 June 2013

9.30 a.m. Got back from school run. Turned on email to deal with the school Sports Day picnic and detonated:

Sender: Brian Katzenberg
Subject: Forwarded email

Yes, you are fired. But they
still want you in the mix.
They're going to set up a
meeting with the new writer. The
movie business!

A new writer? Already? How could they possibly have
found one so quickly?

Phone quacked.

Roxster: <Um, can you find anywhere to stay because
I can't? Everywhere's booked.>

Jerked into action in a frenzy of googling country pubs on
LateRooms.com to find absolutely everything was booked up.

We are like Mary and Joseph with no room at the Inn
except that rather than about to give birth to the Son of
God am about to be broken up with by Joseph.

10 a.m. Just texted Tom who texted back five minutes later.

<LateRooms.com have a treehouse with a terrace
attached to the Chewton Glen hotel.>

10.05 a.m. Oh. Just checked the treehouse. It's £875 a
night.

10.15 a.m. Yayy! Have found a room in a pub.

10.20 a.m. Oh, just called them. It's the Bridal Suite.
Texted Roxster.

<Have found room on river in Oxfordshire.>

<You're ver, ver clever, darling. Do they do Full English Breakfast?>

<Yes. But just one thing.>

<What? It's not either/or with the bacon and sausages?>

<No. But . . . I'm going to have to say it quickly. It's the Bridal Suite.>

<I knew it. That's what you wanted all along. Do they definitely do Full English?>

<*Sighs* Yes, Roxster, they do.>

<So train to Oxford. Get married quickly in Oxford. Then taxi to the pub?>

<Yup.>

<I'll get a ring at lunchtime when I pop out for my sandwich.>

<Shhh. I'm on Net-a-Porter. Dresses: bridal.>

10.45 a.m. No reply. Oh God. Maybe he thinks I'm serious?

<So what do you think?> I braved.

Then decided to give him a way out in case he really just wanted a relaxing setting for the full break-up.

<Or we could just go somewhere close and do a day trip?>

Held my breath . . .

<I say full-on mini-break, Jonesey. I'm fantasizing about it already.>

<Am I in the fantasies at all, or just the food?>

<*Googling menu* Of course you are, my little chicken and mushroom puffball.>

337

11 a.m. Feeling suddenly light and giddy, I booked the room and texted: <I just called them and they said you do actually have to take a marriage certificate.>

Long pause, then . . .

<You're joking, right?>

<Roxster, you are so easy to wind up.>

MINI-BREAK OR BREAK-UP?

Saturday 8 June 2013

Texting has been more high-spirited than ever with Roxby McDuff, full of plans for our trip, so maybe it was just a wobble brought on by the Ellen Boschup toy-boy article, and he is in the Present Moment and everything is all right.

But anyway had better finish packing or will miss train. Ooh, text from Roxster.

<Jonesey?>

Was he going to cancel?

<Yes, Roxster?> I texted nervously.

<*On one knee* Will you be my wife?>

Stared at the phone. What was going on?

<Roxster, is this to do with the food in the prenup?>

<It says I'm due a Full English with eggs, bacon, mushrooms and flambeed sausages every Sunday. Marry me?>

Thought carefully, then, suspecting a trick, I texted:

<The thing is, if we get married, won't that somehow seem like I'm getting too serious?>

<Dunno. I was only thinking about the food.>

Sunday 9 June 2013

Mini-breaks 1, shags 7, alcohol units 17, calories 15,892, weight 193lb (including, feels like, 60lb small animal).

Mini-break was heaven. It was ambrosia. We carried on the marriage joke all weekend. It was balmy, sunny weather and it was blissful being away from the noise and to-do lists. Roxster was at his most cheerful and merry. The pub was tiny, in a hidden valley by a little river. The Bridal Suite was in a separate barn, painted white, with a sloping ceiling and rough wooden beams, and windows on two sides, one side looking straight onto the river and, beyond, a water meadow. Tried to block out memories of Bridal Suite for my real wedding with Mark. But started laughing when Roxster carried me over the threshold, pretending to stagger under the weight, and flung me on the bed.

The windows were open and all you could hear was the river, birds, and sheep in the distance. We had sleepy dreamy sex, then slept for a while. Then we walked along the river and found a little ancient chapel, where we pretended to get married and that the cows were our wedding guests. Eventually we came to another pub, and drank too much beer to quench our thirst and topped it with wine. There was no talk about breaking up. I did tell Roxster about being sacked from *Leaves* and he was so sweet and said they were all mad, and didn't appreciate my rare genius, and he was going to fight them with his beefy arms. Then we ate a meal so gigantic that afterwards I could hardly move. I had this huge . . . thing in my stomach . . . it felt like being pregnant with a strange creature with very protuberant arms and legs.

We went outside to try and walk it off. There was a full moon, and I suddenly thought about Mabel: "There'th the moon. It followth me." I thought about Mark, and all the times the moon had followed us, and all the years when I was sure, sure that he would always be there and that there wasn't heartbreak ahead, just years of being together, stretching before us.

"You all right, baby?" said Roxster.

"I feel like I've eaten a Bambi," I laughed, to cover the moment.

"I feel like I want to eat you," said Roxster. He put his arm round my shoulders and everything felt fine again. We walked along the river a bit, then got into a bog, and decided it was too dark and too far and went back to the pub and rang for a taxi.

When we got home to the room, the windows were wide open, and the room was filled with the scent of blossom and the gentle sound of the river. Unfortunately, though, the Bambi was so huge that all I could do was put on my slip and lie face downwards on the bed, feeling as though there was a massive dent beneath me in the mattress containing the Bambi. Then suddenly a dog started barking, really loudly, right outside the window. It just wouldn't stop. Then the Bambi eased itself slightly and embarrassingly by letting out an enormous fart.

"Jonesey!" said Roxster. "Was that a fart?"

"Maybe just a teensy-weensy little pfuff of Bambi," I said sheepishly.

"Little pfuff? It was more like a plane taking off. It's even silenced the dog!"

It had. But then the bloody dog started barking again. It was like being on a housing estate on the outskirts of Leeds.

"I'll give you something to take your mind off it, baby," said Roxster.

Mmmmmmmmmmmmmmmmmmmmmmmmmmmmmmmm mmmmmmmmmmmmmm.

10 p.m. Back in London now. Blissful. Got home at six feeling like a new woman. Children seemed to have had a really good time and I was delighted to see them again, and was so full of *joie de vivre* and bonhomie that even a Sunday evening, with the panic of forgotten homework, passed in a golden joy of 50s-style hearth and home. *Better, Easier Parenting?* Just get laid a lot.

Ooh, text.

Roxster: <Married life is pretty nice, don't you think, honey?>

Hmm. Suspected a trick. Still wary from the whole confusion/panic attack thing.

Me: <*Farts* Not catching me out being lovey-dovey.>

Roxster: <*Sobs*>

Me: <*Evil cackle* I didn't heart the weekend at all, honestly.>

Roxster: <Not even a teensy-weensy little bit?>

Me: <Well, maybe a minuscule bit only detectable to human eye using nit comb.>

Roxster: <Was it your least favourite Jonesey/Roxster outing of all time, then?>

Me: <If I say no, will you have a panic attack?>

Roxster: <Now that we're married my panic attacks have totally disappeared.>

Me: <You see?>

Roxster: <Do you think it's fair to say I work in Philanthropy on my CV?>

Me: <You mean by marrying me?>

Roxster: <Yes. I could say I'm working for Help the Aged.>

Me: <Bog off.>

Roxster: <Oh, Jonesey. Nighty-night, darling.>

Me: <Nighty-night, Roxster.>

IS IT SNOW OR IS IT BLOSSOM?

Tuesday 11 June 2013

133lb, days since any communication from Roxster 2, amount of day spent worrying about lack of communication from Roxster 95%, mass emails re Sports Day chopped vegetables 76, spam emails 104, combined minutes late for school pickups 9, number of sides on a pentagon (unknown).

2 p.m. Very weird weather—is freezing cold and little white things swirling about. Cannot be snow, surely—is June. Maybe is blossom? But so much of it.

2.05 p.m. Roxster has not called or texted since Sunday night.

2.10 p.m. It is snow. But not nice snow like in the winter. Is strange snow. Presumably world about to end through global warming. Think will go to Starbucks.

Though really ought to find somewhere other than Starbucks that does ham-and-cheese paninis in protest at whole tax-avoidance thing, though maybe irrelevant as world about to end anyway.

2.30 p.m. Mmm. Feel much jollier about everything, now am in world full of people and coffee and ham-and-cheese paninis all huddling together cosy from the cold. The weird unnatural snow has stopped and everything seems normal again. Honestly! Getting in such a stew about everything. Think will text Roxster. I mean, I haven't texted him since Sunday night either, have I?

<Did you know there are 493 calories in a Ham and Cheese panini?>

Roxster: <Busy morning, baby?>

Me: <*Types* Roxster's beefy shoulders glistened in the dappling sunlight like, like . . . beefy shoulders.>

Roxster: <Have you turned to writing Mills & Boon, my precious?>

Me: <*Calmly continues typing* An enormous fart emerged from his bum, which quivered in the blossom-scented air . . .>

Roxster has not replied. Ooh, text.

Was Jude.

<Am on 7th date with Wildlifephotographerman. Does this mean we are going out?>

Texted back: <Yes! You've really earned it. You go, girl!> which wasn't the sort of expression I usually use, but never mind.

2.55 p.m. Still Roxster has not replied. Hate this. Am so confused. And have to pick kids up in half an hour and be all cheerful. OK, have a few minutes to deal with Sports Day emails.

Sender: Nicolette Martinez
Subject: Sports Day Picnic

Sent from my Sony Ericsson
Xperia Mini Pro

We need picnic items for boys/
parents for our class. I've
filled in the parents who have
already volunteered.
Juices: Dagmar
Sliced carrots, radishes and
peppers (red and yellow): ?
Sandwiches: Atsuko Fujimoto
Crisps: Devora
Water: ???
Fruits: ??
Melon balls and strawberries: ?
Cookies (no nuts please!):
Valencia
Black bin liners: Scheherazade
Let us know what you plan to
bring. Thank you.
Please let's all bring picnic
blankets if we have them.

Thanks, Nicolette

Sender: Vladlina Koutznestov
Subject: Re: Sports Day Picnic

I'll bring fruits-probably some
berries and cut-up melons.

Sender: Anzhelika Sans Souci
Subject: Re: Sports Day Picnic

I'll bring sliced carrots, and
radishes. Could someone else do
red and yellow peppers?
Anzhelika
PS Should someone bring paper
cups?

Farzia, Bikram's mum, just forwarded me an email
she'd—in a moment of utter madness—sent to Nicolette.

Sender: Farzia Seth
Subject: Re: Sports Day Picnic

Do you think we all need picnic
blankets-won't a few between us
be fine?

And the one she'd got back from Nicolette, with a note
from Farzia saying, "Shoot me now!"

Subject: Re: Sports Day Picnic

Definitely not. We should all
bring picnic blankets. With two
boys at the school, I do have
some experience of this!

Light-headed and devil-may-care now, I emailed Farzia
"Watch this" and sent:

Sender: Bridget Billymum
Subject: Re: Sports Day Picnic

I'll bring the vodka. We drink
it neat without mixers, all
agreed?

Group email came instantly back.

Sender: Nicolette Martinez
Subject: Re: Sports Day Picnic

Vodka is NOT a good idea at
Sports Day, Bridget. Or ciga-
rettes. Could you manage the red
and yellow peppers? Possibly?
In strips so they'll work with
the dips? It is actually quite
a difficult job organizing the
Sports Day Picnic.

Oh, shit. In the middle of it all suddenly saw email from Imogen at Greenlight.

Sender: Imogen Faraday,
Greenlight Productions
Subject: Ambergris's Notes

Dear Bridget,

Just checking that you got the
notes from Ambergris on the
script for tomorrow's meeting
to meet Saffron. Could you
confirm that you can be at the
meeting to give your notes on
Ambergris's notes for Saffron?

Hope you're not about to slash
your wrists, because I am.

Imogen x

What meeting? What notes? Who is "Saffron"?

Spooled frantically through morass of emails about Sports Day fruits and vegetables, Zombie Apocalypse, Ocado, ASOS, Net-a-Porter, Mexican Viagra, etc., then realized it was time to pick up Mabel.

4.30 p.m. Mabel and Billy just had argument all the way home over whether a triathlon with five sports was called a Quintathlon or Pentathlon.

"It is!"

"It isn't."

Tried to work out feebly how many sides a pentagon had or remember what five was in Latin, and ended up nearly crashing the car and yelling, "Look, will you just shut up?!" then going into paroxysms of guilt while they started on what the five sports were and Mabel said one of them was "Tape measuring."

"Tape measuring?" Billy said incredulously, at which Mabel burst into tears and said, "Dey do do tape measuring."

9.15 p.m. Just read article in the paper about David Cameron saying he keeps getting calls from heads of state when the kids are in the back of the car, recounting putting his hand over the receiver and hissing, "Look, will you SHUT UP?" while talking to the Israeli Prime Minister.

So maybe it isn't just me.

FRANTIC

Wednesday 12 June 2013

8 a.m. Right. Greenlight meeting is at nine so have managed to get Chloe to do school run, and then I will do school pickup instead.

8.10 a.m. Just have to wash hair and get dressed.

8.15 a.m. Disaster. Navy silk dress is at the dry-cleaner's and forgot to ask Chloe to get mountain of red and yellow peppers ready for tomorrow, and still have to wash hair.

8.45 a.m. On bus, nearly there. Feel trussed up like a chicken in black evening dress, which was only clean meeting-like garment could find. Looked OK in mirror because it is corset-like which holds everything in when standing up, giving one a taut hourglass shape, with, admittedly, a lace top, but have put *Grazia* blazer on top, though now boiling, to create pleasingly eclectic *Good Luck Charlie* daughter effect.

However, on glimpsing in shop window realized outfit insane. Now am on bus, remember also that corset-like nature of dress is torture when sitting down. One's rolls of fat are squeezed together like dough being kneaded in a food processor. Also, whole effect has something of the dominatrix about it, which is the last thing I am able to

351

pull off when mental state would be more authentically represented by a duvet, hot-water bottle and Puffle One. Plus hair has gone into weird square bouffe like Mum and Una as if I am wearing a hat.

Did manage to find and read Ambergris Bilk's notes overnight, but now confused because *The Leaves in His Hair* seems, in Ambergris's mind, to have moved to Stockholm. Does she know George is stuck with the yacht in Hawaii because of the stoner movie falling over? And will George think I was trying to talk Ambergris back to Norway and she disguised it as Sweden? Actually, will ask Chloe to get some Pimm's as well as don't see how can otherwise get through Sports Day in sub-glacial temperatures. Gaaah! Text from Roxster.

<Are we having dinner tonight?>

Dinner tonight? Did we say we were having dinner tonight? Oh, shit, now have not got babysitter and . . . had better go to meeting.

3 p.m. Nightmare meeting. "Saffron" turned out to be the new screenwriter, who is, of course, twenty-six, and has just written a pilot—"*Girls* meets *Game of Thrones* meets *The Killing*"—which is about to be "picked up" by HBO (before, I thought with un-Buddhist spiteful hope, it "falls over"). Felt like some embarrassing evening-dress-with-blazer-and-weird-hat-hair elephant in the room. Then accidentally put chair leg on handbag, which, unbeknownst to me, now contained Billy's noise machine from the party bag from the African drumming party, and emitted a very long burp. Nobody laughed except Imogen.

Saffron's opening foray, placing the script on the table

in front of her, was a simpering: "This might just be me, but isn't *Hedda Gabler* actually spelt with one b? *Gabler*? Not *Gabbler*? And isn't it by Ibsen, not Chekhov?"

As everyone stared at me, and I muttered something about anti-intellectualist irony, found self thinking how relaxing it would be to have dinner with Roxster and laugh about it all. Nearly texted him back saying: <I didn't know we were still having dinner tonight.> but thought it sounded petulant so instead, as soon as attention was diverted to Saffron's nauseating theories about how to RUIN my *oeuvre*, I furtively texted: <Chicken pie at my place?>

Roxster: <Mmmmmmmmmmmmmmmmmmmm. About 8.30?>

Instantly regretted saying "chicken pie," as did not have either chicken pie or means to make chicken pie. Also legs were probably hairy, but could not check as in meeting. Was too weak, depressed and bewildered to get into the discussion about Stockholm versus Hawaii so just said that maybe we should "let Saffron do a draft" and see how it "comes off the page." At which George had to run off to get a plane to Albuquerque.

7.30 p.m. Ugh. I rushed home from meeting, managing to squeeze in buying mountain of red and green peppers as did not have yellow, and purchase of chicken pie from overpriced deli, then managed to pick up both children just in time.

As we were driving home, Billy said, "Mummy?"

"Yes," I said vaguely, trying to dodge a cyclist who had just veered out in front of me.

"It's Father's Day on Sunday. We made cards."

"We did too," said Mabel.

As soon as I could, I pulled over and cut the engine. I wiped my face with both hands, rubbing my eyes for a second, then turned to look at them.

"Can I see the cards?"

They scrabbled in their bags. Mabel's was of a family with a daddy, a mummy, a little girl and a little boy. Billy's drawing was contained in a heart, with a little boy playing a game with his father. It said *"Daddy."*

"Can we post dem to Daddy?" said Mabel.

When we got home, I got out all the photos of them with Mark—Billy in a little suit, the same as Mark's, standing together, the same look on their faces, exactly the same pose, one hand in the trouser pocket. Mark holding Mabel up when she was newborn, like a little toy in her onesie. We talked about Daddy, and how I was sure he knew what we were doing, and he was loving us still. Then we went out and posted the cards.

Mabel had addressed hers *"Daddy. Heaven. Space."* In the midst of feeling guilty about everything else I felt guilty about traumatizing the postman.

On the way home Billy said, "I wish we lived in a normal family, like Rebecca."

"That's not a normal family," I said. "They never—"

"Finn has Xbox in the week!" said Billy.

"Can we have *SpongeBob* now?" said Mabel.

They were really tired. They fell asleep straight away after their bath.

8 p.m. Roxster will be here in half an hour. Am going to have a bath and re-wash hair, put make-up on, and try to find something suitable to wear for evening with person who may be about to either break up with me or produce an engagement ring.

8.10 p.m. In bath now. Gaah! Telephone.

8.15 p.m. Jumped out of the bath, wrapped self in towel and grabbed phone, to hear deep, powerful voice of George from Greenlight.

"OK. We're just on the tarmac in Denver. So, look, that went well today, but we don't want you to lose . . . Santa Fe."

"But it's in Stockholm!" I said, suddenly realizing that I hadn't put the chicken pie in.

"Hang on, we're disembarking . . . we don't want you to lose your voice."

What was he talking about? I hadn't lost my voice. Had I?

"Stockholm? No, I'm transferring to Santa Fe." Was he talking to me now, or the air hostess?

"So. We want you to Hedda it up."

"Hedda it up?" What could he possibly mean? Maybe he was talking to the pilot.

"No, sorry, I meant Albuquerque."

"George!" I yelled. "Aren't you meant to be in Albufeira?"

"What? WHAT?"

The phone went dead.

8.20 p.m. Just ran downstairs to put the chicken pie in the oven and the landline rang.

"OK. What was that about Albufeira?" George again.

"It was a joke," I said, trying to open the chicken pie with my teeth. "I can't concentrate on what you're saying, because you're always on a plane or some other mode of transport. Can't we just talk about things calmly for TWO minutes with you in one place?" I said, tucking the phone under my chin, opening the oven door with one hand and shoving the pie in with the other. "I can't WORK with you rushing about like this! I need to concentrate."

George suddenly switched into a purring, sensual, soothing voice I hadn't heard before.

"OK, OK. We think you're a genius. Once this trip is over I'm going to be in the office all the time, all right? You just need to put back the special Hedda voice we love so much into all the Hedda lines when Saffron's finished with them. And you'll have my undivided, calm attention."

"OK, yes," I said frantically, wondering if I could glaze the pie before I dried my hair.

8.40 p.m. Phew. Thank goodness Roxster is a bit late. Everything is fine. Hair is normal. Chicken pie is not only in oven but GLAZED with beaten egg to give pleasing air of some form of cooking. Downstairs is looking all right, and lit by candles, and think silk shirt is OK and not too slutty as we have been sleeping together for months, and also every-thing else is either too uncomfortable or in the wash. Oh God, I'm so tired. Think will just have little sleep on sofa for a few minutes.

9.15 p.m. Gaaah! Is 9.15 and Roxster is not here. Have I slept through the doorbell?

Just texted Roxster.

<Fell asleep. Did I miss the doorbell?>

<Jonesey, I'm so sorry. I ended up having to have a curry with colleagues after work and now the buses are really slow. Should be about 10 more minutes.>

Stared at the text, mind reeling. A curry? Buses slow? Colleagues? Roxster doesn't say "colleagues." And what about the chicken pie? What was going on?

9.45 p.m. Roxster is still not here. Texted: <Estimated ETA?>

Roxster: <About 15 minutes. So sorry, darling.>

FARTING SPORTS DAY

Thursday 13 June 2013

136lb (bloody chicken pie, plus egg glaze), alcohol units 7 (counting last night), hangovers 1 (cataclysmic), temperature 90 degrees, peppers chopped 12, melon balls consumed 35, wrinkles appeared during course of day 45, number of times used word "fart" in texts to Roxster 9 (undignified).

Awoke at first light feeling everything was OK, then suddenly glimpsed the tip of the iceberg of the train wreck of last night. Doorbell rang at 10 p.m. at which I sprayed myself with perfume and answered the door in more or less nothing but the white shirt.

Roxster said, "Mmm, you look so nice," and started kissing me all the way down the stairs. We ate the chicken pie, and downed the bottle of red wine he'd brought. He said I was to sit down on the sofa and relax, while he washed up. I watched him, thinking how lovely everything was, but still vaguely wondering why and how he'd managed to eat a curry and then a chicken pie and not feel or look like he had eaten a Bambi. Then he came over and knelt at my feet.

"I have something to say," he said.

"What?" I said, smiling at him sleepily.

"I've never said this to any woman before. I heart you, Jonesey. I really, seriously heart you."

"Oh," I said, looking at him slightly crazily, one eye closed and one open.

"And if it wasn't for the age difference," he went on, "I'd be down on one knee. I really would. You're the best woman I've ever met and I've hearted every minute we've had together. But it's different for you because you've got your kids and I haven't got my life sorted out. This is just not going anywhere. I really need to meet someone my own age, and I can't do that unless I'm able to do that. Does that make any sense whatsoever?"

Maybe if I'd been less tired I'd have tried to talk it through properly, but instead I immediately turned into Girl Guide mode, launching into a cheery speech about how of *course* he was right! He *must* find someone his own age! But it had been marvellous for both of us, and we'd both learned and grown so much!

Roxster was staring at me with a haunted expression.

"But can we still be friends?" he said.

"Of course," I gushed joyfully.

"Do you think we'll be able to see each other without tearing each other's clothes off?"

"Of course!" I said merrily. "Anyway, chuh! Best be getting off to bed. Sports Day tomorrow!"

I saw him out, with a fixed, cheery smile, then, instead of doing the sensible thing and texting Rebecca and asking her to come over, or calling Talitha or Tom or Jude or anyone, really, I got into bed and sobbed for two hours until I fell asleep. And now, oh, shit, it's 6 a.m., the kids will be up in an hour and I have to take chopped vegetables and both of them to Sports Day, on half a bottle of red wine and four hours' sleep, in the now, freakishly, blazing heat.

6 p.m. Managed to get everyone and everything into car on time, drive to sports ground, and then get everybody and everything out of the car by pretending was soldier in a war combined with the Dalai Lama. Billy and Mabel had forgotten all about the Father's Day trauma and were wildly jolly, running off immediately to charge around with their friends, mercifully forgetting all about their melting-down mother as well.

Unfortunately, however, in the midst of laying out picnic rugs and chopped vegetables, said melting-down mother was suddenly overcome with un-Zen-like rage at Roxster for putting her into such a meltdown and sent off a blistering texting rant which went as follows:

<Roxster. It was fartingly manipulative and selfish to do that like that last night, after you'd pretended to marry me and eaten my GLAZED chicken pie, and you can just stuff your chicken pie and a Full English Breakfast and curry up your own bum and go fart at yourself, you selfish fart-bum.>

Broke off briefly to graciously pour out some of my giant bottle of Pimm's for Farzia and the other mothers.

<You fartingly don't have anyone to think about except your FARTING self at the moment and all I can say is, when you have a baby with some . . . some *Saffron* who will probably not be able to afford on-tap nannies you're going to get a bit of a shock. And if receiving a texting rant makes you feel bad, then good. Because so do I, and I'm at a FARTING SPORTS DAY!>

Then turned back to the group, commenting flatteringly upon the delicious picnic, before returning to my text with an apologetic smile suggesting that I was a very busy and important businesswoman and not just texting farts to a toy boy who had dumped me unequivocally for being too old.

The phone vibrated.

Roxster: <In my defence, I didn't fart once last night, despite having just eaten a curry.>

Me: <Well, I'm just sending the most GIANT FART WITH EXTRA STINK right out of my bum at Sports Day so get ready.>

Quickly checked the children—Billy was running round maniacally with a group of boys and Mabel and another small girl were cheerfully saying obscurely mean things to each other—then returned to my texting exchange.

Roxster: <How do you add extra stink to a fart? Quickly eat a parsnip?>

Me: <Spend the evening with a FUCKING FARTER.>

Roxster: <I just farted into a taxi and told it to go to the Junior Branch sports ground.>

Me: <Yes, well, it's probably airborne by now with the strength of your fart velocity.>

"Enjoying supporting the sporting activities?"

It was Mr. Wallaker, positively *sneering* down at my iPhone. Was just trying to get up, which, because I'd been sitting on my knees for so long, involved crashing onto all fours, when the starter pistol went off for the first race.

In that split second, I saw Mr. Wallaker freeze, and his hand whip to his hip as if for a gun. I could see the powerful body tensed beneath his sports shirt, the muscle in his cheek working, eyes casing the playing fields. As the egg-and-spoon racers wobbled off the starting blocks, he blinked, as if remembering himself, then glanced round sheepishly to see if anyone had noticed.

"Everything all right?" I said, raising one eyebrow in an attempt to mimic his usual supercilious manner, which may not have been entirely successful, owing to my still being on all fours.

"Absolutely," he said, his cool blue eyes levelly meeting mine. "Just a slight issue I have with . . . spoons."

Then he turned and jogged off towards the egg-and-spoon finishing line. I stared after him. What was that about? Was he delusional, dissatisfied with his mundane life and filled with Bond fantasies? Or was he the sort of person who dresses up as Oliver Cromwell and fights pretend battles at the weekends?

As the sporting events got under way, I put the iPhone away and started to focus. "Come on, Mabel," I said, "it's Billy's long jump."

As they measured Billy's jump a cheer went up and he leaped into the air.

"I told you, dammit!" said Mabel.

"What?" I said.

"Dey do have tape measuring in the Kwintoflon."

"Yes, it is an increasingly popular athletic category."

It was Mr. Wallaker and, teetering behind him, a strange, out-of-place woman I hadn't seen before.

"Could I possibly have a drop of that Pimm's?" She was wearing a white, expensive-looking crocheted dress and high-heeled mules with gold *things* on. Her face had that slightly peculiar look which people have when they've had work done which obviously seems fine when they're staring at the mirror but looks weird as soon as they move their face.

"Pimm's?" she said to Mr. Wallaker. "Dear?"

"DEAR?" Could this possibly be Mr. Wallaker's WIFE? How had that one happened?

Mr. Wallaker looked uncharacteristically discombobulated. "Bridget, this is . . . this is Sarah. Don't worry, I'll do the Pimm's, you go to Billy," he said quietly.

"Come on, Mabel," I said, as Billy galloped over like an exuberant puppy, bits of shirt and sash flying in the wind, and buried his head in my dress.

As we started packing up the things before the prize-giving, the weird, drunk Mr.-Wallaker-wife teetered over to us again.

"Could I have some more Pimm's?" she slurred. I began to think I quite liked her really. It's always so nice to meet someone more badly behaved than oneself.

Then she said, "Thanks you," peering at me with her surprised eyes. "Not often I meet someone your age who's still got a real face."

"Someone who's still got a real face"? During the prize-giving I couldn't help regurgitating the phrase. "Someone your age with a real face"? What did she mean? That I was daring to go around without having Botox? Oh God, oh God. Maybe Talitha was right. I was going to die of loneliness because I was so wrinkly. No wonder Roxster had dumped me.

As soon as the prize-giving was over and Billy and Mabel absorbed with their friends, I dived into the clubhouse to recover my composure, stopping in appalled dismay at a poster on the noticeboard:

⟍⟋ Over-50s Trip to Hastings ⟋⟍

And another:

⟍⟋ Over-50s Club ⟋⟍

Every Monday 9.30–12.30

Bingo
Refreshments
Raffle
Coach Trips
Christmas Day Lunch
Tea Dancing
Advice and Support

Furtively typing the Advice and Support number into my iPhone, I stumbled into the Ladies and surveyed myself under the harsh, unforgiving light of an unshaded bulb. Mr. Wallaker's wife was right. The skin around my eyes was becoming, even as I watched, a mass of wrinkles; chin and jowls were sagging, neck like a turkey, marionette lines rushing from my mouth to my chin in manner of Angela Merkel. As I stared I could almost see my hair turning into a tight grey perm. It had finally happened. I was an old lady.

THE DEEP FREEZE

Tuesday 18 June 2013

136lb (inc. 1lb of botulism).

I mean, lots of people do Botox, don't they? It's not like having a facelift. "Exactly," said Talitha, when she gave me the number. "It's just like going to the dentist!"

Went down into basement off Harley Street feeling like was going to back-street abortionist.

"I don't want to look weird," I said, trying to replace the image of Mr. Wallaker's wife with that of Talitha.

"No," said the strange foreign-sounding Botox doctor. "Too many peoples looks weirds."

Felt tiny pricking sensation in forehead.

"Just goweeng to do your mouse now. You are going to laave eet. You don do your mouse, zee face start to droop so you look meeesrable. Like ze Queen."

I thought about this. Actually it might be true. The Queen does quite often look as if she's unhappy or disapproving and she probably isn't really. Maybe the Queen should have Botox in her mouth!

Came out, blinking in the lights of Harley Street and grimacing my face as the doctor had told me to.

"Bridget!"

I looked across the road, startled. It was Woney, wife of Cosmo.

As she hurried across I blinked at her. Woney looked . . . different. Could she possibly have had . . . hair extensions? Her hair was a good six inches longer than it had been at Talitha's party and dark brown, not grey. And instead of her usual high-necked duchess dress she was wearing a fitted peach frock with a beautiful neckline, which showed off her waist, plus high heels.

"You look fantastic," I said.

She smiled. "Thank you. It was . . . well, what you said last year at Magda's drinks. And then after Talitha's party I thought . . . and Talitha told me where to get my hair done and . . . had some Botox, but don't tell Cosmo. And how is it going, with your young man? I've just been sitting next to one at a charity lunch. It's absolutely marvellous, isn't it, doing a bit of flirting?!"

What could I say? Telling her he'd dumped me for being too old would be like telling the troops in the First World War trenches that it looked as though the Germans were winning.

"There's *everything* to be said for the younger man," I said. "You look fabulous."

And she teetered off, giggling, and I could swear, at two in the afternoon, slightly drunk.

Well, at least something good has come out of it all, I muttered to myself. And her Botox looked great, so maybe mine would too!

Friday 21 June 2013

Remaining consonants able to pronounce 0.

2.30 p.m. Oh my God. Oh my God. Something really weird is happening to my mouth. It's all swelling up inside.

2.35 p.m. Just looked in mirror. Lips are sticking out. Mouth is puffed up and sort of paralysed.

2.40 p.m. Billy's school just rang about the bassoon lessons and cannot speak properly. Cannot easily say Ps or Bs or Fs. What am I going to do? Am going to be like this for next three months.

2.50 p.m. Have started drooling. Cannot control mouth so drool is coming out of side of mouth like—ironically enough given objective was to look younger—stroke "victim" in old people's home. Have to keep dabbing at it with a tissue.

2.55 p.m. Called up Talitha and tried to expbflain.
    "But it shouldn't do that. You should go back. Something must have gone wrong. It's probably an allergic reaction. It'll wear off."

3.15 p.m. Have got to do school run. Actually it will be fine. Will simply drape a scarf round my mouth. People don't notice specific bits of other people, they see the whole.

3.30 p.m. Collected Mabel, with scarf draped around mouth like Masked Raider. Took scarf off gratefully in car, and turned round to do usual complex body-contorting movement in order to get the seat belt into the thing. At least Mabel hasn't noticed, munching happily away at her snack.

3.45 p.m. Ugh, traffic is terrible. Why do people drive these enormous SUV things in London? It's like once they're in

367

one, they think they're driving a tank and everyone has to get out of their . . .

"Mummy?"

"Yes, Mabel."

"Your mouth looks all funny."

"Oh," I said, successfully avoiding consonants.

"Why is your mouth all funny?"

Attempted to say "because" but fuffing noise came out: "Pfecase I'pf . . ."

"Mummy, why are you talking funny?"

"It's pfine, Bfafell, just by bouth is a bit pfoorly."

"What did you say, Mother?"

"It's all good, Daughter," I managed. You see, if I can just stick to vowels and guttural and sibilant consonants it's bpffine!

4 p.m. Put scarf round mouth again and took worried-looking Mabel by her little hand, into the Junior Branch.

Billy was playing football. Tried to yell, but how could I say "Bfpilly"?

"Oi," I attempted to shout. "Illy!" Billy glanced up briefly, then carried on playing football. "Illy!"

How was I going to get him out of the playground? And they were having such a nice time running about but then had only got five minutes left on the car because it was in a loading bay.

"ILLYYYYYY!" I yelled.

"Everything OK?"

I turned. It was Mr. Wallaker. "A muffler? Are you cold? Doesn't feel very cold to me," he said, rubbing his hands as if to check out the general temperature. He was wearing a blue businessman-type shirt and I could sense his lean, annoyingly fit body through it.

"Bbdentist."

"I'm sorry?"

I quickly moved the scarf, said "Bbdentist" again and put the scarf back. There was a quick flicker of amusement in his eyes.

"Mummy'th mouth'th all funny," Mabel said.

"Poor Mummy," said Mr. Wallaker, bending down to Mabel. "What's going on with your shoes? Have you got them on the wrong feet?"

Oh God. Was so preoccupied with Botox trauma did not notice. Mr. Wallaker was swapping them efficiently.

"Billy won't come," said Mabel in her deep gruff voice, looking at him with her grave expression.

"Really?" Mr. Wallaker got to his feet. "Billy!" he called down authoritatively. Billy looked up, startled.

Mr. Wallaker jerked his head to beckon him, at which Billy obediently trotted through the gate towards us.

"Your mum was waiting for you. You knew that. Next time your mum is waiting for you, you come straight away. Got it?"

"Yes, Mr. Wallaker."

He turned to me. "Are you OK?"

Suddenly, horrifyingly, felt my eyes filling with tears.

"Billy. Mabel. Your mum's been to the dentist and she's feeling poorly. Now. I want you to be a little lady and a little gentleman and be nice to her."

"Yes, Mr. Wallaker," they said, like automatons, putting out their hands to hold mine.

"Very good. And, Mrs. Darcy?"

"Yes, Mr. Wallaker?"

"I wouldn't do that again if I were you. You looked all right in the first place."

When we reached our road, I suddenly realized I was driving on autopilot and had got the whole way home without noticing anything.

"Mummy?"

"Yes?" I said, thinking, "They know, they know, we're on terribly flimsy ground, and their mother is a Botoxed, failed cougar idiot who's going to crash the car, and doesn't know what she's doing, what she's supposed to be doing or how she's supposed to do it, and they're going to be taken into care by the Social Services and—"

"Do dinosaurs have cold blood?"

"Yes. Ubf, no?" I said as I parked the car. Do they? "I fwmean, what are they? Are they repfhtiles or like phwdolpfhwins?"

"Mummy, how long are you going to carry on talking like this?"

"Can we have spag bog?" said Mabel.

"Yupf," I said, parking the car outside the house.

When we got inside it was all warm and cosy and I soon had the spag bog (supermarket ready-prepared and possibly containing horse but still) bubbling on the stove. They were sitting on the sofa listening to the annoying American-cartoons-where-actors-talk-in-high-pitched-hysterical-voices, but looking so sweet. Leaving the horse spaghetti, I sat down with them and pulled them into a hug-knot, and I buried my frozen face in their messy heads and soft necks, feeling their little hearts beating against mine, and thought how lucky I was, just to have them.

After a while Billy raised his head. "Mummy," he whispered softly, a faraway look in his eye.

"Mbffff?" I murmured, heart overflowing with love.

"The spaghetti is on fire."

Oh dear. Had left spaghetti in the pan with the dry bits leaning over the edge at a sharp angle, intending to squidge them down when the other end softened, but somehow they had tilted down and caught fire.

"I'll get de fire extinglewish," said Mabel calmly, as if this were an everyday occurrence. Which of course it is not.

"Noo!" I said, berserk, grabbing a tea towel and throwing it on the pan, at which the tea towel also caught fire and the smoke alarm went off.

Suddenly felt the splash of cold water. Turned to see Billy pouring a jug of cold water over the whole thing, extinguishing the flames and leaving a smouldering, but extinguished, mess on the cooker. He was grinning delightedly. "Can we eat it now?"

Mabel too was looking thrilled. "Can we toast marshbellowth?"

So (once Billy had turned the smoke alarm off) we did toast barshbellows. On the fire. In the fireplace. And it was one of our nicest evenings.

THAT'S WHAT FRIENDS ARE FOR

Saturday 22 June 2013

136lb, calories 3844, packets of grated mozzarella consumed 2, boyfriends 0, possibility of boyfriends 0, combined alcohol units consumed by self and the friends 47.

"Well, at least she's not a Born-Again Virgin," said Tom. "Rather the opposite if you ask me. More like a Born-Again Nymphomaniac. With a frozen face. Have we run out of wine?"

"There's some more in the fridge," I said, getting up. "But you see—"

"Tom, do be quiet, darling," chided Talitha. "Her face looks really, really good now the drooling's stopped."

"The key thing is, she has to get over the toy boy," said Jude, who is STILL going out with Wildlifephotographerman.

"It's not just that, it's—" I tried to get in.

"It's the ego, it's the ego which is at stake." Tom was pretending to be professional but was completely drunk. "It's not a rejection. A person who goes from one extreme to the other like that isn't rejecting you. He's just caught between his heart and his head and—"

"Bridget, I did warn you that one must never, EVER fall in love with a toy boy," interrupted Talitha. "One has to be in control, otherwise the whole dynamic becomes a total disaster. I forbid you to re-engage with him. Tom, darling, could you just fix me a teensy-weensy vodka with lots of ice and a splash of soda?"

"He's not going to re-engage with me. I sent him a texting rant about farting," I said.

"Number one," said Talitha, "he will re-engage, because his exit was a bang not a whimper, and number two, you are NOT to re-engage or it will become a whimper. Once a man has dumped you, taking him back is a sign of low self-esteem and desperation and he will do NOTHING but fuck you around."

"But Mark took me back and—"

"Roxster," said Tom, "is not Mark."

At this, I burst into silent, gasping sobs.

"Oh God," said Jude. "We have to find her someone else and quickly. I'm setting her up on OkCupid. What shall I put as her age?"

"No, don't," I sobbed. "I have to Take the Stick, like it says in *Zen and the Art of Falling in Love*. I have to be punished. I've neglected the children and—"

"They's fine! You'se gone mad. Where'ye put your iPhoto library?"

"Jude," said Tom, "leave her alone, leave her to me. I. Am ssprofessional. I. Am a doctor of pyscholosphy."

There was silence for a moment. "Thanks you," said Tom. "You are dealing with six things in a relationship. Theirs fantasy about you. Theirs fantasy about the relationship, your fantasy about them, their fantasy about your fantasy about themselves and—how many is that? Oh. Their fantasy about . . . thems!"

Then Tom rose sententiously, walked calmly, if unstead-ily, to the fridge, returned with a packet of chocolate buttons and a bottle of Chardonnay, and pulled a packet of Silk Cut out of his jacket pocket.

"Some things neeever change!" he said. "Nows opens your mouth and takes your medicines. Thassas a good girl."

When I woke up in the morning, I was all tucked up with a selection of soft toys, a copy of *Thelma and Louise*, and a note from all three of them saying: "*We will always love you.*"

However, when I picked up my phone there was also a text from Jude with an OkCupid login and password.

THE YAWNING VOID

Monday 24 June 2013
135lb, texts from Roxster 0, emails from Roxster 0, phone calls from Roxster 0, voicemails from Roxster 0, tweets from Roxster 0, Twitter messages from Roxster 0.

9.15 p.m. Children are asleep. OH GOD, I'M SO LONELY. I miss Roxster. Now that the bubble has burst, and I have realized Mark is still gone, the children still have no father, and all the other complicated, unfixable things, I just quite simply and straightforwardly miss Roxster. Is so weird going from total closeness to . . . nothing. Total cyberspace emptiness. The text is silent. No emails from Roxster. He no longer tweets. I cannot get on his Facebook because to do that I would have to join Facebook which I know is emotional suicide, and then ask to be his friend on Facebook and then find loads of pictures of him snogging thirty-year-olds. Have reread the old messages and emails and there is just nothing left of Roxby McDuff now, at all.

Had not really stopped to think how much Roxster meant to me because I really was being Buddhist and staying in the moment. Had not realized we were building a little world together: the farts, the vomit, jokes about food and our favourite pubs, and the barnacle's penis. Every time something funny happens want to text it to Roxster. And then realize, with cold, lurching remembrance, that Roxster doesn't want to hear about all the funny little things any more, because he's doubtless hearing funny details of the life of someone who is twenty-three and likes Lady Gaga.

10 p.m. Just got into bed. Cold empty boring bed. When am I ever going to have sex again or wake up with someone as young and beautiful as Roxsterrrrrrrr?

10.05 p.m. Fuck him with his fucking curry! I absolutely do not care about Roxster any more whatsoever. Pah! He was simply a curry-eating . . . Callow Gigolo! Have deleted him from contacts and will not correspond with or see or ask to see him ever again ever. He is deleted.

10.06 p.m. But I lurrrrrrrrrrve him.

Tuesday 25 June 2013
Number of mean texts made up to send to Roxster in case Roxster texts me 33.

9.15 p.m. OH GOD, I'M SO LONELY. Keep thinking maybe Roxster will text that we should have a drink, and keep making up imaginary haughty texts in reply:
<I'm sorry, who is this?>
<I'm sorry, but I'm afraid that might prevent me from meeting people who match my own emotional maturity, glamorous social life and stylish designer outfits.>
Or:
<But what if a thirty-year-old walks past in the middle who likes farting and vomiting?>

Wednesday 26 June 2013

9.15 p.m. OH GOD, I'M SO LONELY.

9.16 p.m. Have just had brilliant idea! Will text Leather-jacketman!

9.30 p.m. Texting exchange went as follows:

Me: <Hi! What's up? Haven't seen you for a while. Fancy getting together for a catch-up?>

10.30 p.m. Leatherjacketman: <Hey. Great to hear from you. Lots of changes this end, starting with—I'm getting married in two weeks' time! But maybe we could get together beforehand?>

Thursday 27 June 2013

9.15 p.m. OH GOD, I'M SO LONELY. Maybe will call Daniel and see if he will take me out to cheer me up!

11 p.m. Daniel has not replied. Is not like Daniel. Maybe he is currently getting married.

Friday 28 June 2013

3 a.m. Billy just got into my bed, sobbing. I think he'd had a bad dream. He put his arms round me, all hot and sweaty, and clung to me. "I need you, Mummy."

He does. They do. And there's no one else. I can't afford to get into a mess like this, trying to fill up a void with stupid men. Come on, pull yourself together.

7 a.m. Woke up sleepily and looked at Billy, warm and exquisitely beautiful on my pillow. Started giggling, remembering wailing self-pityingly about Roxster, "When am I ever going to wake up with someone as young and beautiful as that again?"

You see? Simple! Even younger and *more* beautiful.

JUST THE WAY THEY ARE

Friday 28 June 2013 (continued)
10 a.m. Starting to feel worried about Daniel. For all his, well, Daniel-ism, since Mark died he has always got back straight away if I call. Ooh! Telephone.

10.30 a.m. Had forgotten about conference call with George from Greenlight, Imogen and Damian.

"Right—we're all in the office, you'll be pleased to hear," George began. "Now here's the thing." There was sploshing in the background. "If you talk to Saffron about the pages you are not to give her any idea that you are not one hundred per cent in love with Stock—"

"George?" I said suspiciously. "Where are you and what is that sloshing noise?"

"In the office. It's just . . . coffee. OK. Ambergris is into Stockholm so don't—"

There was an odd, rubbery, slithering squeak, a giant splash—I mean, really like something huge had fallen into a large body of water—a muffled shout, then silence.

"Right!" said Imogen. "Shall we see what happened there and call you back?"

11 a.m. Just called Talitha to see if she had spoken to Daniel lately.

"Oh God," she said. "Haven't you heard?"

The thing is, Daniel has always had addictive tendencies, which have got worse as he has got older. There was a period when everyone was saying, "I'm so worried about Daniel," in judgemental voices, as he behaved increasingly outrageously at dinner parties. Various glamorous women tried to "fix" him until eventually he was shipped off to a treatment facility in Arizona and returned looking fresh-faced and a little sheepish. As far as we all knew, he was fine. But it seems a recent break-up with the latest glamorous woman catapulted him into a dazzling spree, taking him through the entire contents of his 1930s cocktail cabinet in a single weekend. He was found in a terrible state last Monday morning by his cleaning lady and now he is in the drugs and drink ward of the same hospital where I went to the Obesity Clinic.

Oh God, oh God, and I let Billy and Mabel stay the night with him.

11.30 a.m. Imogen just called back. It seems that George, rather than, as claimed, being in his office slurping coffee, was in a dinghy on the Irrawaddy River to which he had retreated from his luxury indigenous-style houseboat in order to "get a signal." Somehow, the swell from a passing executive speedboat had unbalanced the dinghy, catapulting George into the murky waters of the Irrawaddy, shortly followed by his iPhone.

George was fine, but the loss of the iPhone was catastrophic. I decided to leave Greenlight to deal with the aftermath and hotfoot it round to see Daniel.

2 p.m. Just back. Scary. St. Catherine's Hospital is a bewildering visual mix of Victorian prison, 1960s doctor's surgery and the Yemen. I wandered, unfocused, until I found the right block, bought Daniel newspapers in the gift shop and a card with a duck on it saying: *"Stay afloat,"* adding in pen: *"Dirty Bastard,"* then impulsively put inside: *"Wherever you go and whatever you do I'll always love you."* One doesn't want to ENABLE, but I could imagine everyone was going to come in and tick him off.

The ward was a "locked ward." Pressed on the green button. Eventually a lady in a burka appeared and let me in.

"I'm here to see Daniel Cleaver."

She didn't seem to recognize the name, just another one on her clipboard.

"Over there to the left. First bed behind the curtain."

I recognized Daniel's bag and his coat but the bed was empty. Had Daniel done a runner? I started trying to tidy up, then a strange tramp-like figure appeared in winceyette hospital pyjamas, unshaven, with wild hair and a black eye.

"Who are you?" he said suspiciously.

"It's me, Bridget!"

"Jones!" he said, as if a light bulb had come on in his head. Just as quickly it went out, and he stumbled over to the bed. "You could at least have told me you were coming. Might have cleaned up a bit."

He lay down and closed his eyes.

"Silly arse," I said.

He fumbled for my hand. He was making a very strange noise.

"What happened? Why can't you breathe?"

A flicker came into his eye, a glimpse of the old Daniel.

"Well, the thing is, Jones," he said, pulling me over to him, "went on a bit of a bender, to tell you the truth. Pretty much drank through everything. I delightedly fastened upon what I took to be a bottle of crème de menthe, you know, the green stuff, drank the whole thing down." His face broke into the familiar rueful smirk. "It turned out to be Fairy Liquid."

We both started shaking with laughter. I know it was a potentially tragic situation but it was pretty funny. But then Daniel started choking, making a wheezing noise, and bubbles started appearing out of his mouth. You could see exactly what had happened. It's like when you run out of dishwasher tablets, and think it would be a good idea to put washing-up liquid in instead and it all froths up inside.

The nurse rushed over and sorted him out. Then he picked up the card and opened it. For a second he looked as if he was going to cry, then he shoved it back down on the table, just as a glamorous leggy blonde appeared.

"Daniel," said the blonde, in a way which made me want to flick my hair at her and give her nits. "Look at you! You should be ashamed of yourself. It has to stop."

She picked up the card. "What's this? Is this from you?" she said accusingly. "You see, this is his problem! All his bloody friends: 'Dear old Daniel.' It's just completely enabling."

"Best be off then," I said, getting up.

"No, Jones, don't," said Daniel.

"Oh, *please*," snorted the girl, just as Talitha appeared carrying a basket of edible gift items, wrapped in cellophane and topped with a big bow.

"You see? You see?" said the glamorous girl. "This is exactly what I mean."

"And WHAT do you mean by that . . . sugar?" said Talitha. "WHO exactly are you and WHAT does this have to do with you? I have known Daniel for twenty years and slept with him, on and off, for most of them . . ."

Almost burst out, "What??" Was Talitha sleeping with Daniel when I was sleeping with Daniel? But then I thought, "What's the point?"

I made my excuses and left, thinking, really, after a certain age, people are just going to do what they're going to do and you're either going to accept them as they are or you're not. Unsure, however, if should altogether leave the children in Daniel's charge again, at least until he's been back to rehab, or can conclusively distinguish a fork from a hairbrush.

LET'S FACE THE MUSIC AND TEA-DANCE

Saturday 29 June 2013

Just set off for Hampstead Heath and had to come back as seemed like giant bucket of water was being emptied on our heads. Weather has been disgusting this summer. Rain, rain, rain and freezing cold, as if there is NO summer. Is completely intolerable.

Sunday 30 June 2013

Gaah! Is suddenly boiling hot. Don't have sunblock or hats and is too hot to stay outside. How are we supposed to manage in this unbearable heat? Is completely intolerable.

Monday 1 July 2013

6 p.m. Right! Am going to stop being so sorry for myself lest I end up accidentally drinking Fairy Liquid. The end of the school year is almost here with its absorbing matrix of plays, school trips, pyjama days, emails about presents for the teachers (including a very strict one from Perfect Nicolette about everyone sticking to chipping in for the John Lewis vouchers and not buying their own Jo Malone candles), and—generating the most unfeasible number of mass emails of all—Billy's Summer Concert. Billy is going to play "I'd Do Anything" from *Oliver!* as a solo on his bassoon. The concert has been organized by Mr. Wallaker, who seems now to be including half the music department in his military-style takeover, and is to be held at sunset in the grounds of Capthorpe House, a stately home up the A11.

Presumably Mr. Wallaker will be dressed as Oliver Cromwell and his "so nice to meet someone with a real face" wife will have had four pints of extra filler put in her face to celebrate. Oops, back in the knife box, Miss Sharp. Must read more of *The Little Book of Buddhism*: *"We do not possess our home, our children or even our own body. They are only given to us for a short time to treat with care and respect."*

Oh, no! I still haven't made the dentist appointment for Billy and Mabel. The longer I leave it, the more I daren't, since clearly their teeth are now riddled with holes, they will end up like extras in *Pirates of the Caribbean* and it will be all my fault.

But at least am treating own body like a temple. Am going to Zumba.

8 p.m. Just back. Usually love Zumba, with young, dark, long-haired Spanish couple, taking it in turns to lead "numbers," flinging their hair about, stomping angrily like horses, transporting one into a world of Barcelona or possibly Basque-coast nightclubs, and firelit Gypsy encampments of undetermined national extraction.

But this week, the thrilling duo were replaced by a zingy-pingy woman with blonde fringe, a bit like Olivia Newton-John in *Grease*. Exotically sexual Zumba moves were strangely juxtaposed with gay, determined grin, as if to say, "Super-dooper, nothing sexual or dirty about this at all!"

On top of that, the grinning woman made us do not only hand-rolling moves, but also "imaginary shaking-off-water-from-wet-hands" moves, not to mention "starbursts." As whole Catalan nightclub fantasy collapsed like house of cards, looked around to realize class was peopled not by wild Gypsy youths, but a collection of women whom members of an unenlightened male-dominated patriarchal society might describe as "middle-aged."

Have sinking feeling that very concept of attending Zumba may be linked to attempt to relive long-gone days of sexual possibility—as evidenced by St. Oswald's House: even there, Zumba has entirely replaced the concept of "tea-dancing."

Staggered upstairs to somewhat galling sight of tall, thin-without-Zumba Chloe cradling children like Leonardo da Vinci's Madonna and reading *The Wind in the Willows*. Children looked up excitedly for usual post-Zumba spectacle of me crawling up, red in the face, on verge of heart attack.

As soon as Chloe left, Billy and Mabel dispensed with *The Wind in the Willows*, to egg self on into hilarious game of throwing contents of laundry basket down stairs. By time had got them to sleep, cleared up overexcited vomit, etc., was so exhausted that stuffed down two giant fried turkey croquettes (cold) and a three-inch wedge of banana cake. Resolved to enrol in proper salsa or meringue class as soon as possible because, actually (airily), it is the purer form of Latin dance which interests me. Merengue, I mean. Not meringue.

GETTING ONLINE

Tuesday 2 July 2013

133lb (thank you, Zumba/tea-dancing), dating sites investigated 13, dating profiles read 87, attractive dating profiles read 0, dating profiles set up 2, number of disastrous relationships Jude has formed online 17, number of promising relationships Jude has formed online 1 (encouraging).

11 p.m. Jude, who is STILL going out with Wildlifephotographerman, just came round after the kids were asleep, determined to make me get online.

I watched her clicking on dating sites with messianic frenzy and making lists: "Scuba-diver," "Likes Hotel Costes," "Read *A Hundred Years of Solitude*"—yeah, right. "You see, you have to make notes, Bridge, otherwise you'll mix them all up when you message them."

"Don't you ever want to just, like, give up?" I said.

"No, or I would have ended up sucking lollipops with a faraway look in my eye."

Realized with embarrassment I had picked up a lollipop and was sliding it in and out of my mouth.

"The thing is, Bridge, it's a percentages game."

Jude, having burst through the "glass ceiling" of the financial world, is, I suppose, bound to see it in these terms.

"You can't afford to take anything personally. You're going to get stood up, you're going to get eighteen-stone people whose pictures are of someone else. But with enough experience—and skill!—you'll weed through that dross."

We then went into a Greatest Hits medley of the online dross Jude had successfully weeded through to find Wildlifephotographerman: Sexualhumiliationman (of course!), Marriedwithbabyman—who took Jude out, snogged her, then included her in the global text saying his wife had had a baby—and SkydiverGraphicdesignerman—who did turn out to be a graphic designer, but also, it emerged, a devout Muslim who didn't believe in sex before marriage, but, bizarrely, also liked to spend his weekends Morris dancing.

"And somewhere," Jude said, "somewhere out there, it'll just take one click, and you'll be home."

"But who would want a fifty-something single mother with two small children?"

"Take a look," she said, signing me in for a free trial on SingleParentMix.com. "They're just normal people like you and me. They're not weirdos. I'll put forty-nine."

A column of photos popped up of strange men in wire glasses and striped becollared shirts hanging over the folds of their stomachs.

"It looks like a line-up of serial killers," I said. "How can they be single fathers? Unless they've murdered the mothers?"

"Yes, well, maybe that wasn't a very good search," Jude said briskly. "How about this?"

She opened up the profile she'd made for me on OkCupid.

Actually, when I looked, there were some really quite cute ones on there. But oh, the loneliness—the profiles giving away months or maybe years of heartbreak and disappointment and insult.

Someone who'd actually picked as their username "Isthereanyoneout_there?" had as their profile:

> I'm a nice normal guy who just wants a nice normal woman. If your photo is from 15 years ago, then MOVE ON! If you're fucked up, married, desperate, passive-aggressive, not a woman, shamelessly gold-digging, emotionally sadistic, superficial, self-obsessed, illiterate, just looking for quick sex, just looking to indulge in endless streams of messaging then not meet, just looking to get a date to massage your ego and stand me up because you can't be bothered, then MOVE ON!

And then there were the profiles from married men quite openly saying they want uncomplicated sex.

"Why don't they just go on MarriedAffair.co.uk?" sniffed Jude.

Wednesday 3 July 2013
8.30 a.m. Billy's football comic just dropped through the letter box and I took it downstairs saying, "Billy! Your Match .com's arrived!"

KBO

Wednesday 3 July 2013 (continued)
133lb, negative thoughts 5 million, positive thoughts 0, bottles of Fairy Liquid drunk 0 (you see? Could be worse).

9.15 p.m. Right. Super! Is school concert tomorrow and is going to be perfectly fine. Mabel is staying at Rebecca's so I don't have to worry about keeping tabs on both of them at the same time. Of course, many, many of the fathers will be away on business, or perhaps busy tapping away on Mar riedAffair.co.uk! And even if Roxster was still around, he wouldn't have come to the school concert, would he? He'd have felt ridiculous with all those people who have children and are so much older than him.

9.30 p.m. Just looked at news online. Whole royal baby frenzy is not helping: perfect young couple of Roxster's age, starting life, doing everything perfectly, in the perfect way and at the perfect time.

9.45 p.m. Went up to check on Billy and Mabel.
"Mummy," said Billy, "will Daddy know I'm doing the concert?"
"I think so," I whispered.
"Will I do it all right?"
"Yes."

I held his hand till he was asleep. There was a full moon again and I watched it over the rooftops. What would it be like now if I was going to the Summer Concert with Mark? He would have leaned over my shoulder the way he used to, whizzed through the mass picnic emails, deleted them and simply replied: "I will bring the hummus and the black bin liners."

I would be one hundred per cent looking forward to it. It would be a one hundred per cent lovely thing. Oh, come on. Brace up. Keep Buggering On.

THE SUMMER CONCERT

Thursday 4 July 2013

We roared up through the landscaped parkland. We were late, because Billy was trying to map the route on the iPhone and we came off at the wrong junction. Clambered out to the smell of cut grass, the chestnut leaves hanging heavy and green, the light turning golden.

Staggering under the weight of the bassoon case, the rug, my handbag, the picnic basket and a second basket with Diet Cokes and oatmeal cookies that wouldn't fit in the first basket, Billy and I headed towards the path marked: *"CONCERT THIS WAY."*

We came out into the open and gasped. It looked like a painting: a gracious, wisteria-clad house, with an old stone terrace and lawns leading down to a lake. The terrace was laid out like a stage, with music stands and a grand piano, and rows of chairs below. Billy held my hand tightly as we stood wondering where to go.

Boys were running around setting up the instruments and music stands, all excited. Then Jeremiah and Bikram shouted, "Billy!" and he looked up hopefully at me. "Go on," I said. "I'll bring the stuff."

As I watched him go, I saw the parents laying out their picnics on the lawn next to the lake. No one was alone. They were all in lovely couples which had presumably not been formed on Match.com or PlentyofFish or Twitter, but in the days when people still did meet each other in real life. Started disastrously imagining being there with Mark again, on time because he'd driven the car and operated the satnav, carrying a modest amount of stuff which Mark would have edited before departure, all holding hands, Billy and Mabel between us. And we'd be together, the four of us, on the rug instead of—

"Did you bring the kitchen table?"

I turned. Mr. Wallaker looked unexpectedly glamorous in black suit trousers and a white shirt, slightly unbuttoned. He was looking towards the house, adjusting his cufflinks. "Want a hand with all that?"

"No, no, I'm fine," I said as a Tupperware box fell out of the basket, spilling egg sandwiches onto the grass.

"Leave it," he ordered. "Give me the bassoon. I'll get someone to bring the rest down. Got anyone to sit with?"

"Please don't speak to me like I'm one of your school-boys," I said. "I'm not Bridget No-Mates Darcy and I'm not helpless and I can carry a picnic basket and just because you've got everything under control, and all lakes and orchestras, it doesn't mean—"

There was a crash on the terrace. An entire section of music stands fell over, sending a cello bouncing off the terrace and down the hill, followed by a shrieking bunch of boys.

"Totally under control," he said, giving a little snort of amusement as a double bass and a tuba crashed over next, bringing more music stands with them. "Better go. Give me that." He took the bassoon and set off towards the house. "Oh, and by the way, your dress," he called over his shoulder.

"Yes?"

"Slightly see-through with the sun behind it."

I looked down at the dress. Oh, fuck, it *was* see-through.

"Good effect," he shouted, without looking back.

I stared after him, indignant, confused. He was just . . . just . . . sexist. He was reducing me to a helpless *sex object* and . . . he was married and . . . just . . . just . . .

I started to pick up the basket when a man in a waiter's outfit appeared and said, "I've been asked to carry these down for you, madam," and another voice called, "Bridget!" It was Farzia Seth, Bikram's mum. "Come and sit with us!"

It was fine, because the husbands all sat on one side talking about business, so we girls could gossip, occasionally shoving food into overexcited offspring who swooped on us like seagulls.

When it was time for the concert, Nicolette, who was, naturally, Chair of the Concert Committee, started the proceedings with an astonishingly sycophantic speech about Mr. Wallaker: "Inspiring, invigorating," etc., etc.

"Arousing. Ejaculating. She's changed her tune a bit since he came up with the stately home," muttered Farzia.

"Is it his stately home?" I said.

"I dunno. He fixed it, anyway. And Nicolette's been completely up his arse ever since. Wonder what the orange wife makes of it."

As Nicolette finally drew to a close, Mr. Wallaker jumped onto the terrace and strode in front of the band, silencing the applause.

"Thank you," he said with a slight smile. "I must say I agree with every word. And now—the reason you're here. I give you—Your. Sensational. Sons."

And with that he raised his baton, the Big Swing Band

burst into an enthusiastic—if slightly out of tune—flourish, and they were off. It was actually completely magical, the light softening, the music ringing out over the grounds.

The performance of "The Age of Aquarius" by the recorder ensemble did not, it's true, *entirely* lend itself to six-year-olds on recorders. We were all giggling helplessly, but I was glad to be giggling. Billy was one of the littlest ones, on near the end, and by the time it got to his turn I was beside myself with nerves. I watched him walk over to the piano with his music, looking so small and scared, and I just wanted to go and scoop him up. Then Mr. Wallaker strode over, whispered something to Billy and sat down at the piano.

I didn't know Mr. Wallaker could play. He started with a surprisingly professional jazz introduction, and nodded to Billy to begin. Although there were no words, I could hear every one of them as Billy puffed his way painfully through "I'd Do Anything," Mr. Wallaker gently following every wrong note and wobble.

I would, Billy, I would do anything for you, I thought, tears welling up. My little boy, with all his struggles.

Applause broke out. Mr. Wallaker whispered to Billy and glanced at me. Billy was bursting with pride.

Fortunately Eros and Atticus were taking the stand to perform their own adaptation of "The Trout Quintet" on their flutes, bending and swooping in a pretentious manner which pulled me back from self-congratulatory and existentially despairing tears to suppressed hysteria again. And then it was all over and Billy rushed up, beaming, for a hug and then ran off with his little gang.

It was a warm, liquidy night: beautiful, romantic. The

other parents drifted off, wandering down to the lake hand in hand. I sat on the rug on my own for a bit, wondering what to do. I was desperate for a drink, but driving. I realized the bag with the Diet Cokes and oatmeal cookies had got left behind. Glanced at Billy. He was still tearing around with his gang, all biffing each other over the head. I headed up to the bushes, found the bag and looked back at the scene.

Slowly, a huge, orange harvest moon was rising over the woods. Couples were laughing together in their evening clothes, hugging their joint offspring, remembering all the shared years which had brought them there.

I stepped into the bushes where no one could see and wiped away a tear, taking a giant slurp of Diet Coke and wishing it was neat vodka. They were growing up. They weren't babies any more. It was all going so fast. I realized I was not just sad, but scared: scared of trying not to get lost driving in the dark, scared of all the years ahead of doing this alone: concerts, prize-givings, Christmases, teenagers, problems . . .

"You can't even get plastered, can you?"

Mr. Wallaker's shirt looked very white in the moonlight. His profile, half in silhouette, looked almost noble.

"You all right?"

"Yes!" I said indignantly, wiping my fist across my eyes. "Why do you keep BURSTING up on me? Why do you keep asking me if I'm all right?"

"I know when a woman is foundering and pretending not to be."

He took a step closer. The air was heavy with jasmine, roses.

I breathed unsteadily. It felt as though we were being drawn together by the moon. He reached out, like I was a child, or a Bambi or something, and touched my hair.

"There aren't any nits in here, are there?" he said.

I raised my face, heady with the scent of him, feeling the roughness of his cheek against mine, his lips against my skin . . . then suddenly I remembered all those creepy married guys on the websites and burst out:

"What are you DOING??? Just because I'm on my own, it doesn't mean I'm, I'm DESPERATE and FAIR GAME. You're MARRIED! 'Oh, oh, I'm Mr. Wallaker. I'm all married and perfect,' and what do you mean, 'FOUNDERING'? And I know I'm a rubbish mother and single but you don't have to rub my nose in it and—"

"Billy!!!!!! Your mummy's kissing Mr. Wallaker!"

Billy, Bikram and Jeremiah burst out from the bushes.

"Ah, Billy!" Mr. Wallaker said. "Your mummy's just, er, hurt herself and—"

"Did she hurt her mouth?" said Billy, looking puzzled, at which Jeremiah, who had older brothers, spurted out laughing.

"Ah! Mr. Wallaker! I was looking for you!"

Oh GOD. Now it was Nicolette.

"I was wondering if we should say a few words to the parents, to—Bridget! What are *you* doing here?"

"Looking for some oatmeal cookies!" I said brightly.

"In the bushes? How odd."

"Can I have one? Can I have one?" The boys, mercifully, started yelling and dive-bombing my bag, so I could bend down, covering my confusion.

"I mean, I thought it would be nice to *round things off*,"

Nicolette went on. "People want to see you, Mr. Wallaker. And *hear* you. I think you're *fiercely* talented, I really do."

"Not sure a speech is quite the thing right now. Maybe just go down there and case it out? Would you mind, Mrs. Martinez?"

"No, of course," said Nicolette coldly, giving me a funny look, just as Atticus ran up saying, "Mummeee, I want to see my therapiiiiiist!"

"Right," said Mr. Wallaker, when Nicolette and the boys had disappeared. "You've made yourself very clear. I apologize. I will go back, to not make a speech."

He was starting to head off, then turned. "But just for the record, other people's lives are not always as perfect as they appear, once you crack the shell."

THE HORROR, THE HORROR

Friday 5 July 2013
Dating sites checked 5, winks 0, messages 0, likes 0, online shopping sites visited 12, words of rewrite written 0.

9.30 a.m. Humph. OhMyGod. Well. Humph. "Foundering"? Man-whore. Lecherous sexist married bastard. Humph. Right. Must get on with Hedda-ing up—i.e., finding all of Hedda's lines in the rewritten version and putting them back to the way they were in the first place. Which is actually quite fun!

9.31 a.m. The thing about Internet dating is, the minute you start feeling lonely, confused or desperate you can simply click on one of the sites and it's like a sweetie shop! There are just millions of other quite plausible people all actually available, at least in theory. Have vision of offices up and down the country full of people pretending to work but clicking on Match.com and OkCupid and somehow getting through the lonely tedium of the day. Right, must get on.

10.31 a.m. Oh God. What was he DOING, Mr. Wallaker? Does he do that all the time? It's completely unprofessional. What did he mean, "foundering"?

10.35 a.m. Just looked up foundering: "to proceed in con-fusion."

Humph. Am going to go back online.

10.45 a.m. Just logged on:

     0 people winked at you. 0 people chose you as their favourite. 0 people sent you a message.

Great.

11 a.m. Look at all these men-tarts. *Married, but in an open relationship.* You see?

12.15 p.m. Jude's Internet dating was a nightmare—strings of communication with strangers suddenly left unanswered. I don't want strange bits of men all over the place. Far better to get on with *Leaves*. Must figure out how the yacht/hon-eymoon could work in Sweden rather than Hawaii. I mean, Stockholm is warm in the summer, right? Doesn't one of the girls from Abba live on an island off Stockholm?

12.30 p.m. Maybe will go on Net-a-Porter and look at the sale.

12.45 p.m. What is happening to me? Just put three dresses into my shopping basket. Then logged off. Then logged on again and realized I felt hurt because none of the dresses had winked back.

1 p.m. Maybe will just look at cute thirty-year-olds on Match.com for a minute.

Mmmm.

1.05 p.m. Just spooled down the line of cute thirty-year-olds and screamed out loud.

There, bold as you please, was a picture of . . . Roxster.

MID-MATCH COLLISION

Friday 5 July 2013 (continued)
"Roxster30" was grinning cheerfully, the same picture he has on Twitter. He is, apparently, looking for women aged twenty-five to fifty-five—so it wasn't because I was too old, it was just because he didn't . . . he didn't . . . OH MY GOD. His profile says he has "particular fondness for walks on Hampstead Heath" and "people who make me laugh" and . . . "mini-breaks in pubs by rivers, with Full English Breakfasts." And he really likes skydiving? SKYDIVING?

I mean, it's OK, isn't it? It's just what people do? It's quite funny, it's . . .

Suddenly doubled over in pain, in my armchair, over the laptop.

1.10 p.m. Roxster is Online Now! But then I'm Online Now too! Oh God.

1.11 p.m. Quickly logged off and paced deranged around the room, stuffing bits of half-eaten cheese and crushed Nutribars from the bottom of my handbag into my mouth.

What am I to do? What is the etiquette? Cannot possibly log on again and have another look at Roxster, or he will think I am stalking him, or worse—better?—looking at pictures of cute thirty-year-olds to smoothly replace him with another toy boy.

1.15 p.m. Just checked my email which is now, of course, as well as being overrun by Ocado emails, and "Staff Present" emails, and emails from various country pubs I have imagined staying in with Roxster, also inundated with endless emails from SingleParentMix.com and OkCupid and Match.com saying: Wow! You're proving popular today! and Someone just checked out your profile! and Jonesey49 Someone just winked at you.

Stared closely at two recent emails from Match.com. Jonesey49 Wow! Someone just checked out your profile.

1.17 p.m. Could not find out who they were from because have not paid to properly sign on to Match.com. One of them was from someone aged fifty-nine. And the other aged thirty. It had to be Roxster. It was too much of a coincidence.

1.20 p.m. Wow! Jonesey49. Somebody just winked at you! Again aged thirty.

1.25 p.m. Clearly, Roxster has clocked that I have checked out his profile. What am I going to do? Pretend it hasn't happened? No, that's just . . . I mean, the whole thing is just . . . You can't pretend something like that hasn't happened, can you? We're human beings and we did care about each other, I thought. And . . . text from Roxster: <Jonesey49, I mean Bridget, I mean @JoneseyBJ?>

Stared at phone, mind spooling through all the texts I'd made up in case he got in touch:

<I'm sorry, who is this?>

<Look, you've made your decision, and expressed it in an unnecessarily brutal way, so bugger off.>

Instead, impulsively texted back:

403

<Roxster30, I mean Roxby, I mean @_Roxster *nervous laughter, gabbles* I just want to make it absolutely clear that I wasn't surfing around Match.com looking for cute thirty-year-olds but doing some important research for *The Leaves in His Hair*. Hahaha! I had no idea you liked skydiving so much! Oh God *lunges at wine bottle*.>

There was a pause. Then another ping on the phone.

<Jonesey?>

<Yes, Roxster?>

There was another pause. What was he going to say? Something kind? Something patronizingly meant to be kind? Something apologizing? Something that would hurt?

<I miss you.>

I stared at it. All those mean things I had planned to say . . . My finger hovered over the phone. And then I simply texted back the truth.

<I miss you too.>

Then immediately thought, "Shit! Why didn't I just put one of the less-mean-but-funny ones? Now he'll just have got his ego-reassurance and bugger off." Text ping.

<Jonesey?>

Another ping.

<*YELLS* JONESEYYYY?>

Me: <*Calm, slightly distracted* Yeeees?>

And we were off!

Roxster: <You've gone awfully quiet.>

Me: <*Airy, dismissive* Well, it's hardly surprising. How dare you draw attention to my age in that impertinent and unnecessary fashion? Oh, oh, look at me, I'm so young and you're so old.>

Roxster: <Oh, oh, look at me, I'm all pleased with

404

myself because I won the "see who can keep the texting silence going longest" competition.>

I laughed. I was indeed pleased with myself. There was such a rush of joy and relief that we were back with that secure feeling of knowing someone cares, and understands your sense of humour, and it wasn't all cold and empty and over, we were still there.

But then at the same time there was a dark, lurking fear of getting back into it.

<Jonesey?>

<Yes, Roxster?>

I waited. Texting ping.

<But I do still think you're really old.>

THAT'S DISGUSTING!! That's absolutely against the rules of . . . of . . . Feel like ringing the police! Surely there should be some sort of DATING OMBUDSMAN who legislates against this sort of thing!

Another texting ping. Stared at the phone as if it was a creature in a space movie. I didn't know what it was going to do next. It might suddenly rear up into a monster, or turn into a gentle little bunny. I opened it.

<Joke, Jonesey. Joke. *Hides*>

Looked eerily from side to side. Another texting ping.

<I have been thinking about the curry/chicken pie night, with some regret, for 3 weeks, 6 days and 15 hours, which if you check in Old Moore's Almanac could technically be described as a calendar month. I was completely confused. And plastered. Please forgive me. You are younger-looking and younger-behaved than any woman I have ever met (including my niece who is 3). I miss you.>

What was he saying? Was he saying he'd rethought the

whole thing and wanted to be with me? But did I want to be with him?

<Jonesey?>

<Yes, Roxster?>

<Will you at least have lunch with me?>

Roxster: <Or dinner?>

And again: <Or preferably lunch and dinner?>

Suddenly had flashbacks to all the delicious dinners and aftermaths we had enjoyed and had to stop self texting back: <And breakfast?>

Maybe Tom was right. Maybe Roxster wasn't just dismissing me as a sad old bag. Texted: <Please be quiet. I am looking out of the window for passing dot-com billionaires wearing walking boots.>

<I am going to come over and fight them.>

<Would I need to be at the lunch or dinner or would it just mainly be the food?>

<We could meet without food if you like.>

This was UNHEARD OF. He must be really, really serious. I needed time to digest this.

Another texting ping.

<If you need time to digest this, if you'll pardon the pun, I'll wait.>

And another.

<Maybe just a packet of crisps?>

Was going to text: <Cheese and onion?> but maybe that suggested I thought he was being cheesy and there were onions hidden amongst the nice stuff.

So, again, I just texted what was true.

<I'd like that. As long as you promise not to fart.>

REKINDLING

Thursday 11 July 2013

Days of continuous sunshine 11, raindrops fallen on head 0 (unbelievable).

2 p.m. Is boiling hot. Still! No one can believe their luck. Everyone is out in the streets, bunking off work, drinking, wild for sex and complaining that it is too hot.

Texting is completely back on again with Roxster and he has been lovely, despite Talitha's dire warnings about taking someone back after they have dumped you. And despite Tom's dire warnings about people who are All Text and No Trousers, and professional warnings about the fact that I could only expect a future of mixed messages, and had I thought about what *I* actually wanted—apart from endless texting and sporadic nights of sex?

Roxster has explained about the curry and lateness on the break-up night, and said he wasn't—as I suspected all along—having a curry with "colleagues." In fact he was sitting on his own, stuffing his face with chicken korma, poppadoms and lager, because he was so confused, and suddenly overcrowded about being a proper boyfriend, and maybe becoming a father figure. And then, after he made his break-up speech, I seemed completely fine about it, almost relieved, delighted to break up, until the farting rant. And then, after that, he didn't know what to do. And he is cheerful and sweet and light and so much better than lecherous married bastards. We are seeing each other on Saturday: for a walk on Hampstead Heath.

BLIMEY

Saturday 13 July 2013

3 p.m. Frantic preparation. Had to deal with Mum, who is taking Mabel and Billy to tea at Fortnum & Mason (good luck with that one, Mum). "Oh, Mabel's wearing leggings, is she? Where do you keep your colanders?"

Dived out for leg wax and toenail polish, then washed hair and put on the Summer Concert see-through floaty dress, then thought it was bad karma, so changed it to a non-see-through pale pink one. Then got text from Farzia, asking if Billy and Jeremiah were going to football tomorrow as Bikram didn't want to go unless they all went, then lost my flip-flops but couldn't wear my other sandals because they'd squash the toenail varnish, then finally got to the pub with two minutes to spare and rushed to the loo to make sure I didn't have too much make-up on like Barbara Cartland. Eventually sat down in the fabulous sunshine in the garden, like a relaxed, on-time Goddess of Light and Calm, and, as Roxster appeared, a seagull shat on my shoulder.

It was so exciting to see Roxster, looking gorgeous in a bright blue polo shirt, and be falling about laughing again about the seagull, and just having fun, and feeling like children on a spree, only more sexy. And we had a couple of beers, and Roxster had his food, and tried repeatedly to get the seagull poo off my boob and I was so . . . happy!

Then we set off for our walk, and the Heath was teeming with people rejoicing in the sunshine and complaining about it, couples in each other's arms, and I was part of one too, arm in arm with Roxster. Then we came to a sun-dappled glade and sat down on a bench we'd sat down on often before. And after Roxster had finished laughing about the red dots he'd noticed on my legs from the leg wax, he looked serious. And he started to say that he'd been thinking, and although he really, really wanted to have children of his own, and really, really thought he ought to be with someone his own age, and didn't know what his friends would say, or what his mum would say, he just didn't think he would find anyone he got on with the way he got on with me. And he wanted to do it all, the whole thing, properly, and climb trees on the Heath, and be a dad to Billy and Mabel.

I stared at him. I did really heart Roxster, I hearted that he was so beautiful and young and sexy, but more than that hearted who he was and what he stood for. He was funny, and together, and light, and kind, and practical, and emotional but contained. But he was also born when I was twenty-one. And if we'd both been born at the same time—how could we know what would have happened? What I did know as I looked at him, was that I didn't want to ruin Roxster's life. And my kids were absolutely without a shadow of a doubt the best thing that I had in my life. I didn't want to deprive him of doing all that for himself.

Crucially, though, I suspected that, even though he wanted to, Roxster just couldn't do it. He would try, but then sometime in a week, or six weeks, or six months, he would go all uncertain again and keep shorting out. And the thing about reaching the advanced age of, er, thirty-five was that I just didn't want all that uncertainty and emotional roller coaster and pain any more. I just couldn't bear it.

Moreover, I did NOT want to be like Judi Dench with Daniel Craig at the end of *Skyfall*, the age difference between whom must be about the same as between me and Roxster. But then, in *Skyfall*, when you think about it, Judi Dench was actually the Bond Girl, not the frizzy-haired one with no character who decided (in a weird anti-feminist twist, surely?) she wanted to be Miss Moneypenny. Judi Dench was the one Daniel Craig really loved, and ended up carrying through the bullets. But then would Daniel Craig actually have had sex with Judi Dench? I mean, if she wasn't dead? How great if they'd done a beautifully lit sex scene with Judi Dench looking gorgeous in a black La Perla slip. Now there would be a rebranding feminist . . .

"Jonesey. Are you pretending not to have an orgasm again?"

I looked back, startled, at Roxster who was now down on one knee. How could I have been so rude as to stare into space for so long when . . . God, he was so, so, so gorgeous, but . . .

"Roxster," I blurted, "you don't really mean all this, do you? You're not actually going to be able to do it."

Roxby McDuff looked thoughtful for a moment, then laughed ruefully, got to his feet, and shook his head.

"No, Jonesey, you're right. I'm actually not."

Then we hugged each other, with lust and happiness and sadness and tenderness. But I knew that, this time, the game was up. It really was over.

As we let go, I opened my eyes and over Roxster's shoulder saw Mr. Wallaker, standing stock-still and staring at us.

Mr. Wallaker caught my eye, impassive, said nothing, and, in his usual fashion, simply strode away.

On the way home, in the midst of confusion, and sadness, and seller's remorse, and overheating, and shock at Mr. Wallaker seeing what looked like an engagement but was actually a break-up, I felt that overwhelming thing that people feel when . . . that I . . . that once again, at a moment of parting, I hadn't . . . that you absolutely have to tell people that . . . and simultaneously, spookily, the text pinged.

<Jonesey?>

<Yes, Roxster?>

Roxster: <Just wanted to tell you that I will always . . . H>

Me: <E?>

Roxster: <A>

Me: <R>

Roxster: <T U>

Me: <M>

Roxster: <E?>

Me: <2 U>

Roxster: <G>

Me: <B>

Roxster: <H>

Me: <X>

I will always heart you. Me too you. Great Big Hug. (Or possibly Hamburger.)

I waited. Was he going to leave me as the final one in the final thread? There was a ping.

<I meant fart, not heart, you understand.>

Then another ping.

<I didn't. And I will. Always. Now don't reply. XX>

Roxby McDuff: a gentleman to the last.

GIVING IN

Saturday 13 July 2013 (continued)

When I got home, there was an hour before Mum was due back with the kids. I sat down, finally, in an armchair, with a cup of tea. And I just gave in and accepted it all. It was really over with sweet, lovely Roxster. And I was sad, but so it was. And I couldn't hold all these balls in the air. I couldn't rewrite a film about an updated Hedda Gabler on a yacht in Hawaii, moved to Stockholm by six different people. I couldn't do Internet dating with weird strangers. I couldn't keep this mad matrix of schedules and Zombie Apocalypses and Build-a-Bear parties in my head, and deal with nearly-confusingly-snogging married teachers at the school, and wear *Grazia*-style clothes and try to have a boyfriend and do a job, and be a mother. I tried to stop myself thinking I should do anything. Check my emails. Go to Zumba. Get on OkCupid. Read the latest insane rewrite of *The Leaves on His Yacht*.

I just sat there and thought, "This will just have to do. Me. The kids. Just let the days flow by." I didn't feel sad, really. I couldn't remember the feeling of not having to do the next thing. Not having to squeeze the last second out of the day. Or find out why the fridge was making that noise.

And I'd love to say something marvellous came out of it. But it didn't, really. My bum probably got fatter or something. But I sensed a sort of mental clarity emerging. A sense that what I needed to do now was find some peace.

"I need to be gentle now," I thought, blinking rapidly. "It's a gentle time. Never mind anyone else, we'll just be us—me, Billy and Mabel. Just feel the wind in our hair, and the rain on our faces. Just enjoy them growing up. Don't miss it. They'll be gone soon."

I stared dramatically ahead, thinking, "I am brave, though I am alone," then realized that the phone was quacking somewhere. Where was it?

Eventually located phone in the downstairs toilet and jumped in alarm, seeing a string of texts from Chloe.

<Just had a call from your mum. Is your phone off? They've been thrown out of Fortnums.>

<She wants you to come. Mabel is crying and she's forgotten the key.>

<She's trying to find Hamleys and they're lost.>

<Are you getting any of my texts?>

<OK. I've told her to get in a taxi and I'll meet them at the house with the key.>

Just then the doorbell rang. Opened it to find Mum with Billy and Mabel—both crying, hot, sweaty and smeared with cake—on the doorstep.

Got everyone downstairs, telly on, computer on, Mum with a cup of tea when doorbell rang again.

Was Chloe, uncharacteristically in tears.

"Chloe, I'm so sorry!" I said. "I just turned the phone off for a little bit to just . . . get over something and missed all your—"

"It's not that!" she wailed. "It's Graham."

It turned out Chloe and Graham had taken out a row-ing boat on the Serpentine, and Chloe had prepared an immaculate picnic hamper with cutlery and china, at which Graham said, "I have something to say."

Chloe, of course, thought Graham was going to ask her to marry him. And then he announced that he had met somebody in Houston on YoungFreeAndSingle.com and was getting transferred to Texas to go and live with her.

"He said I was too perfect," she sobbed. "I'm not per-fect. I just feel I have to pretend to be perfect. And you don't like me either because you think I'm too perfect too."

"Oh, Chloe. I don't! You're not perfect!" I said, throwing my arms around her.

"Aren't I?" she said, looking at me hopefully.

"No, yes," I gabbled. "I mean, not perfect, though you are great. And"—I suddenly felt emotional—"I know middle-class working mothers always say this but I genu-inely don't know what I would do without you helping me, and being so perfe— I mean, so great. What I mean is, it's just a relief that everything in your life isn't completely perfect, though, obviously, I'm very sorry that that FUCK-WIT Graham was so FUCKWITTED as to—"

"But I thought you'd only like me if I was perfect."

"No, I was FRIGHTENED of you because you were perfect, because it made me feel so not perfect."

"But I always think YOU'RE perfect!"

"Mummy, can we go up to our room? Granny's being weird," said Billy, appearing up the stairs.

"Granny'th got a tail," said Mabel.

"Billy, Mabel!" said Chloe delightedly. "Can I take them upstairs?"

"Great, I'll go and see to Granny. Check if she's grown a tail," I said, looking sternly at Mabel and adding reassuringly to Chloe: "You're not perfect."

"Aren't I? You really mean it?"

"No, really, definitely not perfect at all."

"Oh, thank you!" she said. "Neither are you!" and headed up the stairs with the children, looking and being absolutely perfect.

Got downstairs to find Mum, who, if she did have a tail, had hidden it very well beneath the coat-dress, banging through all the cupboards saying, "Where do you put the tea strainer?"

"I use tea bags," I muttered grumpily.

"Tea bags. Durr! I mean, you might have left the phone on! It's only responsible if you have children who can't behave themselves. What have you got on your top? Have you been out in that dress? The trouble with flesh pink is it can wash you out, can't it?"

I burst into tears, straight in her face.

"Now come on, Bridget, you've got to pull yourself together. You've got to soldier on, you can't . . . you can't . . . you can't . . . you can't . . . you can't . . ."

I literally thought she was just never going to stop saying "you can't," but then she burst into tears too.

"You're not helping," I sobbed. "You just think I'm rubbish. You're always trying to change me and think I'm doing it all wrong and make me wear different . . . COLOURS," I wailed.

Mum suddenly snuffled to a halt and stared at me.

"Oh, Bridget, I'm so sorry," she said, almost in a whisper. "I'm so very, very sorry."

417

She stumbled awkwardly, knelt in front of me, put her arms around me and pulled me to her. "My little girl."

It was the first time I'd actually felt Mum's bouffe. It was crispy, almost solid. She didn't seem to mind it being squashed as she held me close. I really liked it. I wanted her to give me a bottle of warm milk or something.

"It was so dreadful. So dreadful what happened to Mark. I couldn't bear to think. You're doing so . . . Oh, Bridget. I miss Daddy. I miss him so much, so much. But you've . . . got to . . . you've got to just keep going, haven't you? That's half the battle."

"No," I wailed. "It's just papering over the cracks."

"I should have . . . Daddy ALWAYS said . . . he said, 'Why can't you just let her be?' That's my problem. I can't let anything be. Everything has to be perfect and it . . . ISN'T!" she wailed. "At least, I don't mean you, I mean you are, you're doing so well . . . Oh, where've I put my lipstick? And Pawl, you know Pawl—the pastry chef at St. Oswald's?—I thought, you know, he was always bringing me little savoury profiteroles . . . taking me into the kitchen. But he turns out to be one of these . . ."

I started laughing then. "Oh, Mum, I could've told you Pawl was gay from the moment I saw him."

"But there's no such things as gay, darling. It's just LAZINESS and—"

Billy appeared on the stairs. "Mummy, Chloe's crying upstairs. Oh." He looked at us, puzzled. "Why is everybody crying?"

Just as Mum, Chloe and I were having a sort of AA-style sharing event over the kitchen table, while Billy played Xbox and Mabel trotted back and forth handing us Hellvanian

418

Fuckoons and leaves from the garden and patting us kindly, the doorbell rang again. It was Daniel, looking desperate and holding an overnight bag.

"Jones, my dear girl, I have been released from the rehab sin bin. I got back to the flat and I . . . Actually, I don't want to be alone, Jones. Could I possibly come into the hellhole for a minute? Just to—" his voice cracked— "be in some sort of human company which I know I'm not going to try and shag?"

"All right," I said, trying to ignore the insult, given the sensitivity of the moment. "But you have to PROMISE you won't try to shag Chloe."

It was quite an odd evening, as social occasions go, but I think everyone enjoyed it. By the time Daniel had finished with her, Chloe thought she was Charlize Theron, and that Graham wasn't fit to touch the hem of her skirt, which he isn't, whoever he is. And Mum, as she cuddled Mabel, eating alternate chocolate buttons with her, slurping red wine and getting completely covered in all of it, was quite coming round to the idea of Kenneth Garside. "I mean, he's terribly charming, is Kenneth. It's just that he's VERY highly sexed."

Daniel, while saying, "And what on EARTH is wrong with that, Mrs. Jones?" turned out to be really, really good at the Xbox. But then he ruined the whole thing in the hallway at the end by putting his hand right up Chloe's skirt. I mean, right up to her knickers.

PART FOUR

The Great Tree

SUMMER OF FUN

Saturday 31 August 2013

133lb (still! Miracle), boyfriends 0, children 2 (lovely), friends loads, holidays 3 (counting mini-break), screenwriting jobs 0, possibility of screenwriting jobs (slight), days till school starts 4, major shocks 1.

It has been a brilliant summer. I called up Brian the Agent and asked him to get me off *The Leaves in His Hair*, and Brian laughed and said, "Finally! What took you so long?" And Brian thinks we should have a go with my new screenplay idea: *Time Stand Still Here* which is an updating of Virginia Woolf's *To the Lighthouse*, only with a bit more *structure*, set in a former Lighthouse and Coastguards Cottages holiday complex from the Rural Retreats brochure, in which Mrs. Ramsay has an affair with a friend of her son James.

Magda and Jeremy invited us to Paxos for a week, where there were lots of friends with kids; and Woney, who has now had liposuction, was parading around in brightly coloured swimsuits and matching sarongs, swinging her hair extensions and frightening Cosmo. And although Rebecca and the kids were away touring with Jake, there were play dates with Jeremiah and his mum, and Farzia and Bikram, and Cosmata and Thelonius. And we tried to do something with the garden, which consisted of planting three begonias.

We went away to a little cottage by the sea in Devon for three nights with Mum and had a great time. And Mum comes over a lot, just to do baking and things with Billy and Mabel, and she doesn't criticize my housekeeping or child-rearing any more, and we all really like it. And she has them to stay, and they love it, though it is a bit late in the day because I've got no one to shag in the empty house now.

But I try to stand like a great tree and take the stick about Roxster—the Love that Could Not Beeeeeeee! as Tom and Arkis have dramatically dubbed it—and just be happy that, even if no one ever loves me or shags me again ever, at least I know it's not completely out of the question.

Now, however, am trying to deal with a growing alarm about going back to school: the different homeworks which will probably be beyond my capabilities, the different days for show-and-tell and shin pads. More alarmingly, find myself looking back over all my encounters with Mr. Wallaker—the tree, the snow, the Sports Day, the Botox, the concert—all his attempts at kindness to me and I feel shallow and think maybe he wasn't just trying to make me feel stupid. Maybe he did really care. BUT HE WAS MARRIED, FOR FUCK'S SAKE, even if it was to an over-plastic-surgeried drunk lady. He had kids. What was he doing nearly kissing me, and confusing me? And I gave him an earful, and he saw me with Roxster, and he thinks I'm a condom-buying, syphilis-infected, shallow cougar and now we are going to have to face each other every day at school.

4 p.m. Just went round to Rebecca's, who is back from the touring, and blurted out the whole confusion about Mr. Wallaker, and the school concert and the Heath.

"Hmm," she said. "None of it adds up. *He* doesn't add up. Have you got a photo? Any other info?"

I spooled through the phone and found a shot of the concert and Mr. Wallaker accompanying Billy.

I watched as Rebecca stared at the photo, frowning slightly. She spooled through some more.

"This is Capthorpe House, right? Where they have festivals and stuff?"

"Yes."

"I know exactly who this is. He isn't a schoolteacher."

I looked at her in consternation. Oh God. He *was* a weirdo.

"He plays a bit of jazz piano?"

I nodded.

She went to the cupboard, slightly dislodging the plastic garden vine woven into her hair, and took out a bottle of red wine.

"He's called Scott. He was at college with Jake."

"He's a musician?"

"No. Yes. No." She looked at me. "That's a hobby. He went into the SAS."

The Special Air Service! He was James Bond! It explained everything. The "One, sir! Two, sir!" Billy jumping and rolling from the tree. The gun reflex at Sports Day. Bond.

"When did he start at the school?"

"Last year—December?"

"I bet it's him. He went off to Sandhurst, then he was abroad a lot, but they kept in touch in a man-friend—i.e., not-very-often—sort of way. Jake ran into him a few months ago. He'd been in Afghanistan. Some bad shit had happened. He said he was back and 'keeping it simple.'" Rebecca suddenly laughed. "He thinks teaching at a London private school is 'keeping it simple'? Has he seen your Quadrant Living chart?"

"And he's married?"

"Not if it's him. He's got two boys, right, at boarding school? He was married, but not any more. She was a nightmare."

"Is she really plastic-surgeried . . . ?"

"Exactly. She turned into a major spender: clothes, charity luncheons, all that bollocks, total plastic-surgery queen. When he went abroad she started sleeping with her personal trainer, filed for divorce and tried to fleece him. That place Capthorpe Hall is the family pile. I think she might have tried to get back with him now she's made herself look like the Bride of Wildenstein. I'll ask Jake. Next time I see him."

BACK TO SCHOOL

Friday 13 September 2013

Minutes late for school pickups 0 (but only as trying to impress Mr. Wallaker), conversations with Mr. Wallaker 0, seconds of eye contact with Mr. Wallaker 0.

9.15 p.m. It seems Rebecca was right. And although I have not breathed a word about any of it (except, obviously, to Talitha, Jude and Tom), the news is out that Mr. Wallaker is not married. Which is awful because now there is a feeding frenzy over Mr. Wallaker. Everyone is trying to fix Mr. Wallaker up with their single friend. Farzia did suggest trying to shove me at him, but it is pointless. Even though my heart leaps now, when I see him on the steps, Mr. Wallaker does not come up and tease me any more. Mr. Wallaker does not run into us on the Heath. The magic is gone. And it is all my own fault.

Mr. Wallaker is in charge of more and more things at the school: sport, chess, music, "Pastoral Care." He is like Russell Crowe in *Gladiator*—when he was a slave and organized the other slaves into an army and defeated all the Greeks or Romans. It's like putting ants down in any situation: ants will just do what ants do. If you put someone really cool and capable down anywhere they will just be cool and capable. And be set up with every unattached woman in sight except me.

Friday 27 September 2013

9.45 p.m. "It's you he loves," said Tom, on his fourth mojito in the York & Albany.

"Look, can we just shut up about Mr. Effing Wallaker?" I muttered. "I've accepted my life now. It's good. It's the three of us. We're not broke. I'm not lonely any more. I'm a great tree."

"And *The Leaves in His Hair* is going to be made!" encouraged Jude.

"What's left of it," I said darkly.

"But at least you'll get to go to the premiere, baby," said Tom. "You might meet someone there."

"If I'm invited."

"If he's not calling you, if he's not texting you, he's just not that into you," said Jude unhelpfully.

"But Mr. Wallaker has never called her or texted her," said Tom squiffily. "Who are we talking about here?"

"Can we please stop talking about Mr. Wallaker? I don't even like him and he doesn't like me."

"Well, you did rather give him an earful, darling," said Talitha.

"But there was so much depth to what was building," said Tom.

"When he's hot, he's hot; when he's not, he's not," said Jude.

"Why don't you get Rebecca to fix you up?" said Tom.

10 p.m. Just went round to Rebecca's. She shook her head. "It never works, that sort of thing. They sense it a mile off, by radar. Just let it unfold."

THE MIGHTY JUNGLE

Friday 18 October 2013
Number of times listened to "The Lion Sleeps Tonight" 45 (continuing).

9.15 p.m. The choir auditions have come round again. Billy is lying in bed singing "The Lion Sleeps Tonight," then going, "Eeeeeeeeeeeoheeeeoheeeeoh" in a high-pitched voice while Mabel yells, "Shut up, Billy, shut uuuuuuuuuuurp."

This year we have been practising hitting actual notes. Was in fact quite carried away with self this evening, teaching them Doh Ray Me, parroting Maria in *The Sound of Music* (I actually do know the whole of *The Sound of Music* off by heart).

"Mummy?" said Billy.

"Yes?"

"Can you stop, please?"

Monday 21 October 2013
Times practised "The Lion Sleeps Tonight" before school 24, hours spent worrying whether Billy will get into choir 7, times changed outfit to pick up Billy from choir auditions 5, minutes early for pickup 7 (good, apart from reasons for same: i.e. impressing hopeless love prospect).

3.30 p.m. Just about to pick up Billy and get choir audition results. Beside self with nerves.

6 p.m. Freakishly was already waiting inside the school gates before Billy came out. I saw Mr. Wallaker emerge onto the steps and glance round, but he ignored me. Was sunk into gloom, realizing that now he was officially single, he feared that all single women, including me, were going to nibble at him like piranhas.

"Mummy!" Billy emerged, grinning the fantastic ear-to-ear grin, as though his face was going to burst. "I got in! I got in! I got in the choir!"

Delirious with joy I encircled him in my arms at which he grunted, "Ge' awfff!" like an adolescent and glanced nervously at his friends.

"Let's go and celebrate!" I said. "I'm so proud of you! Let's go to . . . to McDonald's!"

"Well done, Billy." It was Mr. Wallaker. "You kept trying and you made it. Good effort."

"Um!" I said, thinking maybe this was the moment when I could apologize and explain, but he just walked off, leaving me with only his pert bum to look at.

I just ate two Big Macs with fries, a double chocolate shake and a sugar doughnut.

When he's hot, he's hot; when he's not, he's not. But at least there is always food.

PARENTS' EVENING

Tuesday 5 November 2013

9 p.m. Hmmm. Maybe he isn't not hot. I mean, not completely not hot. Arrived at parents' evening, admittedly a tad late, to find most of the parents preparing to leave and Billy's form teacher, Mr. Pitlochry-Howard, looking at his watch.

Mr. Wallaker strode in with an armful of reports. "Ah, Mrs. Darcy," he said. "Decided to come along after all?"

"I have been. At a meeting," I said hoity-toitily (even though, unaccountably, as yet, no one has asked for a meeting about *Time Stand Still Here*, my updating of *To the Lighthouse*) and settled myself with an ingratiating smile in front of Mr. Pitlochry-Howard.

"How IS Billy?" said Mr. Pitlochry-Howard kindly. Always feel uncomfortable when people say this. Sometimes it's nice if you think that they really care, but I paranoically imagined he meant there was something wrong with Billy.

"He's fine," I said, bristling. "How is he, you know, at school?"

"He seems very happy."

"Is he all right with the other boys?" I said anxiously.

"Yes, yes, popular with the boys, very cheerful. Gets a bit giggly in the class sometimes."

"Right, right," I said, suddenly remembering Mum getting a letter from my headmistress suggesting that I had some sort of pathological giggling *problem*. Fortunately Dad went in and gave the teacher an earful, but maybe it was a genetic disorder.

"I don't think we need to worry too much about giggling," said Mr. Wallaker. "What was the issue you had with the English?"

"Well, the spellings . . ." Mr. Pitlochry-Howard began.

"Still?" said Mr. Wallaker.

"Ah, well, you see," I said, springing to Billy's defence. "He's only little. And also—*as* a writer I believe language is a constantly evolving, fluctuating thing, and actually communicating what you want to say is more important than spelling and punctuating it." I paused for a moment, remembering Imogen at Greenlight accusing me of just putting strange dots and marks in here and there where I thought they looked nice.

"I mean, look at 'realize,'" I went on. "It used to be spelt with a z and now it's Americanized—that's with an 's' by the way. And I notice you're spelling it on the tests with an 's' because computers do now!" I finished triumphantly.

"Yes, marvelous, with a single 'l,'" said Mr. Wallaker. "But, at this present moment in time, Billy needs to pass his spelling tests or he'll feel like a berk. So could you perhaps practise when you two are running up the hill in the mornings just after the bell has rung?"

"OK," I said, looking at him under lowered brows. "How is his actual writing? I mean, creatively?"

"Well," said Mr. Pitlochry-Howard, rustling through his papers. "Ah, yes. We asked them to write about something strange."

"Let me see," said Mr. Wallaker, putting on his glasses. Oh God. It would be so great if we could both put on our reading glasses on a date without feeling embarrassed.

"Something strange, you say?" He cleared his throat.

Mummy

In the mornings when we wake mummy up her hair is crazy. Eeeeek! It blows up! Then she says we are in an army and have to get our kit on One sir, two sir, dont panic! But then EPIC FAIL! she poored the muesli in the washing machine and gave us persil. Mabel was late for Infants they had gone into dissembly. EPIC FAIL LEVEL 2!! Says Attend! like she is a french policman because of the french parant book and now Mabel says it to Saliva and also says dammit EPIC FAIL LEVEL 3!! When mummy is werking she types and talks on the phone at the same time chewing nicorette. When I didn't get in the choir last year said it was not EPIC FAIL but X Factor and next year! It was! And then she found Puffle Two who was MIA missing in action and she cuddled me but then I came down at night she was dansing on her own . . . killer queen. Eek! Graaaaagh!! Strange very strange.

I sank into the chair, dismayed. Was this how my children saw me?

Mr. Pitlochry-Howard was staring down at his papers, red-faced.

"Well!" said Mr. Wallaker. "As you say, it communicates what it's trying to communicate very well. A very vivid picture of . . . something strange."

I met his gaze levelly. It was all right for him, wasn't it? He was trained in giving orders and had packed his boys off to boarding school and could use the holidays to casually perfect their incredible music and sporting skills while adjusting their spelling of "inauspicious."

"How about the rest of it?" he said.

"No. He's—his marks are very good apart from the spelling. Homework's still pretty disorganized."

"Let's have a look," said Mr. Wallaker, rifling through the science papers, then picking up the planets one.

"'Write five sentences, each including a fact about Uranus.'"

He paused. Suddenly could feel myself wanting to giggle.

"He only did one sentence. Was there a problem with the question?"

"I think the problem was it seemed rather a lot of facts to come up with, about such a featureless galactical area," I said, trying to control myself.

"Oh, really? You find Uranus featureless?" I distinctly saw Mr. Wallaker suppress a giggle.

"Yes," I managed to say. "Had it been Mars, the famed Red Planet, with recent robot landings, or even Saturn with its many rings—"

"Or Mars with its twin *orbs*," said Mr. Wallaker, glancing, I swear, at my tits before staring intently down at his papers.

"Exactly," I got out in a strangled voice.

434

"But, Mrs. Darcy," burst out Mr. Pitlochry-Howard, with an air of injured pride, "I personally am more fascinated by Uranus than—"

"Thank you!" I couldn't help myself saying, then just totally gave in to helpless laughter.

"Mr. Pitlochry-Howard," said Mr. Wallaker, pulling himself together, "I think we have admirably made our point. And," he murmured in an undertone, "I can quite see whence the giggling originates. Are there any more issues of concern with Billy's work?"

"No, no, grades are very good, gets on with the other boys, very jolly, great little chap."

"Well, it's all down to you, Mr. Pitlochry-Howard," I said creepily. "All that teaching! Thank you *so* much."

Then, not daring to look at Mr. Wallaker, I got up and glided out of the hall.

However, once outside I sat in the car thinking I needed to go back in and ask Mr. Pitlochry-Howard more about the homework. Or maybe, if Mr. Pitlochry-Howard should, perchance, be busy, Mr. Wallaker.

Back in the hall Mr. Pitlochry-Howard and Mr. Wallaker were talking to Nicolette and her handsome husband, who had his hand supportively on Nicolette's back.

You're not supposed to listen to the other parents' consultations but Nicolette was projecting so powerfully it was impossible not to.

"I just wonder if Atticus might be a little overextended," Mr. Pitlochry-Howard was mumbling. "He seems to have so many after-school clubs and play dates. He's a little anxious sometimes. He becomes despairing if he doesn't feel he is on top."

"Where is he in the class?" said Nicolette. "How far is he from the top?"

She peered over at the chart, which Mr. Pitlochry-Howard put his arm across. She flicked her hair crossly. "Why don't we know their relative performance levels? What are the class positions?"

"We don't do class positions, Mrs. Martinez," said Mr. Pitlochry-Howard.

"Why not?" she said, with the sort of apparently pleasant, casual inquisitiveness which conceals a swordsman poised behind the arras.

"It's really about doing their personal best," said Mr. Pitlochry-Howard.

"Let me explain something," said Nicolette. "I used to be CEO of a large chain of health and fitness clubs, which expanded throughout the UK and into North America. Now I am CEO of a family. My children are the most important, complex and thrilling product I have ever developed. I need to be able to assess their progress, relative to their peers, in order to adjust their development."

Mr. Wallaker was watching her in silence.

"Healthy competition has its place but when an obsession with relative position replaces a pleasure in the actual subject . . ." Mr. Pitlochry-Howard began nervously.

"And you feel that extra-curricular activities and play dates are stressing him out?" said Nicolette.

Her husband put his hand on her arm: "Darling . . ."

"These boys need to be rounded. They need their flutes.

They need their fencing. Furthermore," she continued, "I do *not* see social engagements as 'play dates.' They are team-building exercises."

"THEY ARE CHILDREN!" Mr. Wallaker roared. "They are not corporate products! What they need to acquire is not a constant massaging of the ego, but confidence, fun, affection, love, a sense of self-worth. They need to understand, now, that there will always—always—be someone greater and lesser than themselves, and that their self-worth lies in their contentment with who they are, what they are doing and their increasing competence in doing it."

"I'm sorry?" said Nicolette. "So there's no point trying? I see. Then, well, maybe we should be looking at Westminster."

"We should be looking at who they will become as adults," Mr. Wallaker went on. "It's a harsh world out there. The barometer of success in later life is not that they always win, but how they deal with failure. An ability to pick themselves up when they fall, retaining their optimism and sense of self, is a far greater predictor of future success than class position in Year 3."

Blimey. Had Mr. Wallaker suddenly been reading *Buddha's Little Instruction Book*?

"It's not a harsh world if you know how to win," purred Nicolette. "What is Atticus's form position, please?"

"We don't give form positions," said Mr. Wallaker, getting to his feet. "Is there anything else?"

"Yes, his French," said Nicolette, undaunted. And then they all sat down again.

10 p.m. Perhaps Mr. Wallaker is right about there being always someone "greater and lesser than yourself" at things. Was just walking back to car when posh, exhausted mother trying to wrangle three overdressed children suddenly burst out, "Clemency! You fucking, bleeding *little* c***!"

FIFTY SHADES OF OLD

Friday 22 November 2013
137lb (helpless slide back towards obesity), calories 3384, Diet Cokes 7, Red Bulls 3, ham-and-cheese paninis 2, exercise 0, months since did roots 2, weeks since waxed legs 5, weeks since painted toenails 6, number of months since any sexual experience whatsoever 5 (Born-Again Virgin again).

Am letting self go to seed—un-waxed, un-plucked, un-exercised, un-exfoliated, un-mani-pedicured, un-meditated, roots un-touched-up, hair un-blow-dried, undressed (never, worst luck)—and stuffing face to make up for it. Something has to be done.

Saturday 23 November 2013
3 p.m. Just came out of the hairdresser's where my roots were restored to their youthful glory. Immediately came face to face with a poster at the bus stop of Sharon Osbourne and her daughter Kelly: Sharon Osbourne with auburn hair and Kelly with *grey hair*.

So confused. Is looking old the new bohemian floaty scarf now? Am I going to have to go back, have the grey roots restored and ask the Botox man to add some wrinkles?

Was just pondering this question when a voice said, "Hello."

"Mr. Wallaker!" I said, fluffing up my new hair coquettishly.

"Hello!" He was wearing a warm, sexy jacket and scarf, looking down at me in the old way, cool, with the slightly amused twitch in the corner of his mouth.

"Look," I said, "I just want to say, I'm sorry I said all that at the school concert and was so lippy with you all those times when you were just being kind. But I thought you were married. And the thing is, I know everything. I mean, not *everything*. But I know about you being in the SAS and—"

His expression changed. "What did you say?"

"Jake and Rebecca live across the road and . . ."

He was looking away from me, down the street, the muscle in his jaw working.

"It's all right. I haven't told anybody. And the thing is, you see, I know what it's like when something really bad happens."

"I don't want to talk about it," he said abruptly.

"I know, you think I'm an awful mother, and spend the whole time in the hairdresser's and buying condoms, but I'm actually not like that. Those gonorrhoea leaflets—Mabel had just picked them up at the doctor's. I don't have gonorrhoea or syphilis . . ."

"Am I interrupting?"

A stunning girl was emerging from Starbucks, holding two coffees.

"Hi." She handed him one of the coffees and smiled at me.

"This is Miranda," said Mr. Wallaker stiffly.

Miranda was beautiful and young, with long, shiny black

440

hair, topped with a trendy woollen cap. She had long thin legs in jeans and . . . and studded ankle boots.

"Miranda, this is Mrs. Darcy, one of our school mothers."

"Bridget!" said a voice. The hairdresser who had just done my roots was hurrying up the street. "You left your wallet in the salon. How's the colour? No more shades of grey for you for Christmas!"

"It is very nice, thank you. Happy Christmas," I said like a traumatized automaton granny. "Happy Christmas, Mr. Wallaker. Happy Christmas, Miranda," I said, although it was not Christmas.

They looked at me oddly as I walked shakily away.

9.15 p.m. The children are asleep and I am very old and lonely. No one will ever fancy me again ever, ever, ever. Mr. Wallaker is at this moment shagging Miranda. Everybody's life is perfect except mine.

THE SOUND OF SHELLS CRACKING

Monday 25 November 2013
136lb, number of pounds heavier than Miranda 46.

9.15 a.m. Right. I am used to this now. I know what to do. We do not wallow. We do not descend into feelings of being crap with men. We do not think everyone else's life is perfect except ours, except bloody Miranda's. We concentrate on our inner great tree, and we go to yoga.

1 p.m. Blimey. Started off in yoga, but realized had drunk too much Diet Coke again. Suffice it to say, it didn't go very well during Pigeon Pose.

Went instead into the meditation class next door, which you could argue was a bit of a waste of money because it *had* cost fifteen quid and all we did was sit cross-legged trying to keep our minds blank. Found self looking round the room, thinking about Mr. Wallaker and Miranda, then nearly farted in shock.

I didn't recognize him at first but there, sitting in loose-fitting grey clothes on a purple mat, eyes closed, palms raised on his knees, was none other than George from Greenlight. At least, I was pretty sure it was him, but it was hard to tell. Then I saw the big glasses and iPhone next to the purple mat and I knew it was definitely George.

On the way out, I wasn't sure whether to say hello

or not, but then I thought we had been communing on some sort of level, if subliminal, for the last hour, so I said, "George?"

He put the glasses on and looked at me, suspiciously, as though I was going to force a spec script on him right there.

"It's me!" I said. "Remember? *The Leaves in His Hair*?"

"What? Oh, right. Hey."

"I didn't know you were into meditation."

"Yeah. I'm done with the movie business. It's all studio movies. No respect for art. Meaningless. Empty. Nest of vipers. I was falling apart. Just about to . . . Hang on." George checked his iPhone. "Sorry. Just about to get on a plane. I'm going to an ashram for three months in Lahore. Great to catch up."

"Excuse me," I ventured.

He turned, looking impatient.

"Are you sure the ashram isn't in Le Touquet?"

He laughed then, probably only just remembering who I was, and we had a rather alarming hug, and he said, "Namaste," in a deep movie-producer voice with an ironic expression, then rushed off again, still checking his iPhone. And I realized, in spite of everything, I was actually quite fond of George from Greenlight.

Tuesday 26 November 2013

135lb, number of pounds heavier than Miranda 45 (better), calories 4826, ham-and-cheese paninis 2, pizzas 1.5, tubs of Häagen-Dazs frozen yogurt 2, alcohol units 6 (very bad behaviour).

9 a.m. Just dropped off kids. Feel fat. Maybe will go and get ham-and-cheese panini.

10.30 a.m. Suddenly realized as was standing in the queue that Perfect Nicolette was there, waiting for her hot beverage. She was wearing a white faux-fur jacket and sunglasses and carrying an enormous handbag. She looked like Kate Moss arriving at a black-tie event, only it was nine in the morning. Was tempted to bolt, but had been waiting ages, so, when Nicolette eventually turned and spotted me, I said brightly, "Hello!"

Instead of the frosty greeting I was expecting, Nicolette just stared at me, holding a paper cup in one hand.

"I've got a new bag. It's Hermès," she said, holding up the handbag. Then her shoulders started to shake.

"SkinnyVentiDecafCappkeepthechange," I rattled off, shoving a fiver at the barista and thinking, "If Nicolette's having a breakdown now, then that's it. It's a cut-and-dried case. Everybody, left, right and centre, is a mess of cracked shells."

"Come downstairs," I said to Nicolette, patting her shoulder awkwardly. Fortunately there was no one else in the basement.

"I've got a new bag," she said. "And this is the receipt."

I stared blankly at the receipt.

"My husband bought it for me, from Frankfurt airport."

"Well, that's nice. It's beautiful," I lied. The handbag was mad. It had no rhyme or reason, buckles and straps and loops bursting out everywhere like lunatics.

"Look at the receipt," she said, pointing at it. "It's for two handbags."

I blinked at the receipt. It did seem to be for two handbags. But so?

"It's just a mistake," I said. "Ring them and get the money back."

She shook her head. "I know who she is. I called her. It's been going on for eight months. He bought her the identical bag." Her face crumpled. "It was a present. And he bought the same one for her."

Got home and checked my emails:

```
Sender: Nicolette Martinez
Subject: The school fucking concert

Just to let you know I don't
give a flying fuck who brings
the mince pies or mulled wine
this year and you can all turn
up whenever the FUCK you like
because I don't FUCKING WELL
GIVE A FUCK.

Nicorette
I need it.
```

Think will give Nicolette a ring.

11 p.m. Just had brilliant night at our place with Nicolette, with the three boys running riot on Roblox and Mabel watching *SpongeBob SquarePants* while we had some wine, pizza, cheese, Diet Coke, Red Bull, Cadbury's chocolate buttons, Rolos and Häagen-Dazs, and Nicolette looked at OkCupid, shouting, "Bastards! Fuckwittage!"

In the middle Tom turned up, slightly plastered, going on about a new survey: "It proves that the quality of someone's relationships is the biggest indicator of their long-term emotional health—not so much the 'significant other' relationship, as the measure of happiness is not your husband or boyfriend but the quality of the other relationships you have around you. Anyway, just thought I'd tell you. I've got to go and meet Arkis now."

Nicolette is now asleep in my bed and four kids are all squeezed in the bunk beds.

You see? Don't need men anyway.

A HERO WILL RISE

Friday 29 November 2013

This is what happened. Billy had a football match at another school, East Finchley, a few miles away. We'd been told to park in the street to pick them up, as cars weren't allowed in the grounds. The school was a tall, red-brick building, with a small concrete yard in front of the gates, and to the left, a sunken sports court, four feet down, surrounded by a heavy chain-link fence.

The boys were running round the sports court kicking balls, the mothers chatting round the East Finchley steps. Suddenly, a black BMW roared right up to the school, the driver, an idiotically flashy-looking father, talking on his mobile.

Mr. Wallaker strode to the car. "Excuse me."

The father ignored him, continuing to talk on his phone, engine still running. Mr. Wallaker rapped on the window. "Cars are not allowed in the school grounds. Park in the street, please."

The window slid open. "Time is money for some of us, my friend."

"It's a safety issue."

"Phaw. Safety. I'll be two minutes."

Mr. Wallaker gave him the stare. "Move. The car."

Still holding the phone to his ear, the father angrily slammed the BMW into gear, reversing without looking, turned the wheel with a screech and backed towards the sports court, straight into the heavy steel pole supporting the fence.

As everyone turned to stare, the father, red-faced, jammed his foot on the accelerator, forgetting to take the car out of reverse, and rammed the post again. There was a sickening crack and the post started to topple.

"Boys!" yelled Mr. Wallaker. "Get away from the fence! Scramble!"

It all seemed to be in slow motion. As the boys scattered and ran, the heavy metal post tottered, then fell into the sports court, pulling the fence with it and landing with a terrifying bounce and crash. At the same time the car slid backwards, the front wheels still on the concrete yard, the rear wheels half over the pit of the sports court below.

Everyone froze, stunned, except Mr. Wallaker, who leaped down into the pit, yelling, "Call 999! Weight the front of the car! Boys! Line up at the other end."

Unbelievably, the BMW dad was starting to open his door.

"You! Stay still!" yelled Mr. Wallaker, but the car was already sliding further backwards, the wheels now completely hanging over the drop.

I scanned the boys at the other end of the court. Billy! Where was Billy?

"Take Mabel!" I said to Nicolette, and ran to the side of the sports court.

Mr. Wallaker was below me in the pit, calm, eyes flicking over the scene. I forced myself to look.

The heavy metal post was now wedged at a diagonal,

one end against the wall of the pit and the other on the ground. The fence lay at an angle, buckled, hanging from the post like a ridge tent. Cowering in the small gap beneath the post, caged by the fallen fence, were Billy, Bikram and Jeremiah, their little faces staring, terrified, at Mr. Wallaker. The wall was behind them, the fence trapping them in front and at the sides, the rear of the big car hanging above them.

I let out a gasp and jumped down into the pit.

"It'll be all right," Mr. Wallaker said quietly. "I've got this."

He crouched down. "OK, Superheroes, this is your big break. Wriggle back to the wall and curl up. Brace positions."

Looking more excited than scared now, the boys wriggled themselves back and curled up, arms over their little heads.

"Good work, Troopers," Mr. Wallaker said, and started to lift the heavy fence from the ground. "Now . . ."

Suddenly, with a sickening screech of metal against concrete, the BMW slid further backwards, dislodging bits of debris, the back end swinging precariously in mid-air.

There were screams from the mothers above and the wail of sirens.

"Stay against the wall, boys!" said Mr. Wallaker, unfazed. "This is going to be good!"

He stooped under the car, stepping carefully onto the fallen fence. He raised his arms and thrust the whole of his strength against the chassis. I could see the muscles straining in his forearms, in his neck, beneath his shirt.

"WEIGHT THE FRONT OF THE CAR!" he yelled up to the yard, sweat beading his forehead. "LADIES! ELBOWS ON THE BONNET!"

I glanced up to see teachers and mothers leaping out of their shock, throwing themselves like startled chickens on the bonnet. Slowly, as Mr. Wallaker strained upwards, the rear of the car lifted.

"OK, boys," he said, still pushing upwards. "Stay close to the wall. Crawl to your right, away from the car. Then get yourselves out from under that fence."

I rushed to the edge of the fallen chain-fence, more parents and teachers joining me now. Between us we struggled to lift the buckled metal, the three boys wriggling towards the edge, Billy the last one in line.

Firemen were jumping down, lifting the fence, pulling Bikram out—the metal ripping his shirt—then Jeremiah. Billy was still in there. As Jeremiah wriggled free, I reached forward and put my arms under Billy's, feeling as though I had the strength of ten men, and pulled, sobbing with relief as Billy came free and the firemen pulled us out of the pit.

"That's the last one! Come on!" yelled Mr. Wallaker, still shaking under the weight of the car. The firemen jumped under to support him, stepping on the fence, their weight crushing it down into the space where, seconds before, the three boys had been cowering.

"Where's Mabel?" yelled Billy dramatically. "We have to save her!"

The three boys charged off through the crowd in the yard, with the air of supermen with flapping capes. I followed, to find Mabel standing calmly beside a hyperventilating Nicolette.

450

Billy threw his arms round Mabel, yelling, "I've saved her! I've saved my sister! Are you all right, sister?"

"Yeth," she said solemnly. "But Mr. Wallaker'th bossy."

Incredibly, in the midst of the pandemonium, the BMW dad again opened the car door, and this time he actually climbed out, brushing huffily at his overcoat, at which the whole vehicle started sliding backwards.

"IT'S COMING DOWN!" Mr. Wallaker yelled from below. "GET OUT, GUYS!"

We all rushed forward to see Mr. Wallaker and the firemen jumping clear as the BMW crashed down onto the steel pole, then bounced, rolled and smashed on its side, sleek metal cracking, windows shattering, broken glass and debris all over the cream leather seats.

"My Bima!" shouted the dad.

"Time is money, dickhead," Mr. Wallaker retorted, grinning delightedly.

As the paramedics tried to look him over, Billy was explaining, "We couldn't move, you see, Mummy. We daren't run because that post was wobbling right above us. But then we were Superheroes because . . ."

Meanwhile, chaos was breaking out around us, parents running crazily round in circles, hair extensions flying, enormous handbags lying forgotten on the ground.

Mr. Wallaker jumped onto the steps.

"Quiet!" he shouted. "Everyone stand still! Now, boys. In a second you'll be lining up to be checked and counted. But first, listen up. You just had a real adventure. No one got hurt. You were brave, you were calm, and three of you—Bikram, Jeremiah and Billy—were cut-and-dried Superheroes. Tonight you're to go home and celebrate, because you've proved that when scary stuff happens—which it will—you know how to be brave and calm."

Cheers went up from the boys and parents. "Oh my God," said Farzia. "Take me now"—rather echoing my own sentiments. As Mr. Wallaker passed me, he shot me a smug little look, endearingly Billy-like.

"All in a day's work?" I said.

"Seen worse," he said cheerfully, "and at least your hair didn't blow up."

After the counting, Bikram, Billy and Jeremiah were mobbed by the other boys. The three of them had to go to hospital to be checked out. When they climbed into the ambulances, followed by their traumatized mothers, it was with the air of a newly famous boy band from *Britain's Got Talent*.

Mabel fell asleep in the ambulance and slept through the check-ups. The boys were fine, apart from a few scratches. Bikram's and Jeremiah's fathers turned up at the hospital. A few minutes later Mr. Wallaker appeared, grinning, with bags of McDonald's and went over every detail of what had happened with the boys, answering all their questions and explaining exactly how and why they'd been Action Heroes.

As Jeremiah and Bikram left with their parents, Mr. Wallaker held out my car keys.

"You OK?" He took one look at my face and said, "I'll drive you home."

"No! I'm absolutely fine!" I lied.

"Listen," he said with his slight smile. "It doesn't make you less of a top professional feminist if you let somebody help you."

Back home, as I settled the children on the sofa, Mr. Wallaker said quietly, "What do you need?"

"Their cuddly toys? They're upstairs in the bunk beds."

"Puffle Two?"

"Yes. And One and Three, Mario, Horsio and Saliva."

"*Saliva?*"

"Her dolly."

As he came back with the toys, I was trying to turn on the TV, staring at the remotes. "Shall I have a go?"

SpongeBob sprang into life, and he led me behind the sofa.

I started sobbing then, silently.

"Shhh. Shhh," he whispered, putting his strong arms around me. "No one was hurt, I knew it was going to be fine."

I leaned against him, sniffing and snuffling.

"You're doing all right, Bridget," he said softly. "You're a good mum and dad, better than some who have a staff of eight and a flat in Monte Carlo. Even if you have put snot on my shirt."

And it felt like the aeroplane door opening, when you arrive on holiday, with a rush of warm air. It felt like sitting down at the end of the day.

Then Mabel yelled, "Mummee! *SpongeBob*'th *finished!*" and simultaneously the doorbell rang.

It was Rebecca. "We just heard about the school thing," she said, clattering down the stairs, a string of tiny LED Christmas lights woven into her hair. "What happened? Oh!" she said, seeing Mr. Wallaker. "Hello, Scott."

"Hello," he said. "Good to see you. Headgear unexpect-edly understated . . . but still."

Finn, Oleander and Jake came over and the house was filled with noise and chocolate and Hellvanians and Xbox, and everyone running about. I kept trying to talk to Billy, and help him process what had happened, but he just said, "Mummeee! I'm a Superhero! OK?"

I watched Mr. Wallaker talking to Jake, both of them tall, handsome, old friends, fathers. Rebecca looked at Mr. Wallaker and raised her eyebrows at me, but then his phone rang, and I could just tell he was talking to Miranda.

"I have to go," he said abruptly, clicking it off. "You guys will look after them tonight, right, Jake?"

Heart sinking, I followed him up to the doorstep and started to gabble, "I'm so grateful. It's you who is the Superhero. I mean are. I mean is."

"Are," he said. "And it was my pleasure."

He walked down the steps then turned, added softly ". . . Superheroine," and strode off towards the main road, the taxis, and a girl who looks like she's out of a magazine. I watched him go, sadly, thinking, "Superheroine? I'd still like someone to shag."

'TIS THE SEASON

Monday 2 December 2013
Everything is all right. Took Billy to the child psychologist who said he seemed to have "healthily assimilated it as a learning experience." When I tried to take him for a second time, Billy said, "Mummee! It's you who needs to go."

Billy, Bikram and Jeremiah are enjoying a period of what can only be described as celebrity at the school and have been signing autographs. Their school celebrity, however, is as nothing beside that of Mr. Wallaker.

And Mr. Wallaker is friendly to me now, and I to him. But that's as far as it seems to go.

Tuesday 3 December 2013
3.30 p.m. Mabel just came out of school singing:

> "Deck de halls wid boughs of holly,
> Falalalala la la la la.
> 'Tis de season to be jolly . . ."

It *is* the season to be jolly. Am going to be jolly this year. And grateful.

Wednesday 4 December 2013

4.30 p.m. Oh. Mabel has now changed the words to:

> "'Tis de season to hate Billy."

Thursday 5 December 2013

10 a.m. Thelonius's mother stopped me at the Infants Branch drop-off this morning.

"Bridget," she said, "could you ask your daughter to stop upsetting Thelonius?"

"Why? What?" I said, confused.

It turns out Mabel is going round the playground singing:

> "Deck de halls wid boughs of begonias,
> Falalalala la la la la.
> 'Tis de season to hate Thelonius . . ."

2 p.m. "That'll teach you to plant such an unimaginative flower," said Rebecca. "How's Scott? I mean, Mr. Wallaker."

"He's nice," I said. "He's friendly, but, you know, just friendly . . ."

"Well, are you 'just friendly' to him? Does he KNOW?"

"He's with Miranda."

"A man like that has his needs. It doesn't mean he's going to be with her for ever."

I shook my head. "He's not interested. I think he likes me as a person, now. But that's as far as it goes."

It is sad. But mostly I am happy. It only takes a really bad thing to nearly happen to make you appreciate what you have.

2.05 p.m. Bloody Miranda.

2.10 p.m. Hate Miranda. "Oh, oh, look at me, I'm all young and tall and thin and perfect." She's probably also going out with Roxster. Humph.

THE CAROL CONCERT

Wednesday 11 December 2013

The carol concert was upon us again, and Billy and Mabel both had sleepovers so there was wild excitement combined with the utter hysteria of trying to pack two overnight backpacks, get Mabel and me looking human and festive enough to go to a school carol concert, and get there before it had actually ended.

Was trying to put on my best front, as no doubt Miranda would be in the church cheering on her man. Mabel was wearing a furry jacket and a sticky-out red skirt which I'd got in the ILoveGorgeous sale, and I was wearing a new white coat (inspired by Nicolette, who is currently in the Maldives, where her sexually incontinent husband is begging her forgiveness while she tortures him in a luxury hut on the end of a long wooden walkway, suspended over the sea on stilts, sharks circling below). In the absence of any possibility of blowjobs, I had gone for a blow-dry—though the Disney Princess and Mario backpacks didn't exactly add to the look. Plus Miranda would undoubtedly be wearing an effortlessly sexy yet understated outfit so edgily on-trend that even Mabel would not understand it.

As we came out of the tube station, the "village" looked utterly magical, delicate lights casting shadows in the trees. The shops were all lit up, and a brass band was playing

"Good King Wenceslas." And the old-fashioned butcher had turkeys hanging up in the window. And we were early.

Out of a moment's believing I actually *was* Good King Wenceslas, I rushed into the butcher and bought four Cumberland sausages—in case a poor man suddenly came in sight—adding a sausage bag to the two lurid backpacks. Then Mabel wanted to get a hot chocolate, which seemed like the perfect idea, but then suddenly it was 5.45, which was the time we were meant to be seated by, so we had to run towards the church, and Mabel tripped and her hot chocolate went all over my coat. She burst into tears. "Your coat, Mummy, your new coat."

"It doesn't matter, sweetheart," I said. "It doesn't matter. It's just a coat. Here, have my hot chocolate," meanwhile thinking, "Oh, fuck, the one time I manage to get it together, I fuck it up again."

But the church square was so beautiful, lined with Georgian houses with Christmas trees in the windows and Christmas wreaths on the doors. The church windows were glowing orange, organ music was playing and the fir tree outside was decorated with Christmas lights.

And there were some seats left inside, quite near the front. There was no sign of Miranda. Heart gave a great leap as Mr. Wallaker appeared, looking cheerful yet masterful in a blue shirt and dark jacket.

"Look, dere's Billy," said Mabel as the choir and musicians filed into the pews. We had been strictly instructed by Billy not to wave, but Mabel waved, and then I couldn't help it. Mr. Wallaker glanced at Billy, who rolled his eyes and giggled.

Then everyone settled and the vicar walked down the aisle and said the blessing. Billy kept looking over at us and grinning. He was so proud of himself being in the choir. Then it was time for the first carol and everyone got to their feet. Spartacus, as usual, was singing the solo, and as that pure, perfect little voice rang out through the church . . .

"Once in royal David's city,
Stood a lowly cattle shed,
Where a mother laid her baby
In a manger for His bed."

. . . I realized I was going to cry.

The organ swelled into action and the congregation started to sing the second verse.

"He came down to earth from heaven,
Who is God and Lord of all.
And His shelter was a stable,
And His cradle was a stall."

And all the Christmases before came flooding back: the Christmases when I was little, standing between Mum and Dad in Grafton Underwood village church on Christmas Eve, waiting for Santa Claus; the Christmases when I was a teenager, Dad and I suppressing giggles as Mum and Una warbled overly loudly in ridiculous sopranos; the Christmases in my thirties, when I was single and so sad, because I thought I'd never have a baby of my own to lay in a manger, or more precisely a Bugaboo stroller; last winter in the snow when I was tweeting Roxster, who was probably at this moment dancing to "garage house" music with someone called Natalie. Or Miranda. Or Saffron. Dad's last Christmas before he died, when he staggered out of hospital to go to Midnight Mass in Grafton Underwood; the first Christmas when Mark and I went to church, holding Billy in a little Santa Claus outfit; the Christmas when Billy had his first Nativity Play at nursery school, which was the first Christmas after Mark's brutal, horrible death, when I couldn't believe that Christmas would be so cruel as to actually try to happen.

"Don't cry, Mummy, pleathe don't cry." Mabel was gripping my hand tightly. Billy was looking over. I wiped the tears away with my fist, raised my head to join in:

> "And He feeleth for our sadness,
> And He shareth in our gladness."

. . . and saw that Mr. Wallaker was looking straight at me. The congregation carried on singing:

> "And our eyes at last shall see Him."

. . . but Mr. Wallaker had stopped singing and was just looking at me. And I looked back, with my face covered in mascara and my coat covered in hot chocolate. Then Mr. Wallaker smiled, the slightest, kindest smile, the one smile that understood, over the heads of all those boys he'd taught to sing "Once in Royal David's City." And I knew that I loved Mr. Wallaker.

As we came out of the church, it had begun to snow, thick flakes, swirling down, settling on the festive coats, and on the Christmas tree. There was a brazier lit in the churchyard and the senior boys were handing out mulled wine, roast chestnuts and hot chocolate.

"May I pour some more of this down your coat?"

I turned and there he was, holding a tray of two hot chocolates and two mulled wines.

"This is for you, Mabel," he said, putting down the tray and crouching to hold out a hot chocolate.

She shook her head. "I spilt it before, on Mummy's coat, you see."

"Now, Mabel," he said solemnly, "if she had a white coat on, without chocolate, would she really be Mummy?"

She looked at him with her huge, grave eyes, shook her head, and took the chocolate. And then, quite unlike Mabel, she put down her drink and suddenly threw her arms around him, buried her little head in his shoulder and gave him a kiss: chocolatey, on his shirt.

"There you go," he said. "Why don't you tip a little bit more on Mummy's coat, just for Christmas?"

He stood up, and pretended to lurch towards me with the mulled wines.

"Merry Christmas," he said. We touched paper cups and our eyes met again and, even with the mess of kids and parents thronging around us, somehow neither of us could look away.

"Mummy!" It was Billy. "Mummy, did you see me?"

"'Tis de season to hate Billy!" sang Mabel.

"Mabel," said Mr. Wallaker. "Stop it." Which she did. "Of course she saw you, Billy, she was waving at you, as she was specifically instructed not to. Here's your hot chocolate, Billster." He put his hand on Billy's shoulder. "You were great."

As Billy grinned the fantastic ear-to-ear, sparkle-eyed grin, the old grin, I caught Mr. Wallaker's look, both of us remembering how close Billy had come to— "Mummy!" Billy interrupted. "What did you do to your coat? Oh, look, there's Bikram! Did you bring my bag? Can I go?"

"Me too, me too!" said Mabel.

"Where?" said Mr. Wallaker.

"Sleepover!" said Billy.

"I'm going too!" said Mabel proudly. "Havin' a sleepover. Wid Cosmata!"

"Well, that sounds like fun," said Mr. Wallaker. "And is Mummy having a sleepover too?"

"No," said Mabel. "She'th all on her own."

"As usual," said Billy.

"Interesting."

"Mr. Wallaker." It was Valerie, the school secretary. "There's a bassoon left in the church. What do we do? We can't leave it in the church and it's absolutely enorm—"

"Oh God. I'm sorry," I said. "It's Billy's. I'll go and get it."

"I'll get it," said Mr. Wallaker. "Back in a mo."

"No! It's OK! I'll—"

Mr. Wallaker put his hand firmly on my arm. "I'll get it."

Blinking, head swirling through confused thoughts and emotions, I watched him go off for the bassoon. I packed Mabel and Billy off with their bags and stood by the brazier watching them go with Bikram and Cosmata and their mums and dads. After a few minutes all the other families started leaving too, and I was beginning to feel a bit of a fool.

Maybe Mr. Wallaker didn't mean he was coming back at all. I couldn't see him anywhere. I mean, maybe "Back in a mo" was just the sort of thing people say when they're moving around at a social occasion, though he was going for the bassoon, but maybe he'd locked it in a cupboard ready for the next lesson and gone to meet Miranda. And maybe he just gave me the nice look in church because he was sorry for me because I was blubbing during "Once in Royal David's City." And he only brought the hot chocolate because I was a tragic widow with tragic fatherless children and . . .

I downed a last mouthful of the mulled wine and, chucking my cup in the bin, splattering my coat with red wine to go with the chocolate, set off towards the square, following the last stragglers.

"Hang on!"

He was striding towards me, holding the enormous bassoon. The stragglers turned to look. "It's all right! I'm taking her carol singing," he said, then murmuring as he reached my side, "Shall we hit the pub?"

The pub was all cosy, old and Christmassy with flag-stone floors, crackling fires and ancient beams decked with boughs of holly: though also full of parents looking at us with intense interest. Mr. Wallaker cheerfully ignored the stares, found a booth at the back where no one could see, pulled out my chair for me, put the bassoon next to my chair, saying, "Try not to lose it," and went to get us drinks.

"So," he said, sitting down opposite, placing the glasses in front of us.

"Mr. Wallaker!" said one of the Year 6 mothers, peering round the booth. "I just wanted to say it was the most marvellous—"

"Thank you, Mrs. Pavlichko," he said, getting to his feet. "I deeply appreciate your appreciation. I hope you have a wonderful Christmas, truly. Goodbye." And she scuttled off, politely dismissed.

"So," he said, sitting down again.

"So," I said. "I just want to say thank you again for—"

"So what's with your toy boy? The one I saw you with on the Heath?"

"So what's with Miranda?" I said, smoothly ignoring his impertinence.

"Miranda? MIRANDA?" He looked at me incredulously. "Bridget, she's TWENTY-TWO! She's my brother's stepdaughter."

I looked down, blinking rapidly, trying to take it all in. "So you're going out with your step-niece?"

"No! She bumped into me when she was shoe-shopping. You're the one who's engaged to be married to a child."

"I'm not!"

"You are!" he said, laughing.

"I'm not!"

"So stop squabbling, and dish."

I told him the whole story about Roxster. Well, not the whole, whole story: edited highlights.

"How old was he exactly?"

"Twenty-nine. Well, no, he was thirty by the time—"

"Oh, well, in that case—" his eyes were crinkling at the corners—"he's practically a sugar daddy."

"So you've been single all this time?"

"Well, I'm not saying I've been living the life of a monk . . ."

He swirled the Scotch around in his glass. Oh God, those eyes.

"But the thing is, you see—" he leaned forward confidentially—"you can't go out with someone else, can you? When you're in lo—"

"Mr. Wallaker!" It was Anzhelika Sans Souci. She looked at us, mouth open. "Sorry!" she said and disappeared.

I was staring at him, trying to believe what he'd seemed to be about to say.

"OK, enough school mums?" he said. "If I take you home will you dance to 'Killer Queen'?"

I was still in a daze as we made our way through the parents and the compliments—"Magnificent performances," "Overwhelmingly accomplished," "Fiercely impressive." As we were heading out of the pub door, we saw Valerie. "Have a good night, you two," she said, with a twinkle.

Outside it was still snowing. I glanced, lustfully, at Mr. Wallaker. He was so tall, so gorgeous: the ruggedly handsome jaw above the scarf, the slight glimpse of hairy chest below his shirt collar, the long legs in his dark—

"Shit! The bassoon." I for some reason suddenly remembered, and started heading back in.

He stopped me, again, with a gentle hand on my arm: "I'll get it."

I waited, breathless, feeling the snow on my cheeks, then he reappeared, with the bassoon and the plastic bag of sausages.

"Your sausages," he said, handing them to me.

"Yes! Sausages! Good King Wenceslas! The butcher!" I gabbled nervously.

We were standing very close.

"Look!" he said, pointing above. "Isn't that mistletoe?"

"I think you'll find it's an elm with no leaves," I continued to gabble without looking up. "I mean, it probably just looks like mistletoe because of the snow and—"

"Bridget." He reached out and gently traced my cheekbone with his finger, the cool blue eyes burning into mine, teasing, tender, hungry. "This isn't a biology lesson." He raised my mouth to his and kissed me once, lightly, then again, more urgently, and added, ". . . yet."

Oh God. He was so masterful, he was such a MAN! And then we were kissing properly and it felt, once more, like everything was going crazy inside me, flashes and pulses, and like I was driving a super-fast car in a pair of stilettos again, but this time it was all right because the person actually at the wheel was . . .

"Mr. Wallaker," I gasped.

"So sorry," he murmured. "Did I catch you with the bassoon?"

We both agreed we should take the bassoon safely back to his place, which was a huge flat in one of the lanes off the high street. It had old wooden floors and a blazing fire with a fur hearthrug and candles, and the smell of cooking. A small, smiling Filipino lady was bustling around the kitchen area.

"Martha!" he said. "Thank you. It looks wonderful. You can go now. Thank you."

"Ooh, Mr. Wallaker's in a hurry." She smiled. "I'm on my way. How the concert go?"

"It was great," I said.

"Yes, great," he said, bustling her out, kissing her on the top of her head. "Brass band a bit off but generally good."

"You take care of him," she said as she left. "He the best, Mr. Wallaker, the best man."

"I know," I said.

As the door closed, we stood like children left alone in a sweet shop.

"Look at this coat," he murmured. "You're such a mess. That's why I . . ."

And then he started slowly unbuttoning the coat, slipping it off my shoulders. For a moment I thought maybe this was a practised routine—maybe that's why Martha was so quick to leave—but then he said, "That's partly why . . ." He pulled me close, his hand slipping to my back, starting to slowly undo my zip, "I fell . . . in . . . fell in . . ."

I felt my eyes filling with tears, and for a second I could swear his were too. Then he pulled himself back into masterful mode, and laid my head against his shoulder. "I'm going to kiss away all your tears. All your tears," he growled, "after I've finished with you."

Then he carried on with the zip, which went all the way down, so that the dress fell to the floor, leaving me in my boots and—Merry Christmas, Talitha—black La Perla slip.

When we were both naked I couldn't believe the naughty perfection of Mr. Wallaker's familiar, handsome, school-gates head on top of that incredibly ripped, naked body.

"Mr. Wallaker!" I gasped again.

"Will you stop calling me Mr. Wallaker?"

"Yes, Mr. Wallaker."

"OK. That's a cut-and-dried Caution which is going to lead inevitably . . ." he picked me up in his arms, as if I was as light as a feather, which I am not, unless it was a very heavy feather, maybe from a giant prehistoric dinosaur-type bird, ". . . to a Misdemeanour," he said, laying me gently by the fire.

He kissed my neck, moving slowly, exquisitely downwards. "Oh, oh," I gasped. "Did they teach you this in the SAS?"

"Naturally," he said eventually, raising himself up, looking down with his amused expression. "The British special forces have the finest training in the world. But ultimately . . ."

He was pressing now, gently, deliciously, at first, then more and more insistently, till I was melting like a . . . like a—". . . ultimately it's all about . . ."—I gasped—". . . the pistol."

All hell broke loose then. It was like being in heaven, or other, similar paradise. I came and I came and I came, repeatedly, in a tribute to Her Majesty and the training of Her forces, till finally he said, "I don't think I can hold on any longer."

"Just go, for it," I managed, and finally we both—in a perfect, miraculous, simultaneous explosion of months of desire at the school gates—did.

Afterwards we lay back, panting, exhausted. Then we slept in each other's arms, then woke and did it again, and again, all night.

At 5 a.m. we had some of Martha's soup. We huddled by the fire and talked. He told me what had happened in Afghanistan: an accident, a mistaken attack, women, children killed, finding the aftermath. Deciding he'd done his bit and he was through. And this time, I put my arms around him, and stroked his head.

"I do take your point," he murmured.

"What?"

"Cuddling. Quite good really."

He talked about starting at the school. He wanted to be away from the violence, make life simple, be with children and do some good things. He wasn't prepared for the mothers, though, the competitiveness and the complication. "But then one of them was kind enough to show off her thong when stuck up a tree. And I started to think that life could possibly be a bit more fun."

"And you like it now?" I whispered.

"Yes." He started to kiss me again. "Oh, yes." He was kissing different parts of me between his words. "I . . . really . . . definitively . . . conclusively . . . like it now."

Suffice it to say, when I picked Billy and Mabel up from Bikram's and Cosmata's later that day, I was walking with extreme difficulty.

"Why are you still wearing de chocolatey coat?" said Mabel.

"Tell you when you're grown up," I said.

THE OWL

Thursday 12 December 2013
9 p.m. Just put the children to bed. Mabel was staring out of the window. "De moon is thtill followin' us."

"Well, the thing is, with the moon—" I started to explain.

"And dat owl," Mabel interrupted.

I looked out at the snowy garden. The moon was white and full above it. And on the garden wall, the barn owl was back. He stared at me, calm, unblinking. Then this time he spread his wings, looked for a last moment and flew upwards, his wings beating, almost to the beat of my heart, into the winter night and the darkness and its mysteries.

THE YEAR'S PROGRESS

Tuesday 31 December 2013
*Pounds lost 17

*Pounds gained 18

*Twitter followers 797

*Twitter followers lost 793

*Twitter followers gained 794

*Jobs gained 1

*Jobs lost 1

*Texts sent 24,383

*Texts received 24,284 (good)

*Number of screenplay words written 18,000

*Number of words of screenplay rewritten 17,984

*Number of words of screenplay written and put back like were in first place 16,822

*Number of words of texts written 104,569

*People infestered by nits 5

*Total nits extracted 152

*Price per nit of professionally extracted nits £8.59

*Boyfriends lost 1

*Boyfriends gained 2

*Fires in house 4

*Existing children kept intact 2

*Children lost 7 (counting all occasions)

*Children found 7

*Total children 4

OUTCOME

Mr. Wallaker—or Scott, as I occasionally call him—and I did not have a wedding, because neither of us wanted to get married again. But we did realize that neither of us had christened our children so decided to make it an excuse for a coming-together party at the big country house. That way, we decided, the children would be covered, like insurance, in case it emerged that the Christian God was the True God, even though both Mr. Wallaker and I are slightly Buddhist.

The ceremony was performed in the chapel. The school choir sang, and Scott's sons Matt and Fred—who are no longer in boarding school but at the Senior School—played "Someone to Watch Over Me" on clarinet and piano. I cried most of the time. Greenlight Productions sent a bunch of flowers the size of a sheep; Rebecca had her hair done in an Afro with a lit-up sign saying "*Motel*" and an arrow pointing down at her head; Daniel got drunk at the party and tried to get off with Talitha, leading to Sergei throwing a giant tantrum and storming off in a rage; and Jude—who had, obviously, got bored with Wildlifephotographerman's devotion—got off with Mr. Pitlochry-Howard and then had a terrible time getting out of it afterwards. Tom and Arkis sulked because we hadn't invited Gwyneth Paltrow—even though Jake had once played with Chris Martin—and both flirted outrageously with the senior boys in the big band.

Mum was still slightly annoyed that I hadn't worn something more brightly coloured, but got over it because her coat-dress set was clearly nicer than Una's, and Mr. Wallaker is quite happy to indulge her by flirting outrageously and telling her off when she gets out of line, in a way which just makes her titter. Roxster—who had previously sent me a very nice text saying his heart was broken at the loss of his vomiting cougar, but there clearly was a Dating God as his new girlfriend had morning sickness—texted me on the day to say she wasn't pregnant, it was just that he'd forced her to eat too much food, and she was really annoying. Which was nice.

And somewhere up above it all, I knew in my heart that Mark would be glad. That he really, really would not have wanted us to be alone and in a confused state. And that if it had to be someone, he would be glad it was Mr. Wallaker.

And now I have not two children but four. And Billy has big boys to play Xbox with and comes off perfectly happily and without any discussion about getting to the next level if Mr. Wallaker so much as looks at him. We hang out with Jake and Rebecca and the kids at weekends and everyone has someone to play with. And Mabel, for the first time since she was too tiny a baby to know, has a daddy who is in this world and not the next, and treats her like such a princess that I constantly have to Caution her. And I feel safe and not lonely, and cared for. And we go to Capthorpe House sometimes at weekends, and re-enact the scene in the bushes when the kids are in bed, with a better ending.

And we all live together now, in a big old messy house near Hampstead Heath. And as we can all walk to school from there, we've decided we can manage with just the one car—which makes it SO much easier with the parking permits, though we're still late every morning. Oh, and watch out for *The Leaves in His Hair*, retitled *Thy Neighbour's Yacht*, coming soon as a straight-to-DVD release near you! The children finally went to the dentist and don't have anything wrong with their teeth. And by the way, currently all six of us have head lice.

ACKNOWLEDGEMENTS

Initially it seemed the acknowledgements should be arranged in *hierarchical* order: there are some people without whom I would never have started the book, or who have given a huge amount of material, or just one line, or edited the whole thing. But it was a minefield of possible gaffes, like organizing a seating plan for a wedding in a family with multiple remarriages.

I tried a complex star-rating system, but that seemed somehow . . . strange.

Then I thought it was like award ceremonies when everyone else is bored by the thanking and the only people who care are the thankees. So, finally, I decided just to put it in alphabetical order and hope that's OK.

But you know who you are and where you actually should be in the hierarchical order (first). And I really am appreciative of the help and generous sharing of amusing experiences, and experience, and moral support. And I really . . . I really . . . (bursts into tears) . . . thank you.

Gillon Aitken, Sunetra Atkinson, Simon Bell, Maria Benitez, Grazina Bilunskiene, Paul Bogaards, Helena Bonham Carter, Bob Bookman, Alex Bowler, Billy Burton, Nell Burton, Susan Campos, Paulina Castelli, Beth Coates, Richard Coles, Dash Curran, Kevin Curran, Romy Curran, Scarlett Curtis, Kevin Douglas, Eric Fellner and all at Working Title, Richard, Sal, Freddie and Billie Fielding, my mum Nellie Fielding (not like Bridget's), the entire Fielding family, Colin Firth, Carrie Fisher, Paula Fletcher, Dan Franklin, Mariella Frostrup, the Glazer family, Hugh Grant, the Hallatt Wells family, Lisa Halpern, James Hoff, Jenny Jackson, Tina Jenkins, Christian Lewis, Jonathan Lonner, Tracey MacLeod, Karon Maskill, Amy Matthews, Jason McCue, Sonny Mehta, Maile Meloy, Daphne Merkin, Lucasta Miller, Leslee Newman, Catherine Olim, Imogen Pelham, Rachel Penfold, Iain Pickles, Gail Rebuck, Bethan Rees, Sally Riley, Renata Rokicki, Mike Rudell, Darryl Samaraweera, Brian Siberell, Steve Vincent, Andrew Walliker, Jane Wellesley, Kate Williamson, Daniel Wood.